KT-381-179

OUT OF THE SUN

Also by Robert Goddard

PAST CARING
IN PALE BATTALIONS
PAINTING THE DARKNESS
INTO THE BLUE
TAKE NO FAREWELL
HAND IN GLOVE
CLOSED CIRCLE
BORROWED TIME

Robert Goddard

OUT OF THE SUN

BANTAM PRESS

LONDON · NEW YORK · TORONTO · SYDNEY · AUCKLAND

TRANSWORLD PUBLISHERS LTD
61–63 Uxbridge Road, London W5 5SA

TRANSWORLD PUBLISHERS (AUSTRALIA) PTY LTD
15–23 Helles Avenue, Moorebank, NSW 2170

TRANSWORLD PUBLISHERS (NZ) LTD
3 William Pickering Drive, Albany, Auckland

Published 1996 by Bantam Press
a division of Transworld Publishers Ltd
Copyright © Robert Goddard 1996

The right of Robert Goddard to be identified
as the author of this work has been asserted in accordance
with sections 77 and 78 of the Copyright Designs and Patents
Act 1988.

All of the characters in this book
are fictitious, and any resemblance
to actual persons, living or dead,
is purely coincidental.

A catalogue record for this book is available from the British Library

ISBN 0593 03614X

All rights reserved. No part of this publication may
be reproduced, stored in a retrieval system, or
transmitted in any form or by any means,
electronic, mechanical, photocopying, recording,
or otherwise, without the prior permission of
the publishers.

Typeset in 11/12 ½pt Linotype Times by
Kestrel Data, Exeter, Devon.

Printed in Great Britain by
Mackays of Chatham plc, Chatham, Kent.

For Duncan

READING AREA			
RR	RT	RC	RB
RP	RS	RW	MUS

12/98

WEST GRID STAMP

NN		RR		WW	
NT		RT		WO	
NC		RC		WL	
NH		RB	12/96	WM	
NL		RP	1/98	WT	
NV		RS	6/97	WA	
NM		RW	6/98	WR	6/98
NB		RV		WS	
NE					
NP					

WEST GRID STAMP

OUT OF THE SUN

ONE

If he left now, of course, or even five minutes from now, it would still be all right. The only problem was that he was not going to leave. He knew that. And so did she.

'Top up?'

'Better not. I won't be able to see to paint straight.'

'Then don't try.'

'What about Claude? He won't be pleased if the job's not finished by the weekend.'

'I'll tell him it rained.'

'Will he believe you?'

'Who cares? Now, what about that drink?'

'You shouldn't tempt me.'

'Who says I'm trying to?' She tipped the bottle and gin fizzed into his glass.

'Trying or not,' he said, raising the glass to his lips and swallowing some of the strengthened mixture with deliberate relish, 'you do.'

'Do I?'

'Oh yes. Very much. And I've never been any good at resisting temptation.'

'Haven't you?'

'No.'

'That's funny.'

'Why?'

'Because neither have I, Harry.'

9

Thirty-four years, three months and several days later, Harry Barnett's thoughts found nothing to tempt him as he trudged south along Scrubs Lane into a stiff autumnal breeze soured by traffic fumes and an ammoniated cocktail of industrial pollution. A top up was definitely not in order. Glancing from the crest of the railway bridge out across the pale expanse of Kensal Green Cemetery, its sepulchred ranks an even colder shade of grey than the grimy London sky, Harry would have agreed that just about the last thing his life needed at the moment was an extra dose of any one of its dismal ingredients.

Not the least dismal of those ingredients was his part-time job at the Mitre Bridge Service Station, which lay halfway down Scrubs Lane towards the A40 flyover. He was already late for his five-hour stint of cash-counting and card-swiping, but his right ankle was giving him such gyp following a stumble on the way home from the Stonemasons' Arms last night that acceleration was out of the question. Besides, Shafiq was an understanding fellow. For a Muslim, he was really amazingly tolerant of the scrapes a chap could get into after a few too many. He would complain, of course. That was only to be expected. That was, in a sense, how both of them retained their sanity.

Strangely, however, when Harry turned into the forecourt at Mitre Bridge a few minutes later and made his way none too quickly through the petrol-marbled puddles towards the shop, Shafiq looked up from behind the counter with an expression of puzzled sympathy rather than the over-rehearsed scowl Harry had expected. As a result, before he had even pushed open the door, he was worried. Though not, as it was to turn out, half as worried as he should have been.

'Harry, my friend,' said Shafiq, 'it is good to see you.'

'There's no need to be sarcastic. I got here as soon as—'

'I am not being sarcastic, Harry. How could you think such a thing?'

'Easily. But never mind. I'm here now. You can beetle off home.'

'In the circumstances, I would not dream of it.'

Harry stopped in his tracks, anorak half on and half off. 'What are you on about?'

'Mr Crowther would not object if you went straight to the hospital, I feel sure.'

Shrugging his anorak back on, Harry moved to the counter and leant across it, staring into Shafiq's plump and frowning face. 'Have you been sniffing the anti-freeze, Shafiq? What the hell are you talking about?'

'I am sorry, Harry. I am not explaining properly. But it was a surprise. A shock, actually. I had no idea you even had a son.'

Now it was Harry's turn to frown. 'Son?'

'Yes. They phoned about twenty minutes ago. Your son is in the National Neurological Hospital. I have the room number.'

Birdsong and the scent of fresh paint drifted through the net-curtained window as Harry's breathing returned to normal. From the corner of his eye, he could see the trail of discarded clothes leading from the door to the bed they lay on. In his mind, every tug and twist of their removal was already a delicious memory. Though not as delicious as what had followed. Nor as headily alluring as the pleasures that might still be his to savour.

She was lying on her side, her back turned to him. Ashamed already, perhaps? Regretting, now the spasm was past, the desire she had succumbed to? He reached out and ran his fingers slowly down her spine, then let his hand fan out to cradle her bottom and slide in between her legs. And from the throaty chuckle she gave in response, he knew shame and regret were not going to be a problem. Not for her. And certainly not for him.

'Do it to me again, Harry,' she murmured, parting her thighs in invitation.

'Are you sure you want me to?'

'Didn't my husband tell you to do whatever I asked?'

'Yes, Mrs Venning. He did.'

'Then what are you waiting for?' Her breath was quickening again as he stroked her. 'Once is never enough for a proper finish.'

'How many times would be?'

'I'll tell you later,' she replied, giving way to a moan. 'Much later.'

'I don't have a son, Shafiq. Or a daughter. I don't have any children at all. I'm the last of the Barnetts. Chingachgook without Uncas. The end of the line. The absolute dead end. OK?'

'If you say so, Harry.'

'I do. This bloke who phoned you—'

'It could have been a woman, you know? One of those strange voices you can't pin down.'

'Whoever. Whatever. They've got it wrong. It's some other poor sod's son in that hospital.'

11

'But they had your name. Harry Barnett.'

'There must be dozens of Harry Barnetts around. Hundreds, probably.'

'Only one of them works here.'

'Very amusing. Now shove off, will you? I'm busy.' He nodded towards the forecourt, where three cars had pulled in more or less simultaneously.

'All right. If you're sure.'

'I'm sure.'

Shafiq fondled his moustache for a moment, then sighed to no particular purpose and sloped away. Harry was glad to see him go, hoping that in his absence he could forget the strangely disturbing notion that he might somewhere have a son. Given the kind of life he had led, it was difficult to be as certain on the point as he had claimed to be for Shafiq's benefit. Difficult, if not impossible. On the other hand, the last ten or twelve years had been so predominantly celibate, despite encompassing his only experience of matrimony, that any unwitting paternity on his part must lie so far in the past that it would surely have caught up with him long ago – if it was ever going to.

There was, of course, an easy way to put the matter to rest. Phone the National Neurological Hospital and confirm that the occupant of room E318 was nobody whose father he could possibly be. By any stretch of the imagination.

Quite why Harry felt as reluctant as he did to take this simple step he could not have explained, even to himself. But irritation at his inability to put the incident out of his mind finally overcame that reluctance. And, during a lull between customers, he picked up the telephone and tapped in the number.

'National Neurological Hospital.'

'I've been told a close relative of mine is in room E318 at your hospital, but I think there's been a mistake. Could you tell me the name of the patient in that room? Just to be sure.'

'Hold on, please.' There was a pause, then: 'Room E318, you said?'

'Yes.'

'The patient's name is Venning. David John Venning.'

'Once is never enough,' Iris Venning had said. And she was as good as her word. Marriage to Claude must have been even more passionless than Harry would naturally have supposed to nurture in his wife the yearning for physical release that burst open in

12

Harry's hands that afternoon like some exotic bloom whose flesh was as warm and luscious as its perfume.

What heightened their abandon, he afterwards reckoned, was the shared knowledge of its long-term insignificance. Claude had been his section head at Swindon Borough Council for three years, in which time Harry had met Iris no more than once or twice, fleetingly and usually when the worse for drink at some social gathering. But perhaps his appreciative gaze had even then signalled what she was looking for. Perhaps it was she, not Claude, who had suggested asking him to take a week off to paint their house during a spell of fine weather in July, 1960. Claude was by then two months into a new and better job with Manchester City Council, his connections with Swindon confined to a house he was finding it difficult to sell and a wife who could not follow him north until it *was* sold. A new coat of paint must have seemed like a ploy worth trying. And Harry certainly came cheaper than any professional, which would have appealed to Claude's parsimonious nature. As to what appealed to his wife's nature, both in frequency and variety, that Harry was pleasurably astonished to discover. It was a subject he went on to explore several times, even after the house painting was complete. The summer wore on and a sale still did not come and poor old Claude still slept alone six nights out of seven in his economical Mancunian lodgings. While Harry and the lovely Iris . . .

But idylls always end, preferably, as in this case, just before they stale. September brought a cash buyer. And by the end of the month Iris had joined her husband in Manchester. It was a relief in some ways, probably for Iris as much as Harry. It was the close of a chapter in their lives that was all the more satisfying for its brevity. It was a parting for good, in both senses of the word. Pleasure, with no strings attached. Memory, without reminders.

Occasionally, when he was feeling sorry for himself or had just been given the brush-off by one of the many girls his chat-up lines failed to impress, Harry would recall his spectacularly simple conquest of Iris Venning. Then certain sights and sensations would float into his mind: her flushed face, eyes closed and mouth open, glimpsed in the mirror above the fireplace as they celebrated a gymnastic union on the sofa; the tingling hiss of nylon against flesh as he peeled her black stockings down over her soft white thighs; the cool-skinned fullness of her breasts and buttocks; the fluid urgency with which they came together; above all, her eagerness, magnified in his imagination till his own seemed quite eclipsed; her eagerness – and his enjoyment.

Eventually, as the years passed and other experiences came Harry's way, such recollections faded into the remoter recesses of his memory, seldom if ever to be called upon. A hazy image of her body. A blurred impression of her face. A ghostly whisper of her name. There was nothing else. Ultimately, there would not even have been that. And why should there have been? When probability and common sense decreed that they would never meet again.

Until the moment he handed over to Crowther at the end of his shift, Harry was expecting to walk back up Scrubs Lane to Kensal Green just in time to find Terry sliding back the bolts at the Stonemasons'. That was probably what he should do. That was what common sense suggested. But curiosity – and secret reminiscence – had laid their hands on him. So, instead, he headed south to White City tube station. From there, he took the Central line to Holborn and made his way up through Bloomsbury, where the rush hour was in full swing, to the congregation of hospitals round Great Ormond Street and Queen Square. The National Neurological was a grand old Edwardian edifice, all marble pillars, high ceilings and long echoing corridors. A large modern extension was attached to it like some new shell on an ageing snail, where by contrast bright light and clinical starkness prevailed.

It was to the modern part of the hospital that Harry's steps took him, guided by signs and arrows rather than nurses or receptionists, none of whom did he care to consult. The reasons for his visit did not inspire much confidence, after all. Even, perhaps especially, in Harry himself.

But the signs were easy to follow. And nobody seemed even remotely interested in one plodding downcast figure. So, reaching the third floor and passing an unattended nursing station, he arrived, with little difficulty, at the far end of a short passage lit by a tinted window through which a dusk-smeared flank of the British Museum could be made out across the jumbled roofscape. Room E318. With a card lodged in the name-panel at eye-level: *David Venning*. No mistake, then. But a stranger, even so. Of that Harry remained certain. Unless what seemed like certainty was really only a fading hope.

He pushed the door open and entered. The room was small, but comfortably furnished. Pale wood, pastel carpeting and a large

14

floral-curtained window created as light, airy and normal an atmosphere as could be contrived. But normality stopped at the bed. A youngish dark-haired man lay there motionless, his head resting in the very centre of an otherwise undisturbed pillow, his arms bent at identical angles across the counterpane. He made no sound that Harry could hear, but sound there nevertheless was: the steady rhythmic rise and fall of mechanical breathing. A ventilating device fitted with some kind of bellows sat on a low table next to the bed, linked by a ribbed plastic pipe to a valve fixed to the man's throat and attached to the tracheostomy through which his lungs were being filled and emptied. And without which, Harry's minimal medical knowledge told him, he would die. This did not look good. Peaceful, yes. Almost serene. But very far from good.

Sad as the sight was of an apparently fit and healthy young man lying inert and artificially sustained, it was still no more than that to Harry. It did not involve him. It need not concern him. It was none of his business. Especially since, whoever David John Venning's father was, he could not be Harry. Could he?

'Date of birth,' Harry muttered to himself as he stepped across to the end of the bed and removed a clipboard thick with records from where it was hanging on one of the rails. 'That'll clinch it.' And clinch it, in a sense, it did. Though not in the way Harry would have hoped. *David John Venning. DoB: 10.05.61.* 'Oh, bloody hell.' He had been born the spring after the summer of Harry's long-forgotten fling with Iris Venning.

TWO

By the time he left the hospital, Harry was in no serious doubt that the comatose occupant of room E318 was his own son. Not just on account of the coincidence of dates and names. Nor simply because the proud parents flanking David Venning in a framed graduation photograph on the bedside cabinet were recognizable to Harry as older versions of the Claude he had worked with and the Iris he had been seduced by thirty-four summers ago. It was, after all, possible that the boy had been conceived during one of Claude's weekends home rather than one of his weeks away. Possible, though unlikely, especially given Harry's opinion of Claude's virility relative to his own.

But none of that was really the point. What convinced Harry beyond question was the telephone call. Someone knew for a fact that he was David's father and thought he should be aware of his condition. Which was, a staff nurse warily admitted, serious, if not grave. David Venning had been with them nearly a month and had remained in a deep coma throughout that time. As for the prospects of a recovery, she declined to commit herself, suspicious as she clearly was of Harry's claim to be an old friend of the family who had somehow lost touch. If he did not know the next of kin's address and telephone number, she felt unable to supply them, although one correction she did supply. David's mother was Iris Hewitt, not Venning. Remarriage, then, following divorce or widowhood. Well, the graduation photograph was probably taken more than ten years ago. It was not so

16

surprising. Poor old Claude – one way or the other.

She was scarcely more informative about the cause of David's illness, beyond stating that the coma was diabetic in origin. It seemed a cruelly arbitrary fate to overtake such a good-looking young man. Doubly so, when you considered how fundamentally fit his overweight ne'er-do-well father remained. Harry winced as he glimpsed a reflection of himself in a darkening window. He did not cut a handsome figure. To judge by the photograph, Iris had aged far more gracefully than he had. But that, he supposed, was only to be expected.

A more sympathetic junior nurse told him Mrs Hewitt visited her son every afternoon, usually between two and four. If Harry wanted to see her, that was the time to try. The wisdom of trying was what he debated later over several pints in a nearby pub. Thirty-four years ago, he would have run a mile from fatherhood. In principle, he would do the same now. But that calm still waiting figure in the bed was no principle. It was a person. A body and a soul. A son he had never known. A man he had never met. Till now.

And then there was the telephone call he always came back to. Who could have made it but Iris? She alone would know for certain. It had to be her. If so, the call was a kind of summons. A plea for help, perhaps. An appeal for support. She must have gone to some lengths to track him down. In the circumstances, he could hardly ignore her. But why, if it *was* her, had she left no name or number? Why the anonymity she must have known he would see through? There was, of course, only one way to find out.

Harry called Shafiq from the pub pay phone and asked if he would be prepared to swap shifts with him tomorrow. Pressed for an explanation, he admitted it had something to do with hospital visiting hours, then claimed he was running out of money and rang off before Shafiq could do more than agree.

Since the swap committed Harry to a disagreeably early start, he headed straight home, hoping to find Mrs Tandy had already gone to bed. But no such luck. She was up and about, making cocoa for herself and chopping up sardines to tempt Neptune, her cat, down from a neighbouring rooftop. Though cocoa was not what Harry wanted on top of four pints, no dinner and the sudden discovery of a son, it was what he found himself consuming in the tiny kitchen, while Mrs Tandy stood at the open back door,

17

whistling for Neptune and waving the bowl of sardines in the night air to set his whiskers twitching.

'I don't know why I bother with this cat,' she announced. 'He gets better treatment than most of the children round here.'

Harry choked on his cocoa and wondered amidst his splutters how Mrs Tandy had developed her uncanny knack for making remarks somehow related to whatever he was trying hardest to keep to himself.

'Of course, Selwyn and I were never blessed with offspring. Perhaps if we had been . . . But, then, you can't be sure, can you?'

'What about, Mrs T?'

'How they'd have turned out. What they'd have become. As often a curse as a comfort, I believe.'

'Well, I wouldn't know, would I?'

'No.' She glanced back at him with a disconcerting beadiness about her eye. 'I suppose you wouldn't.'

THREE

Tuesday was Mrs Tandy's Scrabble day. This was a relief to Harry, since it meant the coast was clear for him to return unobserved from Mitre Bridge for a bath, shave and change of clothes before setting off for the hospital. Such midday sprucing-up would have struck Mrs Tandy as highly suspicious. As would the abstention from alcohol that nibbled at Harry's nerves as he made the journey to Bloomsbury. Not to mention the half dozen circuits of Russell Square he completed while making substantial inroads into a pack of *Karelia Sertika* cigarettes. He made a mental note to call at Theophilus's shop off the Charing Cross Road later and collect a fresh supply of the esoteric Greek brand his years on Rhodes had left him with a liking for. Though whether such a banal errand would lodge in his mind in view of all else it might soon have to cope with he rather doubted.

It was nearly three o'clock when he reached the hospital. The third-floor nursing station was staffed this time, but, happily, not by any of the nurses he had met yesterday.

'Is it OK to visit David Venning?'

'Well . . . he already has a visitor, actually.'

'His mother?'

'Yes.'

'Don't worry. We know each other.'

He pressed on down the corridor. The door of room E318 stood half open, a pool of golden sunlight spilling across the threshold.

He stopped just short of it as a voice caught his ear. Iris Venning's. She was reading aloud.

'Cosmologists seem to have taken a Trappist vow in response to such inconvenient data. How can the universe contain stars up to sixteen billion years old when the Hubble telescope measures the age of the entire universe at a mere eight billion? Clearly, there is no easy answer. But scientists are not in business to dodge difficult questions.'

Her voice had not changed. Listening to it, he could almost imagine that if he stepped into the room he would see her as he had last seen her: red-headed, bright-eyed and full-figured, her sensuous lips shaping a come-hither smile or a suggestive giggle. But the photograph had prepared him for what he would actually see. A middle-aged woman with salt-and-pepper hair cut sensibly short, her face grown lined and cautious, her eyes dull and diffident, her smile . . . But she was not going to smile, was she? For there was nothing to smile about.

'How they square this circle may determine the future of astrophysics. The Big Bang may come to be seen as the Big Blunder. A role for the much-derided cosmological constant may suddenly emerge. But that will seem to some awfully like a last resort. What is really needed—'

She stopped the instant he appeared in the doorway. They looked at each other across twelve feet and a gulf of years. Recognition wrestled with disbelief in her gaze. Her mouth fell open in surprise. She slowly removed her glasses, put down the magazine she had been reading from and stared at him, unable to convince herself, it seemed, that it really was him. Had he changed so very much? Or had she thought he would ignore her message?

'I'm sorry,' she said, 'who . . .' She frowned and rose from her chair, stepping round the end of the bed to see him more clearly. 'Do I know you?'

'It's me,' he replied, wishing to God he had thought of something less inane by way of introduction.

'Harry?' Her eyes narrowed. She took another step closer. 'It can't be.'

He shrugged and shaped an apologetic grin. 'I guess this is what letting yourself go means.'

She said nothing, blinking rapidly as she stared at him. She reached out behind her and clasped the bed-rail, as if for support.

'How are you, Iris?'

20

'What . . . What are you doing here?'

'I got your message.'

'What message?'

'About David. About . . . our son.'

Much of the colour drained from her face. A ring on one of her fingers began to tinkle against the hollow metal of the bed-rail. She was trembling, as if fear were slowly replacing shock.

'I called round yesterday. They wouldn't tell me very much.'

'It was *you*?'

'Ah. They mentioned my visit, did they? Surely you must have guessed it was me, then.'

'*Guessed*? Guessed it was you? Of course not. I'd never—'

'Look, why don't we sit down?'

He moved hesitantly into the room. As he did so, Iris suddenly darted to his left and slammed the door shut behind him. Closer to, he could hear the shortness of her breath and sense the turmoil of her thoughts. But he could not fathom it. Her reaction made no sense. 'Let me get this straight,' she said slowly. 'You claim to have got some kind of message . . . about David?'

'You phoned the garage yesterday. Where I work. Just before I arrived.'

'And said what?'

'That my . . . son . . . was here.'

'Your *son*?'

'David.'

'He's no son of yours.' But something in her flickering glance towards the bed was as false as it was evasive.

'Come on, Iris. May sixty-one. I can do the sums.'

'You've done them wrong.'

'What are you saying?'

'I'm saying David isn't your son. I'm saying I made no phone call. And I'm saying I'd like you to leave.'

'What?'

'*My* son is gravely ill. And I'm extremely worried about him. The last thing I need – the *very* last – is somebody I hardly know popping up from the remote past to claim a relationship that exists only in his imagination.'

'Iris, for God's sake . . .' She must have read the bafflement in his eyes. Just as he read the determination in hers. The message had not come from her. The central fact of it was true. David *was* his son. But Iris had no intention of admitting anything. To her, Harry was worse than an enemy and less than a stranger. He was some kind of rival. One she was certain she had the power to defeat.

'Are you going to leave?'

'Not just like—'

She pulled the door open and stepped into the corridor. 'I want to see Staff Nurse Kelly immediately,' she called towards the desk. 'It's urgent.'

'There's surely no need for—'

'You're right,' she said, looking straight at him. 'No need for you to have done this at all. What gave you the idea, Harry? Did you see one of the newspaper articles about David and reckon there might be some money in it for you?'

'*Money?*'

'You look as if you're short. Well, I can't say I'm surprised. But if you think—'

'This has nothing to do with money.'

'I can't imagine what else would bring you out of the woodwork.'

'You *phoned* me.'

'No.'

'Well, somebody did.'

'I don't think so. In fact—' Staff Nurse Kelly strode suddenly into view, a bustling vision of blue-starched efficiency. 'Thank you for coming so quickly, Rachel,' said Iris. 'You met this man yesterday, I think.'

'I did.'

'His name's Harry Barnett.'

'A friend of yours, he said.'

'No kind of friend. And no help to my son at all. I've asked him to leave, but he refuses.'

'I haven't refused,' put in Harry. 'It's just—'

'I want him to go. And I don't want him to come back. Is that clear?'

'It's clear, Mrs Hewitt.' Kelly looked flintily at Harry. 'We do have security staff, Mr Barnett. Am I going to have to call them?'

'No. You're not.'

'This way, then. If you please.'

Harry shaped a final appeal. 'Iris, can't we just . . .' But no. They could not. That was obvious. With a resigned shrug, he walked past them and away down the corridor at what he judged to be a dignified pace.

FOUR

Beer was a lover who never tired of Harry's attentions, a friend who never turned him away. The slurred damn-it-all indifference he could summon up under its influence was his for the rest of the day, expanding with each pub he visited on his erratic route home, until, at his last port of call, even the barman's reluctance to serve him did not dent his sang-froid.

'Don't you think you've had enough, mate?'

'Oh, of many things. But not of beer. "Look through the bottom of a pewter pot, to see the world as the world's not." Truest thing I ever read.'

'We don't allow poetry in here.'

'No? Well, looking at the décor, I can see what you mean. Still, a pint should improve the view.'

'All right. Just one, mind.'

'Absolutely. Just one. As God's my witness.'

It was an oath he regretted breaking next morning, after waking late and leaden-headed to the discovery that even the curtain-filtered light of Foxglove Road, Kensal Green, could be painfully dazzling to those who have just single-handedly boosted several brewers' prospective dividends to their shareholders.

He stumbled to the kitchenette, coughing over his first cigarette. There he filled the kettle, started it boiling, downed a pint of London tap-water and commenced the quest for the Holy Grail of a clean coffee-mug. Before he had abandoned it, the telephone rang.

'Hello?' he said in a gravelly phantom of his own voice.

'Harry?'

'Yes. Who—' It was Iris. Disbelievingly, he fell silent. Surely it could not be. But it was.

'Am I . . . disturbing you?'

'Er . . .' He leant over and turned off the gas. 'No. You're not. Really.'

'The thing is . . . well . . . I'm sorry about what I said yesterday. How I reacted. It was . . .'

'Understandable.' He gave his forehead a vigorous massage with his free hand. It made nothing any clearer. 'Honestly.'

'It was the shock, actually. After all these years. The shock and . . .'

'There's no need . . . to explain.'

'Oh, but I think there is. I think I owe you that much, now you know about David. Could we meet, perhaps?'

'Well, of course. Why not? I mean . . .'

'You mean that's what you wanted to do yesterday and *I* prevented it. You're quite right. I can only apologize. You're probably wondering what's brought about this change of heart.'

'We've both had the chance to sleep on it, I suppose.' Though whether the stupor Harry was still recovering from could be called sleep he was not at all sure.

'Quite. Anyway, I suggest somewhere other than the hospital. I sometimes take tea at the Hotel Russell after visiting David. Do you know it?'

'Yes.' Of course he did. It was the terracotta pile he had passed on his circuits of Russell Square yesterday afternoon. The thought reminded him that he had, as predicted, failed to stock up with Greek cigarettes.

'I'll meet you in the lounge at four o'clock.'

'Fine.' Such a time would necessitate an early departure from Mitre Bridge. Perhaps he would just go sick instead. He felt ill enough to make it almost genuine. Although, strangely, his condition seemed to have improved since picking up the telephone. 'I'll be there.'

'Right. Well—'

'One thing, Iris.' His mind was sharpening now, even without the aid of coffee. A suspicion was growing on him that her conciliatory tone might amount to a confession. 'If you had this number all along, why did you phone me at the garage on Monday?'

'Because I didn't phone you, Harry. I called your mother in Swindon this morning. She gave me this number. Oh, don't worry. I didn't tell her who I was. But the message you got wasn't from me. I realized later how stupid what I said about you being on the make must have sounded. Even if you *had* read about David, you wouldn't have connected him with me, would you? Or with you.'

'Who did call me, then?'

'I don't know. Nobody but David and I know, Harry. That's the point.'

'Know that I'm his father, you mean?'

There was a lengthy silence Harry steeled himself not to break. Then Iris said: 'Exactly.'

FIVE

His neck chafing against the unfamiliar constriction of a tie, his eyes scarcely registering the wood-panelled elegance of his surroundings, Harry took the cup of Assam tea Iris had poured for him and leant back in his chair. He felt as he feared he looked: out of place and ill at ease.

Iris Venning – or Hewitt, as he was struggling to think of her – appeared, by contrast, perfectly in tune with the hushed and alcoved environment. She was wearing a simple but flattering outfit Mrs Tandy would probably have called a tea-dress. It certainly confirmed that Iris had kept her figure. Whereas even a double-breasted blazer could not disguise the paunch Harry had acquired since the summer of 1960, a season his thoughts, and doubtless hers, were bound to return to, however careful they might be to avoid mentioning it directly.

Indirectly, the events of that distant summer were the only reason they had met this wintry afternoon. Without them, David John Venning would never have been born. Nor would he be lying now, comatose and unaware, a few short streets away. Time could devise its revenges from beginnings as well as endings.

'Are you diabetic, Harry?' asked Iris, as he declined the offer of sugar.

'No.'

'I'd thought you might be, you see. I'd thought David might have inherited the disease from you. It developed in his teens. Oh, he came to terms with it readily enough. The injections and the diet. He made no fuss about it. It was just a problem to solve. He's always been good at that. Solving problems. But this time . . .'

'How did it happen? The coma, I mean.'

'I don't know. I don't understand it. He was alone. In an hotel room out at Heathrow. He was staying there overnight before flying back to America. He's lived and worked in the States for, what, nine years now. He's a mathematician, Harry. Quite brilliant, as a matter of fact. But it's all over my head. What he does. What he thinks about. Yours too, I expect.'

'*A brilliant mathematician?*'

'Yes. Amazing, isn't it? At an age when you were still reading the *Beano*, he was devouring Newton's *Principia*. And making things too. Cardboard dodecahedra. Hypercubes. God knows what. He really was a prodigy. Senior wrangler at Cambridge. Ph.D. at twenty-three. We were so proud of him.'

'You and Claude?'

'Yes. Claude died the year after David went to California to do post-doctoral research at UCLA. That's where he met his wife. In Los Angeles.'

'So he's married. Any—'

'No. No children. David and Hope are divorced now, anyway. Maybe you've heard of her. She's married again since. To the film star, Steve Brancaster.'

'I don't think so.'

'It doesn't matter. David was well rid of her. She'd only have held him back.'

'From what?'

'Academic success. She always wanted him to go into the commercial sector. Got her way in the end with the Globescope job. Globescope's an international economic forecasting corporation based in Washington. David was working for them until the spring of this year. But I don't think his heart was really in it. When he came to see us last month, he was full of a new project that was pure research.'

'*Us* meaning you and your new husband?'

'Yes. Ken was a golfing friend of Claude's. He was very good to me after Claude's death. We've been married five years now. He runs an engineering company in Stockport.'

'You still live in Manchester, then?'

'Wilmslow, actually. But I've been staying with my sister in Chorleywood since this happened. Which brings us back to where we started, doesn't it? David had been over here drumming up interest in his new project. He's secured a lot of funding in America already and seemed confident it would get off the ground. A specialist institute to investigate the mathematics of higher dimensions. Don't ask me what *they* are. I've never understood such stuff. But David was full of it. And very excited about the prospects. He could hardly wait to get it up and running. That's what makes the suggestion of attempted suicide so utterly—' She caught his shocked look. 'I'm sorry. Perhaps I should have explained more fully from the start. But it's not easy. Explaining all this to someone I never expected to . . . Someone who never . . .'

'Who never knew he had a son, Iris. Remember that. I had no idea.'

'Would it have made a difference if you had? Would you have stood by me if I'd come back to Swindon a few months after leaving and announced I was carrying your child? I don't think so, Harry, do you?'

He shook his head slowly in surrender to his own memory of himself as much as the force of her argument. 'No. I expect he was better off with Claude as a father. But you said this morning he knows. About me, I mean.'

'I told him after Claude died. I thought he was entitled to know. But he didn't make much of it. Mathematics had always been more important to him than human frailty. Another reason why suicide would never have entered his head.'

'Why do they think it did?'

'Because the coma was precipitated by an overdose of insulin. Too big an overdose for him to have taken accidentally. If a chambermaid hadn't found him when she did, he'd certainly have died. As it is . . .' She sighed. 'They don't think he's going to recover, Harry. They don't think he's ever going to wake up.'

So that was it. The final irony. Perhaps a disembodied voice of fate had left the message for Harry. So he could learn he had a son only when it was too late to claim him. 'There's no hope?'

'Realistically, not much. So the doctors tell me, anyway. Miracles do happen, of course. But they reckon the chances of a full recovery are virtually nil. And that, even if he did emerge from the coma, he'd have permanent brain damage. Can you imagine what that would mean for a brilliant mathematician?'

'I'm not sure I can, no.'

'They've suggested taking him off life support.' She looked straight into Harry's eyes. 'Letting him die.'

'I see.'

'Do you? Do you really see where that leaves me?'

'Torn, I imagine.'

'Yes. Torn very nearly in two.' She glanced away. He was tempted for a moment to reach out and take her hand. To offer physical comfort where words seemed likely to fail him. But they had not touched each other in David Venning's lifetime. And perhaps they never would. 'I sometimes wish . . .'

'Don't say it.'

'I'm sorry,' she said briskly, looking back at him. 'This isn't your problem.'

'Isn't it?'

'No. Absolutely not. Ken and I will—'

'What does Ken think you should do?'

She pursed her lips. A flicker of weakness passed across her face. Harry reckoned he knew what Ken thought without her needing to say. If he was right, Iris might have made the anonymous telephone call after all – so that she could enlist his help without having to beg for it.

'I don't think you should let yourself be talked into taking any action you might later regret.'

'How very level-headed of you, Harry.'

'Whoever left that message for me obviously thought—'

'It wasn't me.'

'Then who?'

'I simply don't know. I'm more or less certain David kept what I told him to himself.'

'He might have confided in his wife.'

'You wouldn't say that if you'd ever met her.'

'Or a close friend.'

'No. I was nervous about telling him. But I needn't have been. He made it obvious he regarded it as a matter of no importance.'

'You can't be sure of that.'

'No? Well, did he track you down, Harry? Did he seek you out when he had the chance?'

'He might have found that difficult. I was living abroad.'

'Yes. In Rhodes.' Her look hardened. 'I read about you in the papers. Six years ago, wasn't it? Something to do with a girl who disappeared on holiday.'

With weary fatalism, Harry confronted the moment he had known was coming all along. The skeleton in his cupboard that was no skeleton at all. And yet so much more famous than the

29

real ones. 'Something, yes. But the press made more of the mystery than its solution. As they always do.'

'Well, I shouldn't think the story made the American papers. And I didn't send David any cuttings. So he was probably blissfully unaware of your brush with notoriety.'

'Iris, you can't think—'

'How exactly did you end up in Rhodes? I'd always imagined you whiling away life as a council clerk.'

'I left the Council five years after you moved to Manchester. Opened a car sales business in Marlborough Road with an old National Service chum, Barry Chipchase. Went bankrupt, I'm afraid.' He decided not to mention his partner's treacherous role in the episode for fear he would not be believed. 'After that, I worked for a marine electronics firm in Weymouth. The job fell through after a few years.' The phrase was another triumph of reticence. He did not think Iris was ready to hear how he had been falsely accused of embezzlement. 'A friend offered me a caretaking job at his villa on Rhodes around the same time, so . . .'

'This friend would have been the disgraced government minister – Alan Dysart?'

'Yes. But he wasn't a minister then. And he hadn't been disgraced.'

'How did you come to know him?'

'He worked for Barry and me when he was a student.' Harry shifted awkwardly in his chair. 'Look, where's all this getting us?'

'The present, Harry. *Your* present.'

'I live at 78 Foxglove Road, Kensal Green. I have a flat on the first floor. My landlady and her cat live downstairs. I pay the rent by working part-time at a nearby garage. I get by. I live from day to day. I survive. What more do you want to know?'

'Never married?'

'Since you ask, yes. Just a few years ago.'

'But you don't live together?'

'She moved to Newcastle to find a job. She has a cousin who's a solicitor there. He took her on as a secretary.' Growing caution prevented Harry explaining that he had married Zohra in order to save her from being deported back to Sri Lanka. It had been an act of unambiguous generosity. But somehow he did not think it would sound like it. 'That's enough about me. What about you? And David?'

She drank some tea, palpably playing for time before answering.

'There's something you need to understand, Harry. Something that isn't easy to say. What happened between us thirty-four years ago had an . . . ulterior motive.'

'What do you mean?'

'Claude and I had been trying to have children for a long time. Without success. And I wanted children. Badly. Claude was a good man. I loved him. But . . .'

'He couldn't get you pregnant?'

'No. Whereas . . .'

'I could.'

'It sounds awful, doesn't it? So clinical. So . . . calculating.'

'I thought we were having fun. Simple uncomplicated fun.'

'Simple, yes. Uncomplicated, no.'

'So, the realization that you were pregnant by me wasn't a horrible shock so much as a satisfactory outcome. Did you tell David that?'

'Yes. Which is why he would never have come looking for you.'

'Well, thanks,' he said, allowing the bitterness to break through in his tone. 'Thanks a lot for making my son understand I was just a means to an end.'

'Your *son* in the strictest biological sense only.' She threw back her head, as if in search of calm as well as logic. 'I won't stop you visiting him, Harry. I could, but I won't. On the other hand, I'm not going to let you invade his life. Or mine.'

'How long do I have before you switch him off?'

'It's not like that.'

'Will you at least warn me . . . when you reach a decision?'

'Yes.' She looked at him gravely. 'I will.' She took a tiny notebook from her handbag, tore out a page, wrote something on it and slid it across the table towards him. 'My sister's address and telephone number. You can contact me there . . . if you really need to.'

'Does she know about me?'

'She will.'

'And Ken?'

Iris shook her head. 'I'm not going to answer any more questions, Harry. You already know as much as you've a right to. Probably more.'

'Not in the opinion of whoever left me that message.'

'If there was a message.'

'You said yourself I couldn't have found out any other way.'

'I suppose not. It's just another mystery.'

31

'Like the overdose? If it wasn't a suicide attempt and it couldn't have been an accident . . .'

'Stop it.' She had raised her voice for the first time, sufficiently to attract a curious glance from a nearby table. 'I'm tired of such speculation. Don't you think I've been through it all in my mind, over and over again? In the end, the whys and wherefores don't matter. They won't help him breathe or eat or speak or walk. Nothing will.' She was trembling now, her eyes brimming with tears. 'Could it be some kind of punishment for deceiving Claude, I wonder? I asked myself that about his diabetes when it was first diagnosed. Now this. It makes you think.'

'You know that's ridiculous.'

'Yes.' She dabbed at her eyes with a handkerchief and blew her nose. 'Of course I do. Like hoping he'll recover. Ridiculous. But I can't help doing it.'

'Neither can I.'

The remark, with its hint of intimacy, seemed suddenly too much for Iris. 'Why should you care?' she snapped. 'He's nothing to you.'

'Perhaps because I have no-one else to care about.'

'Exactly.' There was harshness in her expression, honed by the anguish she had endured. 'If you had a family of your own, you wouldn't be interested, would you? You wouldn't want to know.'

'It's easy for you to say that, knowing I can't disprove it.'

'That's not good enough.' She glanced at her watch. 'I really must be going. Blanche will be wondering what's become of me.' Rising hurriedly, she took a ten-pound note from her handbag and dropped it onto Harry's side of the table. 'Would you mind paying the bill for me? That should cover it.'

'There's no need—' But catching her eye as he stood up, Harry realized there was a compelling need from her point of view. She did not want to owe him any kind of debt, however trivial. Lest it remind her – and him – of what they could not help owing each other.

'Goodbye, Harry,' she said with cool finality.

SIX

Room E318 at the National Neurological Hospital seemed as warm and muffled as a womb next morning. The ventilator pumped out its measured maternal breaths and a vase of fresh irises spread its symbolic cheer; while the distant sounds of calm voices and familiar movements compressed themselves into an institutional universe of care and compassion. It surrounded Harry on all sides, enclosing him and his silent son, encompassing their pasts and however much of a future either of them had.

'Your mother's lifted her ban on me,' Harry remarked, trying another gambit in his one-way bedside conversation. 'So you'll be seeing quite a bit more of me. As long as you don't mind, that is. Say if you do. We've got a lot of catching up to do, of course. I'll tell you about myself, if you like. There's nothing remarkable to say. Nothing out of the ordinary. Not like you. I mean, mathematics? I wouldn't know where to begin. The square on the hypotenuse is equal to the sum of the squares on the other two sides. I know a joke about that, involving squaws and hippopotamuses. Or is it hippopotami? Well, I don't suppose you want to hear it anyway. What would you like to hear? My life story? That can be arranged. I'd like to hear yours. As well as your thoughts on one or two things that have been troubling me. The message I received. If it wasn't from your mother, who was it from? And what was it supposed to make me do? Ask how you ended up like this, perhaps? An accident's out of the question, apparently. And attempted suicide? I can't see it. Not for a

33

son of mine. The Barnetts are often unlucky. But never self-destructive. What, then? What happened in that hotel room? I'd try to find out – I promise I really would – if you'd just tell me where to begin.'

But David could tell Harry nothing. And Iris, even if she could, had made it clear she did not intend to. Which left Harry to interrogate Shafiq about the person who had left the message for him at Mitre Bridge – to no avail. Shafiq remained uncertain about the sex of the caller. Nor could he remember any particular accent.

'Didn't you think to ask for their name?'

'Of course I did, Harry. Do you take me for a fool?'

'Well, what did they say?'

'Nothing. That was when they rang off.'

'Oh, marvellous.'

'Well, I'm sorry. Would you have done any better?'

'Maybe. For a start, I might have recognized them.'

'If they'd known that was likely, they would not have called while you were here, would they?'

'No. No, they wouldn't.'

'In which case . . .'

'They must have been studying my movements. They must have been watching me.'

It was a disturbing possibility. So much so that Harry decided to unburden himself to Mrs Tandy. He chose his next day off, when, as usual, he accompanied her to Kensal Green Cemetery as flower porter and water carrier. Mrs Tandy's had been a marriage of cousins, as a result of which her late husband's relatives and her own were inextricably intertwined. And more numerous, it sometimes seemed to Harry, than the weeds that grew between their overgrown plots.

Recuperating on a bench after a vigorous tour of the scattered outliers as well as the main cluster of Tandy memorials, Harry explained his predicament as non-committally as he could. He felt Mrs Tandy should be made aware of the situation. But he was not sure he wanted her to understand how deeply it had affected him. His uncertainty, however, took little account of the keenness of her insight.

'Quite a shock for you, I imagine. Discovering you're a father so late in life.'

'Only *technically* a father.'

34

'But the man who believed he *was* David's father is dead, isn't he? So perhaps the technicalities are irrelevant.'

'Not according to Iris.'

'Whose need is greater, Harry? David's – or his mother's?'

'David's, of course.'

'Then perhaps you should do something to help him.'

'What do you suggest?'

'Find out what caused his coma and what can be done to cure it.'

'How?'

'Speak to his doctor. And to those who know him best. His friends and contemporaries. His fellow mathematicians. Anybody who might understand his state of mind when he booked into that hotel. Or know of any reason why others might have wished him harm.'

'But Iris—'

'Is his mother. What would she know? Have you told *your* mother, for instance, that she has a grandson?'

'Of course not. What would be the point?'

'See what I mean?'

'But his friends . . . are probably all in America.'

'His ex-wife, for instance?'

'For certain, I should think.'

'Should you?' She grinned mischievously. 'You ought to read more of the newspapers than the racing page, Harry, you really ought. Fetch yesterday's *Telegraph* from the bin over there, would you?'

'But I screwed up the dead flowers in it.'

'Then unscrew them. You want page three or five.'

With shrugs and sighs of reluctance, Harry crossed to the bin, fished out the bundle in which he had disposed of the whiffy accumulation of sodden stems, flattened out the paper on the path and tried to separate the damp pages. 'What exactly am I looking for, Mrs T?'

'Bring it over here.'

Leaving the mess of rotten foliage behind, he carried the paper back to the bench, where Mrs Tandy had already put on her glasses. She took it from him with a supercilious smile and arched back her head to improve her focus.

'Let me see, let me see.' Two wet-edged pages were carefully parted. 'Ah, here we are. There was a film première the night before last at the MGM Cinema in Shaftesbury Avenue. I doubt it had the panache of those I attended before the war, but never mind. The point is that one of the stars of *Dying Easy* is none other than Steve Brancaster, pictured here arriving at the event with his glamorous wife Hope.'

Harry sat down beside her and stared at the photographs. There were three of them in all, the largest showing a young Royal disgorging from a limousine. But one of the accompanying shots was what drew Harry's eyes. As the caption confirmed, the tall faintly lupine figure in tuxedo and open-neck dress shirt was the actor Steve Brancaster. Beside him, blond hair cascading over bare shoulders, a dazzling smile and sparkling eyes competing for attention with a neckline that displayed a truly startling amount of cleavage, stood Hope Brancaster, formerly Venning, formerly God knows what.

'I expect they're still here,' said Mrs Tandy. 'Premières can be very exhausting.'

'You think so?'

'Oh yes.' She peered closer. 'I should try the Dorchester if I were you.'

SEVEN

Mrs Tandy's estimate of the Brancasters' taste in hotels turned out to be spot on. With his fraying blazer and faded tie once more to the fore, Harry strode into the Dorchester late that afternoon, asked as confidently as he could for Mrs Brancaster and was rewarded with confirmation that she was indeed a guest there. Unfortunately, she was also out.

'Can I take a message for her, sir? Or would you prefer to wait?'

'Well, er . . .'

'Oh, actually, there's no need.' The concierge glanced over Harry's shoulder. 'Here's the lady now.'

Harry turned to see Hope Brancaster making an eye-catching entrance in wide-brimmed hat, flared raincoat and high-heeled bootees. A porter was bringing up the rear with two Bond Street carrier bags in either hand and a fifth looped over his shoulder.

'This gentleman's been asking for you, Mrs Brancaster,' said the concierge as he held out her key.

'And you are?' said Hope in a Californian drawl. She was close enough to Harry for the headiness of her perfume and the flawlessness of her complexion to be abundantly apparent.

'Harry Venning,' he replied at once, smiling earnestly. Noticing a flicker of doubt in Hope's eyes, he added: 'David's uncle.' The lie had been planned to get him as far as Hope's room. Now, committed to using it face to face, he wondered if she might know for a fact that David had no such uncle. If so, he could be about to make a forced and ignominious exit.

But his luck was in. Luck – and something else he could never have anticipated. 'You've got his smile. You know that?'

'You think so?'

'To the life. But it's odd. I don't recall David ever mentioning you.'

'I've been out of touch with the family for quite a while. Doing my best now . . . to rally round.'

'Yeh, right.' She rattled the key in her hand as if to signal his time was nearly up. 'So, what can I do for you?'

'I was hoping to talk to you . . . about David.'

'That could be kinda difficult.' She glanced ostentatiously at her watch. 'I'm on a tight schedule.'

'It really is rather important.'

She hesitated for a moment, then said: 'OK. But I need to freshen up. I'll meet you in the bar in ten minutes.'

Half an hour had passed, during which Harry had finished one extravagantly priced lager and started another, when Hope Brancaster deigned to join him. Her schedule, it seemed, was nothing like as tight as the PVC jeans she had somehow managed to wriggle into in the interim. There was a faint squeak as she descended into the chair opposite Harry, who could not suppress a pang of disappointment at how well her loose-fitting T-shirt camouflaged those remarkable breasts he remembered from the newspaper photograph. She ordered a Virgin Mary and cast a hostile glare at the ashtray, where smoke was still curling up from the remnants of a *Karelia Sertika* cigarette.

'You smoke those things?' she enquired with no hint of irony. 'Or cure fish with them?'

'Sorry,' he said with a shrug.

'Not as sorry as you should be. I dislike liars every bit as much as nicotine addicts.'

'That's all right, then. I'm neither.'

'Cut the bull. I gave Iris a call. She recognized your description. But not your name.'

'Ah.'

'Advised me to throw you out. Without listening to a word.'

'Did she?'

'Which is what I would do . . .'

'Except?'

'You really do remind me of David. Weird, I'd say, if you're no kind of relative. Which Iris assures me you're not.'

38

'I'm his father.'

'Your death was just an ugly rumour, right?'

'Iris and I . . . had a brief affair . . . the summer before David was born.'

'Well, well. Did you now?'

'David never mentioned this to you?'

'He never even *hinted* at it.'

'I see.'

'Well, I don't. Haven't you left it awful late to play the paternal card?'

'I only found out about it myself a few days ago.'

'Iris looking for an ally, was she?'

'How d'you mean?'

'She's in a minority of one in wanting to keep David alive. I'm guessing she thought you might back her up. But the way she talked about you makes me suspect you disagreed with her. Am I right?'

'You think he should be allowed to die?'

'It's not for me to say, is it? David and I are ex in every way. But I went to see him in the hospital for old times' sake and it looked pretty hopeless to me. I mean, nobody actually said so, but you could see that's what they thought. It must be hard for Iris. Only child and all. But you have to face it, don't you? For David more than anyone, life with half a brain would be infinitely worse than death.'

'Why more than anyone?'

'Because thinking's what he's spent most of his life doing. Resolving all those damned equations in his head. Searching for the answers to questions most of us don't even know how to ask. Math, math, math. There never was room for much else.'

'You're not a mathematician yourself?'

'What do you think? Do I look like a mathematician? Maybe if I had been . . . But you don't want to hear about that.'

'If it helps me form a picture of what David . . . what my *son* is really like, I do want to hear.'

'Ask his mother. You'll only get a biased picture from me.'

Harry grinned ruefully. 'Iris hasn't exactly been forthcoming.'

'Come to regret involving you, has she?'

'She didn't involve me. An anonymous informant told me about David. Any idea who that might have been?'

'Somebody who knew more than me. Who cared more than me, maybe.' There was a hint of resentment in her voice.

39

'You have somebody specific in mind?'

Hope paused to sip her drink, then clunked the glass back onto the table with exasperated force. 'Listen, Harry. You want to understand the son you never knew you had? Obsession's the key to it. The man I married was charming, witty, good-looking, sharp as a nail and fun to be around. That's what attracted me to him in the first place. But then there was his other side. His *mind*.' She tapped her brow. 'Out of this world. Literally. Complex numbers. Higher dimensions. Quantum physics. And something wrapped up in it all that he was looking for. Something that always drove him on. You could say I never understood a word and that would be true. But then he didn't deal in words. Numbers. Symbols. Equations. Formulae. Sometimes not even that. Sometimes he'd sit for hours, not speaking, not moving, just thinking. His "unwritten theorems", he called them. After a while, I couldn't cope. With Steve, I only have to worry about the latest actress who's trying to get into bed with him. With David, things were more complicated. If you want to know what made him tick, look through his notebooks. He carried them with him wherever he went, page after page crammed with his damned mathematical hieroglyphs. Why, I've even known him bring them to the dinner table in a restaurant.' She sighed. 'Yeh, you take a stroll through them, Harry. Iris should have the latest set. They'll have been in his hotel room. Probably under his pillow. You'll need a mathematician to interpret them for you, of course. And even then . . .'

'Who would I ask?' Harry enquired, doing his best to suggest he was motivated by intellectual curiosity rather than an eagerness to glean as much information as he could about David's circle of friends.

'You're serious?'

Harry shrugged.

'Well, the Dane, I suppose. Torben Hammelgaard. A physicist rather than a mathematician, but it comes to the same thing. He and David worked together at Globescope.'

'On what?'

'Forecasting, I guess. Isn't that what Globescope do?'

'You tell me.'

'Well, forecasting covers it. Economic projections. Climatic predictions. How many more billions there'll be to sell cheeseburgers to in 2020. It's pretty big business. If David had taken it more seriously, he might never have ended up like this.'

'Why not?'

'Because he'd have been in Washington earning good money, not skulking in a hotel room at Heathrow wondering where his next fund-raising scheme was coming from.'

'Iris said he'd secured the backing to set up some sort of research institute.'

'That's what he told her. Who in their right mind would fund research into higher dimensions? What you can't see you can't sell. It's a lesson David never wanted to learn. But since he was fired from Globescope—'

'Fired?'

'The way I heard it, yuh. Along with Hammelgaard. And David's very good friend Donna Trangam.'

'Who?'

'A neurobiologist. An expert on brains who fancies herself as an expert on hearts as well. Funny how her friendship doesn't seem to have extended to offering help with David's treatment. Something of a specialist in comatose conditions, I believe. But nowhere to be seen when most needed. Odd that, wouldn't you say?'

'You mean . . . she really might be able to do something for him?'

'It's possible.'

'Then where is she?'

'Your guess is as good as mine. Well, maybe not. She used to be at Berkeley. I'd lay money she crawled back there after Globescope fired her.'

'Why were they fired?'

'I wouldn't know. In David's case, he was probably spending too much of the corporation's time on his own research. As for the others . . . I really can't imagine.' She moved forward in her chair. 'And I *do* have to be going, fun as this has been. If you want to do something for your son, Harry, persuade Iris to let go of him. He isn't coming back. Not as he was, anyway. And that means not at all.'

'Tell me,' said Harry, holding her gaze for a moment with his own, 'how do you think he came to take an overdose of insulin?'

'I think he's been going nowhere fast since leaving Globescope. And I think he may have realized that. But don't take my word for it. Ask Adam Slade. From what I hear, he had dinner with David at his hotel the night it happened. If anyone can tell you David's state of mind at the time—'

'Who's Adam Slade?'

41

'You've never heard of him?'

'No.'

Hope rolled her eyes in mock surprise. 'I thought you'd only been out of David's life for thirty years, not the world in general. Adam Slade the *magician*. Doesn't the name mean anything to you?'

Harry shook his head.

'Well, who'd have believed it? Not Adam, that's for certain. He's really quite big. Here *and* in the States. Claims to perform some of his tricks by manipulating higher dimensions. Hence David's interest in him. Amazing how a brilliant scientist can be taken in by a crude con artist, don't you think?'

'I don't know what to think. I don't even know what higher dimensions are.'

'No. I don't suppose you do.' Hope flashed him a smile of apparently genuine amusement. 'Why don't you see for yourself? Adam had the gall to send Steve and me a couple of tickets for tomorrow night's show. He's doing a short season of what he calls "Pure Magic" at the Palladium. We won't be going, so you may as well be our guest.' She plucked a small envelope from her tote-bag and dropped it onto the table between them. 'Take a friend.' With that she rose and was gone, soft light shimmering on taut PVC as she strode swiftly away. Leaving Harry to realize, a second after he had lost sight of her, that he would have to pay the bill for their drinks. There was, it seemed, no such thing as a free ticket.

EIGHT

A measure of Adam Slade's eagerness to ingratiate himself with the Brancasters was the excellent location of the seats Harry and Mrs Tandy found themselves occupying at the Palladium the following night. The centre of the stalls, half a dozen rows back from the stage, could hardly have been bettered as a vantage point from which to admire the man's magical talents. The admiration of a Hollywood luminary and his no less luminous wife was, of course, well worth such generosity. Adam Slade was not to know that the Brancasters' tickets had been passed on to a part-time employee of the Mitre Bridge Service Station and his elderly landlady.

On the other hand, Mrs Tandy was unquestionably cutting a dash in aubergine organza and pearls. She had been delighted to accept Harry's invitation, even though it had briefly and tearfully reminded her of theatrical outings with her husband long ago. But that was more than could have been said for Harry's only previous recorded proposal of a social evening: karaoke night at the Stonemasons' Arms. 'Pure Magic' at the London Palladium was definitely more to Mrs Tandy's liking.

And to Harry's, he would freely have admitted. Professional illusionism had clearly come on apace since his last exposure to it: a trip with Uncle Len to see the Great Caldenza at the old Empire Theatre in Swindon not far short of fifty years ago. Caldenza had not entered amidst deafening rock music and pink-lit swirls of dry ice. Nor had he been accompanied by a quartet of curvaceous blondes in diaphanous costumes. And he had definitely not embodied Adam Slade's curious mixture of Mephistopheles and the boy next door.

High-octane charm with a jagged edge appeared to be Slade's stock-in-trade. Short and slightly built, with sharp features and a ready smile, he could have been every mother's ideal vision of a son-in-law, but for the dark crew-cut hair and the carefully judged five o'clock shadow. Confident he certainly was, as well as slick, witty and hugely egotistical. His routine was fast-moving and entertaining. But come the interval Harry could not help feeling disappointed. Tricksy lighting effects, whizz-bang technology and calendar-girl assistants apart, Slade's repertoire was basically the same old magician's routine of disappearing and reappearing, levitating and predicting, card-sharping and pea-shuffling. True, he sawed himself rather than a leotarded lady in half. And, equally true, Harry had not the first idea how he did any of it. Nor, presumably, had the audience member whose birthday Slade guessed. Not to mention the nervous volunteer whose gold wristwatch Slade apparently smashed to smithereens before suddenly reassembling it. But that it was all a trick – all a clever sleight-of-hand – Harry did not doubt.

And what of higher dimensions? 'They've not even been mentioned,' Harry complained to Mrs Tandy in the bar.

'You should have read the programme,' she said reprovingly. 'They're billed as the highlight of the second half.'

'Oh.'

'And they'll need to be. So far, I haven't seen anything you couldn't learn how to do from dear Selwyn's *Secrets of Houdini* book. It's somewhere in the attic at home.'

The second half opened bemusingly to subdued lighting and melancholic music. Slade entered unsmiling and alone, moved to a corner of the stage, advanced to the edge, sat down and gazed out at the audience.

'What you've seen so far this evening,' he announced, 'has been an illusion. I design my tricks for your enjoyment and mystification. But they are only tricks. Yet I find they prepare me better than solitude or meditation for the execution of genuine magic, which is what you're about to see. Unlike my fellow illusionists around the world, I possess the ability to manipulate objects in dimensions other than those of length, breadth and depth. It's an ability I inherited from my great-grandfather, Henry Slade, an American who visited this country in 1877 and was convicted of fraud on the basis of the demonstrations he gave of his hyper-dimensional powers. His conviction was unjust, as my grandfather and father both maintained throughout their lives. But only now, with the reappearance of his powers in my generation, can that injustice be proved. I shall perform this evening variations of three of the hyper-dimensional demonstrations Henry Slade gave. And I will add a couple of my own.'

The music gathered pace. The lights came up bright and clear. Three of the blondes, more conservatively costumed than before, brought on the props: a tray bearing a silver coffee-pot and a cup and saucer, a pair of wooden hoops about six inches in diameter and a length of rope, which they arranged on a circular pedestal table. Volunteers were asked for and a forest of hands shot up, Harry's among them. He was not one of those chosen, but the view from his seat was distinct and unobstructed. Whatever hyper-dimensionality was, he would soon see it in action.

Slade welcomed the volunteers – two men and a woman – onto the stage, elicited their names, cracked a few mood-lifting jokes, then picked up the rope. 'Professor Zöllner of the University of Leipzig set my great-grandfather several tests of hyper-dimensionalism, all of which he passed, though not necessarily in the way Professor Zöllner had asked him to. The Slades, it seems, have always had a sense of humour.' He grinned, handed one end of the rope to each of the men and asked them to stand just far enough apart for it to hang between them in a semi-circle. 'Who can tie a figure-of-eight knot in this rope without Mark or Neil letting go?' Nobody responded. 'For those bound by three spatial dimensions, it's impossible. For those who are not, it's as simple as fastening a shoelace.' He reached out, ran his hand round the bottom of the loop, hooked his index finger over it, performed a sudden twisting movement and . . . hey presto, as the Great Caldenza would probably have said, there was a well-formed figure-of-eight knot in the rope, tied without either end being released. And there too was a storm of applause.

'Coffee for the lady,' said Slade, swooping over to the table and filling the cup. He handed it to the woman and, when she had taken a sip, said: 'How long have you been married, Amanda?'

'Eighteen months,' she replied hesitantly.

'And you've worn an engagement ring as well as a wedding ring all that time?'

'Yes.'

'Always the same way round – wedding ring first, engagement ring second?'

'Yes. Of course.'

'Until tonight.'

'What? No, I—' But when she looked at her wedding finger, she so nearly dropped her cup in surprise that Slade had to take it from her.

'Which way round are they tonight, Amanda?'

'The . . . the other way.'

'If I'd tried to slide them off while handing you the cup, you'd have noticed, wouldn't you? Besides, it's quite hot in here, so they'd probably stick a bit. But not if you simply lift them up and swap them over.'

Amanda seemed as genuinely shocked as the audience was genuinely impressed. Harry did not know what to think. But, before he had the chance to ponder the point, Slade had moved on.

'It's OK, Amanda. Your rings are completely unharmed. Finish your coffee. It'll calm you down.'

She took the cup from him, raised it obediently from the saucer to drink, then stopped. 'It's empty,' she said in amazement.

'So it is,' said Slade. 'Now, what did I do with that?' More applause.

'Never mind. I'll pour you another.' Amanda by now resembled somebody in a hypnotic trance. After filling the cup and giving it back to her, Slade ambled over to Mark and Neil. 'You can let go now, gentlemen,' he said, taking the rope away and handing them each one of the wooden hoops. 'It's time for a little healthy competition. The coffee-pot's solid silver. And it's yours if you can toss your hoop over it. Fairground stuff, eh? In fact, a piece of cake. Test the hoops first. Make sure they're solid. Stretch them. Twist them. Bite them if you like.' When Mark and Neil had tapped and strained to their satisfaction, he stepped back and waved them into action. 'Fire away. Would you like to go first, Mark?'

But priority made no difference. From the far side of the stage, with nerves ajangle, it turned out to be too much for both of them. Mark's fell dismally short, while Neil's went way over the top. Slade retrieved them with eye-rolling expressions of mock disgust, then took careful aim himself, as if intent on showing the audience how it should be done. But what he showed them was rather different. The first hoop flew low and fast through the air, striking the table-leg about halfway up and ricocheting away. 'If at first you don't succeed,' remarked Slade unabashed, 'try something else.' He tossed the second hoop almost nonchalantly. It too struck the table-leg, but did not rebound from it. Instead, it somehow looped itself around the leg and could suddenly be seen rattling to rest round the base. Some people stood up. Others gasped in astonishment. Even Harry was taken aback. He was not at all sure that *Secrets of Houdini* would contain an explanation of what he had just seen. He was not at all sure it *could* be explained. But it had happened.

Amidst resounding cheers, Slade discharged the volunteers from the stage, stopping Amanda just as she was leaving and asking her to check her rings again. To her crowning astonishment, universally shared, she discovered they had been switched back to their original positions.

Then the props were removed and the music assumed a frolicsome beat. Two clowns rode onto the stage on monocycles and completed a couple of wobbly circuits. One of them dismounted, handed his machine to Slade and capered off. A cable was lowered, which Slade clipped to the saddle before standing back to watch as the cycle was raised about six feet off the floor. The same procedure was then followed with the second clown's cycle, except that it was suspended a few inches higher. The two machines now hung about twelve feet apart, with their wheels at right angles to each other. An ominous tone came into the lighting and music as Slade set the wheels spinning. Then the cables began slowly to converge, Slade racing across the ever decreasing gap between them to sustain and accelerate the spin. What would happen when the wheels met seemed obvious: a simple collision of rubber tyre and metal spoke. But Slade was jumping back and forth as if set on some ambitious twist to the plot, head swivelling from side to side, hands flicking at the tyres almost as fast as they were rotating. The music soared, turquoise smoke billowed up at the back of the stage and, suddenly, the two wheels met and came abruptly to rest locked together, tyre threaded through tyre, spoke through spoke.

At first, there was silence. Then, as people realized what had happened, tumultuous applause. When it had died and the bizarrely tangled cycles had been raised out of sight, Slade said: 'My great-grandfather never got around to doing that with a pair of penny-farthings. Pity, don't you think?'

The audience agreed enthusiastically. To groans of

47

disappointment, Slade then announced that his hyper-dimensional powers were exhausted for the evening. A few self-confessed tricks with playing cards, handcuffs and white rabbits in black hats were all that remained before he signed off by vanishing from inside a seemingly escape-proof safe, only to reappear in the midst of the audience before springing back onto the stage to take his final bow.

'What did you think, Mrs T?' Harry asked as the cheers died and they rose to leave.

'Impressive. Truly impressive. But if he really can . . . what did he say . . . manipulate objects in higher dimensions . . . why bother earning his living in such a demanding fashion? Why not simply help himself to some gold bars next time he's passing the Bank of England?'

It was a reasonable question, to which Harry was still trying to think of an answer when they reached the aisle, where a nervous-looking young man in evening dress was waiting to buttonhole them. 'Mr and Mrs Brancaster?' he asked doubtfully.

'Certainly not,' said Mrs Tandy.

'But close friends of theirs,' put in Harry. 'Here on their behalf, you could say.'

'Oh, well, in that case . . . I suppose it might still be all right if . . . You see, Mr Slade was hoping the Brancasters could join his party for supper after the show.'

'Why, yes,' said Harry. 'They mentioned it to us. Remind me where it's being held.'

'La Chasse-Marée. In Beak Street.'

'Of course. Well, thanks. We'll go straight there.'

'What can you be thinking of, Harry?' demanded Mrs Tandy as the young man hurried away. 'We are *not* friends of the Brancasters. And it could prove to be extremely embarrassing when that becomes obvious. As I'm sure it will to a man of Mr Slade's talents.'

'I know,' said Harry, winking at her. 'In fact, I'm counting on it.'

NINE

Harry did not blame Mrs Tandy for backing out of the rest of the evening's entertainment. Gate-crashing a late-night supper party, after all, had not featured in his original invitation. Besides, it was way past her bedtime, Neptune would be expecting his sardines and, secretly, Harry preferred to go it alone.

After seeing her off in a taxi, he walked unhurriedly round to Beak Street, judging Slade would need to shower and change before joining his guests. La Chasse-Marée turned out to be one of Soho's classier and least garishly lit establishments, a French fish restaurant with blue-washed walls and everything from lamp-shades to ashtrays cunningly disguised as sea-shells. The Slade party were immediately identifiable as the glamorously dressed dozen monopolizing the bar to whom champagne was being liberally dispensed. Harry needed to do no more than nod and smile at a waiter to find himself included in the hospitality.

'One of his best, wouldn't you say?' enquired a tall long-nosed brunette between heavy-lidded draws on a cigarette. 'I mean, he was really *there* tonight.'

'Actually, it was the first time I'd seen him on stage. It was quite a revelation.'

'Would be. I'm Tina, by the way.'

'Hi. I'm Harry.'

'How'd you come to know Adam, Harry?'

'It's complicated. But not as complicated as higher dimensions. I'm not sure I understand what they're all about.'

49

'Explain higher dimensions to Harry, Malcolm,' she said, pulling a loud young man away from the nearest conversation.

'You're not into them?' asked Malcolm, flicking his hair out of his eyes.

'Are you?'

'Not like Adam. But I get the picture.'

'And what is the picture?'

'Well, it's an extra way of seeing, isn't it? Like parts of the spectrum ordinary humans can't detect. Like if we only existed in two dimensions, say length and breadth, we couldn't see height, could we? And we wouldn't understand what had happened if something was picked up and put down again rather than slid forwards or sideways. It would disappear and reappear somewhere else like . . . like magic.'

'Like the hoop on the table-leg?'

'Yeh. And the wheels. Adam says it's easy to thread all those spokes together when you know how. Like shuffling cards. It's just . . . what he does.'

''Course,' put in a burly red-faced man who had overheard them, 'it makes no difference whether Malcolm's in two dimensions or three or bloody seventeen . . .' He slapped Malcolm hard on the head with the theatre programme. 'Things still tend to fall on him from a great height.' The walls of the restaurant seemed to rock with his guffaws. Then, with merciful abruptness, he stopped laughing.

The reason was the arrival amongst them of Adam Slade, magician and hyper-dimensionalist. Strolling through the door in black suit and open-necked red shirt without any apparent effort to stage a grand entrance, he nevertheless drew people's gaze instantaneously. Then the cheers and welcomes rang out. The crush at the bar parted before him like the Red Sea before the tribes of Israel. And Harry found himself, to his great surprise, standing at the elbow of a human phenomenon.

'Brilliant show, Adam,' said Tina as she moved in for a kiss.

'Thanks, darling.' Slade gulped down some iced mineral water. 'Shattered?'

'Yeh. But I'll soon bounce back with my friends here to revive me.' He noticed Harry for the first time and frowned slightly. 'Do I know you?'

'That's Harry,' said Tina. 'Bit of a sceptic, I reckon.'

'The name's Barnett,' said Harry, smiling defiantly and offering his hand, which Slade studiously ignored.

'Never heard of you.'

'You surprise me. I mean, if you have all these additional dimensions of perception, isn't it obvious who I am? Can't you call on one of them to work it out?' Harry had not planned to antagonize the man, but, desperate to hold his attention, he seemed to have lapsed into doing precisely that.

'Spare me the effort.'

'All right. I'm David Venning's father.'

'I don't think so.'

'It's true. Why else would his mother have told me about your dinner date with him last month?'

'I don't know. And I don't much want to know.'

'But I want to know. About how he was that night. About what was on his mind.'

'I came here to relax. Not to be interrogated.'

'Understood.' Harry tried another grin, but it did not seem to be infectious. 'Perhaps we could meet tomorrow.'

'I have a better idea. Phone my agent on Monday.'

'This has nothing to do with your agent.'

'Really? Well, I happen to know David's father died nearly ten years ago. Which makes you an impostor. And probably a journalist. Thought this charade would get you an exclusive interview, did you? For the sort of paper that would employ you, I should think it would be a real scoop. Except it isn't going to happen.'

'I can assure you—'

'Don't bother.'

'I only want to know what you and David talked about over dinner. It's hardly a state secret.'

'No. But it was between him and me. And it's going to stay that way.'

'My son's in a coma, Mr Slade. Has been since the night he had dinner with you. He took an overdose of insulin and nobody seems to know why. Surely you can see—'

'What I can see is an uninvited guest creating a disturbance at a private party. If you were really David's father, you'd know I told his mother everything I could. You wouldn't have needed to come here and give me a hard time. Which means your story's just an excuse. One that isn't going to wash.'

'Looks like you've been rumbled, Harry,' said Tina.

'You can walk out of your own accord. Or I can ask a couple of my friends here to throw you out. They keep themselves pretty

51

fit.' Slade prodded Harry's paunch. 'But they can always use some extra weight-training.'

Harry grimaced. 'I'll go quietly.'

'Thought you would.'

'But David won't. If that's what you were hoping.' It was a hollow threat, based more on anger than suspicion. Yet the mere saying of it made Harry's exit seem, at least to him, less like a headlong retreat than a strategic withdrawal. 'I'll make sure he doesn't.'

TEN

A mild grey Sunday afternoon of light traffic and scant custom had given Harry ample opportunity to review what he had so far achieved and might yet attempt on his son's behalf. The more he thought about it, the more futile his efforts seemed destined to be. And the more misdirected. Hope Brancaster had probably been right. Depressed by a series of career reverses, David had deliberately taken an overdose of insulin and was now in an irreversible coma. There had been no foul play. There would be no miracle cure. It was as simple as that.

It was not even difficult for Harry to see through his own reluctance to accept such a conclusion. A son might give some purpose to an otherwise feckless life. To discover that purpose only for it to be snatched away again was too much to bear. Hence the digging for secrets; the probing for mixed motives and flawed accounts. So far, he had turned up nothing beyond the usual grab-bag of human weaknesses; nothing any more discreditable than his own role in the tragedy. So, why add to Iris's agonies of mind by hounding overworked doctors and hunting down lapsed friends? Why not simply accept what everybody else had already realized and Iris was well on the way to understanding: that David must be allowed to die?

Because of all Harry had missed, of course. The sleepless nights and playful days; the beaming baby and the sulking toddler; the growing boy and the full-grown man; his aspirations and achievements; his humours and his honours: everything that made and

53

marred him. The life, in short, of David John Venning. The thirty-three years he and Harry had shared on this planet without meeting. The bond that had never been broken because it had never been forged. It was a hard lesson and a worse penance. Once before, he had said to himself: '*This is the worst, Harry, the least and lowest.*' But it had not been. Because this moment had still been lying in wait.

A pick-up truck drew into the forecourt. A curly-haired man in jeans and lumberjack shirt clambered out and began filling her up. A racing-green Jaguar pulled in behind him. Harry felt dismally grateful for the flurry of custom. Any interruption to his solitude, however short-lived, was to be welcomed. But the Jag moved on past the pumps and coasted to a halt by the air-line. Typical. They were not even going to buy a pint of milk, let alone a gallon of petrol. Then he realized who was sitting in the passenger seat, staring at him through the drizzle-spotted window: Iris. Her face was grey and expressionless, her gaze directed straight at him but somehow unfocused. She looked tired and drained and close to some unmarked limit of tolerance.

The driver's door slammed. A tall thick-set man in tweed jacket and cavalry twills rounded the bonnet and strode towards the shop. He had low-peaked dark hair slicked down in an old-fashioned style. His face was set and flushed, cheeks quivering with the force of his tread. His eyes were small and intent, swivelling to meet Harry's as he walked. He was everything Harry had feared Ken Hewitt would be: tough, remorseless and accustomed to getting his own way. Harry had met his type before, all too often. More often, he sometimes thought, than he deserved. It was already certain that this encounter would not go well.

'Harry Barnett?' The words were out of Hewitt's mouth before the door had clunked shut behind him.

'Yes. You must be Ken Hewitt.'

'That's right.' He marched up to the counter, seemingly in doubt until the last moment whether to haul Harry out from behind it. But both of them could feel the weight of Iris's attention through the glass. The only force they could afford to use was that of personality. In which department Harry was heavily outgunned. 'I've decided to put a stop to your meddling in my wife's affairs.'

'I'm not meddling.'

'Hope told us about your visit. Don't you call impersonating a non-existent relative meddling?'

'I *am* a relative.'

'Not in law. Not in practice. And not in my opinion.'

'An opinion you plan to impose on Iris, no doubt.'

'You're the one imposing, Barnett. And it's got to stop.'

'I don't think that's for you to say. If you were Claude, it might be different. But Claude's dead. I reckon that leaves me the closest to a father David has.'

'*You* reckon? I'll tell you what *I* reckon—' He broke off as the man from the pick-up came in and sauntered over to the magazine rack. Hewitt lowered his voice and leant across the counter. 'I love Iris. I respect her. I don't think you've ever done either. Otherwise she wouldn't have kept you at arm's length. *Leave her alone.*'

'All I'm trying to do is—'

'Make yourself seem important. Make Iris think you matter. But you don't. You never have and you never will. You're just a mistake she made too long ago to be worth remembering.'

'Where does that leave David?'

'Where he's been for the past month. Beyond help. Especially yours.'

'Does Iris think the same?'

'She was just coming round to thinking it – when you crawled out from under a stone.'

Harry smiled grimly. 'Sorry about that.'

'You will be. If you don't crawl back there.'

'That's a threat, right?'

'I'll get a court order if necessary, Barnett. I'll stop you interfering. One way or the other.'

Harry sighed. 'What did she ever see in you?'

'What do you think? Look in the mirror and work it out.'

'You want him switched off, don't you?'

'I want him put out of his misery. I want Iris to stop hoping for what can never happen and to start mourning her son. You're an obstacle to that process. One I intend to remove.'

'Why do you think he took the overdose?'

'Stay out of it.'

'Or did someone . . . make him take it?'

'Don't try to put crazy thoughts like that into Iris's head, Barnett. I'm serious. *Don't.*'

'This lot and twenty Rothmans king size,' said the man from the pick-up, dumping a four-pack of cokes, two sausage rolls, a Mars bar and a girlie magazine between them. 'Plus ten quids' worth of four star.' He glanced warily at Hewitt. 'Not interrupting, am I?'

'No,' said Hewitt levelly. 'We've finished.'

55

Harry watched him leave, then turned to look out at the car. But Iris was staring straight ahead at the list of recommended tyre pressures hanging on the boundary wall of the forecourt. And she went on staring at it as Hewitt climbed into the driver's seat and started away. They exchanged neither word nor glance. For Harry it was a fleeting victory to set against looming defeat.

'Do you rent out videos, mate?' asked the man Harry was supposed to be serving.

'Er . . . yes. Over there.' He pointed to the rack.

'Oh, right. Only, I was wondering if they'd brought out the story of your life on video. Sounds like it could be a real corker. Bit of a change from all that sex and violence. Know what I mean?'

ELEVEN

Harry trudged homeward along Scrubs Lane in a mood matched by the sullenness of the slow-moving clouds. This, he supposed, was how it ended: in a creeping acceptance of the inevitable. He would go to the hospital tomorrow afternoon and make his peace with Iris. He would let her decide what was best for David and respect her decision. He would let his resentments and his suspicions die with David. And then? Why then, no doubt, he would get very very drunk.

Unfortunately, the small matter of twenty-four hours lay between him and this pragmatic acceptance of other people's wisdom. Worse still, it was Sunday, which meant the Stonemasons' was not yet open. So, there was nothing for it but to return to the solitude of his flat and wait for seven o'clock. It was just as well, he reflected as he turned into Foxglove Road, that he did not own a cut-throat razor. Otherwise, lying on his bed while *Songs of Praise* seeped up through the floorboards to a back-beat of next door's reggae music might be just what was needed to tip him over the brink.

Songs of Praise had not in fact started when he entered the house. Harry was not sure whether this was good news or bad, but his consideration of the point was soon replaced by puzzlement. A letter was waiting for him on the hall table, where Mrs Tandy normally left his post. But this was Sunday. How could there be any? He picked it up and squinted at the handwritten address. It was not from his mother. Or from Zohra. Then who? He did not recognize the hand. And the postmark was

57

too smudged to decipher. He looked into the sitting room and flapped the envelope at Mrs Tandy, who glanced up reluctantly from the Peter James horror novel her niece had sent her for her birthday.

'Where did this come from, Mrs T?'

'I don't know, Harry. It arrived just after you left for work. Perhaps a neighbour dropped it round. You know how many wrong deliveries we've had since our regular postman retired.'

'Can't say I'd noticed.'

'That's because you get so little post.'

'You mean I should be grateful for small mercies?'

'Perhaps you should. Now, do you mind? I'm in the middle of a decapitation.'

Reckoning that might mean he would be spared at least a few hymns, Harry started slowly up the stairs, opening the envelope as he went. There was a newspaper cutting inside, folded in three, but no note or letter to indicate who had sent it. Closing the door of his flat behind him, he propped himself against it and unfolded the cutting. It was *The Sunday Times* of three weeks ago, the top half of an inner page sporting a four-column headline: *Forecasting scientists meet with unforeseen accidents*. Eagerly, Harry read the article beneath.

> The death last Tuesday of Dr Marvin Kersey, a Canadian biochemist, brings to three the number of scientists formerly employed by Globescope Inc., the Washington-based forecasting corporation, to have been struck by fatal or near-fatal accidents in recent weeks. The President of Globescope, Byron Lazenby, has dismissed suggestions of a link between the rash of accidents and their victims' work for his organization as 'fanciful nonsense' and so far there is nothing beyond coincidence to connect them.
>
> But the coincidence is nevertheless compelling. On September 13, Dr David Venning, an English mathematician, was found in a diabetic coma in his room at the Skyway Hotel, Heathrow Airport. He had apparently taken an overdose of insulin. Nine days later, Gerard Mermillod, a French sociologist, fell in front of a Paris Metro train at Pigalle station and was killed. Witnesses described the nature of his fall as 'bizarre'. Then, last Tuesday, Dr Marvin Kersey was found dead at his apartment in Montreal. Police believe he was poisoned by carbon monoxide fumes emanating from a faulty central-heating system. All three had worked for Globescope

as members of their specialist scientific staff until April of this year. Mr Lazenby attributed their simultaneous departure to 'normal turnaround'. Dr Kersey had subsequently returned to a lectureship at McGill University, Montreal, from which he had originally been seconded to Globescope, while M. Mermillod had taken up a post at L'Institut des Hautes Études Scientifiques in Paris. Dr Venning held no academic position at the time of his illness.

Staff at Globescope have been instructed to say nothing about their former colleagues. One employee who was prepared to talk off the record said everyone hoped these events really were coincidental. The thought that they might not be, he admitted, 'makes you kind of jumpy'. No plausible motives for suicide have been put forward so far and neither the Paris nor the Montreal police are thought to regard the circumstances of the deaths as suspicious. Dr Venning remains in a coma at the National Neurological Hospital in London. His condition is described as 'grave but stable'. At Globescope, meanwhile, the task of predicting the future is beginning to look a whole lot simpler than interpreting the present.

Less than an hour later, Harry was striding along the corridor leading to room E318 at the National Neurological Hospital. The visit seemed unlikely to serve much purpose, but his thoughts were now so restless that physical activity, whether purposeful or not, was essential. The phone call and the letter; David's coma and the deaths of two other men; at least five scientists dismissed from Globescope last spring, of whom two were dead and one nearly so: all, surely, part of a pattern. Iris must have realized that. But she had chosen to keep it from him. She had pretended there *was* no pattern, that David's illness was a tragic but uncomplicated misfortune. What had she said? *'I'm not going to let you invade his life.'* It had seemed fair enough at the time, but now . . . Everyone was so very eager to let David die, yet so very reluctant to understand what had happened to him. Their unanimity made Harry's blood boil. Where were they when he needed them? If Harry himself had only known he had a son, he would have—

He pulled up sharply, barely avoiding a collision with a man leaving the room just as he was about to enter it. Approximately Harry's height and weight, with more muscle and less fat, he had a handsome if slightly battered face, large blue eyes and short spiky blond hair. He could have passed for a night-club bouncer but for the dark Savile Row suit and red silk tie. He cocked one

59

eyebrow and ran a glance of fleeting scrutiny over Harry, then brushed past and strode away.

Harry stepped into the room and glanced across at David. There was no change in his blank and peaceful expression, no hint of awareness, however slight. He could not hear, he could not see, he could not respond. He remained dead to the world. But maybe, deep inside, not quite dead to his own father. Harry sat down beside the bed, reached out and laid his hand over David's where it was resting on the blanket. 'I'll try, son,' he murmured. 'I truly will. I'll see your mother tomorrow. And your doctor if possible. It's time I found out exactly—'

David's doctor. Of course. The man he had nearly bumped into had the right authoritarian air to be a consultant. And Harry had let the opportunity slip through his fingers. Swearing under his breath, he jumped up and rushed into the corridor. But the fellow was nowhere to be seen. A nurse was bustling about behind the previously empty counter further along, though. Harry waved and hurried down to speak to her. He was known to the staff now and she gave him a welcoming smile.

'Hello, Mr Barnett. You're in late.'

'Not the only one. Was that David's specialist I just met leaving his room?'

'No. Mr Baxendale won't be in again till tomorrow. That was just another visitor. David's been very popular today.'

'Who was he?'

'He didn't give a name. A colleague, I think he said.'

'A colleague of David's?'

'Yes.'

'From Globescope?'

'Globescope? What's that?'

The nurse's uncertainty made no difference. If the man was a colleague of David's, he had to be from Globescope. And if so . . . But a jog as far as the main entrance yielded only severe breathlessness and dismal news from the receptionist, who vaguely recalled a man matching the description Harry panted out leaving a few minutes earlier. Outside, in the drizzly London night, there was naturally no sign of him.

Harry lit a cigarette to ease his frustration and stood smoking it in the shelter of a pillared porch looking out across Queen Square. A missed chance to speak to somebody with inside knowledge of Globescope was bad enough. But a more tantalizing possibility was already worming its way into his thoughts. Could David's unidentified colleague also be responsible for the letter and the telephone call? Could he be the nameless messenger who seemed to know more about Harry's past than Harry did himself?

TWELVE

'We'll see what your mother has to say about this, shall we, David? I'm prepared to give her the benefit of the doubt, you know. Ken could be the real problem. I realize that. I expect you do too. Is he pressurizing her, do you think? Only he's certainly trying to pressurize me. But don't worry. In my case, it isn't going to work.' Harry smiled in acknowledgement of his own stubbornness. It was stubbornness, after all, that had kept him at the hospital since mid-morning, awaiting the maternal visit David was bound to receive, a visit that would give Harry the chance to put to Iris some of the questions that were troubling him. He could have telephoned her, of course. But she might have refused to speak to him. He could have gone out to Chorleywood to see her. But she might have slammed the door in his face. Ken certainly would have. Except Harry was hoping Ken had gone back up to Manchester to captain his segment of industry. All of which left David's hospital room as the most certain ground on which to confront Iris.

Spending most of Monday there had already enabled Harry to squeeze some information out of David's specialist. But Mr Baxendale, a kindly if cautious man, had only confirmed his worst fears. 'There is no realistic prospect of a recovery from such a profound coma, Mr Barnett. Sooner or later, Mrs Hewitt is going to have to decide how to deal with that fact.' As for the alleged neurobiological expertise of Donna Trangam, Baxendale was politely dismissive. 'She visited David once, shortly after his admission, and offered me her fairly radical opinion on coma treatment. But she had absolutely no clinical experience. Besides, she returned to the United States almost immediately thereafter and I haven't heard from her since.'

'When was this?' Harry had asked. 'I mean, exactly.'

'Hard to say. David was transferred here from Charing Cross on the fifteenth of September. A few days after that, I suppose.'

'And another few days before she left?'

'Probably.'

Unlike his son, Harry was no mathematician. But simple arithmetic was not beyond him. Donna Trangam's sudden departure for the States coincided more or less with Gerard Mermillod's death in Paris on 22 September. Of course, her destination was an assumption on Baxendale's part. She might actually have gone to Paris. Or *via* Paris. Either way, it did not sound like the workings of chance. Not much did to Harry any more. Conspiracy. Concealment. Confusion. They were the prevailing echoes.

'What happened to you, David?' he asked, crouching forward in his chair and gazing into his son's softly closed eyes. 'Did you inject the insulin into your bloodstream? Or did somebody else? The same somebody who pushed Mermillod from the Metro platform and tampered with the heating system at Kersey's apartment? The same somebody who could be hunting down your other friends while you lie there and I sit here, while they run and we wait? Is that what—'

He looked up and saw Iris standing in the doorway, fresh flowers cradled like a child in her arms, a smile frozen on her face. She had heard what he was saying, but seemed not to know how to respond. They stared at each other for a long silent moment. Then she lay the flowers gently down on a table, their cellophane wrapper squeaking above the respiration of the ventilator, and drew up a chair facing Harry across the bed.

'Hello, Iris. Surprised to see me?'

'A little.'

'Ken confident he'd seen me off, was he?'

'He thought he'd made you understand, yes.'

'But he never mentioned this.' Harry took the newspaper cutting from his pocket and passed it across to her. 'Nor did you.' He saw her swallow hard as she scanned it. 'Why was that?'

'How did you find out?'

'That doesn't matter. What matters is what it means.'

'Nothing. It means nothing.'

63

'Come on, Iris. What was David doing at Globescope? What were all these people doing?'

'I don't know. I've absolutely no idea.'

'Haven't you even wondered?'

'Globescope predict the future. Companies – even some governments – pay them to forecast economic developments. David worked on something called predictive modelling. What else is there to say?'

'Did he work with Kersey and Mermillod?'

'He may have done. He never mentioned their names to me. Why should he? I wasn't that interested.'

'Aren't you interested now?'

'I'm interested in doing what's best for David.'

'So am I.'

'Then do as Ken asked. Leave us alone.'

'How can I when you seem so reluctant to find out the truth?'

'The truth is that David took an overdose of insulin, probably accidentally. If somebody had . . . if somebody had done what you obviously suspect . . . there'd have been signs of a struggle in his hotel room. But there weren't any. He'd have had ample time to get medical help in those circumstances anyway. Unless you're suggesting he was bound and gagged till the insulin took effect to stop him raising the alarm. Again, there'd have been signs. But there weren't. There wasn't a mark on him. Not one. He was alone when it happened, Harry. Don't you see? This journalist is just cobbling together a story to fill a space. There's nothing to it.'

'So you think these two deaths are . . . purely coincidental?'

'What else can they be?'

'Why was David sacked by Globescope?'

'He wasn't, as far as I know. He told me he'd resigned, in order to concentrate on—'

'Higher dimensions? A talking point at his dinner with Adam Slade, no doubt. Something else you omitted to mention.'

'Because of how you might react, Harry. Because of how you *are* reacting. Mr Slade was actually most solicitous. And as helpful as he could be. Whether he really does have these powers he claims I rather doubt. But there's nothing sinister in his meeting David to discuss them.'

'What about Donna Trangam's flying visit? Don't you see anything sinister in her sudden departure?'

'Not at all. She had a teaching post at Berkeley to return to. Once she'd satisfied herself there was nothing she could contribute

64

to David's treatment, she and Mr Hammelgaard—'

'The Dane was here too?'

'Briefly. Then he went back to Princeton. What's so strange in that? They're friends of David. They wanted to help him. But they realized they couldn't.'

'They told you that, did they?'

'Not in so many words. I only met them once. Here, a few days after David's admission. I wasn't in a state to take much in, but it seemed obvious—' She broke off and pressed two fingers to her forehead, then said in a calmer voice: 'They simply went their separate ways, Harry. People do.'

'When? When did they go?'

'I don't know. They didn't *notify* me. Why should they?'

'But they arrived within a week of David being taken ill and left again a few days later?'

'Well, yes, I suppose so. But what—'

'Have you heard from them since?'

'No.'

'Are they still all right, do you think?'

'All right? Well, of course. Why shouldn't they be?'

'For the same reason Kersey and Mermillod aren't, I should have thought.'

'That's nonsense. Kersey's death was accidental. Carbon monoxide poisoning kills hundreds of people every year. Probably thousands worldwide.'

'And throwing yourself under a train is a common method of suicide.'

'Well, so it is.'

'But within a fortnight of each other? Among a small group of scientists sacked from the same company at the same time for—'

'*David wasn't sacked!*' Iris glanced round at her son, as if afraid she might have disturbed him. But she need not have worried. His rest was impenetrable. 'He resigned. Of his own accord.'

'That's not how Hope tells it.'

'What would she know? They were divorced by then.'

'She implied there could have been something between David and Donna Trangam.'

'Well, what if there was? They're both adults.'

'You agree there may have been, then?'

'I suppose it's possible. They're both attractive people. They have a lot in common. It would certainly explain why he telephoned her that night.' She tensed. 'That is . . . I mean . . .'

65

'He telephoned her from the Skyway Hotel?'

Iris looked solemnly across at Harry. 'Yes. He did.'

'How do you know?'

'Because the hotel had the effrontery to send me David's bill for settlement. It showed a phone call he made just after eleven o'clock that night. I dialled the number and it turned out to be the university switchboard at Berkeley. San Francisco's eight hours behind us, so—'

'What did Donna say when you asked her about it?'

'I never had the chance to ask. She'd gone by the time the bill came through.'

'But you must have spoken to her since.'

'No. I haven't.'

'Why the hell not?'

'Because she isn't there any more.'

'Not there? What do you mean?'

'She's not been seen at Berkeley since taking leave on the fifteenth of September. That must have been when she heard about David.'

'And she's not been back since?'

'Apparently not. They gave me her home number, but it's just an answering machine. She's not responded to any of my messages.'

'Could she be with Hammelgaard?'

'Possibly.'

'Have you tried to contact him?'

'Yes.'

'At Princeton?'

'Yes.'

'And?'

'Same story. Absent without leave.'

'You mean missing?'

'Well, yes, I suppose I do.'

'For God's sake!' Harry jumped up and strode to the window, where he took a few calming breaths before turning to look back at Iris. His anger drained away at the sight of her crushed expression. She seemed suddenly old and fallible and in need of help. She was not going to ask for it, of course. But that did not mean she would refuse it. Even from him. 'A few moments ago, you said there was no reason to think they were in any danger.'

'There isn't.'

'You don't believe that.'

'Ken advised me to drop it. He said there was no point pursuing the matter. He said it couldn't help David to antagonize his former employer.'

'Well, good old Ken.'

'But he's right, isn't he?'

'I don't know. Maybe. I do know one thing, though. The least – the very least – we owe David is to find out how this happened to him. And why. Did Donna say anything when you met her to give us a clue?'

'Not that I can remember. We discussed David's condition. Nothing else.'

'But she didn't mention the telephone call?'

'No.'

'Which means either he didn't get through to her or—'

'The call cost more than ten pounds, Harry. I should think he must have got through to somebody. Miss Trangam's the obvious candidate.'

'Then she can't have wanted you to know what he said, can she?'

'No. It seems not.'

The thought clearly hurt Iris. But in her sidelong glance at David Harry detected a fear he was equally eager to stifle. Could the call have been a farewell message to a former lover? In that case, her reticence would not merely be forgivable, but admirable. 'What about Hammelgaard? Did he say anything when you met him?'

'Not much. He offered his sympathy, of course. Apart from that, I don't recall . . .' She shrugged. 'He seemed preoccupied with the whereabouts of David's notebooks, actually, but—'

'His *mathematical* notebooks?'

'Yes.'

'The ones Hope said he was never parted from?'

'Well, I don't know about—'

'Weren't they in his hotel room?'

'No. As a matter of fact, they weren't.'

Too taken aback to speak for a moment, Harry walked slowly across to the bed and sat down in his chair. There was a flush of guilt in Iris's cheeks when he looked up at her. 'You mean they're missing?'

'I mean he didn't have them with him.'

'Did he have them with him when he came to see you in Wilmslow?'

'I don't know. I didn't search his luggage.' She shook her head. 'I'm sorry. I assume he must have left them at his house in Washington.'

'Has anybody checked?'

'I haven't. Perhaps Mr Hammelgaard has since.'

'Only we can't ask him because he's gone missing.'

'Apparently so.'

'Hope specifically told me they went everywhere with him.'

'Well, she would know that much, I suppose.'

'So, if they weren't in his hotel room, either somebody removed them or he didn't take them there in the first place. Could he have left them somewhere else – for safekeeping?'

'Why should he have done?'

'Because he thought they might otherwise fall into the wrong hands. Because he foresaw circumstances in which he could no longer protect them.'

Iris looked at Harry long and hard. 'You realize what you're suggesting?'

'Oh, I realize. But I don't understand. The abstract jottings and abstruse calculations of a higher mathematician. What value would they have?'

'None you or I are capable of comprehending.'

'But it would be a different story for Hammelgaard, wouldn't it?'

'Yes. I imagine so.'

'What did you tell him?'

'That I had no idea whether or not the notebooks were in David's possession while he was staying with us. I suggested he should contact Athene Tilson, David's old tutor at Cambridge. David mentioned he'd been to see her before coming on to us. She's a mathematician, of course. He might have shown her his latest work.'

'Or left it with her?'

'That too, of course.'

Harry leant forward across the bed. 'Where can I find her, Iris?'

'Southwold. On the Suffolk coast. She's retired there.'

'Have you heard from her since David's illness?'

'No. Strangely enough, I haven't.'

'Then don't you think it's time *she* heard from *us*?'

'Perhaps.'

'Don't you want to know what she has to say?'

'That depends on what it is.'

68

It was the earlier fear re-echoed. A man preparing to make a voluntary exit from this life might well leave the fruits of his most recent intellectual endeavours with his trusted mentor. Just as he might pay a last visit to his mother and make a farewell call to his ex-lover. Before hanging up the DO NOT DISTURB sign outside his hotel-room door and filling a syringe with enough insulin to stretch his night's sleep into eternity. That was really why Iris had shrunk back from probing the mystery of her son's final hours. Because she was not sure the truth was preferable to not knowing. Because ignorance was safe – even if it could not be blissful.

'You don't have to do this, Harry. You can still take Ken's advice. Stay out of it. Leave well alone.'

'I don't think so,' he replied, glancing round at David's calm unchanging face. 'I really don't think that's an option any more.' He looked back at her. 'Do you?'

THIRTEEN

Harry reached Southwold by bus from Ipswich on a bright breezy morning of fluffy fast-moving clouds and wide blue East Anglian horizons. Local poets might have been moved to verse by the bustle of the High Street and the gull-loud air of seaside purposefulness. But Harry was in far from poetic mood. He had just the sort of leaden headache and incipient liverishness he might have expected as a result of a heavy night at the Stonemasons', a bolted breakfast and a rush-hour tube journey to Liverpool Street. He was troubled by the memory of Crowther's sarcasm when agreeing to let him take the day off – 'Working here isn't making too many demands on your time, is it, Harry?' And he was not at all sure that flogging out to the marshy margins of Suffolk was actually going to achieve anything he could not have accomplished in a telephone conversation.

He *had* phoned Dr Tilson, of course, but had spoken only to a housekeeper, through whom he had managed to fix an appointment without having to say more than that he was a friend of David Venning's mother. Reticence had seemed only prudent till he could meet David's old tutor and weigh her expression along with her words. Now, trudging out to the seafront and reeling before the brain-scouring force of the wind, he could not help doubting whether he had played his hand wisely.

Avocet House was a high-gabled Victorian villa set behind gale-carved hedges at the southern end of the town. It looked more like some whiskery admiral's final mooring than an academic's hideaway. Why Dr Tilson should prefer this patch of salt-sprayed obscurity to the wood-panelled college rooms Harry found it easy to imagine she had left behind in Cambridge was at first sight a mystery.

The mystery did not evaporate when Harry was greeted at the door by the housekeeper he had spoken to on the telephone. Younger than he would have predicted, she was short and plump, with a startlingly clear-skinned face and a mass of marmalade-coloured hair. The plain dress and headband were consistent enough with the position Harry had assumed she held, but the quivering air of insecurity was not.

'You must be Harry Barnett,' she said in a breathless voice. 'Come in.' Harry stepped into the cavernous hallway. 'Athene's in the conservatory.' *Athene*, Harry noted. Not *Dr Tilson*. 'Come on through.'

He followed her along the hall and into a dowdily furnished drawing room which gave onto the conservatory. She left him at the doorway with an offer of coffee. He accepted, failing to specify the strong black brew that he badly needed, and went on alone.

The conservatory was clearly contemporary with the house; terracotta lozenge tiles underfoot, grimy glass and cast iron overhead. Cacti and assorted frond-leafed exotics occupied most of the floor space, their thick green stems planted firmly in fat red pots. There were no statuettes or figurines, no grinning gnomes or frolicking cherubs. The place would, in fact, have seemed more like a working greenhouse than a domestic conservatory but for the wicker chairs and table set in a kind of arbour at the far end.

Seated on one of the chairs was a thin grey-haired woman who looked up as he approached. She was wearing stout shoes, corduroy trousers and a guernsey, with what looked like a tennis shirt underneath. Her hair was short, her face lined and free of make-up. She made no effort to rise, which Harry assumed the pair of walking-sticks propped against the table explained, but her dark piercing eyes engaged him more directly than any word or gesture.

'Mr Barnett?'

'Yes. Dr Tilson?'

'Indeed. Come and sit down.' There was a hint of sharpness in her voice that made the invitation sound more like an instruction. 'Has Mace offered you anything?'

'Er . . . yes. Coffee.'

'Coffee? How unexciting.' She watched him closely as he sat

down. 'Well, it can't be helped. We have no beer in the house. And cigarette smoke would disturb the plants.' Catching his frown, she added: 'The waistline is a giveaway, Mr Barnett. And I have a keen enough nose to detect the aroma of a cigarette recently smoked. Not English, I think. Italian?'

'Greek, actually.'

'Really? How disappointing. For me, I mean. For you, I imagine, it was a considerable pleasure.' She smiled with surprising warmth. 'A touch of emphysema means tobacco is a banned substance in this house, I fear. And it's a ban Mace polices rigorously.'

'Well, the sea air must be . . . good for . . .'

'Clarity? Yes, it is.' She glanced out through the window, where the fall of the land and the lie of the garden hedge disclosed a sun-winking wedge of the North Sea. 'Clarity of thought as well as respiration.' She looked back at Harry, then down at the book she had been reading. *Shadows of the Mind: A Search for the Missing Science of Consciousness* by Roger Penrose. It looked a fat and formidable work. 'I don't suppose you're familiar with Professor Penrose's . . . No, of course not. You're not a mathematician, are you, Mr Barnett?'

'No. I'm afraid not. But I'm here about a mathematician.'

'David? Yes. Poor boy. I really was so very sorry to hear what had happened to him. It would always be sad, naturally. But for the possessor of such a first-class brain . . . Well, you're a friend of the family, so I need hardly elaborate.'

'Actually, I don't know David at all. To be honest, I don't think you could really call me a friend. Of any member of the family.'

'Could one not? Well, well. You do intrigue me.' She grinned mischievously as Mace brought in his coffee. 'Mr Barnett is here under false pretences, Mace. What do you think of that?'

'I think it's not so unusual,' said Mace. She placed the cup at Harry's elbow and left again without looking at either of them, the hem of her dress brushing past the plants like a forest breeze.

Dr Tilson chuckled. 'You didn't want sugar, did you, Mr Barnett?'

'Er . . . No.'

'Just as well. Mace obviously decided it would be bad for you.' Her gaze narrowed. 'But don't let me distract you from explaining yourself.'

Harry sipped evasively at the coffee before replying. It tasted insipid enough to be decaffeinated. 'I'm David's natural father.'

Dr Tilson nodded reflectively as she absorbed the information,

72

then said: 'Why don't I find that as surprising as I should?'

'A resemblance, perhaps. David's ex-wife thought she noticed something in my smile.'

'Yes. I think she's right. Put three stones and twenty-five years on David and I suppose you're something like what one would get.'

'Thanks very much.'

'Take it as compliment, Mr Barnett. I met Mr Venning once. David's legal father, as I suppose I should call him. You represent an improvement, believe me. But let's come to the point. What brings you here?'

'Some of David's possessions seem to be missing. Which makes the circumstances of his insulin overdose look less straightforward than most people seem to think.'

'Which . . . possessions . . . in particular?'

'His mathematical notebooks. I gather he always carried the latest few around with him. Did he have them with him when he last visited you?'

'Yes. Most certainly he did. We glanced through some of his recent work. I'm flattered to say he still values my opinion. Mathematicians peak early, Mr Barnett. David would be thought by some to be past his best already, even without . . . As for a septuagenarian like myself, well, the present generation look upon me as a museum piece. Those that don't assume I'm long dead, that is. David is exceptional in his ability to disregard the fashions of the moment when assessing mathematical significance. It's an ability that did little for his career. But as for posterity, that could prove to be a vastly different matter.'

'You mean David's on the track of some important discovery?'

'Maybe. To be honest, some of his calculations proved to be a little beyond me. My mind simply isn't as agile as it once was. I can't help hoping emphysema will claim me before Alzheimer's does.'

'But you did see what he was working on?'

'Some of it. He was reluctant to show me everything. He said much of the material was too speculative to be shared. But there was certainly plenty of it. The freedom he's enjoyed since leaving Globescope had evidently been put to good use.'

'Did he say why he left Globescope?'

'Not exactly. He was recruited by them a couple of years ago, along with half a dozen or so specialists from other disciplines, to work on the corporation's most ambitious project yet. Project

Sybil, it was called, presumably after the prophetess of antiquity. The objective was to assemble a detailed and accurate model of the state of the world fifty years from now. A consortium of international companies wanted to take a long-term look at where they should be going and how they should be planning to get there. Futurology is something of a fad in big business at the moment, I believe. Blame the imminence of the millennium. I dare say Ethelred the Unready was up to something similar a thousand years ago. But he didn't have Globescope to hire, did he?'

'Was the project finished, then?'

'I had the impression not. But David said very little about it. He referred airily to some sort of disagreement with the President of Globescope and left it at that.'

'The same disagreement that led four other scientists to leave, two of whom have since died?'

Dr Tilson started with surprise. 'Died?'

'A Canadian biochemist, Marvin Kersey, and a French sociologist, Gerard Mermillod. Within a fortnight of David's . . . accidental overdose. Their deaths were accidental too. Makes you think, doesn't it?'

'Yes. It does.'

'Did David mention them in connection with Project Sybil?'

'Not that I recall. But then, you see, Globescope – and Project Sybil – were just means to an end to him. They paid well. And he needed money – the sort of money only American entrepreneurs seem able to come up with – to finance his brainchild: a hyper-dimensional research academy. HYDRA, it was to be called, appropriately enough. That's what was on his mind when he came here. The world of higher dimensions, not futurology.'

'And that's what his recent work was about?'

'Of course. In a sense, it's what all his work's been about. Ever since he was an undergraduate. His promise was immediately obvious to me. But so was his interest in higher dimensions. Sometimes it . . . unbalanced his achievements.'

'What *are* higher dimensions, Dr Tilson?'

'They're what particle physicists tell us are necessary to explain the fundamental structure of matter. I don't suppose you're acquainted with superstring theory?'

'You suppose right.'

'Well, superstrings are about the most satisfactory way physicists have come up with for harmonizing Einsteinian relativity with quantum mechanics, a difficulty that's dogged them for most of this century. For superstrings to work mathematically it's necessary to accept the existence of dimensions additional to the four we get on with from day to day: length, breadth, depth and time. Superstring theory tells us there are at least another six out there somewhere.'

Harry nodded. 'I went to see Adam Slade's magic show. He claims to be in touch with them.'

Dr Tilson clicked her tongue. 'A charlatan, Mr Barnett. Neither more nor less.'

'Does David see him that way?'

'Not as clearly as I should like. David has always been eager to seize upon evidence of the actual physical existence of higher dimensions. It's a deeply unfashionable concept. Superstring theorists prefer to dispose of the problem by arguing that the additional dimensions were compactified at the point of origin of the universe into a space so minute that they can never be detected. *Quod erat disponandum.* Neat, don't you think?'

'Er . . . I suppose it fits the facts.'

'Quite so. But beware convenience. It's often a treacherous ally. If you really want to understand higher dimensions, without recourse to compactification, you could do worse than my own foray into the subject. It earned me a limited kind of fame when it was first published, but it was fame of an impermanent nature. David was the first undergraduate I came across who'd read it in, oh, ten years at least.'

'But his recent work has gone beyond even your grasp?'

'Yes. Largely because of the new notational techniques he's been obliged to deploy as a consequence of . . .' She stopped and smiled. 'I'm getting out of my depth as well as yours, Mr Barnett. If I understand you correctly, what concerns you is the absence of David's notebooks from the hotel room where he was found in a coma. Did you wonder if he left them with me?'

'It would account for them, certainly.'

'Well, he didn't. I have to second your informant on that point. I doubt he'd be voluntarily parted from them. As I told Mr Hammelgaard—'

'Hammelgaard came to see you, then? Iris – David's mother – said she'd referred him to you.'

'Oh, he came. About a week after I heard of David's illness. He definitely worked on Project Sybil. And he was also familiar with David's hyper-dimensional speculations. He was almost David's equal in his enthusiasm to set up HYDRA. He could see and understand the potential of it, he told me. But where were the notebooks? The question troubled him even more than it troubles you. It left little room for other issues. He never mentioned these fatal accidents you referred to, for instance.'

'They hadn't happened then. If they had, Hammelgaard might have found the disappearance of the notebooks even more suspicious.'

'You can't be suggesting . . . foul play?'

'I don't know what I'm suggesting. The fact is they've vanished. Along with Hammelgaard.'

'You must be misinformed, Mr Barnett. Mr Hammelgaard told me he was returning to Princeton. I think you'll find—'

'He's been absent without explanation since the middle of last month.'

'Odd. I seem to recall he was quite specific about his intentions. And it was certainly later than the middle of the month when he came here.'

'Mermillod died on the twenty-second, Kersey on the twenty-seventh. I think news of their deaths changed Hammelgaard's plans.'

'Well, it's easy enough to check the sequence of events. Mr Hammelgaard phoned ahead, as you did. I'll have made a note of our appointment in my diary. It's in the study. Let's go and take a look.' Levering herself out of the chair involved such an effort that Harry jumped up to assist her. But she shook him off impatiently. 'I'll make my own way, thank you, Mr Barnett. Decrepitude's not to be appeased, but faced down.' Grasping a walking-stick in either hand, she made a wheezy start towards the door. 'Tell me . . . about these . . . accidents . . . as we go.'

Harry had ample time to relate everything he knew about the deaths of Mermillod and Kersey during their creeping progress to the study, a journey which took them back through the drawing room and down the hall. Indeed, he was able to throw in a mention of Donna Trangam's disappearance and David's mysterious dinner date with Adam Slade before they arrived.

'*Prima facie* . . . the connection with Globescope . . . and Project Sybil . . . appears compelling . . . Mr Barnett . . . But it's all . . . circumstantial . . . isn't it? Highly . . . circumstantial . . . Ah, here we are.'

The study was not the book-lined retreat from the world Harry had unconsciously expected. Books there certainly were, filling most of one wall. But the furniture was modern, with the contemporary appurtenances of computer and fax machine much in evidence. There were Venetian blinds at the window as well as heavy green curtains. A blackboard was fixed to the opposite wall, the narrow shelf beneath it crammed with sticks and stubs of yellow chalk. They must have been used recently, for there was a faint scent of chalk-dust in the air, a scent that instantly transported Harry back across the years to the classroom at Commonweal School in Swindon where Howell-Jones, the Welsh maths teacher, had striven by logic, sarcasm and occasional brutality to drum the basics of geometry and algebra into his recalcitrant charges. In Harry's case, as in most others, he had striven in vain.

'Let me see . . .' said Dr Tilson, lowering herself into a swivel-chair behind the desk and pausing to recover her breath. 'Where did I put that diary?'

Equations, written in a swirling hand, filled the greater part of the blackboard. Harry ran his eye over their familiar but impenetrable form, the brackets and braces, the pis and psis, the signs and symbols of a language he could not speak. Then he moved across to the blocked-up fireplace and leant against the mantelpiece, waiting as patiently as he could while Dr Tilson prised a desk diary from beneath a sheaf of computer paper and began leafing through its pages. His gaze shifted to a framed photograph hanging above the mantelpiece. It was of a gathering of middle-aged and elderly men, lined up in two rows for the benefit of the camera, one standing, the other sitting. They were dressed in the fashions of forty or fifty years ago and looked as if they might be the staff of a down-at-heel public school. Then, almost simultaneously, Harry noticed three things. Firstly, there was a woman among the baggy-suited males, a slim but not particularly elegant young woman dressed in tweeds and brogues, with a severe hairstyle and a stiff smile. Secondly, he recognized her, by the set of her features and the intensity of her expression, as none other than Athene Tilson. And thirdly, he recognized the man seated next to her. Because he was the one mathematician whose face everybody knew. He was Albert Einstein.

'Tuesday the twentieth of September, Mr Barnett.'

'Sorry?'

'Mr Hammelgaard came to see me on Tuesday the twentieth of September.'

'Oh . . . Right.'

'Which rather supports your contention that his plans to return

77

to Princeton could have been abandoned in the light of Monsieur Mermillod's death two days later.'

'Yes. I suppose it does.'

'Strangely enough, though, you don't seem to be particularly interested.'

'No. I am. Honestly. It's just . . . This *is* Albert Einstein, isn't it? And this *is* you next to him.'

'Yes. On both counts.'

'How did you . . . I mean, where . . .'

'Einstein spent the last twenty-two years of his life at the Princeton Institute for Advanced Study. I was there in the early fifties. That photograph was taken in, oh, 1953, I think.'

'And this is where Hammelgaard's based now?'

'No. Mr Hammelgaard is – or was – at Princeton University. The Institute for Advanced Study is an entirely separate establishment. No students, you see, Mr Barnett. No teaching. No timetabled work of any kind. Only thought. Pure and profound thought. In theory, at any rate.'

'You knew Einstein well?'

'He was good enough to spare me some of his time. That book of mine I mentioned to you contained some material he found interesting. It was what led to my invitation to join the Institute. I jumped at the chance, naturally. Some of the greatest scientific brains of the century were there during that period. On my other side in the photograph you'll see a thin not to say gaunt gentleman doing his best to fracture the camera lens with his glare.'

'I see him.'

'Kurt Gödel. Most famous perhaps for his Incompleteness Theorem. But also notable for his alternative solutions to Einstein's gravitational field equations. He demonstrated the mathematical consistency of a universe that is homogeneous but not isotropic. His paper on the subject had just taken the scientific world by storm when I joined the Institute. Are you with me, Mr Barnett?'

'None of the way, I'm afraid.'

'Never mind. Elsewhere in the photograph you'll find John von Neumann, the man who developed the first electronic computer, and Benoit Mandelbrot, the inventor of fractal geometry. Great names.' She sighed. 'With which you appear to be unfamiliar. Well, look at the middle of the front row. Somebody tall, lean, flinty-eyed, short-haired and evidently angst-ridden. Got him?'

'Yes.'

78

'J. Robert Oppenheimer. Director of the Institute. Formerly—'

'Father of the atom bomb.'

'Well, midwife, let's say. Also philosopher – to his ultimate detriment. But enough of *my* past. What about *your* future? What do you propose to do next?'

'I don't know. I'd like to speak to Hammelgaard. Or Donna Trangam. But I've no idea where they are.'

'You think they're in hiding?'

'I think it's possible. But in hiding from what?'

'Mr Hammelgaard did have the air of a worried man. Perhaps even a hunted one. And that was before he knew about either Mermillod or Kersey. You seem to be onto something, I can't deny. But to pursue it you'll surely have to find Hammelgaard. He's David's closest confidant. If anyone knows what's going on, he does.'

Harry shrugged. 'Exactly. Hopeless, isn't it?'

'Not necessarily. Apply some simple logic to the problem. If Mr Hammelgaard *is* in hiding, where would he be most likely to have chosen to go to ground?'

'Search me.'

'He's Danish, Mr Barnett. A little conspicuous in Princeton, I should think. But not in his native country. He had a glittering career at the Niels Bohr Institute in Copenhagen before he moved to the United States. If he couldn't return to Princeton, why not Copenhagen instead?'

'Yes, why not?' Harry frowned. 'You could be right. But . . . it's a big city.'

'With a small academic community. I would start at the Niels Bohr Institute. You might learn nothing, of course, but . . .'

'Nothing ventured, nothing gained.'

'Mathematically as well as proverbially, that is axiomatic. But before I forget . . . Would you be so kind as to fetch a book for me?' Dr Tilson pointed at the bookcase, to which Harry obediently crossed. 'Fourth shelf down. Far end. A slim volume. Buff-covered. *The Implicate Topology of Complex Numbers*. You have it?'

Harry pulled the book out and checked the title. 'Yes. I've got it.' Then he saw the author's name: A. H. Tilson.

'Take it as a gift, Mr Barnett. I have several spare copies.'

'That's very kind of you. But . . . I won't understand a word. Let alone a number. Complex or otherwise. I never got past differentiation at school.'

'Perhaps you were a late developer.'

'Very late. It still hasn't happened.'

Dr Tilson chuckled. 'There's always time.'

'Not enough for me, I'm afraid. But . . . you said David read this?'

'Yes. It was one of the stimuli of his interest in higher dimensions.'

'Then I *would* like to have a look at it. Thanks very much.'

'Let me autograph it for you.'

Harry took it to the desk and watched as Dr Tilson turned to the title page and signed her name in brown ink with a large old fountain pen. She added a dedication which Harry was unable to decipher before she closed the book and handed it back to him.

'Will you go to Copenhagen?'

'Probably. It seems I've already come too far to turn back. I may achieve nothing, but that'll be better than wondering what I *might* have achieved.'

'Good luck.'

'Thanks. For the book, too. Very generous.'

'Not really.' She smiled. 'But if you want to repay the favour . . . Come back and tell me what you find out. That's all I ask.'

'I will. It's a promise.'

'And one piece of advice . . .'

'Yes?'

'Try the Lord Nelson before you leave town. I believe they keep an excellent pint.'

Half an hour later, with Athene Tilson's recommendation amply vindicated and the question revolving in his mind of whether there would be time for a third pint of Adnams' Broadside before the Ipswich bus pulled out, Harry remembered to look at the dedication in his copy of *The Implicate Topology of Complex Numbers*. He pulled the book from his pocket and turned to the title page. *For Harry*, Dr Tilson had written. *May you find as well as seek.*

FOURTEEN

'Why couldn't we meet at the hospital?' Harry complained when
he returned from the buffet queue to the corner table Iris had
selected. Tea and biscuits in the no-smoking zone of the British
Museum cafeteria was not his idea of fun, although for confidentiality it was probably unrivalled. The dozen identically
dressed French teenagers gathered round the nearest occupied
table were all speaking at once – and very loudly.

'I'm sorry,' said Iris. 'It's just . . . Well, you'll think it stupid, but
. . . I sometimes feel I can't speak freely . . . in front of David.'

Harry smiled sympathetically. 'I don't think it's stupid. I talk to
him as if he can hear and understand what I'm saying. I know you
do too. It's only natural. But . . . what is it you can't bring yourself
to say in front of him?'

'Never mind that for the moment,' she said briskly, sipping at
her tea. 'Tell me about Dr Tilson.'

'There isn't much to add to what I said on the phone. She doesn't
have David's notebooks. She agrees their absence is suspicious.
She confirms Hammelgaard thought the same. And she thinks he
may have gone to ground in Copenhagen.'

'With Miss Trangam?'

'Maybe. Either way, he must know where she is.'

'I still can't believe she can help David in any practical way,
Harry. If she could, she'd have told me when we met.'

'She did offer Baxendale some advice, didn't she?'

'Yes, but of a highly theoretical nature. The findings of some

81

research she'd done into the meaning of consciousness. According to Mr Baxendale, it was all about precisely where and how in the brain consciousness functions. Given enough precision, it might be possible to stimulate those areas surgically and snap a patient out of a coma. But the necessary techniques simply don't exist. And won't for the foreseeable future.'

'It's at least worth talking to her, isn't it?'

'I suppose so. But you must understand just how long a shot it is. David stopped breathing shortly after the chambermaid found him. It was twenty minutes before the paramedics got his heart beating again and put him on a respirator. The consensus of opinion is that there's nothing to revive.'

'Why didn't you agree to let him die some time ago, then?'

'Because a mother can't help hoping.'

'Well, believe it or not, Iris, neither can a father.'

She looked at him for what seemed a long time without speaking, then said: 'This isn't really about saving David though, is it, Harry? This is about blaming somebody for what's happened to him.'

'It's about both.'

'Ken has been very generous, you know. All Claude left me was a bungalow and a widow's pension. Without Ken I wouldn't be able to pay for David's room. Let alone the twenty-four-hour care he receives. But I can't impose on his generosity indefinitely. Not when there's no reasonable prospect of an improvement in David's condition. It simply wouldn't be fair.'

'Would leaving even a single stone unturned be fair to David?'

'Put like that . . .'

'All I'm asking you to do is nothing – until I've had a chance to speak to Hammelgaard and Donna Trangam.'

'You've got to find them first.'

'Which is why I'm going to Copenhagen.'

'When?'

'As soon as possible. Next week, I suppose. I'll have to give my boss a few days to arrange cover for me.'

'Your boss at the garage?'

'The very same.'

'It didn't look much of a place.'

'And it's not much of a job. But it's the only one I've got.'

'What's the pay like?'

Harry grinned. 'Put it this way. If Labour ever get in and introduce a national minimum wage, I'll be due a substantial rise.'

Iris chuckled. 'You always did have a good sense of humour, Harry. I remember that. David would have—' She broke off and flushed, then reached evasively for her tea.

'Would have liked me?'

She swallowed some tea and clattered the cup back into its saucer.

'You never mentioned I have his smile.'

'What would have been the point? You're never going to see him smile, are you?' She closed her eyes tightly for a moment, then opened them and said: 'I asked about your wages in case you need some money. Travelling expenses. That sort of thing. I mean, in a sense you'll be going to Copenhagen on my behalf, won't you? So—'

'I don't need to be paid to help my son, Iris. Keep your money. Put it towards the hospital bill.' Their eyes met. Thirty-four years of mutual indifference contended with the bonds and necessities of the moment. And a silent truce was concluded. 'I'm sorry. There's no point us arguing. That won't help David.'

'I'm sorry too. I never meant to suggest . . .'

'It doesn't matter. What matters is whether you'll give me the time I need.'

'I'll do nothing until I've heard from you. Nothing without . . .' She paused a long while before using the word that somehow dignified their pact. 'Without consulting you first. Good enough?'

Harry nodded. 'Good enough.'

They parted in the gateway leading from the museum forecourt into Great Russell Street, where Harry proposed to wait until Iris had set off by cab for Marylebone before sliding into the pub on the other side of the road. But Iris hung back, as if there were still something to be said.

'I have a present for you,' she said, delving into her handbag. 'I wasn't sure if . . . But I think you should have it . . . It's not much, but . . . Like what we're doing, I suppose. Better than nothing.' She handed him a small brown envelope, its flap unsealed, its contents thin to the touch. 'It's a photograph of David. The most recent I have. Taken at Edale. We went there for a walk when he came up to see us last month. Just the two of us. David used to love the Peaks, you know. Anyway, I got a duplicate for you in case . . . Well, in case you wanted it.'

'Thanks, Iris. I appreciate this. I really do.'

'It's only a snapshot. And . . . Well, you'll see.' She turned and hailed a cab. One pulled in immediately. As she opened the door, she looked back and said: 'Be in touch soon, Harry.'

'I will be.'

The door slammed, the cab pulled away and Harry slid the photograph out of its envelope. David, tousle-haired in jeans and a skiing jacket, was pictured leaning against a dry-stone wall with some slab of Pennine scenery behind him, bathed in watery sunlight. It was, as Iris had implied, an unremarkable snapshot. But the event it had preceded by only a few days gave it a patina of unattainability, a quality of longing as well as loss. And something else struck Harry at once. Something he knew must have made Iris wonder in the end whether she should hand it over after all. David was smiling. Broadly and affectionately. As a son would at his mother. Or his father.

FIFTEEN

Rain spat at the window of room E318. Beyond the glass lay a wet and windy London night. Harry stared glumly out at the refracted lights of the city – red and white, green and amber – then turned back to the bed and looked down at David, his unmoving unknowing son, to whom all weathers were one, all changing moods and variations a single grey shapelessness. Did he dream? Harry wondered. Did his mind stray where his body could not? Was there really, was there truly, nothing to retrieve?

'I'll be off soon,' said Harry, slumping down into the bedside chair. 'Got to be at Victoria by ten. Think of me, bucketing across the Channel, while you're tucked up here, all snug and warm. It's my own fault, of course. If I'd taken up your mother's offer, I could probably have flown to Copenhagen in about an hour and a half. Instead of which, it'll be this time tomorrow night before I arrive. Assuming the ferry makes it to Ostend, of course. In this weather, you can't take that for granted. Still, I once came back to London from Athens by train and that took two and a half days, so twenty-two hours to Copenhagen shouldn't kill me, should it? Of course, I was younger then. Well, a bit younger. Lately, I've been getting too set in my ways. Perhaps this trip will do me good.

'But I'll have to watch the pennies. Or the kroner. I won't have a job to come back to, you see. Crowther turned down my request for time off. Said it wasn't "convenient". Said if I insisted on going he'd "look on it as a resignation". Well, I insisted. So apparently I've resigned. Can't say I'm sorry. I'll miss old Shafiq, but that's

85

about it. I think he'll miss me too. We went for a farewell drink, but it wasn't an uproarious send-off, not with Shafiq sticking to orange juice and muttering about the gloomy employment prospects for a man of my age.

'We'll have to see about that, won't we? First I have to find your friend Torben Hammelgaard. Maybe Donna Trangam as well. Your mother doesn't think she can help you, but I'm not so sure. She might be staying away because she's afraid for her life. After what happened to Kersey, Mermillod and you, you couldn't blame her. Not that I know *exactly* what happened. To them or to you. I went out to the Skyway Hotel, you know. Your mother gave me the room number. I talked the management into letting me take a look inside. Drew a blank, of course. There weren't any notebooks strapped to the bottom of the bed or wedged behind the cistern. I checked. If I say so myself, I was pretty thorough. And there was definitely nothing. But they *were* there, weren't they? They were there with you.

'What's in them, David? What makes them so important? If they *are* important. If they're not just a red herring. I mean, higher dimensions? Who the hell understands them, let alone cares about them? I tried Dr Tilson's book, but I couldn't get past the first page. I had to borrow Mrs T's dictionary just to work out what the title meant. Topology is the mathematics of abstract spaces, right, which can change size or shape while still remaining the same? So implicate topology is about abstract spaces wrapped around each other, twisted together somehow. And complex numbers are numbers that can't be mathematically defined, like the square root of minus one. So Dr Tilson's book is about tangled-up abstract spaces created with numbers that don't exist. Well, hell's teeth, what does any of that actually *mean*?'

Harry sighed and leant forward, resting his elbow on his knee and his chin on his palm. 'My guess is higher dimensions don't come into this. They weren't what you were working on at Globescope, were they? Dr Tilson told me about Project Sybil. The future. That's what it's all about, isn't it? The new millennium and what it holds. Something you realized. Something you discovered. Something you *foresaw*. That could be in the notebooks too, buried in the hyper-dimensional hocus-pocus. Two dead. Two in hiding. And you. How many others? Two? Three? Four? You know, don't you? But you're not going to tell me. They must all know what it is. That's why they're all in danger.

'Your mother's given me a snapshot of you. You don't mind,

do you? It's only a copy. It's the last picture she took of you, when you went to Edale with her a few days before . . . You used to go there a lot, so she tells me. When you were younger. You and her and . . . Claude, of course. So many happy family outings. You didn't know about me then. She hadn't told you. But even when she did, you didn't come looking for me, did you? Why not? You could have found me easily enough. My mother . . . your grandmother . . . could have given you my address in Rhodes. You could have come out for a holiday. Or written me a letter. But you never did. Thought there was no point, I suppose. Thought there was nothing to be gained. I can understand that. Well, now's my chance to prove you wrong, isn't it? Now's my once-in-a-lifetime opportunity.

'It doesn't feel much like it, though. It feels more like a fool's errand. But I've run those before. And I haven't always regretted it. So we'll just have to see what comes of it, won't we? We'll just have to give it a go.'

Harry sat back and looked at his watch. 'Nearly time I was off. I'd better make sure I catch that train, hadn't I? I only hope there's a buffet on board. A clear head isn't what I need for a midnight sailing in a force ten gale. Think I'll find Torben in Copenhagen? I reckon you've a fair idea of my chances. Well, perhaps it's better if you don't tell me. Odds generally depress me. Basically because they're seldom in my favour. I suppose it's been that kind of a life. Only child, like you. Never knew my father. He died when I was three, crushed under a locomotive wheel at the GWR works in Swindon. A bit like you again, I suppose. Except you thought you did know your father. Only to find out after he was dead that he was an impostor. An unwitting impostor, it's true, but still not the real thing. Not the shabby inadequate genuine article.'

Harry reached out and patted David's hand where it lay on the coverlet. 'That's me,' he said, smiling gently in something between affection and self-mockery. 'Your last best only hope.' He rose, picked up his bag from beside the bed and moved to the door. 'I'll do what I can,' he said, stopping to look back. 'However little, however much.' He smiled again. 'It's a promise.' Then he turned and walked out into the corridor.

SIXTEEN

Harry's storm-tossed Channel crossing was but a distant memory when he stumbled out of the Hovedbanegården in Copenhagen the following evening to confront a city every bit as damp as London and several degrees colder. Illuminated hotel signs lured him west, but he had reached the fringes of the red-light district before he spotted an establishment that looked on a par with his budget. Sandwiched between a Turkish grocery and a tattoo parlour, the Hotel Kong Knud clearly had no pretensions to grandeur, but its foyer struck Harry as decent enough to promise clean sheets while dowdy enough to guarantee a modest tariff.

It turned out to have a small bar as well, whose gloomy custodian recommended Tuborg's special winter brew with the urgency of somebody who recognizes a good customer when he sees one. Too many bottles of Julebryg later, Harry headed for bed. A broken-backed mattress and noisy copulation in the adjoining room did precisely nothing to delay his descent into log-like slumber. When he woke next morning, stiff-limbed and dry-throated, he was nevertheless ready for action.

The Niels Bohr Institute was a huddle of anonymous-looking greystone buildings a mile or so out of the city centre. Harry asked the taxi driver to drop him just beyond the entrance, but the fellow either misunderstood or pretended to, because Harry found himself clambering out in the Institute's forecourt amidst a flurry of flaxen-haired students steering their bicycles adroitly round him despite armfuls of files.

There was some sort of time-lock mechanism on the main door, but so many people were coming and going that Harry was able simply to stroll in. The fact that he was about three times older than most of them did not seem to make much difference. Whether they took him for a professor or a janitor was hard to tell.

He reached an ill-lit foyer with corridors off and a large noticeboard crammed with handwritten advertisements for cheap accommodation and cut-price textbooks. Through a sliding glass partition next to it, he could see into a postroom where two figures were sifting lethargically through binloads of parcels and padded envelopes. Encouraged by a fleeting smile on the face of one of them, Harry tapped at the glass.

'*Kan jeg hjaelpe med noget?*'

'Um . . . I'm looking for, er, a member of staff here. Torben Hammelgaard.'

'*Undskyld?*'

'Torben Hammelgaard.'

The fellow shrugged and shook his head. '*Jeg forstår det ikke.*'

'He used to teach here. Ham-mel-gaard.'

Another shrug. Then his colleague, the one who had smiled, intervened. 'You are looking for Torben Hammelgaard?'

'Yes. I am.'

'He has gone. Four years. Five, maybe. To America. Where all the clever ones go.'

'I heard he'd come back.'

'No.'

'Not necessarily here, to work. But to Copenhagen.'

'I don't think so.'

'Is there anybody he might have been in touch with? A friend, maybe?'

There was a sudden debate between the two men in Danish. Glum mutterings and frowning glances at Harry. He did not understand a word, but the suspicion began to form in his mind that they had been asked such questions before. Eventually, the debate resolved itself.

'Nobody has seen Torben Hammelgaard here, sir. We don't know his friends.'

'Family, then?'

The fellow deliberated for a moment, then said: 'He had a sister. A . . . *blomsterhandler*. Flowers, you understand? She gave me . . .

en rabat . . . a good price.' He grimaced. 'I sent flowers one time. Not any more.'

'Sorry? You mean . . . you sent flowers to Hammelgaard's sister?'

'*Nej, nej.*' He grabbed what looked fat enough to be the yellow pages for the whole of Denmark, thumbed through the book, then turned it round to face Harry, his finger stabbing at a boxed advertisement. Where a flower-basket emblem next to a familiar name finally surmounted the language barrier. Hammelgaard's sister was a florist. With a shop in Copenhagen.

It was an up-market establishment on Strøget, the pedestrianized spine of the city centre. The assistants were polite but unhelpful. Margrethe Hammelgaard was away from the shop. Harry was advised to try again about four o'clock.

He filled the time with a liquid lunch and a tramp round the harbour. Copenhagen at the onset of winter was a chill and cautious city, offering as little as it denied: skies, streets and marine horizons of unyielding grey. On his way back along Strøget, still killing time, he wandered into a bookshop and scoured the academic shelves for some scientific work by Torben Hammelgaard, brain-drained lion of the Niels Bohr Institute. To his surprise, he found not just one, but two. Higher maths leavened with Danish prose rendered them doubly incomprehensible, of course, but there was a dust-jacket photograph of the author to reward his efforts.

Torben Hammelgaard was a prematurely balding young man in an open-necked black shirt, earnest and unsmiling behind steel-rimmed glasses and a precisely delineated beard. *Han er født i 1957*, the biographical blurb began. So, he was four years older than David. And the photograph looked to be at least ten years out of date. *Københavns Universitet. Niels Bohr Institutet.* So was the information. It led Harry nowhere.

The store-cum-office at the rear of Margrethe Hammelgaard's shop just after four o'clock held more promise, however. The lady in question had returned. She was busy on the telephone when Harry was shown in. Slim, short-haired and snappily dressed, she looked and sounded like a highly efficient businesswoman. Too efficient to welcome rambling enquiries about her errant egg-head brother, Harry feared. But at least she spoke fluent English. That was some kind of a start.

The telephone call ended. She looked up at him enquiringly. '*Ja?*'

'My name's Harry Barnett, Miss Hammelgaard. I . . . er . . . I'm looking for your brother.'

'My brother?'

'Torben.'

'And you are?'

'Harry Barnett. You don't know me. Nor does your brother. But . . . it's important I find him.'

'Torben lives in America. Princeton University.' She looked at him a little as the pair in the postroom had. 'Copenhagen wasn't big enough for him.'

Harry stepped closer and lowered his voice. 'Miss Hammelgaard . . .'

'I can't help you. Torben—'

'Left Princeton about six weeks ago and hasn't been back since.' He tried to sculpt a reassuring smile. 'It's all right. I know what's going on. Some of it, anyway. I'm no kind of threat.'

'I don't know what you're talking about.'

'If he's here, he must have been in touch with you.'

'Like I said, Torben—'

'I'm David Venning's father.' The name meant something to her. That was clear. 'I'm trying to help my son. And I'm trying to help your brother as well. He's in danger. You know that, don't you?'

She studied him silently for several seconds, then said: 'You introduced yourself, just a moment ago, as Harry Barnett. Not Venning.'

'It's a long story.'

'I don't have the time for this, Mr . . . Barnett.'

'Fine. You're busy. I understand that. You're busy and I'm in a hurry. Maybe Torben is too. If not, I reckon he should be.' Her frown was deepening towards impatience. He did not have long to make an impression. 'Look, Miss Hammelgaard, if I was going to *pretend* to be David's father, I'd call myself Venning, wouldn't I? That's what an impostor would do. But I'm not an impostor.'

'What are you, then?'

'A father. Trying to understand what's happened to his son. David's in a coma, you know. Has been since—'

'I know all about that,' she snapped irritably.

'Because Torben told you?'

91

She gave him a long hard stare. 'I read about it.'

'It made the Danish papers? You surprise me.'

She looked away: a sign of weakness, of doubt as much as surrender. 'What do you want, Mr Barnett?'

'A message passed. To your brother.'

'What is the message?' The question came in a whisper, loud with unspoken admission.

'We need to talk. As soon as possible. Time's running out – for everybody. I'm staying at the Hotel Kong Knud on Istedgade. Have him come there tonight.'

'It doesn't work like that, Mr Barnett.'

'How does it work, then?'

'You'll have to wait and see, won't you?'

'How long?'

'A day or two, maybe.'

'That's too long.'

'Then don't wait.' She turned to meet his gaze. 'It's your choice.'

Harry waited – as he was bound to. The rest of that day and most of the next. While Copenhagen's strange mixture of licence and austerity chewed at his nerves. And the irrational conviction grew that he was being watched, followed, tracked every step of the way. He mooched round the sex shops of Istedgade, trying to work out what the more exotic items on display were actually for. He sat in bars drinking Julebryg and staring at David's photograph until he had memorized every detail of the boy's expression. He experimented with Danish cigarettes to eke out his dwindling supply of Greek ones, while watching the comings and goings of the car ferries down at the harbour. And every now and again he would find himself glancing nervously over his shoulder. But never quite quickly enough. If there was something there beyond his own baseless fears, it was always too fast for him.

'Letter for you,' announced the misanthropic manager of the Kong Knud as Harry shambled into the foyer late on Thursday afternoon. He slid a crumpled brown envelope across the counter along with the key. Harry grabbed the letter and tore it open as he moved towards the lift. There was a tourist street-map of Copenhagen inside. He looked back at the manager. 'Did you see who delivered this?'

'No. There was nobody on the desk when it arrived.' Hammelgaard then. It had to be.

Harry unfolded the map. Kongens Nytorv, the square at the eastern end of Strøget, had been circled in red ink. And one word had been written in the margin, unmissably large. MIDNIGHT.

SEVENTEEN

It was cold. There was rain in the air. And a chill stirring of rigging against masts down in the harbour reach that ended at a wharf on one side of the square. The dregs of the opera crowd had dispersed from the Royal Theatre. The last diners had quit the street-front restaurant of the Hotel d'Angleterre. The traffic had dribbled away. Harry felt exposed and far more conspicuous than he really was, circling the darkened centre of Kongens Nytorv. He lit another cigarette – one of his precious *Karelia Sertika* – and held the match close to his watch to read the time. Midnight had come and gone. But there was no sign of Torben Hammelgaard.

Harry drew on the cigarette and mixed a sigh with the smoke as he breathed out. Despite a lengthy soak in a bar halfway along Strøget, he felt completely sober. At this hour of the night, it was a particularly disagreeable sensation. Not least because he had so little experience of it.

Suddenly he spun round, convinced there was somebody close behind him. But no. It was just his nerves playing up again. Damp cobbles and glimmering tram-lines curved away towards the harbour, yielding nothing to his gaze. A late and empty bus sped by in a rush of sound. He turned back. And was no longer alone.

A short square-shouldered figure in black stood about six yards from him, hands thrust deep into the pockets of a donkey-jacket, face partially obscured beneath a fur-peaked cap. But the steel-framed glasses and trimmed beard were enough to clinch his

94

identity. He took a slow deliberate step into better light and nodded in greeting.

'Hi, Harry.' The voice was soft and low, an odd fusion of Danish and American. But it was not the accent so much as the hint of familiarity that Harry found confusing.

'Torben Hammelgaard?'

'Of course. Don't you recognize me?'

'Well, yes. From a photograph in one of your books. But how did—'

'Don't you recognize me from the last time we met, I mean.'

'We've never met.'

'You must remember.'

'No. Our paths have never crossed. Why should they have?'

'Why? I'd have thought you'd know the reason well enough.'

'I don't know what you're talking about.'

'Rhodes, Harry. August eighty-eight. The bar in Lindos where you used to work. What was it called?'

'The Taverna Silenou?'

'Yes. That's it.'

'You went there?'

'Yes. I went there. And I didn't go alone.'

Dread seized Harry's thoughts. A sickening guess began to form in his mind. 'Who were you with?'

'Two friends. A girl who was keen on me at the time called Hanne. And . . . somebody else.'

'August eighty-eight, you said?'

'Yes. That's what I said.'

'And this . . . Hanne . . . was Danish?'

'Yes. I was still at the Niels Bohr Institute then. Most of my friends *were* Danish. But not all of them.'

Some things never went away, never diminished, never faded. They just grew and worsened, swelling like a tumour in the memory. A drunken misunderstanding one broiling summer's day in Lindos should have been inconsequential. But three months later it had counted against him during the police investigations into the disappearance of Heather Mallender. And now, more than six years on, it had returned again to mock him.

'It wasn't your fault, Harry. Hanne was trying to make me jealous by flirting with you. She probably thought you were harmless. When things got out of hand, she made a fuss. She was always making a fuss. She manages a geological field station in Greenland now. That should have cooled her down.'

'Who was your other friend?'

'You know who he was.'

'But I can't remember. You or him. I suppose I thought you were all Danish. I was . . . too drunk to pay much attention.'

'He never said a word. He let me talk Hanne into dropping it. He was . . . very subdued. At the time, I couldn't understand why. Going to Lindos was his idea, of course, but I thought we chose the bar at random. We didn't though, did we? David made the choice. He wanted to see you. To find out what you were like. That has to be it.'

And what had David seen? After making the effort Harry had thought he had spurned to track down his father? He had seen a middle-aged ex-pat making a drunken fool of himself. And if he had been planning to make himself known, he had surely changed his mind then. When he had realized what he would be making himself known *to*.

'We should be glad, I suppose.'

'Why?'

'Because otherwise I wouldn't have believed the story you told Margrethe. I wouldn't have recognized the man I watched entering and leaving the Kong Knud. And I wouldn't have kept this appointment. You told my sister I was in danger and you were right. But you don't know how much danger. You can't. If you did, you wouldn't have come here. You'd have been mad to.'

'Why?'

'Because they'll be after you now as well as me. If I've walked into a trap tonight, Harry, then so have you.'

They headed west, by ever narrower and emptier streets, Hammelgaard choosing such a maze-like route that to Harry it seemed aimless – and utterly disorientating. Not that it mattered where they went. Their words were their destination. Hammelgaard wanted to know how Harry had become aware of his son's existence, let alone his condition. He wanted to know what had led him to Copenhagen. And what he heard he did not like.

'The telephone message. The newspaper cutting. Communications you have no explanation for. But I have. Carrot and stick, Harry. With you as the donkey. And me as the target. They must have known you'd be able to flush me out. But how? How could they know that? And why didn't they follow you tonight? Nobody trailed you to Kongens Nytorv. I made sure of that. But why not? What are they waiting for?'

96

'Who is it you're talking about?'

'Globescope, Harry. Byron Lazenby. Or whoever he's employing to do this. They killed Gerard and Marvin. They put David in a coma. And they won't stop there.'

'What's this about?'

'The future. And who owns it. Lazenby would trademark it if he could, then sell it to the highest bidder.'

'You mean Project Sybil?'

'That was just the spark. It's what we did because of Project Sybil that's led to this.'

'Tell me what you did.'

'No. It's safer for you not to know. What you don't know you can't tell.'

'Why did you agree to meet me, then?'

'Because I have to get a message to the others. And you're the only way I can do it. You could have been set up. Perhaps I should abandon the idea. But I can't afford to. It's their only hope. And mine. I could be wrong. Maybe your informant *was* some well-meaning relative. Maybe they're not onto us at all. I can't be sure. But I have to take the chance. I'm not going to get another.'

'I'm carrying no messages until I hear the truth.'

Hammelgaard glanced round at him. 'What's happened to you since we last met, Harry? Barflies shouldn't be as tough as this.'

'You got me on a bad day.'

'A pity. For you *and* David.'

'I'm trying to make up for it now.'

'For his sake?'

'For mine as well.'

'There's clearly more to you than meets the eye. David thought you weren't worth bothering with, I'm afraid. He was depressed when we got back to Rhodes Town. In a really black mood. That's how he could be sometimes. For no reason. The price of genius, he used to say. Modesty was never one of his faults. But it was different that night. Deeper. Sharper.'

'Why were you on the island?'

'To discuss higher dimensions and have a holiday at the same time. I first met David at a conference at Los Alamos earlier that year. He was already planning a summer gathering for people who shared his enthusiasm for the subject. The venue was his suggestion. It seemed inspired. Now I know by what.'

'The man he'd thought of as his father died in eighty-six. That's when his mother told him about me.'

'And two years later he decided to go take a look at you.'

'So it seems. But he obviously didn't like what he saw.'

'I'm sorry, Harry. Really.'

'Don't be. Just tell me what you and he were mixed up in.'

'You don't want to know. Believe me. David doesn't come out of it a hero.'

'I want to understand. I think I need to.'

They emerged into a small square with the outline of a church looming ahead of them, a starker black than the sky. Hammelgaard pulled up and glanced around, as if checking the route. Then he cast a long look behind them. 'All right,' he said. 'I'll tell you. Some of it, anyway. On one condition. That you agree now – in advance – to take a message for me to the others. They're in hiding in the States. I can put you in touch with them.'

'Why don't you just phone them?'

'Because phones can be tapped, computers hacked, letters opened and read. And my face can be recognized. Globescope has the power to do all of those things. But it's possible – just possible – they don't know about you. I may have been dealt a losing hand, but you could be the joker in the pack.'

'What's the message?'

'Will you take it?'

'Is Donna Trangam one of them?'

The pale hint of a smile appeared on Hammelgaard's face. 'Yes, Harry. She's one of them. But she has no magical powers. I can't promise she'll be able to rouse David from his coma. If that's what you want to hear me say . . .' He shrugged. 'Agree or not. But don't ask me to lie. I've told too many lies already. I'd say your chances of ever speaking to David again are pitifully small. But there *is* something you can do for him. Donna and the others are in danger because of David and me. We betrayed them. By helping them, you'd be settling a debt for your son. And the message I'm asking you to carry *will* help them. As just about nothing else can. So what do you say? Yes or no?'

The question was chance and challenge combined. A chance to play the part of a good father, however briefly, however obliquely. And a challenge he was probably unequal to. But he could not have one without the other. He could not wipe away the shame of six years ago without risking failure in the present. It was, as Hammelgaard had said, yes or no. And though he might regret saying yes, it was certain he would regret saying no even more. 'OK,' he murmured. 'I'll do it.'

98

They crossed the square and turned into what was scarcely wider than an alley. Hammelgaard's voice sank nearly to a whisper, forcing Harry to stick close to his shoulder and cock his head to catch the words.

'What turns people into traitors, Harry? Money? Sex? Or some other kind of greed? David and I dreamt of masterminding the single most significant step in human evolution. We dreamt of unlocking the power of higher dimensions. Splitting the atom gave the human race hydrogen bombs and power stations and nuclear waste. But access to higher dimensions would transform our minds along with our lives. Nothing would be beyond us. And no honour would be denied those who had found and opened the door. Most scientists believe the technology required to generate the energy we would need to unlock that door lies many centuries in the future. But David believed he was on the way to finding a short-cut. Some of his mathematical insights were beyond me, but I could see where they were leading. We needed time and help and money to carry them through. That's why we were so keen to set up HYDRA. Because with enough mathematicians and physicists working on the problem full-time, we were certain it could be solved. And that certainty convinced us almost any sacrifice was justifiable to achieve our objective. Friendship. Loyalty. Integrity. What do they matter – what do they count for – when you think the destiny of the entire species lies in your grasp?'

They emerged from the alley onto a broad canalside street. Beyond the canal lay the floodlit roofs and courtyards of Christiansborg Castle. Hammelgaard kept to the shadows of the shuttered buildings to their right as they went on.

'Globescope started in a small way, about ten years ago. Lazenby had a partner then, later disposed of. Under his sole control, the corporation grew and extended itself, selling guesses about the future to whoever wanted to listen. Plenty did. The future's such a hostile place you'd take advice on what to go armed against if you thought the advice was good, wouldn't you? And Globescope's was good. The Soviet Union to collapse at the end of the eighties but the Chinese version of communism to adapt and endure. That was their call. And calling right earned them a lot of credit. As well as a lot of customers, commercial *and* political. I wouldn't know whether it was good luck or good judgement. I wasn't with them then. But it turned them into a big-time operation. And Byron Lazenby into a very wealthy man.'

'When *did* you join them?'

'Two years ago. When Project Sybil was set up. David recommended me. Ostensibly because of my expertise in technological applications of quantum effects. Actually so we could work closer together on higher dimensions.'

'Dr Tilson said the purpose of the project was to predict in detail the state of the world in 2050.'

'Correct. On behalf of a consortium of international corporations Lazenby never identified. Confidentiality is another of his watchwords. Secrecy is what it feels like. We were forbidden to discuss the project, even with other Globescope staff. The money was good, of course. The money was enough to buy a lot of silence. Particularly in the light of Lazenby's reputation as a litigator. He had us tied up with all sorts of contracts. And he was prepared to enforce them.'

'You didn't have to sign.'

'No. But we did sign. For the money, the prestige and the job itself. It was a genuinely exciting opportunity.'

'How many of you were there?'

'Seven. David and I. Gerard Mermillod and Marvin Kersey. Donna Trangam. Makepeace Steiner. Rawnsley Ablett. It was an impressive line-up. A mathematician; a physicist; a sociologist; a biochemist; a neuroscientist; a computer scientist; and an economist. With two years and Globescope's facilities at our disposal, we aimed to form a clear and specific picture of the middle of the next century. How it would be. What it would feel like. What sort of lives we'd all be leading. How the world and the human race would be faring. You have to understand. This was no rush-job. No superficial sketch of the future. This was weighed and analysed reality. As close to the truth as you could come, with allowances for all the variables. This was as accurate as prediction ever gets.'

'And how will it be in 2050?'

'You won't hear that from me. You'd gain nothing from knowing what we predicted. You'll be long dead by then. So will I. It's a burden you don't need to carry, believe me. And it's not the point. It's not really why we're here.'

'Why are we, then?' —

'Because last spring the seven of us presented our preliminary conclusions to Lazenby. And he didn't like them. He said they were incompatible with Globescope policy and weren't what his clients required. He didn't dispute their accuracy. He didn't bother

100

to. He simply told us to change them. To make them . . . commercially acceptable.'

'But if you changed them, they wouldn't be—'

'Right? Exactly. We realized then, as we should have sooner, that Lazenby's guiding principle – the key to his success – was to tell clients what they wanted to hear, not what they needed to know. Neither he nor his clients were going to be around to argue the point in 2050. What they were paying for was reassurance for their shareholders. Proof that they were looking to the future in a responsible manner. Lazenby never identified the corporations involved, but we knew they had to be big multinationals with interests in all the global staples. Oil. Automobiles. Chemicals. Arms. Aerospace. Pharmaceuticals. Whatever it was, our predictions were clear. None of that kind of business would be going on in the same way in 2050. The world wouldn't be recognizable to the corporate kings of today – or suited to their survival. It's not nice to be told your days are numbered. It's not popular. And Lazenby decided it wasn't profitable either. So, he instructed us to . . . adjust our parameters, as he put it . . . in order to produce a more palatable result. We refused. Seven high-minded scientists took an ethical stand. We weren't going to be pushed around. Instead, we were pushed out. Dismissed on the spot. Told to be off the premises within half an hour. Watched throughout that time to ensure we took nothing with us. And forcefully reminded that discussion of any aspect of Project Sybil with a third party would constitute breach of contract. We could crawl back to the comfortable academic institutions we'd come from and keep our mouths shut. Or we could shoot them off and get taken to court.'

'Surely the project generated records? If not on paper, then on computer. Couldn't you have used them to defend any court action?'

'Shredded and/or wiped. Probably the day we left. Makepeace hacked into the Globescope system later and confirmed our files had been deleted. Eighteen months' unique analysis of the future had been flushed down the toilet.'

'What did you do?'

'At first, nothing. We were all a bit shell-shocked, I think. I went back to Princeton. The others dispersed too. Gerard returned to IHES, Marvin to McGill, Rawnsley to Harvard, Makepeace to Caltech and Donna to Berkeley. Only David stayed in Washington. In his little house in Georgetown, within walking distance of Globescope. He wasn't in any hurry to leave.'

101

'What about him and Donna? His mother seems to think . . .'

'Yes, they had a thing going. They lived together for a while. But that ended about the same time. What can I tell you? Donna went back to California and David didn't follow her. Neither of them wanted to talk about it. But they were civil to each other when we all met up last summer in Florida. The gathering was Donna's idea. She wanted to know how many of us felt the same as her. That we should do something to publicize our findings and expose Globescope as a corrupt organization. Well, we all went along with that. Our predictions for 2050 were truly frightening. But they weren't inevitable. Our whole point was that concerted action *now* could improve the picture immeasurably. But we no longer had enough detailed facts and figures to back up our claims. Lazenby had destroyed them. So, what could we do? Donna's answer was typical of her. She can be a terrier when she wants to be. Her proposal was that we each reassemble our own contribution to the project from scratch. It wasn't as bad as it sounds. We knew where to find the information. But it meant a lot of hard painstaking work, at evenings and weekends, for no immediate reward. Nevertheless, we all agreed. It was worth it, after all. We were talking about the kind of world our grandchildren might grow up in. We were unanimous. We reckoned it would take six months to put Project Sybil back together. Then we could offer it – and the whole story – to the scientific press. Until then, we had to work and communicate in secret. It was vital Lazenby shouldn't learn what we were planning.'

'But he did?'

'Oh yes. He learnt about it.'

Christiansborg was still on their left, but the wind that had been at their backs was blowing in their faces now. They had circled the castle and were heading towards the harbour, the rain dying as the wind rose, star-pricked windows opening in the churning sky.

'A couple of weeks after I got back from Florida, David came to see me. He was in one of his elated moods, when he could make you believe nothing was beyond him. He had an idea. A good one, he persuaded me. We could go to Lazenby and make a deal with him. We could offer to break ranks with the others and publicly contradict them. Dispute their predictions and say Globescope had behaved impeccably throughout. That would effectively kill the story. In exchange, we would require Lazenby to finance the establishment of HYDRA. It would cost him several

102

million dollars, but that would be a fair price to pay for preserving Globescope's reputation.' Hammelgaard glanced round at Harry. 'Perhaps you think I should have turned him down there and then. But there was our dream, you see. A dream suddenly made attainable. With an elegant justification built in. Access to hyper-dimensional powers might help to solve many of the problems that Project Sybil had shown the future held. Whereas the reaction to the Globescope story when it broke might be just as ineffectual as all those other high-sounding appeals to safeguard the planet. Remember the Earth Summit? Long-term achievements nil. What made David's idea so hard to resist was that it made sense. We could waste our lives applying for funds to this worthy body and that. There would never be enough to set up an institution that would actually work, actually *succeed*. Whereas, with the kind of money Lazenby could tap into . . . We'd be doing our friends a favour, David argued. In the end, they'd thank us. Around the same time as we won the Nobel Prize for Physics.'

They reached the harbourside road and turned left, still following the floodlit ramparts of Christiansborg. For a minute or so, neither of them spoke. Harry felt sick and fuddled, sated with knowledge, much of which he would have preferred not to possess. A peril-strewn future. And friendship betrayed by his own son. For the sake of half a chance, maybe less, of discovering something Harry had not the slightest hope of ever understanding. Yet something took the edge off his gloom, something he could never have brought himself to admit. The score was closer between him and David now. Condemnation and forgiveness were owed on both sides.

'We should have told the others. We should have consulted them first. It would have worked equally well as a put-up job. But we were afraid they'd veto the idea. Donna disagreed strongly with David's theories about hyper-dimensional capability in the brain. And none of the others really understood them. It was too risky to seek their agreement. We decided to keep them in the dark.'

'You went to Lazenby together?'

'Yes. At the end of August.'

'What did he say?'

'He agreed to our terms. There was a lot of bluff and bluster, but eventually he caved in. Or so we thought. It's obvious to me now he was just buying time. He wasn't prepared to be black-mailed. Or to risk exposure. He decided to apply the ultimate sanction. To pick us off one by one. That has to be it. There's no other possible explanation. I don't know how they arranged David's overdose. The circumstances sounded entirely accidental. I certainly believed it *was* an accident. But when Gerard died, then Marvin, I realized what was happening. We were being eliminated. The threat we posed was being neutralized. The others thought the same. I flew to New York with Donna. We met with Rawnsley and Makepeace at a hotel near the airport and agreed we'd have to go into hiding until we could finish our work on Sybil Two. Without David, Gerard and Marvin, it could never be as wide-ranging as before, but there was nothing else we could do. Accusing Lazenby of commissioning murders would get us no-where if we couldn't put forward a plausible motive.'

'But you didn't stay with them?'

'No. I said I'd prefer to work alone. I said they'd find it easier to hide without a Dane for company. But that was just an excuse. I sound as American as the next guy on the subway. I couldn't have stuck with them, though. Not knowing all the time that I was partly responsible for the situation we were in. I had to get away. To think the problem through. To find a solution.'

'And have you found one?'

'Maybe. As I see it, our only hope is to strike back. To cut the ground from under Lazenby's feet.'

'How?'

'That's where the message comes in, Harry. The one you've agreed to carry.'

'You'd better tell me what it is.'

'If it works, you won't just be repairing the damage David caused. You'll be avenging what was done to him. You realize that, don't you?'

'I've said I'll do it.'

'All right. But remember. It's dangerous. The insulin overdose. The Metro accident. The faulty heating system. Whoever set those up is patient and resourceful. I have no way of anticipating what they may try next. Nothing's happened in over a month. They're waiting for us to show ourselves.'

'But you won't be showing yourself. I will.'

'You're wrong. We have to distract their attention to give you a reasonable chance of success. As soon as you're on your way, I shall contact Lazenby and tell him I want to speak to him. Here. In Copenhagen.'

'You expect him to agree?'

104

'No. I expect him to send his people after me. While they're chasing me round this city I know so much better than they do, you'll be delivering a message to my friends. Unobserved.' He chuckled. 'With any luck.'

They had left Christiansborg behind now and were about to pass under one of the bridges spanning the harbour. Hammelgaard nodded at the steps leading up onto the bridge and turned towards them. 'What if they get to you before your friends get to them?' asked Harry.

'Then it's *god nat, København*. This really is the only way out, Harry. I've spent the past month trying to think of an easy answer. There isn't one.' They reached the bridge and started across it, the wind tugging at Harry's hair and sloshing the water at the piers beneath them. 'This is Knippelsbro. The other side is Christianshavn. We part here. Come back this time tomorrow – one a.m. – and wait at the top of the steps. I'll tell you then what arrangements I've made to get you to the States. If I reckon it's too risky to come myself, I'll send a friend. Olaf Jensen. Tall and thin as a lamppost, with a ginger beard. Difficult to miss. You can trust him.'

They came to the middle of the bridge and stopped. Hammelgaard leant against the railings and gazed down into the harbour. He stayed like that for several seconds, saying nothing. Then Harry broke the silence. 'What's the message, Torben?'

'Sorry. You're right. We mustn't waste time. Tell Donna and the others everything I've told you. Then add this. When David and I went to see Lazenby, I was wired. A state of the art high-resolution micro-recorder. We wanted evidence of whatever Lazenby agreed to, you see. And we got it. But Lazenby's always more suspicious than you reckon possible. He insisted we be searched before leaving. I knew they'd find the tape, of course. So, while we were waiting for Fredericks, the head of security, I disconnected the recorder, slipped it out of my pocket and stuffed it down the side of the chair. They'll remember those huge squashy armchairs in Lazenby's office. It was the one nearest the window. Down by the right arm. The recorder's no bigger than a box of matches. It was safe there. I hoped to be able to retrieve it later. The microphone was inside a pen, which on its own didn't arouse any suspicion. But we were shown the door straight after Fredericks had frisked us, so I had to leave the recorder where it was. There should be enough on the tape to make some kind of case against Lazenby. Even if it doesn't stand up in

105

court, it'll ruin him. And that's the only way to stop him now.'

'That's it?'

'Yes. I don't know how they can lay their hands on the cassette, but they have to. It's—'

'A recording you've never listened to? Hidden in an *armchair*? Lazenby may have found it and destroyed it by now. It may not have been working properly, for God's sake.'

'It's not likely to have been found,' said Hammelgaard calmly. 'And I made sure it was working before we went. It's a recording of everything said, up to the moment of disconnection, by David, Lazenby and me in Lazenby's office at Globescope on the afternoon of August twenty-ninth. Project Sybil. HYDRA. The whole deal. Everything. We spoke candidly, I can assure you. Very candidly. The recording won't leave any room for doubt. It'll destroy Lazenby.'

'*If* it's still there. *If* it can be retrieved.'

'It's if against when, Harry. *If* you can pull this off. Against *when* they track us down. Take your pick.'

'But I already have, haven't I? I've already agreed to go.'

'I can't force you to honour that agreement. Walking away from this may still be an option. For you, anyway.'

'But not for you and the others. And not for David.'

'No. Not for us.'

'Then I seem to have no choice.'

'You'll be here tomorrow night?'

'Yes. I'll be here.'

Hammelgaard stared at him for a moment, his expression indecipherable in the darkness. Then he said: 'Thank you, Harry. This means a lot. And not just to me.'

'That's what worries me.'

'Good. Worried men make good messengers.'

'How do I deliver the message?'

'I'll explain tomorrow. I have a lot of arranging to do.'

'If you say so.'

'I do. And one more thing. About David's notebooks. I assume they were taken in case they contain references to Project Sybil. It's not likely they do. They're actually a record of his hyper-dimensional work. Of no possible interest to Globescope. A precaution on their part, we must suppose. But it's puzzling. Why go to such lengths to fake the circumstances of an accidental or suicidal overdose, then spoil it all with a pointless theft?'

'It doesn't seem to have aroused much suspicion.'

106

'No. Except mine. Nothing was taken from Gerard or Marvin, but they would have had papers about them as well. Gerard carried a lap-top with him wherever he went. It was found intact on the Metro platform after he fell under the train. Why not take that too – as a precaution?'

'Because there were witnesses?'

'Maybe. Maybe that's it.'

'Iris thought David might have left the notebooks in Washington, but Dr Tilson—'

'Confirmed they were with him. I know. That's what . . .' Hammelgaard lowered his voice still further. 'Listen to me, Harry. This has no bearing on anything else. We'll keep it personal between us, OK? Iris gave me the keys to David's house in Washington. In case I wanted to check for the notebooks. I didn't, of course. It would have been too risky. Anyway, Dr Tilson had already told me I wouldn't find them there. But there might be other papers – other records – of his most recent work. He was close to a breakthrough. Anything that can be salvaged could be . . . hugely significant. When this is all over, I want you to go there and remove all the disks and documents you can find. Everything. Then take it to Dr Tilson. She might appreciate its importance. I'm not sure anyone else will. Here are the keys.' He grasped Harry's hand and pressed three keys held on a ring into his palm. 'Don't lose them.'

'Why not search the house yourself? Like you say – when this is all over.' But Harry knew the reason. He knew it as surely as Hammelgaard.

'Just do it, Harry. As soon as it's safe. The tape will destroy David's reputation along with Lazenby's. Don't let everything he achieved be destroyed as well. He was close. He was nearly there. He was on the brink of history.'

'He might still be able to carry on the work, you know. In person.'

'A fine hope, Harry. A father's hope.' Hammelgaard stood upright and glanced around. 'Time to go. No more to be said. Here. Twenty-four hours from now. You *will* come, won't you?'

'Yes.'

'Till then, lie low.'

'I will.'

'Goodnight, Harry.' Hammelgaard shook his hand firmly. '*Held og lykke.*' Then, catching his frown, he added: 'I'm wishing us both luck.' With that, he turned and walked swiftly away across the

107

bridge, without once looking back. Harry watched him go, then lit a cigarette and smoked it through, standing on the bridge above the dark plashing water, letting nicotine and solitude slow the turmoil of his thoughts. Till he too was ready to walk away, weary and confused, sure of nothing except his promise to return.

EIGHTEEN

Friday was cold and grey in Copenhagen. Harry wandered its wintry streets, trying not to think about the foolhardy mission he had agreed to undertake. Which proved possible, but only at the expense of surrendering to the tug of a comfortless memory.

Lindos, August 1988. The beach as crowded as the town. A burning sun striking the white roofs like a hammer. Every bar packed, every craft shop crammed. Noise and heat and too much jostling humanity. At the Taverna Silenou, Harry was more than a little drunk. Wisely, Kostas had told him to go home and sleep it off: absent waiters were better than inebriated ones. Taking his resentful leave, Harry had fallen into flirtatious conversation with a Danish girl. What about he could not remember. Nor could he remember the exact sequence of subsequent events. He thought he might have tripped on a chair-leg, but it could as easily have been a deliberately extended human foot. Either way, his hand, flailing for support, had ended up grabbing the front of the girl's loosely buttoned blouse, ripping it open as he toppled to one side. He had already noticed she was not wearing a bra. Now everybody else noticed as well. The resulting scene – blouse buttons flying, breasts bouncing, Danish voice shrieking, faces staring, arms restraining – was a merciful haze. It was only the following day that Kostas had told him how seriously the girl had threatened to report him to the police for indecent assault; her companions had evidently dissuaded her.

Ah yes, her companions. There had been two men sitting at her

109

table. That much Harry could recall. But his memory could dredge up no details of their appearance. They seemed now in his mind's eye to be obscured by the sort of shimmering blur deployed in television interviews for the benefit of spies and supergrasses. He knew who they were, of course. He had met them both since. But still he would have liked to be able to form a distinct picture of them that day. Of one of them, anyway. The one he could only otherwise envisage as a motionless figure in a hospital bed. The son he had met and probably spoken to without realizing it; who had seen him, red-faced and barely coherent, clinging to the trunk of a fig tree as he offered a fuddled apology along with an unconvincing denial; who had studied him and judged him and gone on his way unannounced.

Three months later, shadowed by a far more serious allegation, his pleas of innocence once again disbelieved, Harry had left Rhodes, never to return. But the circularities of life wound him in as they had before. It was only in the physical sense that he had not returned. In the same sense, he had not visited the Venning house in Swindon since the summer of 1960. But memory was a traveller who acknowledged no barriers. And whose journeyings could not be avoided. So to the Taverna Silenou and Iris Venning's bed his thoughts slipped back with disconcerting ease as the Copenhagen day wore on. Somebody should have told him – they really should – how complicated life becomes the more there is of it to look back on. How complicated – and how intractable. By mid-afternoon he had consumed enough Julebryg to guarantee a few hours' sleep before a long and unpredictable night began. He went back to the Kong Knud actively looking forward to the escape from remembrance slumber would provide.

It was a twin-bedded room, an arrangement he distrusted on account of some superstitious saying of his mother that to sleep in a room with another made-up bed in it was unlucky. He had actually gone to the lengths of stripping the other bed his first night there, only for the slatternly chambermaid to make such a fuss that he had decided to ignore his mother's advice. Not for the first time, he came to regret it.

It seemed to him that he woke at dusk and, rolling over to look towards the window, saw the shape of a human figure beneath the other bedspread, lying supine and inert, like a corpse beneath its shroud. It seemed to him that, gripped by horror, he rose, crossed the room, reached out and grasped the edge of the bedspread, then pulled it back to expose . . .

110

Nothing. He was awake, staring down at an undented pillow and undisturbed sheets, his heart pounding, his face bathed in sweat. He stumbled to the window and threw it open, leaning out to breathe the cold unhaunted air. NON-STOP SEX, the neon sign blinked at him from the other side of the street. STRIP AROUND THE CLOCK. Night had fallen in the real world. Darkness had welcomed him back. Death was only a dream.

A capacity audience comprising several hundred Danish teenagers – plus Harry – watched the late-night showing of *Natural Born Killers* at the Palads Cinema. Harry felt perversely grateful for being sickened by such a wallow in pointless violence. It at least distracted him from anxious anticipation of his 1 a.m. appointment on Knippelsbro.

He wandered along Strøget, forced down some coffee in a bar, then made his way to the harbour. It was still some minutes short of one o'clock when he reached the foot of the steps leading up onto the bridge. But it was better to be early than late. Glancing up at the parapet, he thought he saw a figure leaning on the railings, looking down at him. It was too dark to tell if it was Hammelgaard. He raised his hand cautiously and the figure moved instantly back out of sight. Suddenly anxious for no definable reason, Harry ran up the steps two at a time. At the top, he had to stop to recover his breath. But he had got there fast enough to be sure of seeing the figure, whoever it was and whichever direction it had been heading in. Yet there was nobody on the bridge. Nobody approaching him or retreating. Nobody at all.

He was trembling as he fumbled for a cigarette. Cursing his nerves, he wedged a *Karelia Sertika* between his lips and struck a match. Only to be seized by a conviction very close to a visual certainty that somebody was standing beside him. He whirled round to confront nothing but thick cold air. The match blew out. And the box slipped from his grasp. He made a grab for it as it struck the railings, but succeeded only in stubbing his thumb against a bar. The box bounced through and vanished. Then, a few seconds later, came a dismal plop as it hit the water. 'Thanks a lot,' he muttered. 'That's all I need.' In an irritated spasm, he snatched the cigarette from his mouth and flung it in after the matches, then instantly regretted doing so. Hammelgaard would probably have a light.

But where was Hammelgaard? It was surely one o'clock by now. As if on cue, some distant church clock struck the hour. Harry

111

shivered and decided to walk to the middle of the bridge in the hope of seeing Hammelgaard approaching from the other side. The still night magnified his footfalls as he moved. The steam of his breath made him think longingly of cigarette smoke. His thumb began to throb.

Then he saw a huddled shape on the pavement ahead of him, at the Christianshavn end of the bridge. He broke into a run. It was a man, dressed in black, lying face down close to the railings. His cap had slipped off, revealing the pale crown of a bald head, but the collar of his coat was turned up, obscuring his features. There was still just a chance, as Harry stooped over him, that he might be a stranger. A slim fading ghost of a chance. Harry reached out and grasped the edge of the collar, then pulled it back to expose . . .

Torben Hammelgaard. Eyes staring. Mouth sagging. And no breath frosting on the air. There was no pool of blood, no sign of violence. But the unblinking eyes and crumpled limbs told their story. Before Harry could feel at his wrist for a pulse or turn him over and listen for a heartbeat, he knew what he would find. Torben Hammelgaard was dead.

NINETEEN

Fear is a winged chariot. Harry ran farther and faster than he ever had in his life before from that unmarked corpse on Knippelsbro. He ran until his chest was a tightening hoop of pain and he could run no more. Until he staggered into some dank doorway in Christianshavn and sank down on his haunches among the dog-ends and burger cartons, wondering if at any moment the shadow of his pursuers would fall across him.

Pursuers there surely had to be. They had killed again, in their unique undetectable way. They had killed the man Harry had led them to. And now it must be his turn. At any moment, from any direction, they were bound to come for him.

But they did not come. As the minutes passed and Harry slowly recovered, the hope formed in his mind that somehow he had evaded them. He struggled to his feet and peered out from the doorway. Nothing was moving anywhere. Nothing was waiting for him to emerge.

He set off again, this time at no more than a fast walk, glancing around and behind him as he went, clinging to the shadows, heading wherever the next turning took him. He badly wanted a drink and a cigarette. He was not absolutely sure which he wanted more. But it hardly mattered, since his chances of getting either seemed for the present remote.

What to do. Where to go. How to deal with what had happened. The need to be decisive wrestled in his mind with the impossibility of deciding. Hammelgaard was dead. Harry had a message to carry

113

for him, but no way of delivering it. And he was in peril of his life. Or was he? Perhaps they had been following Hammelgaard for some time. Perhaps it was just a coincidence they had chosen to strike when he was on his way to meet Harry. If so—

But he could not take the chance. He could not afford to assume anything. He should leave Copenhagen as soon as possible. But leave it to go where? And leave it how? The airport and the railway station could easily be watched. And his passport was still in his room at the Kong Knud. That too could be watched.

Yet flight was his only sane choice. Hammelgaard's body would be found by morning. If he had any identification on him, the police would soon trace his sister. And she would tell them about Harry. Harry could end up wanted for murder, with no alibi and a lot of suspicious behaviour to explain. That made one decision at least easier to take. He could not go to the police.

Who could he turn to, then? Without help, he was finished. He might as well turn himself in to the police and hope they believed him. At least he would be safe in their custody. But what about Hammelgaard's surviving friends in America? What about the message he had sworn to take to them?

Margrethe Hammelgaard. Of course. She was the answer. She might know how to contact Donna Trangam and the others. She might believe Harry where nobody else would. But how was he to find her? Her shop on Strøget was a conspicuous place to wait. It would not open for another seven hours or more. And there was no guarantee she would be there when it did. It was better by far to go to her home, wherever that might be.

Spotting a telephone kiosk ahead, he headed straight for it and rang directory enquiries. The person on the other end spoke English and did her best to help, but no M. Hammelgaard was listed. Maybe she lived out of town. Maybe the number was in her husband's name. If she had a husband. Harry did not know. But he knew she had a brother. He might have a diary or pocket-book on him, with his sister's address recorded in it.

And so, reluctantly and uncertainly, Harry began to retrace his steps towards Knippelsbro. He knew what he was doing made sense, but he also knew he was asking a lot of his threadbare nerves. Added to which, he was completely disorientated. The road he thought led to Knippelsbro in fact ended in an apartment complex at the edge of the harbour. As he reached the waterfront and looked to his left, he could see the bridge no more than a quarter of a mile away. But there were blue and red lights now as

114

well as white marking its span across the harbour. There was a ghostly wail of a siren in the air and a faint crackle of radio static. Uniformed figures were moving in headlamp beams at the Christianshavn end of the bridge. Torben Hammelgaard had been found. Along with whatever he was carrying.

TWENTY

The Pussy Cat night club in Helgolandsgade at half past four on Saturday morning was a smoky den filled with electronic music and stale lechery. On the small floodlit stage, three girls wearing nothing beyond tasselled G-strings and bored expressions were dutifully playing out some pseudo-lesbian routine. At the table next to Harry's, an over-tired businessman had fallen asleep in his chair, leaving his topless hostess to sip champagne in grateful silence. In private rooms around him, Harry supposed, the night was reaching a more energetic climax. But out here the only cause of wide-eyed wonderment was the bill he had just been handed. Should he telephone the Guinness Book of Records and ask if such a charge for four beers, two coffees and a box of matches warranted inclusion in the next edition? Or should he just pay up politely on the grounds that for a man in his position it was actually a bargain? Where else would have offered him refuge at such an hour with no questions asked? Where else in all of Copenhagen could he have taken shelter?

Ruefully, he stacked the requisite number of hundred kroner notes on the tray and signalled to the frilly-aproned waitress at the bar. She came across and took the money, smiling stiffly, then minced away with a desultory wiggle of her exposed bottom. There was nothing like fear, Harry reflected as he watched her go, to sap the sexual appetite. Somebody should have marketed it as a contraceptive long ago.

But even fear has its limits. And fatigue has a way of finding

116

them. Too weary to think, Harry rose and made for the door. The Kong Knud was just round the corner. It was too soon for the police to have tracked him there and so late that anybody else watching the place would surely have given up and gone home to bed. This, on a balance of doubtful probabilities, was the time for Harry to collect his belongings – especially his precious passport – and go. He still had no idea where he would or should be going, but in his present condition one step was all he could take at a time.

He mounted the basement steps, footsore from the circuitous route he had followed from Christianshavn in order to avoid using Knippelsbro. The street was still and cold and empty, a bass rumble floating up behind him from the Pussy Cat. He lit a Danish cigarette and started walking. Helgolandsgade led straight into Istedgade. In five minutes he would be at the Kong Knud. And in another five he could be away again.

He paused at the junction and peered along Istedgade towards the hotel. Everything looked all right. No figures moving. No bulky shapes in kerbside cars. No sinister profiles in shadowy doorways. He started along the street, moving at a steady pace, glancing across to the opposite pavement as he went. Then, as the familiar unlit frontage of the Kong Knud came into view, he took his pass-key from his pocket, threw away his cigarette and darted abruptly across to the door, only to spoil the effect by trying to jam the key in upside down. A moment later, he had the door open. A moment after that, it was closed behind him.

The foyer was in darkness, save for a feeble night-light behind the desk. Harry navigated by it to the key-board, took the key to his room and made for the stairs. They creaked to his tread, but no other sounds broke the reassuring silence.

His room was as he had left it, his few belongings scattered amidst the meagre furnishings. The bedspread was still pulled back from the pillows on the spare bed. And still they were undented.

It took him no more than a few minutes to pack. Then and only then did he feel capable of deciding what to do next. It was nearly five o'clock and something was bound to start moving on the rail network soon. Something that could take him out of Copenhagen – and Denmark – before the police traced him to the Kong Knud. Yes, that was it. He would go to the railway station and buy a ticket for the first train out. Patting his chest to confirm his passport was now safely stowed in his pocket, he picked up his holdall and left the room.

117

Down in the foyer, he deposited his keys where they could not be missed, spared a mournful thought for the unexpired portion of the week he had been obliged to pay for in advance, then slipped the latch on the street door and stepped out into what remained of the night.

He had covered about twenty uneventful yards and begun to contemplate lighting a cigarette when he heard the ticking of a cooling engine close by. Suddenly and silently, the rear door of a parked car swung open across the pavement directly in front of him, blocking his path. Before he could react, he sensed a presence at his shoulder and heard a voice whisper in his ear: 'What are you waiting for? Get into the car.'

TWENTY-ONE

The sight of a bearded man had never given Harry such pleasure, even in the days when he smoked Senior Service cigarettes. Olaf Jensen looked immensely and encouragingly tall in a long grey coat and hat, his ginger beard just about level with the top of Harry's head. 'Go on,' he hissed, glancing along the pavement. 'Move, will you?'

'Sorry. It's just . . . I wasn't . . .'

'We must go. Now!'

'Right. Sorry.' Harry scrambled into the car and made fleeting eye contact with the driver in the rear-view mirror. The look conveyed neither warmth nor menace, merely relief that he was finally aboard. Jensen slammed the door behind him and, a second later, climbed into the front passenger seat. He muttered some-thing to the driver in Danish and they started away. 'You are . . . er . . . Olaf Jensen, aren't you?' Harry asked nervously.

'No,' said Jensen glancing back at him. 'I'm Søren Kierkegaard. What's the matter with you? Torben told you the plan, didn't he?'

'Not . . . er . . . exactly.'

'He must have done. You came out at five, as agreed.'

'Yes, but . . .' They did not know. That was obvious. And it was equally obvious Harry would have to tell them. But would they believe him? Somebody had murdered Torben Hammelgaard. And there was a chance his friends might suspect that somebody was Harry. 'You ought to know I . . . er . . . went to the rendezvous as agreed, but . . . er . . .'

119

'But what?'

'I found Torben on the bridge. Knippelsbro. He was . . . dead.'

'*Hvad?*'

'Torben's dead. They've killed him.'

'How?' There was shock but no great surprise in Jensen's tone. Dismay – but not disbelief.

'I don't know. There didn't seem to be a mark on him. No signs of a struggle. Nothing.'

'That's not possible. Torben would not allow it to be easy.'

'I can only tell you what I saw.'

Jensen's chin fell onto his shoulder where he was resting it on the back of his seat. They were moving fast now, along empty residential streets, the lamplight strobing across Jensen's mournful face. Harry thought he could see a glistening of tears in the man's eyes.

'The police were there when I left. Do you think they'll be able to identify him? I mean, should you . . . or somebody . . . contact them?'

'*Måske, måske.* But we must be . . . very careful. You saw the police on the bridge?'

'Yes.'

'Did they see you?'

'No.'

'You're sure?'

'Nobody saw me.'

'Unless it was somebody *you* did not see.'

'Well, I—'

'Like Torben. He hid good. He ran fast. But they caught him and killed him. Without a struggle. Who are these people?'

'I'm not sure. Torben thought—'

'*Nej.*' Jensen made a sudden slashing gesture with his hand. 'His words were true. Knowledge kills. He told me to stay out. To help you, but to stay out. I will keep my promise. That is enough. The rest . . .' He shook his head. 'I don't want to know.'

'I need to contact some friends of his in America.'

'*Ja, ja. Amerika.*' Jensen sighed. 'You are a lucky man. Torben and I grew up together. Then we grew different. But a friend is a friend. You want to understand the universe, like Torben? *Beklager.* I can't help you. You want to leave the country with no fuss and a new identity? Different story. That's what I do. Arrange things. Normally for big money. This will be free. You are one rabbit among a lot of foxes. But I think we'll get you through.'

120

'How?'

'We are going to my house. A man is waiting for us there. He takes photographs. Sometimes he puts them on passports. So, you are about to change your name. Choose one you like. Then I give you breakfast – and put you on the road.'

'The road to where?'

'Sweden. First rule of travel. Never start in the direction you want to go.'

They reached Jensen's house about twenty minutes later. Harry had an impression of well-to-do suburban spaciousness in the setting, but it was still dark and not much traffic was moving. As to whether they were north, west or south of the centre, he had not the vaguest notion. They drove straight into a vast garage, parked between a Porsche and some sort of land cruiser and entered the house by a communicating door. Harry glimpsed a huge pine-panelled kitchen and a broad airy hallway, then he was ushered down into a strip-lit basement. There, a small bald moustachioed man with the clipped manner of a minor government official transcribed some details from his passport and made a careful note of his chosen *nom de voyage*: Norman John Page. He positioned Harry in front of a screen, took some photographs, then told him to wait upstairs.

The driver was drinking coffee and munching a croissant in some sort of ante-room to the kitchen. He nodded Harry through to where Jensen was standing by the kitchen window, one hand holding a telephone to his ear, the other cradling a coffee-cup. Harry studied his own reflection in the glass as Jensen's conversation wound up. Even by the standards of passport mug shots Norman Page's likeness was going to be a grim sight for immigration officers.

'Done?' said Jensen, putting down the telephone. 'Good. Want some breakfast?'

'What I'd really like is some information.'

'Ah. Yes, it is time, I suppose. OK.' He lit a cigarette, lit another for Harry, walked up and down a few times, scratched his beard, then said: 'We'll drive you to Helsingør. It's about thirty-five kilometres north of here. You can take the ferry from there across to Sweden.' He glanced at his watch. 'There's one just after eight. You take a train from the other side through to Stockholm. You get in about four. Plenty of time to catch the overnight ferry to Helsinki. It sails at six.'

121

'*Helsinki?*'

'The capital of Finland.'

'I know where it is, for God's sake. What I mean is—'

'Torben wanted you out of Copenhagen. On the move, he said. For a few days. Till his friends in America could make arrangements. So, that's what I do. Get you going. On a route nobody will guess. Now listen. The ferry gets to Helsinki at nine tomorrow morning. Go straight to the airport. There's a flight to New York at eleven twenty. Be on it. It's due into JFK at one thirty. When you get there, call this number.' Jensen handed him a box of matches on which a seven-figure number had been written in red biro. 'The person who answers will tell you what to do next.'

'What's this person's name?'

'I don't know. And you don't need to know. Just call when you get in. They'll be waiting by the phone.'

'Yes, but—'

'And this.' Jensen held out a bulging envelope for Harry to take. 'Twenty thousand kroner, mostly in hundred kroner notes. For your ferry, train and air tickets. Plus unscheduled expenses. But don't spend too much on beer and cigarettes. You can't use cheques or credit cards now. They can be traced too easily. Cash only.'

In other circumstances, Harry might have been amused by Jensen's overestimation of his credit-worthiness. The truth was that his foray into cashless economics had ended in the forced surrender of his flexible friend nearly three years before, poignantly quartered with Mrs Tandy's embroidery scissors. He was about to proffer his thanks for the money, incapable though he currently felt of calculating its sterling equivalent, when the man from the basement slipped into the room and attracted their attention with a clearance of the throat.

'Your passport, Mr Page.'

Harry took the flimsy burgundy-covered booklet and glanced at the photograph and personal details. His bleary-eyed *doppelgänger* stared unconsolingly back at him. 'Looks fine,' he said. 'Thanks.'

'You should sign it.'

'Oh, of course. I . . . er . . .'

'Pen?'

'Thanks.' He leant forward to rest the passport open on the worktop and signed his new name as fluently as he could.

'*Mange tak, Herre Boel,*' said Jensen, with a polite hint of dismissal. It was a hint Hr Boel promptly took.

122

'Look, about the money,' said Harry. 'I'm very grateful. Really. God knows how I'll pay it back, but—'

'I am giving it for Torben, not you. I do not want gratitude. It would be inconvenient for both of us if you tried to repay it. Our dealings end at Helsingør.'

'All right, but even so—'

'I telephoned a contact of mine in the police while you were downstairs. There will be no record of our conversation. He told me a body was found on Knippelsbro last night. It has been identified as Torben Hammelgaard, former associate professor of theoretical physics at the Niels Bohr Institute.'

'It didn't take them long, did it?'

'They knew the name before they picked him up. An anonymous telephone call. Did you make that call?'

'Of course not.'

'His killers, then. Making life difficult for us. You're lucky we got to you before the police. Are you always so lucky?'

'Not so you'd notice.'

'Why don't you ask me how Torben died?'

'Do the police know?'

'No. They will make an autopsy later today. But why haven't you asked me? It's the obvious question.'

Harry shrugged. 'Because I guessed the answer, I suppose. There have been other deaths. They looked like accidents or suicides or . . . anything but what they were. There's something behind this I don't understand. Torben thought he understood, but he was wrong. He was sure nobody could be following us, me or him. But somebody must have been.'

'Nobody was watching the hotel. We left clean. A second car followed us to make sure. There was nothing. *Ikke noget.* Take my guarantee.' Jensen smiled cautiously. 'This is my profession. To carry valuable cargoes. I know what I'm talking about.'

'Have you been sheltering Torben?'

'I fixed him a place to stay. So shelter, yes. But you mean protection. He never asked for that.' Jensen refilled his cup from a coffee-pot on the stove and poured Harry a cup as well, then topped both up with brandy. 'You think it would have been no good, don't you? You think they're too clever for us. Always a step in front.'

'They have been so far.'

'Nobody will guess Sweden. Nobody will follow you onto the ferry. I do my work well. Extra well for a friend.'

123

'I expect you're right,' said Harry doubtfully, swallowing some of the laced coffee. 'And I'm sorry about Torben, really I am.'

'*Ja, ja.*' Jensen pleaded for reticence with a faint motion of his hand. 'Finish your coffee. Then we go. While it's still night. Second rule of travel. Always leave in the dark. That way, nobody will even know you've gone.' He looked round at the blank black window. 'If you're lucky.'

'Right.' Harry gulped down some more coffee. The brandy was making him feel better already. 'Well, that should be no problem. You said I was a lucky man.'

'*Ja,*' said Jensen reflectively. 'But luck is like gasoline. When you run out, you're always a long way from a filling station.'

TWENTY-TWO

'They'll be waiting by the phone,' Jensen had said. If so, they had to be deaf to ignore its ringing for so long. Harry stood at one of a row of pay phones in the arrivals hall at JFK Airport, listening with ever mounting anxiety to the distant electronic bleat in his ear, trying desperately not to think what he would do if there never was an answer. He did not know who he was ringing. Strictly speaking, he did not know why he was ringing. Exhausted by a day and a half of trains, boats and planes, of changing time zones and money and just about everything except his clothes, unshaven, hung over and more thoroughly drained than a Hebridean roof in winter, he needed someone to pick up that phone, whoever they were, wherever it was.

He was late, of course. That might be the explanation. Half an hour stacked in the sky, waiting for a landing slot. Another half hour collecting his luggage, then emptying it for the satisfaction of a customs officer who clearly thought Norman Page had a smuggler's face. Plus a full forty minutes in the immigration queue clutching his coffee-stained visa waiver form. All in all, it had not been a New World arrival to eclipse Oscar Wilde's.

He had been worn down by something more insidious than mischievous circumstances, however. What had really stretched his nerves was an uncertainty he knew he would have to live with for a little longer yet. Were they on to him? Had they followed him in spite of all Jensen's precautions? Logic and observation said no. But something more primitive than either, something that

125

raised the hairs on the back of his neck whenever he surrendered to it, sang its own sinister song.

'Yuh?'

The voice interrupted his thoughts with such gruff abruptness that Harry was for a moment struck dumb, unable to recall how he had planned to introduce himself.

'Who the hell is that?'

'I . . . er . . . This is Harry Page. Christ, sorry, I mean Barnett.'

'You're sure now?'

'Yes. My name's Harry Barnett. It's just— It doesn't matter.'

'It might matter to me.'

'I think you've been expecting to hear from me.'

'Yuh. Most of the afternoon. Why wait till I'm in the john?'

'Sorry. Delayed.'

'Then I'd better not delay you any longer. Got a question first, though. Torben said you'd be able to answer it. You and nobody else. When you first met Torben, a few years back, who was with him?'

Harry sighed. 'David Venning. And a girl called Hanne.'

'On the button. Seems you're Barnett even if you're not sure yourself.'

'Yes, I am. And you are?'

'A cautious guy, Harry. Listen good. Where are you now?'

'The airport.'

'OK. We'll meet in one hour at the United Nations Building. You know it?'

'Not really. I—'

'You got an hour to find your way there. Four o'clock. Don't be late, 'cos I won't linger. Wait out front by the flags. You're from Denmark, right? So wait under the Danish flag. That way there can't be any mistake.'

'Hold on. I don't—' The burr of a disconnected line stopped Harry in mid-protest. He had never been to New York, let alone the UN Building, before. And he would not have been able to identify the Danish flag if it was wrapped round a Viking. But he supposed an hour was sufficient to cope with both disabilities. There might even be time—

He looked at the telephone clutched in his hand and wondered, as he often had since leaving Copenhagen, if he should try to call Iris. He would have liked to assure himself there had been no deterioration in David's condition. Maybe, just maybe, there had even been an improvement. Beyond that, he was aware that sooner

126

or later Iris would learn Hammelgaard was dead and assume Harry's attempt to contact him had failed. What she would make then of his failure to contact *her* he could not guess. As to the possibility that the Danish police might suspect him of Hammelgaard's murder and request Scotland Yard's help in tracking him down, his mind reeled helplessly before the welter of consequences. Should he alert Mrs Tandy as well as Iris?

No was of course the answer. 'Don't contact your friends or relatives,' Jensen had advised him. 'Don't give yourself away. Run silent; run safe.' Good advice, but hard to follow. Yet follow it he would. He dropped the telephone back into its cradle, grabbed his bag and headed off across the concourse, scanning the overhead displays as he went for directions to the taxi rank.

TWENTY-THREE

A cloudless sky was beginning to lose its colour and the still.air such warmth as it may have had as Harry trudged along the line of flags hanging listlessly at their poles outside the United Nations Headquarters. Up the steps on the esplanade, in front of the General Assembly Building, some tourists were posing in front of a sculpture of a gun with a knotted barrel while others gaped across the East River at a giant Pepsi-Cola sign on the opposite shore. But Harry had neither aesthetics nor commerce on his mind. The man on the gate had told him which end the alphabetical sequence of flags began at, but as to which was Denmark's, he was on his own.

Time was short, his taxi-driver having turned out to know New York's road system scarcely better than he knew the English language. They had jolted in from the airport along a succession of drab expressways before bridging the East River and becoming snarled in north-creeping traffic between towering skyscrapers and trash-strewn sidewalks. The stuff of Harry's New York imaginings, fed by fifty years of Hollywood indoctrination, had blended with the bustling blaring reality of Manhattan on a winter's afternoon: camera-slung tourists threading through the hotdog-vendors and the shoeshine boys, the lost souls and the lavish spirits, while steam rose like dragon's breath from the manhole covers and sunlight twinkled on the soaring cliffs of steel and glass.

At length, excessive length it seemed to Harry, they had reached their destination. Leaving Harry no spare moment in which to goggle at his surroundings. A clue was what he needed. And it duly arrived in the form of the Canadian maple leaf. That he certainly recognized. It should, he thought, be a simple matter to count down through the letter C to D, if he could only remember how many countries started with a C. Chile, of course. And China. Colombia, whence came Mrs Tandy's favourite coffee. Cuba, where Barry Chipchase had always claimed the world's finest cigars were rolled on the world's finest thighs. But hold on. Was Cuba actually a member of the UN? If not—

'That's the Ivory Coast.'

'What?' Harry whirled round from his skyward squint to find a large gum-chewing face glaring at him through the open passenger window of a rust-pocked old Cadillac.

'You Harry Barnett?'

'Yes.'

'Get in.' He pushed the door open and fell back into the driving seat, leaving Harry little option but to obey. 'Toss it in the back,' he said, nodding at Harry's holdall. Then he took off with such a tyre-squealing lurch that Harry nearly dislocated his shoulder while hoisting the bag over his seat. 'Woodrow Hackensack,' he announced, raising one ham-like palm from the steering-wheel in greeting. 'Sorry about the flag stunt. Bit of a specialty of mine. Denmark's red with a white cross. Ivory Coast couldn't be more different if it tried.'

'I must have gone straight past Denmark,' said Harry, craning over his shoulder for a glimpse of the flags only to find they were already out of sight.

'Nah. You were still in the Cs. Ivory Coast's Francophone. Goes officially by its French name. Côte d'Ivoire. Get it?'

'Ah, yes.' Hackensack was a paunchy shambles of a man, dressed in ill-assorted outsize sports clothes, rounded off with a baseball cap that even at maximum adjustment could do no more than perch on his crew-cut crown like a howdah on an elephant. His appearance somehow made his sarcasm harder to bear. 'Was that pantomime really necessary?' complained Harry.

'I've never done pantomime. All my work's been on the cabaret circuit.'

'Really? As a comedian, presumably.'

'No. Conjuring, illusionism, escapology. The whole bag. Plus feats of memory. Some involving instant identification of obscure national flags.' He grinned. 'I like to keep my hand in.'

'You're a magician?'

'Was. Been retired a few years now. Couldn't take the pace.' Though pace on the streets of New York seemed to be a different matter. They were dodging and weaving between lanes to an accompaniment of protesting horns. But if Hackensack heard them, he did not seem to care. 'Torben tells me you're David's old man.'

'Yes, I am.' Harry knew he ought to break the news of Hammelgaard's death straightaway, but Hackensack's white-knuckle driving style seemed one good reason to delay doing so. 'How did you and David come to be acquainted?'

'Pure chance. A lucky chance for me. David pulled me out of a hole I dug myself into, deep as they come, a couple of years back. He and Donna showed me some real kindness. That's why I'm trying to help them out best I can. And why you've got me as your chauffeur.'

'Where are you taking me?'

'Upstate.'

'Where upstate?'

'Albany. About a hundred and forty miles. I'm putting you on the train there tonight to Chicago. Donna's orders. You could have caught the train in New York, but we're going to take an after-dark cruise round the back roads to shake off anybody who *might* be following you.'

'Nobody's following me.'

Hackensack studied the rear-view mirror for a moment. 'I'd say you're right, but Donna doesn't take any chances.'

'She's in Chicago?'

'Will be tomorrow.'

'Is that where they're hiding?'

'Could be. I wouldn't know. I'm just a mailbox. I pass messages, same as you. And, incidentally, I don't want to know what your message is. Keep it to yourself. It must be important as hell to run these risks for, though.'

'What makes you think we're running any risks?'

'Torben sounded twitchy as a Broadway débutante on the phone, so risks I reckon there have to be.'

'There's something I have to explain,' said Harry as they plunged into the dark mouth of an underpass. Several long black seconds elapsed before he added: 'Torben's dead.' Silence followed again, broken at intervals by a double thwack of the tyres as they crossed the seams in the road surface. 'He was killed the night before last.'

130

'Jesus,' murmured Hackensack, raising one hand from the wheel to cross himself. 'I never thought they'd get him.'

'You knew him well?'

'No, but— How'd it happen?'

'I'm honestly not sure.'

'Like before, then.'

'How much do you know about this?'

'Hardly a thing. When I heard about David, I assumed it was just an accident. You must have too. You've got my sympathy, Harry, you really do. David's got a fine mind. How's his mother bearing up?'

Clearly Hackensack had no idea how ambiguous Harry's paternal status was. 'She's coping.'

'It can't be easy.'

'When did you learn it wasn't an accident?' They emerged from the tunnel and climbed back into the Manhattan twilight.

'When Donna came to me six weeks back and told me about Kersey and the Frenchman. She asked me to act as a line of communication between her and Torben. Between all of them and the outside world, come to that. Nobody at Globescope was aware she and David had made friends with me. That's why I was the ideal choice, I guess. I'm just an over-the-hill old magic-man nobody gives a damn about. Cover doesn't come any better than my kind of obscurity.'

'How did they meet you?'

'Long story, Harry. But since we've got a long drive ahead of us . . .' Hackensack gave the rear-view mirror a hard stare and nodded to himself in evident satisfaction. 'You may as well hear it. I'm surprised you haven't heard it from David. But maybe that just goes to show what you probably already know.'

'Which is?'

'That you've got a son to be proud of.'

TWENTY-FOUR

Woodrow Hackensack apparently considered an autobiographical preamble essential to his account. A couple of attempts to urge him on having failed, Harry resigned himself to learning more than he really wanted to about the former illusionist's childhood in a southern Vermont village where his parents ran the general store; his frustrated intellectual yearnings; his adolescent rebellions; his friendship with a cantankerous old vaudevillian who taught him some conjuring and card tricks; his short-lived career as an insurance clerk in Boston; his tentative forays into show business; his love affair with the daughter of a Polish acrobat; their marriage and peripatetic life together; his precarious prime as 'Mr Nemo, Man of Magic'; his wife's death in a trapeze accident; and his subsequent decline into drink-sodden drug-sapped unemployability.

They had been on the road more than an hour before Hackensack mentioned a name Harry recognized. By then they had left New York far behind, the sun had set and their promised back-road tour had begun: a serpentine cruise along pot-holed routes between nowhere much and nowhere else. Hackensack's story had rambled with it into the limbo of his recent past: a roach-ridden apartment on New York's Lower East Side; subway rides to Coney Island with his wife's ghost; drugged days and drunken nights lived on the crumbling brink of vagrancy; a twilit spiral of self-pity and self-destruction. And then, one evening, in a Bowery bar, he picked up a discarded newspaper and read about the latest Off-Broadway sensation: English magician Adam Slade.

'I can't recall whether it was his grinning photograph or his horseshit claims about higher dimensions that made me angry. Maybe it was both. Or maybe it was his lack of respect for fellow professionals. Magicians deal in tricks and illusions. They should admit that. They should claim credit for it. But Slade wants the dime *and* the doughnut. He wants people to admire his talents *and* believe he's got inherited powers. That's probably what got my goat. So, I tidied myself up and went along to one of his Friday night shows, at a theatre in Greenwich Village, just to see for myself. And d'you know what I saw? A lot of gullible people. And a few clever tricks.'

'I saw Slade in London recently,' put in Harry. 'He *was* impressive.'

'So was I in my day. Without resorting to hyper-dimensional hogswill. We're magicians, not messiahs. We're entitled to applause, not worship. We don't need it. We're too good to need it. Or we should be.'

'You don't think Slade is?'

'Matter of fact, I do. The guy's a natural. Slick and dexterous. But that only makes it worse. He adds these higher powers onto his act as a come-on, as a way of saying he's better than the rest of us without having to prove it.'

'Doesn't the act prove it?'

Hackensack grunted dismissively. 'The act proves nothing. Hoops round table legs and those other stunts? Jesus, I could do them in my sleep.' He paused. 'Well, maybe not. But I *could* do them, with enough practice. I don't exactly know how he does them. But there'll be a way. There always is. With time and patience, I could work it out.'

'That's easy to say.'

'Don't believe me, Harry? Healthily sceptical, are you? Good. Tell me this, then. When you saw Slade in London, did he do any mind-reading?'

'Not as such.'

'When I saw him, he did. Another demonstration of higher dimensions, y'see. The way he explained it, one of these dimensions accessed the thoughts and memories of people around him. So he fretted a bit and furrowed his brow and announced stray recollections he'd picked up from the audience to see if any fitted. Which, naturally, they did. If there was no response, he put it down to shyness on the part of the person concerned. Most everybody there seemed to swallow the thing. He summoned up a memory of small-town Nebraska for some girl who'd grown up there. Even had the first name of the best friend she'd gone to school with. Persuasive stuff. She nearly passed out.'

'But you weren't persuaded?'

'I know the tricks of the trade. And I could see Slade was getting over-confident. Maybe believing his own publicity. So, when nobody claimed some half-assed memory of a favourite uncle making model aeroplanes, I put up my hand and said, "Jeez, that must be Uncle Ira." Slade went for it in a big way. Had me nodding like a donkey to some crap about Uncle Ira standing in for my dead pa. He'd been killed in Korea, seemingly. I still kept his medals in a tobacco tin. Polished them every Veterans' Day. It was something, believe me. Till I up and said, "See here, Mr Slade, I may as well own up. That was all a crock of lies. I've never had an Uncle Ira. Or a war hero for a father. What made you think I had? I mean, why didn't your hyper-dimensional insight tell you I was lying?" '

'What did he say?'

'Oh, the obvious. That I'd claimed somebody else's memory simply to make mischief. That I could lie, but his instincts couldn't. He was shaken, but he hid it well. Most of the audience probably believed him. They *wanted* to believe him, y'see. They certainly didn't rush to my support when the security goons threw me out. I was shouting back over my shoulder at Slade all the way. About how I was a real magician who didn't try to deceive his customers. About how I'd forgotten more tricks than he'd ever learn. Pretty unoriginal. But I was mad at him by then. For being so brazen as well as so successful. And for not recognizing me. I guess that hurt more than his lack of ethics. Still, it taught him a lesson. Mind-reading's been sidelined from his public performances since then. He only does it with carefully vetted audiences. And they don't include the likes of me.'

'Did the press make anything of your set-to with him?'

'Nah. He wasn't quite famous enough then. But it didn't go completely unnoticed. Some guy followed me out onto the street and asked if he could buy me a drink in exchange for my considered opinion of Slade's hyper-dimensional powers. Nice feller. Young, good-looking, friendly. Had his girlfriend along with him.'

'David and Donna?'

'You got it. We went to a bar and he pumped me for details of

134

how Slade could do those things *without* special powers. Since he kept the drinks coming, I didn't mind obliging with the answers. Well, the hunches, anyway. My guesses about how he did it. David wasn't convinced. I could tell that. Even then, I could tell he wanted it to be true. Donna saw it differently. She was real eager for me to discredit Slade. I think David's belief in him worried her. That's how I read it later, anyway. At the time, I was just happy to sound off. Turned out Donna had seen my act once, in Seattle, where she grew up. But she hadn't recognized me as Mr Nemo. I'd changed too much. That really broke me up. That or the drink. In the end, they had to take me home in a cab. By then, I was babbling about Anna and the day she fell from the high trapeze. Next morning, I couldn't remember much about it. I reckoned one thing was certain, though. I wouldn't see either of them again. And there I was dead wrong. They came to see me that afternoon. They were up from Washington for the weekend and didn't want to go back without checking how I was. Seems my theories about Slade's act had got to David. And those old Mr Nemo posters peeling off the walls of my mildewed apartment had got to Donna. They wanted to help. Get me off the juice and put me back on the rails. They wanted to rescue me. Can you believe it? It was like the Salvation Army without the tambourines.'

'But it worked?'

'Yeh, it worked. You see beside you a sane overweight stimulant-free man. David and Donna pulled some strings with a doctor they knew at a clinic out on Long Island. Got me admitted free of charge and pretty much put back together. Then they helped find me a part-time job. Caretaker at the Vanderbilt Law School. It's not exactly Wall Street wages, but I've stuck it. Hell, with what I've saved on booze and dope alone, I've been able to move to a better apartment. Well, a *habitable* apartment, leastways. Plus this stylish vehicle you're currently resting your butt in. Anna would be proud of me. And it's all down to two people who don't owe me a damn thing. One of them your son. Who's evidently been too modest to tell you about it.'

'We've rather lost touch recently.'

'That a fact? Some kinda disagreement, was there?'

'More a lack of understanding.'

'It happens. I hope you get the chance to put it right, Harry, I surely do. Y'see, all this academic ambition, this career building, isn't the whole man, is it? At bottom, David's one of the good guys.'

135

'Trustworthy? Loyal? Reliable?'

'Sure is. That's why I'm doing this. Why the hell else would I?'

'No reason.'

Hackensack slowed gently to a stop at the side of the road, turned off the lights and looked back over his shoulder. Then he lowered the window and listened for a moment. 'Nothing,' he finally pronounced. 'Not a dog's barked since we left the Taconic State Parkway. This is a clear run, Harry. You don't have a thing to worry about.'

Hackensack's confidence was such that he reckoned they could safely lay up at an inn he knew for a couple of hours before heading on to Albany. It was a quiet well-kept place near the centre of a scattered settlement of trimmed farmyards and prosperous residences. Harry was by now as clueless as to their whereabouts as he was uncaring. The inn supplied food, drink and warmth in an atmosphere of old-fashioned hospitality, all of which he badly needed. His other requirements were at the mercy of plans hatched for him by strangers. And for the moment he was content to leave them that way. His curiosity on another subject was very much alive, however.

'Tell me more about David, Woodrow.'

'He's your son, Harry. Hell, you talk as if you've never met him.'

'Pretend I haven't. Describe him as you would to somebody who never had.'

'OK. If you want me to. He seems lightweight at first acquaintance. Genial and accommodating. Then you realize there's a remoteness behind the smile. You could take it for aloofness, even arrogance. But that's not it. It's just half his mind is always somewhere else. Floating round those damned equations. He'd be attractive to women, I guess. But they'd have to be on his scientific wavelength. Like Donna, y'know? She told me he'd been married to some Hollywood social climber and it's no surprise that was a disaster. Mathematics is more than his profession. It's an obsession. He believed in Slade's hyper-dimensional powers because he was mathematically satisfied that higher dimensions exist and therefore, theoretically, should be accessible to us. Well, you'd have to call that single-minded, wouldn't you? Whatever he was doing for Globescope, I can assure you it didn't command much of his attention. Last time I met him, he was still on that hyper-dimensional duck-hunt.'

136

'When was that?'

'Oh, a couple of months back. Just before he flew to England. Start of the Labor Day weekend. Early September.'

'In New York?'

'Yeh. He turned up at my apartment just as I was leaving for work Friday evening. He looked fine, but he sounded kinda odd, kinda . . . spaced out. Asked if he could stay over. Well, that was no problem. Least I could do. Then, Saturday morning, he asked if I'd do him a favour and go upstate with him to see somebody. Well, that was no problem either. I was happy to go along for the ride. We headed for Poughkeepsie, just west of here, down on the Hudson.'

'Who did you see?'

'An inmate of the Hudson Valley Psychiatric Center. Guy name of Dobermann. Y'know? Like the dog. Carl Dobermann.'

'Who's he?'

'Well, no dog-breeder, that's for sure and certain. A head case. Chronically wacko. Been in that hospital more than thirty years. On the way up to Poughkeepsie, David told me a bit about him. A bit about why he wanted to see him. Not all, though. He was holding something back. I could tell by his manner. Shifty. Nervy. A mite ashamed of himself. Anyway, it seems Dobermann's been locked up at Hudson Valley since he was a student at Columbia back in the fifties. So long nobody's sure why he was locked up there in the first place. Lately he's been allowed to mix with other inmates more. To walk around the grounds. Even leave them under escort. I guess that's why the rumours started. Visitors began saying they'd seen him do the weirdest things. Move objects without touching them. Appear as if out of thin air, then disappear the same way. Predict the arrival in the car park of a certain make and colour of automobile before anyone else could see it. I mean, bizarre stuff. Seriously screwball.'

'What was David's interest in him?'

'Can't you guess? He thought it was possible Dobermann had hyper-dimensional powers. Might have gone crazy because of them. But might still possess them. That was the point. He wanted to check him out. And he wanted me – as a confirmed sceptic – to be there when he did it. To authenticate whatever happened.'

'What did happen?'

'Not a thing. Oh, we met Mr Dobermann. He seemed real pleased to see us. He's about sixty. Looks it, leastways. Lean as a hoe, with a hospital tunic several sizes too big hanging off him like a sail from a mast on a windless day. Grins a lot. Twitches a hell of a lot more. But says near to nothing. I mean, out of touch isn't in it. He still thinks Eisenhower's in the White House. This is not a together guy. As for walking through walls, forget it. The special effects were off-line.'

'A wasted visit, then?'

'Not exactly. After a while David took him for a walk round the grounds. Told me he thought I might be making Dobermann nervous. So I waited in the car park. When David came back, he seemed, well, satisfied about something. He didn't say much, other than Dobermann hadn't gone up in a puff of blue smoke. They'd talked about Columbia mostly, he said. About Dobermann's studies there.'

'Was Dobermann a . . . mathematician?'

'Hole in one. Carl Dobermann was studying for a doctorate in mathematics when he had his breakdown. He was writing a thesis on higher dimensions and David had got hold of an early draft of his work. That was as much as he told me on the way back to New York. But I reckon there was a hell of a lot more he wasn't telling. I didn't get the chance to find out, though. He flew to England that very night.'

'Never to return,' murmured Harry, half to himself.

'I don't know about *never*. While there's—'

'How far is the hospital from here?'

'Oh, about fifteen miles.'

'Take me there, Woodrow. Please.'

Hackensack grimaced. 'No can do. I've got to put you on a train at Albany.'

'When does it leave?'

'Twenty after ten.'

'And how long will it take us to get to Albany?'

'Hour, maybe. Hour and a half.'

Harry glanced at his watch. 'There's time, then.'

'Not enough. Besides, it's too risky.'

'You said yourself there was nothing to worry about.'

'There isn't. So long as we don't take any senseless detours.'

'This isn't senseless. I just want to talk to Dobermann. To ask him what he told David.'

'He'll clam up. You may as well talk to the wall.'

'I just want to try.'

'Sorry, Harry, but I can't do it. Donna told me to be careful. I aim to oblige her.'

138

'Fine. I understand.' Harry grinned. 'I'd better call a cab, hadn't I?' Hackensack flung up his hands in a gesture of pleading. 'Unless you think that's even riskier.'

'I guess I do.' Hackensack pulled a grubby white handkerchief from his pocket and flapped it in front of him. 'You win, Harry. We'll go pay Mr Dobermann a visit.'

TWENTY-FIVE

Did the Hudson Valley Psychiatric Center admit visitors after seven o'clock on a Sunday evening? This was the kind of practical question Harry did not pause to consider until he and Hackensack were standing in the lofty foyer of the establishment, waiting for the man behind the counter to drag his attention away from a televised football game. But the glossy brochures on display and the coming and going of people who certainly looked as if they had a stake in the outside world encouraged him to be optimistic, as did Hackensack's confidence that he could talk their way past any number of bureaucratic obstacles.

'You want to see *who*?'

'Carl Dobermann. We're friends of his.'

'That so?'

'Yuh. But we're not often in the neighbourhood, so we'd sure appreciate it if . . .'

'Wait over there. I'll see what I can do.'

They sat down on a couch, where Hackensack muttered contemptuously at the assorted ineptitudes of the televised footballers while Harry studied an artist's impression of the hospital's picturesque setting on the banks of the Hudson, something he would have to take on trust, having seen nothing beyond the floodlit car park. Then the man returned and announced somebody would be out to have a word with them shortly. A few minutes later, somebody arrived. A small spring-heeled slick-haired fellow in a far smarter suit than Harry would have supposed the night-shift at Hudson Valley really warranted. He did not actually have *Public Relations Officer* stamped on his forehead, but his sparkling smile signalled a certain expertise in that direction.

'Would you two gentlemen care to step along to my office?'

'No problem,' said Hackensack. 'But we only called by to see a friend. Don't want to cause any trouble.'

'It's just there are one or two points about after-hours visiting I need to clear.'

Hackensack glanced round at Harry, giving him the chance to pull out there and then. But Harry was not about to give up so easily. 'I'm sure it won't take long. Let's go.'

It was a short walk along blank peach-walled corridors to their smiling host's office. He introduced himself en route as Glendon Poucher, a member of the hospital's administrative staff. His manner was brisk but accommodating. There seemed no reason to think trouble was his middle name. Or to suppose that closing his door behind them signified anything beyond habitual politeness.

'Gather you want to see Carl Dobermann.'

'Yuh,' said Hackensack. 'But, look, it's no big deal. Just a . . .'

'A whim,' said Harry.

Poucher frowned. 'You're friends of his?'

'That's right,' said Hackensack. 'From way back.'

'How far back?'

'Pardon me?'

'I ask because Carl was admitted to this hospital thirty-six years ago. Since his parents died, he's received very few visits and the only friends he's made have been among his fellow residents. You're not former patients, are you?'

'No, sir, we're not.'

'But you *are* friends of his?'

'In a manner of speaking.'

'Would you mind telling me when you last visited him?'

'Well, I don't rightly . . . I'm not exactly . . .'

'September third, perhaps?'

'Oh no. Not as recent as that.'

'Definitely not,' put in Harry.

'Two gentlemen came to see Carl that day,' Poucher continued. 'We don't know their names and we wouldn't ordinarily be interested. It wouldn't be significant. Except for the fact that, two days later, Carl Dobermann absconded from this hospital.'

'He did what?'

'He ran away. Something he hadn't tried to do in all those thirty-six years. He went over the wall. And he hasn't come back.'

TWENTY-SIX

Harry's expectations of America, he was coming to realize, were largely shaped by film and television. He had unconsciously assumed the train he was to join at Albany would resemble the one Cary Grant had seduced Eve Marie Saint on in *North by Northwest*. But just as Harry was no longer the Brylcreemed buck who had taken Doris Crowdy to the cinema one Saturday night long ago to see the latest Hitchcock, so the Twentieth Century Limited was no longer a stylish conveyance laden with romantic possibilities. If anything, it had aged less gracefully than Harry: a fact which gave him no comfort whatever.

Nor, come to that, did the diabolically sprung seat he was currently slumped in. Sleep would have been a risky enterprise for those with stronger backs than his. Fortunately, sleep was not on his agenda. There were too many mysteries piling up in his path for rest to be a serious option. And one of them was why he had allowed himself to become involved in all the other mysteries in the first place.

He knew the reason well enough, though. On the other side of the aisle, a boy of eight or so had fallen asleep on the elbow of his father, who glanced down fondly at him from time to time through heavy lids, but refrained from moving for fear of waking the boy. This unremarkable piece of paternal generosity symbolized for Harry all the things he could and would and should have done for the son he had never known he had. Fatherhood as an idea had never interested him. His estate was not the kind that required a will, let alone an heir. As for parental bonding and other such notions trumpeted on the covers of glossy magazines he had often glimpsed arrayed by the supermarket check-out while doing service as Mrs Tandy's bag-carrier, he was frankly contemptuous. Or had been. Till the physical and factual reality of his son's existence burst into his life. It could not be ignored. It could not be shrugged off or disowned. It was a piece of truth he would carry with him to the end of his days.

But what was the truth about David John Venning? He had alienated his wife and probably his lover too. He had betrayed his friends and their principles. He had set a murderous conspiracy in motion. And all to serve his obsession with a scientific puzzle he could never hope to solve. So much was undeniable. But he had been Woodrow Hackensack's saviour. And maybe in a sense he was Harry's too. Only somebody as helpless as David now was could accept whatever was done for him so unconditionally. He could not walk away from Harry, as he had done once before. And Harry was not about to walk away from him.

Precisely what he was going to do instead remained unclear. His visit to the Hudson Valley Psychiatric Center had only served to complicate an already confusing situation. Carl Dobermann's unknown whereabouts and unguessable motives had been added to an insoluble equation. Why did David go to see him? What did they talk about? And where, two days later, after thirty-six years of placid immobility, did Dobermann go?

His flight had clearly surprised the hospital authorities, as Glendon Poucher had freely admitted. 'It's unusual, if not unprecedented, for a long-stay patient like Mr Dobermann to decamp. His was a carefully planned covert departure, taking advantage of reduced staffing levels and high visitor density during the Labor Day holiday. There's been no trace of him since. I should add that he was not a voluntary patient, so any light you gentlemen can shed on his probable movements would be greatly valued.' But light they could not have shed even had they wanted to. Their hastily assembled story might only have helped cover Dobermann's tracks. No, they definitely were not the pair who had visited him on 3 September. Their connection with him dated from using the same Upper West Side bar back in the fifties. Poucher was welcome to their names and telephone numbers – at any rate the false ones they supplied. They would certainly be in touch if anything else occurred to them.

'Do you think he believed us?' Harry had asked once they

were safely back in the car, driving towards the main gate.

'Maybe. He's not exactly likely to guess the truth, is he? Just as well we both look as if we could have been propping up bars since . . . when the hell was it?'

'Some time in 1958. Dobermann was here right through the sixties, the seventies and the eighties. He never showed any signs of even *wanting* to leave.'

'Until two days after David hauled me up here. Jeez, I thought at any moment some orderly was gonna come in and say, "Yup, this is one of the guys who came to see Mad Dog Carl all right."'

But was Dobermann mad? And, if so, what form did his madness take? Poucher had been cagey on the point when Harry mentioned the strange rumours surrounding his fugitive patient. 'I've heard no rumours. As far as I'm aware, Mr Dobermann's dementia has remained intractable since his admission. His condition certainly hasn't altered of late. As to why he was admitted in the first place, that is naturally confidential. We are presently concerned with locating him, not re-examining his diagnosis. Insanity frightens many people, gentlemen. You would be surprised what outlandish explanations they devise for its symptoms.'

From the computerized security of Poucher's office, that no doubt seemed as sensible a view as it was convenient. But to Harry, turning occasionally to stare at himself in the night-blanked window of the train, Dobermann was more than an errant madman. He was one with the blurred presence Harry had glimpsed at his shoulder in Copenhagen, the figure on the bridge, the shape beneath the sheets, the fading pitter-patter of following footsteps. He was the shadow of whatever had reached out from the darkness to overwhelm Hammelgaard – and might reach out again.

'Would you do me a favour when you get back to New York, Woodrow?' Harry had asked when they were about halfway between Poughkeepsie and Albany.

'Depends.'

'Try and find out what happened to Dobermann in 1958. Why he was locked up in that hospital.'

'How the hell am I supposed to do that?'

'I don't know. Sweet talk your opposite number at Columbia. Caretakers go back longer than professors. Check the local papers for that year. See if something . . . unusual . . . occurred at the university.'

145

'Students going cuckoo ain't exactly unusual.'

'This must have been different. It has to be what led David to him.'

'Nah. I told you. That was the scraps of Dobermann's thesis. Plus the rumours, o'course.'

'Ah yes, the rumours. You've heard them yourself, have you?'

'No. But—'

'Nor had Poucher. So he claimed, anyway. Maybe David invented them for your benefit.'

'What are you getting at?'

An alternative explanation for the crop of deaths among former Globescope staff. That was where Harry's fears were beginning to drag his thoughts. Did it start in Lazenby's office on 29 August? Or at the Hudson Valley Psychiatric Center on 3 September? If the latter, then hunting down incriminating tape recordings was a pointless diversion. But no. That made no sense. The future would not matter to a man who did not even have a past. And yet . . . He looked round at the empty seat beside him and shivered. *'He was close,'* Hammelgaard had said. *'He was nearly there. He was on the brink of history.'* Where was Dobermann? Far away? Or close by, all too close, all the time?

'I'll see what I can dig up about the guy,' Hackensack had reluctantly agreed. 'I'll ask a few discreet questions.'

'Thanks.'

'But don't complain if I come up with damn all. We're talking about the fifties. To most people today, that's as remote as the Ice Age.'

'It seems clear enough in my mind.'

'That's because you're not most people.'

'What do I do when I get to Chicago?'

'I'll tell you at Albany.'

'Tell me now.'

'Donna said—'

'Just tell me, Woodrow. It's my neck, remember.'

But was it? Gazing from the train as it drew slowly out of Albany–Rensselaer Station to see Hackensack standing by his Cadillac in the car park, Harry had wondered if carrying a message to Donna Trangam was actually any riskier than asking questions about Carl Dobermann. He had wished for a moment that Hackensack had refused to do him such a favour, a wish not far short of a premonition. Well, perhaps he would phone him from Chicago and tell him not to bother. There would be time enough for that once his appointment with Donna had been kept.

'OK, Harry. Have it your way. The train gets into Chicago at one o'clock tomorrow afternoon. Take a cab to the John Hancock Center. Ride the elevator to the top floor. There's a restaurant up there, and a bar. Should be pretty busy around lunchtime. Buy yourself a drink, take a seat and admire the view of Lake Michigan. Donna will contact you there.'

'How will she identify me?'

'She's gonna call me in the morning. I'll describe you to her. But I doubt I'll need to.'

'Why not?'

' 'Cos, like I told you, you're not most people.'

He was not most people. How Harry wished he could be at this low midnight ebb of his confidence. He struggled out of his seat and made his way to the vestibule, where he broached his last pack of *Karelia Sertika* and smoked one slowly through with the window pulled open to admit a freezing gale of air. He took David's snapshot from his wallet and stared at his son's smiling face in the sickly yellow lamplight. All he had learnt about this distant stranger-child was contained in the knowing warmth of his photographed gaze. An untold joke; an unshared secret; an unsolved mystery. They were waiting for Harry, somewhere out there. They were beckoning him on. They had neither time nor place in any printed schedule. But already they were fixed points in his future.

TWENTY-SEVEN

Harry did fall asleep in the end, just as day was breaking. Breakfast, along with substantial tracts of Ohio and Indiana, passed by in a drowsy haze and alertness only returned when the conductor announced they would shortly be arriving in Chicago. Stumbling out into the echoing maze of Union Station with a parrot-cage mouth, a fuzzy head and a sandpaper chin, he somehow managed to locate the taxi rank and mumble his destination before sitting back to blink at the glaring blue sky, the mufflered pedestrians, the ice-limned stormdrains and the sunlight flashing off the towerblock walls.

The John Hancock Center was a black-steel giant at whose fat-girdered feet Harry was in due course delivered. The lift rushed him to the top, which was as busy and panoramic as Hackensack had promised. Retreating into the bar as far from the dazzling view as possible, Harry ordered a beer and commenced sizing up the solitary females as surreptitiously as he could for one that might be Donna Trangam. There were not many candidates, but one blond-haired woman in a grey suit and pink blouse looked across at him with what seemed like significant deliberation before putting a cigarette to her mouth and flicking at a lighter with ostentatious lack of success.

'Can I help?' asked Harry, strolling across to her table, glass in hand, at what he judged to be a casual pace. 'Matches never let you down.' He took the box with Hackensack's number written on it from his pocket and rattled the contents.

'Thanks,' she said, accepting the light. She was older than Harry would have expected, quite a bit older than David, with a hardness to her features that fear might have solidified. Her high-fashion suit and chunky jewellery were far from the blue stocking stereotype. Perhaps, he supposed, that was the point of them. 'It's good to know there's one man left in Chicago who hasn't kicked the habit.'

'Actually, I've only just arrived.'

'That sure isn't a Midwest accent.'

'Mind if I join you?'

'Not at all. I'm feeling kinda lonely.'

As Harry sat down, she turned slightly in her seat to face him, crossed her legs and smiled coolly. 'Where you from?'

'England. I'm Harry, Donna.'

'Pleased to meet you, Harry.'

'You've spoken to Woodrow today?'

'Pardon me?'

'Woodrow.'

'The only other man I've spoken to today is my shmuck of a husband. Soon to be ex-husband. That's if you count him as a man. Which I'm not sure I do.'

In the same instant that Harry realized he had made a ghastly mistake, a movement caught his eye on the far side of the room, by the windows looking west across the city. A slim dark-haired woman, dressed anonymously in jeans, trainers and a multi-coloured brushed-wool sweater, raised one hand in cautious recognition. She did not smile. Indeed, there was a purse-lipped look of puzzlement on her face that assumed a tinge of irritation as he met her gaze.

'Glad to hear you're not a Chicagoan, Harry. I've had it with the men of this city. Too damn smooth for my liking. There comes a time when a girl needs something rough to scratch her back on. Wouldn't you say?'

Harry's mouth sagged open as the ironies of the situation reverberated inside his head. She was a good-looking woman, smartly turned out and eager for company. His company, amazingly enough. And rather more than company, if he read the signs correctly. As the studiously sensuous manner in which she drew on her cigarette convinced him he did. It was the fulfilment of a lifelong fantasy. Or it promised to be. Unfortunately, he had waited forty years to be picked up by a glamorous middle-aged nymphomaniac only for opportunity to knock just when he could least afford to seize it.

149

'My name's Carmen, by the way. Like the opera. It was my mother's favourite. It appealed to her passionate nature.'

'Which you inherited?'

'Matter of fact, I did.' As she spoke, she applied a carmine-nailed forefinger to a minor itch somewhere high on her thigh, flicking up the hem of her skirt in the process. 'What line of business are you in, Harry?'

'No kind.' He took a deep regretful breath. 'I've just been released from a lunatic asylum.'

She smiled nervously. 'You're joking.'

'If only I were.'

'That's, er, kinda surprising.' She eased back in her chair and tugged the hem of her skirt down towards her knee. 'How long . . . were you in there?'

'Thirty-six years.' He saw her jaw drop. 'Oh, there's my daughter. She's waiting to take me home. You'll have to excuse me.'

'Sure,' said Carmen, nodding numbly.

Harry picked up his beer and walked slowly across to the window, letting a shudder of deprivation come and go. As he reached Donna Trangam's table, she rose to meet him. A slightly built woman of thirty or so, with bobbed brown-black hair and a pale peaceful face in which eyes as dark and rich as teak glistened behind small gold-framed glasses, she frowned reproachfully and murmured: 'What the hell were you playing at?'

'Telling a goose I didn't like golden eggs. Not much of a game, I can assure you.'

'You were supposed to be careful.'

'I had to settle for being good instead. My mother would have approved.'

'Let's get out of here.'

'Suits me.'

'I'll meet you by the elevator.'

Harry returned to his original table by a semi-circular route that avoided any possibility of eye contact with Carmen. There he plonked down some money for his beer, grabbed his coat and bag and headed for the lift. Donna was waiting by the doors in a short red coat and black beret. The simultaneous departure of a lunch party meant she and Harry could say nothing to each other then or during the descent, even though they were jammed together in a corner of the car. In the circumstances, Harry thought it best to stare fixedly at the floor indicator.

Eventually, they reached the ground, where Donna led Harry out by a side-exit into the teeth of a cold blast of Lake Michigan air. 'We don't have long,' she said. 'Certainly not long enough for stunts like that.'

'It wasn't a stunt.'

'I spoke to Woodrow this morning. He told me about Torben. He also told me about your trip to Poughkeepsie. That was a stupid thing to do.'

'You reckon so?'

'What I *reckon* is that I should never have responded to Torben's message if your behaviour so far's any guide. He was probably killed because of you.'

'I don't think so.'

'But do you think at all? That's the question.'

'Listen to me!' Harry snapped, grabbing her by the shoulder as anger flared up at the memory of all he had so far endured on account of this woman and her friends. 'I didn't ask to be your bloody carrier-pigeon. I didn't ask to become involved in any of this. Since I am, and since whoever's fault it is it damn well isn't mine, I'd be grateful if you didn't treat me like a student who's handed in a shoddy essay. I'm sorry about the woman in the bar. It was a mistake. I make them from time to time. I imagine you do too. Otherwise you wouldn't be in such a mess. *Would you?*'

'No.' The cool logician and the frightened loner met in her sudden wincing admission of weakness. 'You're right, of course. I'm sorry. It was—' She broke off and turned abruptly away. For a moment, Harry thought she might burst into tears.

'I'm sorry too,' he mumbled. 'I didn't mean to upset you.'

'The news about Torben was a terrible shock. I don't think I've quite taken it in yet. We thought we'd outwitted them. We thought we were safe for as long as we needed to be. Then this. And then something else.'

'What else?'

'Your smile when you went over to that woman's table. I can't tell you. It was so . . . so . . . very like . . .'

'David's?'

'Yes.'

'I *am* his father.'

'That's another thing I'm having trouble taking in.'

'Me too.'

She looked back at him and shaped a hesitant smile of her own. 'You have something to tell me, Harry. Why not get on with it?'

151

'It's a little . . . complicated.'

'I'm a scientist. I'm used to complexity.'

'All right. But can't we go somewhere warmer?'

'Somewhere even colder would be safer. There's a beach two blocks north of here. In this weather, we'll have it to ourselves. No chance of being overheard.'

'No chance of being heard at all if I'm too cold to speak.'

'Then walk as fast as you talk. You look as if you could use some exercise.'

TWENTY-EIGHT

It had taken an hour and several aimless miles of lakeshore walking for Harry to relate the events and discoveries that had led him to Chicago. Sustained by chain-smoked cigarettes and Donna's remorseless questioning, he had doled out every fact and supposition he held in his mind. Now, cold, hungry and drained of secrets, he sat beside her on a low wall enclosing a harbourside esplanade, staring out vacantly into the clear blue distance while traffic roared by on the expressway behind them and the skyscrapers to north and south kept up a looming vigil like some gathering of respectful giants.

'So David and Torben betrayed us,' said Donna, as neutrally as if confronting a scientific proof.

'It seems so.'

'For that foolish dream of theirs.' She shook her head and briefly closed her eyes. 'How sad. Yet how predictable. I should have guessed.'

'Why?'

'Because of the part it played in David and me breaking up. He wanted so badly to prove he was right and I was wrong. I suppose this must have seemed an opportunity too good to miss.'

'You broke up over a scientific argument?'

'Partly. A fundamental difference of professional opinion doesn't do much for a relationship. He wouldn't back down, wouldn't admit his theories could be flawed in any way.

153

He wouldn't compromise at any price.' Her chin drooped. 'That used to make me mad as hell.'

'I don't think he or Torben saw it as a betrayal.'

'No. But we can all devise a justification for our actions if we try hard enough, can't we? They thought they knew better than the rest of us. Well, where judging Byron Lazenby's character is concerned they were wrong. Push him and he pushes back. Play dirty and he gets his retaliation in first. That's the kind of man he is.' She paused. 'The murderous kind.'

'What will you do now?'

'Go back to Makepeace and Rawnsley and discuss what they think we should do. It'll be a joint decision.'

'Where are they?'

'A long way from here. A long safe way.'

'But what do *you* think? About the tape.'

'I think we'd have to be pretty desperate to pin our hopes on half a chance of recovering it and less than that of finding enough on it to make a case against Lazenby.' A moment passed before she added: 'And I think we *are* pretty desperate.'

'You're sure Lazenby's behind this?'

'I'm sure. Forget Carl Dobermann. He's just some poor mad guy on the run. I expect David's questions stirred up a lot of memories he'd have been better off forgetting. David never has let anyone else's needs stand in the way of his crusader quest. Believe me. I'm an expert on that side of his character.'

'Torben took it seriously.'

'Yes. And look where it got him.'

'You didn't see his body. I did. There wasn't a mark on him. Just as there wasn't on David. How was it done?'

'I don't know. But I know how it wasn't done. Higher dimensions don't exist in a way the human mind can manipulate. They aren't there. You can't reach out and touch them. For heaven's sake—' She bent her head back and sighed in a slow release of impatience. 'I used to have this argument with David. And it never got us anywhere. God, I was still having it the very last time we spoke.'

'When he phoned you from the Skyway?' She frowned at him in surprise. 'It was on his bill. A long call, evidently.'

'Long and pretty incoherent. He wanted to expound his latest hyper-dimensional theories, whereas I—' She sighed, impatience mixing with her regret. 'There was nothing in his manner to suggest suicidal depression. Absolutely the reverse. He seemed . . .

154

unnaturally exuberant. Full of how exciting the future was going to be. Not in the least curious about *me*. Which only made me more determined not to listen. If I'd known : . .' She shook her head. 'I thought later he might have got so caught up in his theorizing that he took an accidental overdose.'

'But you don't think that now?'

'What I think, Harry, is that your son was chasing an illusion. While something much more solid and threatening was chasing him.' She sighed again. 'Do you know what the essence was of our findings for Project Sybil? Hunger. Plague. Sterility. Social disintegration. Economic collapse. Global catastrophe. People talk about such things every day as generalities. But this was a detailed point-by-point explanation of why and how it'll happen if we go on as we are. Lazenby believes us. That's the amazing part of all this. He thinks we're right. But he doesn't care. He wants to tell today's clients what they want to hear about tomorrow, not what they need to know. He isn't trying to suppress our findings about the future of the world because he thinks they're extreme or alarmist. He's trying to suppress them because they can be used to prove Globescope is a corrupt organization. It's his commercial reputation he's worried about. And the irony is that we wouldn't much mind if his reputation survived unscathed, so long as we could publish our predictions. It's incidental. But it's become the crux of the whole thing. And now . . . either he goes under . . . or we do.'

'Then you have no choice but to try for the tape.'

'Not true. We could remain in hiding and stick to our original plan. Reassemble Project Sybil nut and bolt, then publish and be damned. They've no idea where we are. Nobody could have followed you from Copenhagen given the precautions we took. And Woodrow's certain nobody got on the train at Albany after you.'

'They might have *seen* me get on.'

'Not good enough. You could have got off at any one of a dozen intermediate stops. You could be anywhere from Syracuse to Sandusky. How would they know?'

'All right. But I still think—'

'I'll tell you what I think, shall I?' She turned her head to look at him, her eyes wide and appraising. 'I think you want this over and done with quickly, in the hope that I'll be able to go back to England with you and wave a magic wand over David.' Now she had said it he knew it was true. Preposterously frail as the hope

155

was, it was the one he had been clinging to. Not just because David represented his last chance of the only kind of immortality life has to offer – a stake in the next generation – but because, if David *did* recover, it would be partly thanks to Harry. The father David had once turned his back on would have come to his rescue.

'What's wrong with hoping, Donna? You're the only one who's ever talked as if he *can* be saved.'

'Saved *in theory*. It's true some research has been done at Emory University in Atlanta which suggests deep coma retrieval *might* become a practical possibility. They're working with Hector Sandoval, the pioneering neurosurgeon, to refine the necessary laser-surgical techniques. But they haven't even reached the experimental stage yet. And even if we could get Sandoval interested in treating David, he'd be crazy to agree when the risk of failure's so high. Better from his point of view to maintain David on life support for as long as it takes to be optimistic about the outcome.'

'You mean . . . there's a strong case . . . for doing that?'

'Yes. And I'd have been impressing it on Iris if I'd had the chance.'

'But she's actively considering letting him die. Her husband's trying to talk her into it. And David's doctor backs him up.'

'I know. That was the way things were shaping up when I was over there. But what can I do? Lazenby's just waiting for one of us to show ourselves. I don't enjoy living like a fugitive. I have a mother, father and two sisters in Seattle who probably think I'm dead. Makepeace has a daughter in Minneapolis who hasn't heard from her in over a month. This isn't easy on any of us.' Her face had flushed and her chin was quivering. Tears were suddenly close. She whipped off her glasses and rubbed her eyes, then looked at him with reimposed self-control. 'Persuade Iris to hold off taking a decision, Harry. Can you manage that?'

'I think so.' It was both an exaggeration and a simplification. Iris had promised to do nothing without consulting him first. And one sure way to hold her to her promise was to avoid being consulted. Offhand, in fact, he could think of no better way. 'For a while, at least.'

'And how long does a while need to be? You want me to say, don't you?' Donna frowned thoughtfully for a moment, then said: 'I think you'd better meet the others, Harry. That's the only way to settle it.'

'So what do we do?'

156

She glanced at her watch. 'I have a return flight booked for later this afternoon. I need to be on it.'

'Shall I come with you?'

'No,' she said, a little too hurriedly for his liking. 'Travelling together would be complicated. And risky.'

'Why? You said yourself—'

'We'll go on as we've started, all right?' Was petulance the price she had to pay for suppressing her vulnerability? Or was she playing a deeper game than Harry could grasp? He had no way of knowing. And no alternative but to agree, as he signalled with a nod. If David had a chance, it lay in her hands. She could win the medical arguments Harry could not even present. She could call in the best in the business to help his son. *If* she wanted to. 'Stay in Chicago tonight. Fly out in the morning.'

'Where to?'

She deliberated for what seemed like several minutes during which her large dark eyes studied him coolly. Then she said: 'Dallas.'

'You've been there the whole time?'

'There's a hotel right by the terminal,' she went on, calmly ignoring his question. 'The Hyatt Regency. Book into it when you arrive. We'll contact you there.'

'When?'

'By Wednesday at the latest. What name are you travelling under?'

'Norman Page.'

'Right.' Once more she glanced at her watch. 'I have to go.' But the urgency was synthetic. Harry felt sure she would have allowed more time than this for their meeting. She was not hurrying to catch a plane so much as to cut short their exchanges before they could stray beyond what was strictly necessary.

She rose and headed across a frozen patch of grass to the expressway crossing. He followed, noticing for the first time how quick and determined her movements were. Catching her up as she pressed the pedestrian button, he said: 'I wanted to ask you more about David.'

'I know,' she replied, keeping her eyes fixed on the red pictogram of a man on the far side of the road. 'But I can't trust myself to say more. I loved him once.'

'But you don't now?'

'He made that impossible.'

'I'm sorry. I've no right to intrude. It's just . . .'

157

'You want to know what kind of son Iris bore you. I understand that. Strangely enough, I'm not sure I could tell you even if I wanted to. He's always kept too much of himself hidden. Take you, for instance. He told me his father was dead long after he knew you were alive. He even told me about the visit to Rhodes with Torben and the scene in Lindos. I remember them joking about it one night over dinner. He never hinted . . . never implied . . .' She shook her head. 'He never trusted me with the truth.'

Before Harry could respond, the traffic lurched to a stop, the red man changed to green and Donna set off across the road at a clip. Harry had to break into a trot to keep up. At the other side she carried straight on, up a quieter road leading towards the city centre. 'Maybe he just couldn't bring himself to admit it,' he panted. 'As fathers go . . . I suppose I take a bit of owning up to.'

'You didn't fit his image of himself. You were a potential embarrassment.'

'I'm not sure which of us that's harder on.'

'Not you.' She pulled up and turned to face him. 'Whoever it was who thought you ought to know about David was doing him a bigger favour than you. Who else would have come this far on his account? Who else could have won my confidence?'

'Have I won it?'

'Amazingly, you have.'

'But how?'

'By being the real thing.'

'What do you mean?'

She came closer to smiling then than she had since they had first met. 'You'll fly to Dallas tomorrow?'

'Yes.'

'*That's* what I mean.' With no further word of explanation, she turned and hurried on to the junction, where the road met a busier thoroughfare. Harry watched as she raised her hand and a taxi pulled up for her. She climbed in, leant forward for a word with the driver, then fell back in her seat. She did not look in Harry's direction as the car started away, but he had the strangest impression – which light, shade and distance could all have falsified – that she was crying as the taxi vanished from sight behind a building on the corner.

TWENTY-NINE

Wednesday morning in Dallas was grey, still and drizzly. It had never looked like this on Kostas's television set at the Taverna Silenou, courtesy of which Harry had clocked up nine years' random exposure to the everyday melodramas of Texan oil folk. They had left him with an abiding impression of blue skies, high winds and a city peopled with sexually incontinent megalomaniacs talking in badly dubbed Greek. The reality, as viewed from a hotel room at Dallas–Fort Worth Airport, was reassuringly drab by comparison. Jets descended slowly from the louring cloudbase and ascended slowly into it, while a polluted mizzle encroached on the featureless horizon. It was movement without event, place without location: a transportational limbo in which Harry felt unnaturally secure.

Raising his coffee-cup to his lips only to discover that the coffee had gone cold, he grimaced and reached for a cigarette instead, then returned to leafing through his complimentary copy of the *Dallas Morning News*. If there had been any further developments in the strange affair of Globescope Inc. and its accident-prone former employees, they evidently did not warrant a mention when there were so many homegrown murders, football games and unique customized realty opportunities to report to the citizens of Dallas. Which was probably just as well when he considered the disturbing tone of the front-page article he had chanced to spot at a news-stand in the departure lounge of O'Hare Airport the previous day. An article whose headline – GLOBESCOPE SHARE PRICE

159

FALLS ON REPORT OF THIRD STAFF FATALITY – had caused him to abandon his intention of buying an out-of-date copy of the *Sunday Express* there and then in favour of an up-to-date *Wall Street Journal*.

Harry rose, walked across to the bed and sat down amidst the rumpled sheets. He bent over to retrieve the paper from where he had discarded it last night and scanned once more the sparse contents of an article he could by now have made a reasonable attempt at reciting from memory.

> The macabre crop of fatalities and near-fatalities among recently released employees of Globescope Inc., the Washington-based socio-economic forecasting corporation, impacted on Globescope's share price on the New York Stock Exchange yesterday, which lost $2½ to close at $11¼. This followed a report in yesterday's *Berlingske Tidende* that the Danish-born physicist Torben Hammelgaard, retained as a researcher by Globescope until April of this year, had been found dead on a bridge across Copenhagen Harbor in the early hours of Saturday morning.
>
> An autopsy has proved inconclusive as to the cause of Mr Hammelgaard's death and the results of a second autopsy are presently awaited. The Copenhagen police have said they would like to interview a middle-aged Briton going under the name of Barnett, who is thought to be the last person to have seen Mr Hammelgaard alive. Mr Barnett vanished from his Copenhagen hotel on Saturday.
>
> In Washington, a Globescope spokesperson said they had no knowledge of or dealings with Mr Barnett. Byron Lazenby, President of Globescope, was reported to be confident that the corporation's share price will recover as soon as the circumstances of Mr Hammelgaard's death are clarified.

Harry tossed the paper back onto the floor and took a long nerve-settling drag on his cigarette. If a second autopsy showed Hammelgaard had been murdered, the Copenhagen police would do more than express a polite wish to interview him. They would come looking for him. Just as well then that Norman Page, not Harry Barnett, had booked into the Hyatt Regency. And that the *Dallas Morning News* remained firmly parochial in its concerns. Nevertheless—

Harry grabbed the telephone at the first ring, praying it would be Donna's voice he would hear on the other end. But it was not.

'Mr Page?'

'Yes.'

'This is the front desk. Your cab's here.'

'What cab? I never—' Then he realized what the taxi's arrival must mean and did his best to suck the surprise out of his voice. 'Yes, of course. Thanks. I'll be right down.'

THIRTY

'You from outa town, sir?' asked Otis McSweeney of the Yellow Checker Cab Company as they cruised through a part of Dallas the television cameras had never focused on, a part where vacant lots, weed-pocked pavements, peeling clapboard and rusting metal meant the houses tended not to have their photographs splashed across the *Dallas Morning News* property pages.

'Yes. A long way out.'

'Only Fair Park, it's kinda quiet this time o' the year. You'll have the Cotton Bowl jus' about to yourself.'

'Is that a fact?'

'Yessir.' Otis laughed. 'Near a fact as they come.' He seemed to be enjoying the joke. But since asking for an explanation would involve Harry revealing that he did not know where they were going, it seemed best to grin and say nothing.

A few minutes later, they slowed for some lights, then took a left through an imposing flagpoled gateway and entered Fair Park. A seemingly infinite expanse of large unattended buildings and wide empty roads revealed itself through the drizzle. They passed a sign reading *749,000 square feet available for lease for conventions, rodeos, concerts, ice events, etc*, swung past a vista of shuttered Art Deco pavilions and steered towards a distant ferris wheel presiding forlornly over a silent funfair.

Otis turned left into a road box-canyoned by the soaring flank of a sports stadium and slowed to a halt. 'Cotton Bowl jus' for you, sir,' he announced. 'That'll be eighteen dollars and fifty cents.'

162

Harry handed Otis a twenty-dollar bill, then clambered out into the mild damp-rag day. He watched the taxi perform a slow U-turn, followed it back out onto the main boulevard and stared after it as it cruised away towards the exit. Beyond the gates, a sprawling metroplex went about its business. But in the 749,000 square feet of Fair Park on a wet November morning, time stood still. Emptier than any prairie, a desolation of unused space stretched its circumference around Harry, hollow with the memory of summer multitudes, loud with the absence of their voices.

Then, as the thrum of the taxi finally faded into the gentle hiss of the drizzle, another sound came to Harry's ears, that of a higher-pitched car engine, approaching slowly from behind him. He turned to see a mud-brown camper-van heading towards him from the funfair. It was fitted with a reflective windscreen, behind which the driver remained invisible. Harry stepped back, wondering if he had walked into an elaborate trap. If so, it had been adroitly sprung. He was alone and far from help of any kind.

The camper-van coasted to a stop in front of him and the side-door slid open. To Harry's immense relief, Donna looked out from the rear seat and beckoned for him to climb in. He did so without a word, sitting down beside her to find the occupants of the front seats staring at him over their shoulders. The driver was a thin frowning woman with black curly hair and an olive complexion, dressed in jeans and a leather fleece-lined jacket. The passenger was a tubby little man wearing a large hooded anorak over shirt, tie, razor-creased trousers and thin gold-buckled shoes. Snow-white hair flopped schoolboyishly over his brow, but his eyes were rheumy, his face lined like dried mud.

'Makepeace Steiner and Rawnsley Ablett,' said Donna by way of superfluous introduction. 'Harry Barnett.'

'Hi, Harry,' said Steiner.

'You should know I think this is crazy,' said Ablett without the hint of a smile. 'But I was outvoted.'

'We're grateful to you for coming,' put in Donna, laying her hand briefly on Harry's forearm. 'All of us.'

'We think you can help us,' said Steiner.

'How?'

'We'd better keep moving. You tell him, Donna.' Steiner started away, driving just as slowly as before. 'Then *he* can tell *us*.'

'Tell you what?'

'Whether you'll do it,' growled Ablett.

'It's like this, Harry,' said Donna. 'We've talked it over. Over *and* over. Sooner or later, Lazenby will track us down. What happened to Torben proves that. It took them six weeks to find him. Even if it takes them twice that to find us, we still won't be ready for them. The tape may be a lifeline. A short-circuit. Who knows without listening to it? But we can't listen to it without retrieving it from Lazenby's office. And we can't just walk in and help ourselves. If we try to break in and get caught, it'll be tantamount to suicide. So there's no way *we* can realistically attempt to get the tape.'

'You mean—'

'You have a chance, Harry,' Donna went on. 'One we don't. Lazenby doesn't know you. Fredericks doesn't have your face on file. To Globescope you're nothing. If you could talk your way into Lazenby's office . . .'

'You're not serious.'

'I am. Two of you have an excellent chance of pulling it off. One distracts Lazenby while the other—'

'*Two* of us?'

'You and Woodrow.'

'You've asked Woodrow?'

'Not yet. But he'll agree, I'm sure of it.'

'It's you we're not sure of,' put in Ablett.

'You're crazy.'

'That's what *I* said,' Ablett threw back at him.

'But *we* said it could work,' Steiner contributed as she took a leisurely right round a redundant roundabout.

'How could it work? How could we even get onto the premises?'

'It can be done,' said Donna in her softest most reasonable tone. 'We set you up as chairman and managing director of a London-based investment company. Woodrow poses as your American partner. You fax Lazenby saying you're going to be in Washington for a few days and want to discuss using Globescope's services. You quote some big figures. Lazenby invites you in. Woodrow keeps him talking while you retrieve the tape. Then you go away to think over his offer, taking the tape with you.'

'Can we be sure he'd agree to see us?'

'I think so. He's about as resistant to business as a cat is to fish.'

'But *what* business? He'd expect to have heard of our company, surely.'

'And he will have done. We know which database he buys into for background information about clients. And Makepeace has a friend on the senior technical staff there who'd be willing to insert a fake company file for us. So, when Lazenby consults them about you, he'll learn what we want him to learn: enough to make him bite.'

'You just have to pray he doesn't ask around more widely,' said Ablett. 'And learn enough to make him bite your heads clean off.'

'We won't give him time,' Donna countered. 'Besides, it's not his way. He likes to play his cards close to his chest.'

'But what if he recognizes Woodrow? He may have seen him perform on stage, for God's sake.'

'Unlikely. And even less likely that he'd realize who Woodrow was even if he *had* seen Mr Nemo.'

'What about me, then? My name's been in the papers in connection with Torben's death. Globescope have been asked if they know me. It won't be long before a photograph of me's in circulation.'

'Nice point,' sneered Ablett. 'But it doesn't stand up. The result of the second autopsy on Torben came through this morning.' He paused, scanning Harry's features as if for some hint of fore-knowledge. 'Natural causes.'

'*Natural causes?*'

'Some kind of brain haemorrhage, evidently.'

'That's absurd.'

'Maybe. But it puts you in the clear. The Danish police won't want to interview you now, will they? So there'll be no photograph of you sliding out of fax machines around the world.'

'Even so—'

'Unless you think there's some other reason why Lazenby should recognize you.'

'What do you mean?'

'He means he doesn't trust you,' said Steiner over her shoulder.

'But *we* do, Harry,' said Donna. 'And Rawnsley's willing to go along with us.'

'True,' said Ablett. 'Largely on the grounds that if you *are* working for Lazenby we're finished anyway – and the tape's nothing but a figment of your imagination.'

'I'm not working for anyone.'

'Prove it, then. Go and get the tape.'

'We can't force you to do this,' said Donna. 'We're not trying to blackmail you.'

'No? Well, it seems to me that's what you *are* doing, whether you want to or not. If I don't co-operate, you won't try to get Sandoval interested in David's case, will you?'

165

'I won't be *able* to.'

'But is blackmail worse than treachery?' Ablett fixed Harry with an accusing glare. 'Remember it was your son who obliged us to bury ourselves in this hell-hole. So don't get picky about the methods we employ to dig ourselves out.'

'Don't mind him,' said Steiner. 'He's just a grouchy old Bostonian with withdrawal symptoms.'

'It's true Texas doesn't agree with me,' Ablett replied. 'But then neither do traitors. Or their fathers.'

'You seem to have as big a mouth as you do an opinion of yourself,' Harry snapped. 'If there's something personal in this you want to settle, then I'll be happy to oblige.'

'This we don't need,' Steiner intervened. 'Jesus, will you listen to yourselves?'

But Ablett went on staring straight at Harry. 'Put up or shut up.'

'That's no problem,' Harry replied, not stopping to consider the consequences. 'If Woodrow's game, then so am I.'

'Listen to the details first,' said Donna, twisting round in an effort to make Harry look at her rather than Ablett. 'I want you to be satisfied the plan will work.'

'I don't need to be satisfied.'

'For heaven's sake, Harry—'

'I'll do it, OK? What more do you need to know?'

Steiner braked sharply to a halt and turned to look at him. 'We need to know you mean it,' she said with quiet emphasis.

'I mean it,' said Harry, returning her gaze. He glanced across at Ablett. 'OK?' Ablett nodded. Leaving Harry to close the circle by fixing his eyes on Donna's and letting them rest there for as long as it took for his intention to be as clear as it was irrevocable. 'I mean it.'

THIRTY-ONE

It was early Friday evening and the revolving lounge in the dome at the top of Reunion Tower was three-quarters filled with Dallasites celebrating the arrival of the weekend. Below them, a trail of headlamp beams marked out the snarled freeways like an illuminated street-map, while at eye level the downtown skyscrapers showed off their spotlit profiles against the inky Texan sky.

Customarily, at this time on a Friday, Harry would have been standing at the bar of the Stonemasons' Arms, Kensal Green, with a pint of London Pride in his hand. Contrary to what he would have predicted, the thought was unaccompanied by any sense of deprivation. Given the sarcasm his new hairstyle would have attracted from the clientele of the Stonemasons', he was in some ways relieved to be surrounded by strangers. Also, the Reunion Tower waitresses were much prettier than Terry's unalluring assortment of barmaids. And Shiner Bock beer was turning out to taste better with every bottle he drank. Which was just as well, considering how many bottles he *had* drunk since Wednesday. A consistent state of mild inebriation had enabled him to maintain an attitude of blithe optimism about what he had agreed to do. So much so that when he saw Makepeace Steiner striding towards him along the slowly rotating aisle between the tables, the last thing he wanted to hear her announce was that the whole madcap scheme was off.

'Hi, Harry,' she said, sliding quickly into the seat opposite him. 'How's it going?'

167

'Extravagantly. I've blown two thousand dollars of your money on three sea-island cotton shirts, two silk ties, a designer suit, a cashmere overcoat, a pair of lounge lizard shoes, a fancy suit-case and something called an executive grip. Plus the haircut, of course.'

'Yuh. Very Harvey Keitel.'

'You recommended the salon, as I recall.'

'True. Don't worry. It looks great. Exactly what you need.'

'I *do* need it, do I?'

'Yuh.' She nodded. 'It's on.' She broke off to order a drink, then took one of his cigarettes, lit it and said: 'I seem to have taken these up again. Stress, right?'

'Aren't I the one who should be feeling under stress?'

'You won't have the chance. By this time next week, it'll be all over.' She leant forward and lowered her voice. 'Donna called a few hours ago. She had no difficulty persuading Woodrow to help us. Seems he sees this as an ideal outlet for his untapped acting abilities. Undertook to rig himself out at Bloomingdale's this weekend. We're bankrolling him too. On Monday, you both fly to Washington and book into the Hay-Adams Hotel. Ritzy sort of place just across from the White House. There are reservations for a week in the names of Norman Page and Bill Cornford of the Page-Muirson Investment Company. A fax will reach Lazenby the same day asking if the two of you can meet with him soonest to discuss applying Globescope's predictive techniques to the Far East and Latin American markets you're thinking of diversifying into. This is a print-out of what he'll find on the Page-Muirson file my friend has set up for us.' She slid a stapled tranche of papers across the table. 'Along with extracts from recent press and investment magazine articles about the kind of business you'll be claiming to be in. Futures trading. Arbitraging. Interest-rate swaps. The whole derivatives jungle. Try to get familiar with the phrase-ology. Then you'll at least sound as if you understand it. Keep the whole thing general, though. Avoid specifics. But don't worry too much. Lazenby will talk as if he knows much more about it than he really does. You can afford to bluff a little. Depending how well you do your homework. Probably best to leave most of the talking to Woodrow. That's his forte. Concentrate on getting hold of the tape. If you can walk out of there with the tape in your pocket, it doesn't much matter if you leave Lazenby thinking you're the biggest dope he's ever met.'

'Just as well.' Harry leafed sceptically through the pages, the abundance of graphs and pie-charts giving him a queasy sense of inadequacy. 'How do we know Lazenby will respond?'

'Because the information we've planted paints Page-Muirson in his favourite colours. Cash-laden and unworldly. I've accessed his appointments file and confirmed he's in town all week, with a lightish schedule. My guess is he'll go for this before his Monday morning coffee's cooled. There'll probably be an answer to your fax waiting for you at the Hay-Adams.'

'What about Donna? Will she be waiting for us at the Hay-Adams?'

'No. She can't risk being seen in Washington. She'll stay in Baltimore. But that's less than an hour away by train. When you reach Washington, she'll call and give you a contact number. For use when you get hold of the tape.' Makepeace smiled stiffly and clunked her bourbon on the rocks against his beer glass. 'Here's to your success.'

'Would Rawnsley share the toast if he were here?'

'Leave me to worry about Rawnsley, Harry. Just get the tape if it's there to be got.'

'I'll do my best.'

'How about better than your best?'

'OK. I'll try for that as well.'

'Great.' The stiffness dropped out of her smile and she took an unladylike gulp of bourbon. 'That I like the sound of.'

THIRTY-TWO

Norman Page, chairman and managing director of Page-Muirson Ltd, financial adviser to the quality, flew into Dulles Airport early the following Monday afternoon. His suit was dove-grey, his shirt powder-pink, his tie richly striped, his hair elegantly styled. A pre-hired limousine sped him and his brand-new luggage through twenty-six miles of damp green Virginia and across the Theodore Roosevelt Memorial Bridge into the spacious heart of Washington. He glanced up at the pale slopes of Arlington Cemetery as he passed, down at the grey waters of the Potomac and all around him at the tree-screened federal buildings, the low-rise office blocks, the trimmed and trained regularities of the capital. At length he was delivered to the door of the Hay-Adams Hotel, just the sort of lavishly appointed establishment to which such a gentleman would naturally be used, and was ushered into its walnut-panelled lobby.

After signing his name in a vellum-paged register, he was escorted to a suite overlooking Lafayette Square. The view of the White House, though not the intervening vista of the homeless camping out in the park, was drawn to his attention. The push-button availability of multiple electronic media was deferentially explained to him, as were the hot-and-cold mysteries of the marbled bathroom. He administered a five-dollar tip and was left alone pending the arrival of his suitcase. This brief interval allowed him to peer at the framed reproduction above the fireplace of L'Enfant's 1792 Plan for the Federal City, test the broad acres of the firm yet yielding bed and squint in awe at the printed tariff on the back of the door.

The suitcase delivered and another five-dollar tip dispensed, he telephoned reception and asked if his colleague, Bill Cornford, had yet booked in. He was told he had not. Mildly surprised, he proceeded to unpack and take a leisurely bath. He emerged from the bathroom an hour or so later to find an envelope had been slipped beneath his door, addressed to him by name and room number. It turned out to contain a fax. From Byron Lazenby, President of Globescope Inc., predictive consultant to the corporate élite.

Dear Norman Page

I would be delighted to meet with you during your stay in Washington and to outline the kind of forecasting package my organization could offer a company such as yours. Perhaps you would call my secretary, Ann Mather, to fix a date.

Sincerely
Byron E. Lazenby

It was not yet five o'clock and Harry was tempted to telephone Ann Mather straightaway. 'If it were done when 'tis done, then 'twere well it were done quickly' surfaced in his mind as a sound principle more than forty years after its accidental absorption during a desultory reading of *Macbeth* in the dying days of his school career. In the end, though, the only call he made was to reception, to learn that Bill Cornford had still not arrived.

Harry was now beginning to feel badly in need of a drink. He could not risk going in search of the bar for fear of missing Donna's promised call. The mini-bar it therefore had to be, yielding two bottles of Budweiser and a Jim Beam chaser for each. Leafing through Makepeace's notes under the influence of this self-assembled cocktail, he felt the onset of a strange illusion: that he was actually developing a grasp of high finance. The pros and cons of the Mexican bond market as against Californian earthquake futures started to resemble a subject he could coherently discourse on. Then the telephone rang.

'Hello?'

'Hello, Harry.' It was Donna. 'Everything OK?'

'Not exactly. Do you want the good news or the bad news?'

171

'Just tell me.'

'Lazenby's sent a fax agreeing to see us.'

'Great.'

'But Woodrow hasn't shown up.'

'He hasn't? Oh, I don't suppose there's anything to worry about. He may have had to put in some time at work. He's coming down on the Metroliner. Probably already on his way.'

'If you say so.'

'Have you made an appointment with Lazenby?'

'Not yet. I thought I'd wait for Woodrow.'

'OK. But we don't want him to think you're not interested.'

'And we don't want him to think I'm over-eager either. I'll phone his secretary first thing in the morning and suggest some time tomorrow or Wednesday.'

'OK. Keep me informed. The number here's 410-939-2745. It's a small hotel.'

'Got it.'

'Speak to you soon. And Harry—'

'Yes?'

'Be careful, huh? Just for me.'

But Harry did not want to be careful. What he required was more of the drunken confidence he already had. He ordered a bottle of wine to maintain the state as long as he could and to wash down a room-service dinner, abandoned Makepeace's notes in favour of the television set and gazed blearily out of the window at the floodlit portico of the White House and the illuminated obelisk of the Washington Monument. Eight o'clock came. Then nine. Then ten. But word of Bill Cornford did not come.

Harry descended to the lobby, a flushed and rumpled travesty of the suave man-about-town who had booked in seven hours earlier. He quizzed the concierge about Metroliner services from New York and established that the last of the day arrived at eleven o'clock. He then walked out to a waiting clutch of taxis, climbed into the nearest and asked to be taken to Union Station.

Half an hour later, Harry stood forlornly beneath the cathedral-like roof of the station concourse, an empty polystyrene coffee-cup in one hand, a cigarette in the other, as the straggling remnants of the eleven o'clock Metroliner's payload vanished from sight. Woodrow Hackensack was not among them.

His absence did not yet constitute a crisis. There were later

172

stopping services. And something called the New England Express due in around two. But in Harry's mind a certainty had formed like concrete, cold and hard and heavy, that Woodrow was not coming. Then or later. That night or any other.

He could not properly have explained why. It had something to do with his last sighting of Woodrow, a lone figure in the car park at Albany–Rensselaer station a week before; something to do with the premonition of disaster Harry had felt as he watched him from the train window. First Torben. Now—

Harry marched across to a deserted row of phone-booths, glanced back self-consciously over his shoulder, then put a call through to Woodrow's New York number. It rang. And it went on ringing. But there was no answer. Woodrow was not going to pick up the phone. That fact blared louder than any unheeded bell. He was not going to respond. Maybe because he was no longer able to.

THIRTY-THREE

'Globescope Incorporated. Martina speaking. How may I help you?'

'Ann Mather please.'

'Who shall I say is calling?'

'Norman Page.'

'Putting you through, Mr Page.'

A few seconds of synthesized Sibelius, then: 'Ann Mather here, Mr Page. Mr Lazenby's very much looking forward to meeting you. When can you come in? Later today, perhaps?'

'Today's a little . . . difficult.'

'Tomorrow, then?'

'Well . . . er . . .'

'The end of the week's filling up awful fast for Mr Lazenby.'

'All right. Tomorrow.'

'Ten thirty?'

'Could we make it later? I . . . er . . .'

'Four o'clock?'

'Yes. OK. Four o'clock.'

'I'll enter it in his diary. Mr Lazenby will see you and your colleague at four tomorrow afternoon, Mr Page. Thank you for calling.'

'Right. Well, thank—' Harry stopped as soon as he realized he was talking to himself. He had never found it a profitable exercise. Besides, soliloquies came ruinously expensive at Amtrak's on-board call rates. He put the telephone down, extricated himself from the cramped cubicle and rocked and rolled to the rhythm of the Metroliner back to his seat.

The train was about halfway between Philadelphia and New York. It was just after ten o'clock the following morning. Harry glared out at an anonymous stretch of overcast New Jersey hinterland, as if holding it personally responsible for this journey he should not have had to undertake. But argue it out with himself however he pleased, there really was no alternative. He had to find out what had happened to Woodrow. Preferably, he had to find him. Before the appointment he had just made with Lazenby.

Perhaps he should not have made the appointment at all. But to have delayed any longer would have looked odd. And it is a short step from oddness to suspicion. Perhaps he should also have consulted Donna before leaving Washington. She could have boarded the train at Baltimore and shared whatever difficulties or dangers awaited him in New York. But she might have insisted on going *instead* of Harry. Probably would have, given how crucial his safety was to their plans. So maybe some old-fashioned concept of gallantry was actually the key to his behaviour.

The train slowed fractionally as it swept through a station. Peering out, Harry managed to catch its name. Princeton Junction. He was not far from the University, then, where Torben Hammel-gaard had worked. Nor from the Institute for Advanced Study, where Athene Tilson had swapped high-flown theories with Albert Einstein forty years ago. And maybe not far from the answer either, if only he could learn what the question was.

Harry paused long enough on arrival at Penn Station to lift Woodrow's address from a telephone directory. Then he jumped into a taxi. The driver had to spend several minutes studying a pocket atlas of the city before starting off and Harry soon lost his bearings in the skyscrapered grid. They headed east and south from Penn, crossing Broadway and finishing up in a narrow defile between steepling soot-smeared apartment blocks. Fifth Avenue it emphatically was not.

Woodrow's apartment was in a five-storey building most of the way along. Six bell-pushes and their respective wires clung to the doorpost courtesy of a few strips of rain-loosened insulation tape. Harry went through the motions of ringing Woodrow's. Then, after a responseless few moments, he tried the bell next to it. The speaking grille, on which somebody had apparently been sick

175

recently, spat out some static. Harry bellowed back an enquiry about Woodrow's whereabouts. More static was followed by silence. Then, almost as an afterthought, the door-lock buzzed open.

The hall was narrow and ill-lit. A pool of grey dusk descended from some lofty fanlight onto brown lino and the lower treads of seemingly endless stairs. Harry craned his neck to look up them as he entered. And met the gaze of a swarthy stubble-chinned fellow in a grubby T-shirt, who was staring down at him from the second-floor landing.

'You sure you're the Harley-Davidson type?' he asked, leaning out over the banisters. 'I wanna sell it to a serious biker, y'know.'

Harry grinned defensively. 'I'm not here about a motorbike. I'm looking for Woodrow Hackensack.'

The man in the T-shirt scowled. 'That case, we're both outa luck. He ain't here.'

'Do you know where I'd find him?'

'Bellevue, the paramedics said. But he could be in the morgue by now for all I know. Looked a candidate for it when he left here, that's a fact.'

'What happened?'

'Fell down the stairs. Did himself quite a bit of damage. But what d'you expect, when a man that size starts high-diving without a pool to land in?' He sniggered. 'An accident-prone escapologist. Ain't that something?'

'You're sure it was an accident?'

'What else, man?'

'You saw it happen?'

'No. I was out. Came back to find an ambulance out front and old Woodrow being hauled through the door on a stretcher.'

'Who called the ambulance?'

'Martha Gravett. Door across the hall from where you're standing. She'll tell you all about it. Just so long as you don't mind her telling you all about her frigging family tree as well.'

Martha Gravett, a frail but dignified old lady attended by an almost equally frail but dignified Cairn terrier, proved much more succinct than her neighbour had predicted.

'I heard an almighty thump about eleven o'clock yesterday morning and when I came out here there was poor Mr Hackensack, all crumpled up on the floor at the foot of the stairs. He was out cold. And it looked to me like his leg was broke. I came straight

176

back in here and dialled 911. Then I stayed with him until the ambulance arrived.'

'Did he say anything?'

'He came round a bit and started mumbling. But nothing you could understand.'

'He was definitely alone when it happened?'

'Of course. What can you be—' Her expression changed. 'Well, now you ask, I suppose . . .'

'What is it?'

'It's just . . . When I came out here and found him, I thought I saw, out of the corner of my eye . . . the door to the street swinging shut, as if . . . somebody had just left. But I guess I must have been mistaken. If there had been someone, they'd have stayed to help. Wouldn't they?'

THIRTY-FOUR

Woodrow Hackensack was not in the morgue. He was actually sitting up perkily in bed on a mound of fluffy white pillows in a modern air-conditioned wing of Bellevue Hospital, munching a bagel and surveying a view of the East River through an adjacent window. Had it not been for his bandaged forehead and the thigh-to-ankle plaster on his right leg, he would have looked like a man occupying a hospital bed under false pretences. As it was, his immobility should have worried Harry more than it did. For the moment, he was simply relieved to find him alive.

'Great to see you, Harry. I tried to call you earlier but you'd already left. I reckoned you might be on your way here. Sorry I wasn't in touch yesterday. Matter of fact, I wasn't in touch with much after that fall. Concussion, so they tell me. But I'm feeling fine now.'

'What about the leg?'

'Broken tibia. Plus some wrenched knee ligaments. No big deal. I should be up and hopping around by the end of the week.'

'I've arranged to meet Lazenby tomorrow afternoon.'

Hackensack grimaced. 'That's kinda soon for me. Can't you put it off?'

'Till when? Our fax said we'd only be in Washington for a few days. I don't think so, do you?'

'I could try and talk the doc into letting me out on crutches. Just for the day, maybe.' He caught Harry's eye and nodded ruefully. 'Well, maybe not.'

'I'll have to go alone.'

'That's crazy. Deception works by distraction: the illusionist's big secret. With me along to distract Lazenby, you have a chance. Without me . . .'

'I don't see what else I can do.'

'Donna won't let you take the risk.'

'Donna needn't know. Have you spoken to her?'

'Nah.' He glanced meaningfully around at the other occupants of the ward and lowered his voice to a whisper. 'Too many ears on stalks. Deafness sure ain't these people's problem. I only called *you* as a last resort.'

'There you are then.'

'But I'll call Donna if I have to.' Hackensack was suddenly serious. 'Don't do it, Harry.'

Harry shrugged. 'All right.'

'You mean that?'

'Tell me about the fall. How did it happen?'

'Plain stupidity. I was leaving in a hurry. Aiming to catch the noon train. Taking the stairs two at a time. I guess I must have missed my footing. Simple as that.'

'You *guess*?'

'Well, it's all a mite hazy. Short-term memory loss is pretty common with concussion, they tell me. To be honest with you, I don't remember much between setting off down the stairs from my apartment and waking up in here. The rest is kinda like the Chinese flag: red with a lot of stars.'

'Martha Gravett thinks there may have been somebody on the staircase with you.'

'Does she? Well, Martha thinks her dead sister from Jersey City calls by for tea most afternoons. I wouldn't set much store by anything she says.'

'She seemed sane enough to me.'

'You don't live above her. There was nobody with me, Harry. Believe me.'

'But you just said you couldn't remember.'

'I'd remember being pushed, if that's what you're getting at.'

'Would you?'

'You think the people who caught up with Torben caught up with me?'

'Maybe.'

'They must be losing their touch, then. As fatal accidents go, mine was pretty ineffective.'

179

'Perhaps you just got lucky.'

'You call this lucky?' Hackensack rolled his eyes. 'I spent the entire weekend turning myself into a well-dressed financier. Only to finish up in here, with the pants of my Wall Street suit ripped from ass to ankle and my memory shot full of holes. Most people would reckon that was about as *un*lucky as a guy gets in an average day.'

'OK, OK.' Harry held up his hands appeasingly. 'I'm on your side. Remember *that*?'

'Sure. And I remember the favour I agreed to do for you too. How could I forget? It's partly because of it that I slipped on the stairs.'

'How do you make that out?'

'I went up to Columbia last week and asked around about your friend and mine, Carl Dobermann. Drew a blank. There's nobody on the manual staff who goes back that far. Nobody on the academic staff either, far as I could figure out. And Dobermann ain't the stuff of local legend. Like I told you, students go loco for a pastime. Memorable it is not. I trawled through the 1958 index for the *Times* and *Post*. No entry for Dobermann. He's a dog without a scent.'

'What's this got to do with falling downstairs?'

'Jeez, sorry, I keep losing my drift.' Hackensack bounced the heel of his hand off his bald patch in self-reproach. 'I got the name and address of a lab technician who'd been at Columbia more than forty years. Retired about eighteen months ago. Isaac Rosenbaum. Lives with his daughter now, down in Philadelphia. That's the point. I knew you'd want to hear what I'd found out, so I planned to stop off in Philadelphia and look the old guy up. That's why I was in such an all-fired hurry to catch the noon train. So I'd have time for the stopover. And this' – he tapped his plaster-cast – 'is where hurrying got me.'

'Which means I'm to blame?'

'Sure. And you can make up for it by reducing my stress levels. They need to be rock-bottom to expedite a swift recovery.'

'How can I do that?'

'Call off your meeting with Lazenby.'

'Didn't I say I would?'

'You did,' Hackensack grinned. 'But I didn't believe you.'

When Harry left half an hour later, he had still not convinced Hackensack he meant to cancel his appointment with Lazenby.

This was hardly surprising, since he had not convinced himself either. Why turn back when he had come so far? Why give his nerves the chance to fail? They might hold for twenty-four hours. But they surely would not last until Hackensack came out of hospital. In the end, it did not matter if Hackensack knew he was being fobbed off. There was nothing he could do about it, apart from contacting Donna. And there was nothing she could do about it even if he did.

Harry boarded the four o'clock train back to Washington, armed with Isaac Rosenbaum's address and a firm intention of stopping off in Philadelphia to hunt him down. But fatigue proved stronger than his intentions. He had slept little and eaten less since his anxious vigil at Union Station the night before. Now, his anxiety relieved on one score at least, he plunged into the deep sleep of a body running on empty. To be woken by the conductor three hours later in Washington.

It was out of the question to return to Philadelphia at that stage. Irritating as it was, Harry concluded that his business with Mr Rosenbaum would simply have to wait. He trudged out into the Washington night and headed for his hotel.

Halfway along E Street, he was lured into the Hard Rock Café by the doorman's promise of draught Bass. The beer turned out to be of such excellence that he found himself reminiscing to the barman about the arrival of the first juke-box in Swindon and his youthful admiration for Elvis Presley. As a result it was nearly ten o'clock when he entered the lobby of the Hay-Adams, walked unsteadily to the desk and asked for his key. Only for sobriety to pay him a sudden and unexpected call.

'Glad to see your colleague was able to join us after all, Mr Page,' the clerk said cheerily.

'What?'

'Mr Cornford. I wasn't on duty when he booked in this afternoon, but I see from the register—'

'*Cornford?*'

'Yes, sir. We gave him the room next to yours.' He glanced at the key-board. 'And it looks like you'll find him in.'

THIRTY-FIVE

Harry lit another cigarette and gazed up at the southern façade of the Hay-Adams Hotel, checking his calculations for the umpteenth time. Those were definitely the windows of his room on the third floor. And those were just as definitely the windows next to them of the room occupied by whoever was posing as Bill Cornford. Golden lamplight seeped through the thick curtains, but no hand twitched them back to reveal the identity of his impersonator. Whether, strictly speaking, appropriating somebody else's alias qualified as impersonation was a point Harry did not propose to dwell on. He glanced nervously over his shoulder and commenced another circuit of Lafayette Square, pummelling his weary brain into some kind of logical thought.

What should he do? Get as far as possible from the Hay-Adams as quickly as possible? Or walk up to the third floor, knock boldly on the door next to his and see who opened it? The answer might be revealing as well as dangerous. So much that had dogged his path since leaving England had been unseen and unattestable, a threat made more potent by its elusiveness. Now, within the reassuringly solid walls of the Hay-Adams Hotel, there was a chance to corner his foe, to look him in the eye and know him for who and what he was. And it was a chance he knew he had to take.

Ten minutes later, Harry emerged from the hotel lift and walked slowly along the third-floor corridor, easing his key from his pocket

182

as he went. He paused by the door before his, but heard nothing, not even a footstep, within. Then he moved on to his room, slid the key gently into the lock, turned it and entered, closing the door softly behind him.

The walls were thick enough to absorb most sound. And a maid had already been in to switch on the lights, draw the curtains and turn down the bed. He went straight to the bedside table, picked up the telephone and dialled room service.

'Page here. Room 331.'

'Yes sir?'

'Could I have a bottle of champagne and two glasses. Right away.'

'Certainly, sir.'

'Delivered to room 330. I'll be there.'

'Be with you directly, sir.'

Harry replaced the handset and sat slowly down on the bed. Then he lit a cigarette and listened to the silence in which his heart beat louder and faster than a funeral-drum. It would not be long now, though it would seem for ever. Five or ten minutes. Maybe fifteen. Then he would know.

Or would he? A sudden crazy thought formed in his mind. Perhaps there was nobody in room 330. Perhaps there never had been. Like whatever had visited David at the Skyway Hotel and met Torben on the bridge in Copenhagen; like the push on the Metro platform, the trip on the stairs, the blocked flue in Montreal: it could touch but not be touched; it could see but not be seen.

He rose, circled the bed and leant his head against the wall, willing his ear to detect something, anything, that would tether his anxieties to physical reality. Somebody was in there. They had to be. They had signed the register, ridden the lift and tipped the porter. They existed. Yet he could hear nothing. Absolutely nothing. It was as if—

Then he did hear a sound, though from a different direction. The opening and closing of the service lift, followed by footsteps in the corridor: a firm waiterly tread. He padded swiftly across the room. As he reached the door, there was a tap at the next one along. 'Room service,' a voice announced.

Harry turned the handle, edged the door open and peered out round the jamb. The waiter had his back to him, one hand fanned beneath a tray on which a bottle of champagne stood in an ice-bucket flanked by two glasses, the other hand raised, index knuckle cocked. 'Room service,' he repeated. Before he could knock again, the door opened, hinged to Harry's blind side. It snagged on a chain. There was a mumbled remark from within. The waiter smiled, shrugged and pulled out a chit. '330,' he said. 'Champagne ordered by Mr Page. Took the order myself.'

A momentary pause. The door closed, the chain was slipped and it opened again, wider. Harry stepped cautiously out into the corridor. The waiter caught sight of him and frowned. Then Harry lunged into the doorway in front of him, flinging the door wide and swinging round to meet—

'You.' The door rebounded from its stop and jogged his shoulder as he stared in astonishment.

'Well? Who did you expect?'

'But they said . . . Bill Cornford had . . .'

'The champagne was a really nice idea, Norman.' Donna gave him an exasperated smile. 'Why don't you come in and help me drink it?'

THIRTY-SIX

'What the hell did you expect me to do?' demanded Donna as she paced the plush-carpeted length of the room in voluminous towelling bathrobe and matching mules, hair still damp and face flushed from the shower she had been taking when the champagne arrived. 'You and Woodrow had both vanished. Anything could have happened. I couldn't just sit in Baltimore and wait for you to call.'

'I might have aged less rapidly if you had.'

'Bad luck. If you'd called me, you'd have got the message I left for you. Then Wilhelmina Cornford wouldn't have come as such a big surprise.'

'I didn't want to worry you.'

'Silence *was* worrying.'

'Sorry. I just needed time to work out what to do.'

'Pity you didn't put it to better use. Woodrow's right. We have to postpone.'

'How can we?'

'We don't have a choice. We get one shot at this. Just one. Sending you in single-handed isn't the way to do it.'

'Nor is giving Lazenby an opportunity to smell a rat.'

'He won't. Not in a week. And that's all Woodrow needs, doesn't he?'

'So he reckons. But he'll be in plaster. On crutches. Maybe in a wheelchair. What happens if something goes wrong and we need to make a run for it?'

'Jesus, I don't know. Why did he have to fall down the stairs in the first place?' She made a despairing gesture with her hands and turned towards the curtained window. 'It's all going wrong. All falling apart. That's the truth.'

Harry had thought the same. But this was not the time to say so. If Donna suspected that going back into hiding was now the only sensible thing to do, it was not a suspicion he could afford to echo. For David's sake – and his – they had to go on. Without delay. 'Have some champagne,' he said, filling her glass. 'You may as well.'

Donna sighed. 'Champagne,' she murmured. 'You crazy fool, Harry.' She walked over, took the glass and sat down on the sofa beside him. 'You really would go through with this, wouldn't you?'

'Yes.'

'But you're not going to.'

'Aren't I?'

'Phone Globescope in the morning and call it off.'

'Are you sure you want me to?'

She half-smiled. 'I'm sure I don't want you to. The thought of ending all this running and hiding. The thought of it being over by this time tomorrow. Can you imagine how attractive that is? But I can't let you do it. I can't let you take the risk.'

'Why not?'

'Because the odds have changed. And you don't owe us enough to gamble on them. In fact, you don't owe us anything at all.'

'David does.'

'And you reckon *you* owe *him*, do you?'

'I reckon I must. Fathers don't come much more neglectful than me.'

'But you didn't know you *were* a father.'

'That's no excuse.'

Donna sipped her champagne and gazed at him thoughtfully. 'Do you have any other children?'

He grinned self-consciously. 'Not that I know of.'

'Ever been married?'

'I *am* married. Technically. But it's not what you'd call a love match.'

'Has there ever been a love match?'

Forced to survey the emotional desert of his middle years, Harry shrugged. 'No. There hasn't.'

'That's what you're looking for, isn't it? All this about debts,

186

duties and paternal obligations is just . . . camouflage. It's love you're after. Human warmth. An end to loneliness.'

'I'm not lonely.' Even as he spoke the words, he was aware of their hollowness. Donna was closer to the mark than he would have thought their brief acquaintance had made possible.

'Yes you are. I know the signs.'

'From personal experience?'

'Maybe. But let's not talk about me.'

'Why not? You're more interesting than I am.'

'Not seen from over here. I'm just a straightforward neurotic-obsessive scientist. Childless feminist and lapsed Lutheran. It's a well-worn groove. Whereas you're . . . unclassifiable. A genuine puzzle. Just too sensitive, too intelligent, too stubborn to be the ambitionless nonentity you claim to be. A few years ago, you were a drunken potman in a Greek taverna. So how come you're capable of even trying to play the white knight with a rusty sword? What have you done with your life in the meantime?'

'It's thrown me a few challenges.'

'And you measured up to them?'

'Most people wouldn't think so.'

'Tell me about it.'

'Why?'

'Because I'm curious. Because you want to know about me and David and I'm willing to trade. Because whatever we decide to do it can't be done till morning and I don't want to spend the whole night arguing about it.'

'Then don't argue. I'll go back to my room. We could both use some sleep, I expect.'

'Is that what you want to do?'

'No.' The one word admitted a shared wish: a relief from solitude; a lowering of the defences. 'I don't want to leave. You know that.'

'Do I? I'm not sure what I know any more. All these months . . . Running and hiding . . . Christ, so long I've almost . . .' She was convulsed by a sudden wrenching sob. Instinctively, Harry reached out to comfort her and she fell against him, her shoulders heaving.

'It's OK,' he said, sliding his arm around her. 'It really is OK.'

'I'm sorry.' She pulled back, dabbing at her damp cheeks with the cuff of her robe. 'This is so . . . so very stupid.'

'No. Just human.'

'I've had to judge every move. Measure every risk. Pretend for

187

Makepeace's sake – even Rawnsley's, I suppose – that I really am in control.' The tears were flowing freely now. And she was making no attempt to staunch or conceal them. 'But I'm not. Am I?'

'You're as much in control as anyone else.'

'And how much is that?'

Harry risked a smile. 'Hardly at all.'

She laughed through her tears. 'You're such a fool, Harry. Such a dear sweet fool. If only David could have known.'

'Maybe he still can.'

'Maybe.' She wiped her eyes with the heel of her hand and smiled back at him. 'Here, now, with you, at this moment . . . I almost believe he will.'

THIRTY-SEVEN

For a second, when Harry woke and glimpsed the first grey fingers
of dawn prising between the curtains, he was uncertain where
he was. Kensal Green? Copenhagen? Dallas? No. Suddenly, as he
turned slightly on the pillow and saw Donna asleep beside him,
realization and recollection collided. He closed his eyes and sighed.
It had seemed such a natural progression at the time, from giving
comfort to sharing pleasure. But what had seemed then simply too
good to be true seemed now altogether too complicated for
comfort. An accusatory voice of middle-aged responsibility whispered in his ear: *'You're old enough to be her father, Harry. What
would your son say if he knew? How would you explain it to him?
How would you justify it?'*

It was clear to him now. She had been, in some curious way,
entrusted to him. And he had abused that trust. She had endured
more than two months of a fugitive existence, guarding her tongue,
stifling her anxieties, bottling up her emotions. It was understandable that the dam should eventually burst. He had merely
been there when it had. And he had been lonely and fearful in
his own right. But he should still have had the sense – the maturity
– to foresee and avert the consequences of surrendering to his
instincts – and allowing Donna to surrender to hers. They were
obvious now. As obvious as they were disturbing.

It had been a night of mental as well as physical intimacy. A
meeting of minds as well as a joining of bodies. Harry had told
Donna more of the truth about himself than he had divulged to

189

any other living soul. And Donna had been similarly revealing about herself.

Born in Seattle thirty years ago, the youngest of three daughters of an aeronautical engineer, Donna, like so many of Globescope's victims, had been an academic prodigy, absorbed into the hothouse world of scientific research just as computers were making that world their own. From the Neurosciences Institute in New York, where she had cut her teeth on the quest to create artificial intelligence, she had gone on to teach at Berkeley. There, during a conference about the definition of consciousness, in the fall of 1990, she had met David Venning. Their immediate and mutual attraction had foundered on Donna's fallacious assumption that David loved his wife. When they had met again, at Globescope two years later, David and Hope were in the throes of a divorce. It soon became apparent that he had recommended Donna to Lazenby as a suitable recruit partly in order to renew their acquaintance, which had swiftly ripened into love. They had set up house together. They had planned to marry. They had talked about children. They had been happy. And then, just when David's divorce made it possible for them to implement their plans, something had gone wrong. A rift over scientific theory had articulated for Donna her suspicion that David thought his intellectual potential necessarily greater than hers, that motherhood and domesticity would win for him the arguments he might otherwise lose. Complicated by the brewing confrontation with Lazenby, their relationship had fallen apart. She had moved into an apartment of her own. They had ceased to understand each other, even though a form of armed truce had enabled them to continue working together.

Then the crisis at Globescope had broken – and made their differences irretrievable. David must have seen his secret deal with Lazenby as a way of proving his point once and for all: proving himself cleverer and subtler than Donna while saving her from herself. The collapse of their relationship and the reasons for it seeped into his fateful decision to betray her along with the others.

And there, for Harry, was the harshest rub of all. He was supposed to be helping his son, not seducing the woman his son had loved. This was worse than desertion. This was dereliction. How, if David recovered, would Harry explain it to him? How would he make it sound other than shameful?

It was his fault and nobody else's. Donna would say otherwise, of course. She would say that what had happened between two frightened lonely people required no explanation and conferred no blame on either party. She would be as gently realistic as Harry suspected she always was. But she would be wrong. Because realism had been overtaken by the tangled reproaches of Harry's past. From a house in Swindon to a hotel room in Washington, across thirty-four years during which he should so often have known better, the thread stretched taut. But it did not break.

Decisiveness came to him then, undisguised as certainty. When Donna woke, she would try to talk him into calling off his appointment with Lazenby. And she was so tenderly reasonable that she might well succeed. Even if she failed, Harry would be left playing the part of her heroic protector, which was the worst possible way of ensuring that what had begun last night did not continue. The answer was clear. He must not be there when she woke. He must not be near her till his business with Lazenby was settled.

Slowly, he slid out of his side of the bed, uttering a silent prayer of thanks for the high quality springing of the Hay-Adams's mattresses. Donna stirred faintly, but did not wake. Looking down at her, sleeping the sleep of peaceful exhaustion, one arm and a smooth-skinned flank exposed by the flung-back sheet, he shook his head in regret.

He dressed swiftly and cautiously, watching her all the time. But her eyelids did not so much as flicker. She slept on, unaware. When he was ready to go, he felt a sudden impulse to kiss her forehead, clear and cool and unfurrowed as it was beneath the ruffled fringe of her hair. But he resisted. This leave-taking was between him and his conscience only.

He moved to the door, eased it open, stepped out into the corridor and closed the door softly behind him. He paused in case there should be a tell-tale noise from within, a puzzled murmur of 'Harry, where are you?' But there was nothing. With a nod of satisfaction, he walked along to his own room and made as surreptitious an entrance as he had just made an exit.

He stripped, showered and shaved hurriedly, then put on the clothes he had kept back for the challenge this day held. Within twenty minutes, he was on his way, as slickly senatorial in appearance as he was queasily apprehensive in mood. All was still quiet in the corridor. Silently, he wished Donna a late untroubled waking. Then he headed for the lift.

Downstairs, businessmen's breakfasts were being wordlessly

consumed in the restaurant overlooking the park. But hungry as he was, and badly in need of coffee, Harry did not linger any longer than it took to extract directions from the concierge to Globescope's offices at 25 Dupont Circle. 'Time spent in reconnaissance,' Flight Sergeant Hughes had never tired of telling him during his RAF career, 'is seldom wasted.' And Harry had plenty of time to put to use.

He headed north along 16th Street, west along K, then northwest up Connecticut Avenue, straight as an arrow towards Dupont Circle, past shops and offices not yet open for business, knots of commuters stamping their feet at bus stops, hooded joggers flexing their muscles against fire hydrants, ragged down-and-outs emerging from their cardboard nightclothes. The city stretched and yawned around him, sniffing dubiously at the dankish day. It paid him no heed. And he returned the compliment.

Dupont Circle lay at the junction of Massachusetts, Connecticut and New Hampshire Avenues. The traffic generated by these three roads surged round a bedraggled cluster of trees and benches, overlooked by an assortment of stylish old Beaux-Arts mansions and sleek new office blocks. The Globescope Building contrived to keep a foot in both camps. Its seven storeys of glass and concrete were clearly modern, but its mansard roof, intricate pedimenting and mock balconies paid architectural homage to the past. For the headquarters of an organization that concerned itself with the future, it seemed curiously ambivalent about which direction it was looking in.

Harry surveyed it from the crowded refuge of Starbucks Coffee Shop, sipping at a cup of scalding espresso and chain-smoking Marlboro cigarettes, which as far as he was concerned the cowboys could keep, while pretending to read a copy of the *Washington Post* somebody had left on his stool. It was a window-seat, giving him an uninterrupted view across a corner of the park of the Globescope Building's main door and the shuttered entrance to its underground car park. Two or three cars had descended into it since he had taken up this position, their drivers waiting on the threshold for the shutter to be raised, and twenty or so workers of indeterminate status had arrived on foot, using security cards of some kind to open the door. Passers-by were clearly not encouraged to wander in off the street. And the office windows were tinted reflectively to prevent idle glimpses of what went on behind them. The building, at first glance stolidly anonymous, revealed under prolonged scrutiny an air of well-mannered secrecy.

It was not what Harry had expected. And this made his visit to Lazenby's office that afternoon seem a more uncertain prospect than ever. How was he going to pull it off? *Exactly* how? With Woodrow riding shotgun, the plan would have been clear. Now there was no plan at all. Just a hopeful bet on Harry's powers of improvisation.

His gloomy train of thought was suddenly derailed by a snatch of conversation between the man and woman who had occupied the pair of stools beside him. They were dressed in off-the-peg executive garb and were sharing a pre-nine-to-five dose of cappuccino and office gossip. Gossip in this case about a colleague who had died recently in mysterious circumstances, supposedly of a brain haemorrhage.

'Do you really buy that?' the woman asked in a guarded undertone.

'Could be true,' the man muttered back, breaking off to bite open his sugar sachet. 'Can't be healthy to be as cerebrally charged up as he always seemed to be.'

'But it makes four out of seven. I trained as an actuary, Roger, and I have to tell you that's way off any mortality scale I ever saw.'

'Seven's an unrepresentative sample. You oughta know that. Anyhow, there are only three actual deaths, so we're still below fifty per cent.'

'Three deaths and one deep coma, if we're going to be picky. It still stinks.'

'But of what?'

She shrugged. 'How should I know?'

'Do you think he could enlighten us?' Roger gestured through the window with his cup as a pale-blue Rolls Royce purred into the circle and tracked slowly round towards Globescope. Reclining in the back seat, with a telephone to his ear, was a broadly built, spiky-haired figure whose eyes virtually matched the paintwork of the car. Recognition hit Harry almost as a physical blow, shocking him into a throat-singeing gulp of coffee. It was the man he had encountered leaving David's hospital room, the man he had mistaken for a doctor till corrected on the point by a nurse. A colleague of David's, she had said. Well, maybe that was what *he* had said. Because *colleague* was so much simpler than *former employer*. Simpler – and less suspicious.

'How does he stay so cool?' the woman pondered.

'Dunno. Wish I had his secret, though.'

'But which secret? There are so many to choose from.'

The Rolls pulled up in front of the Globescope Building. The chauffeur jumped out and opened the rear door for Byron Lazenby to make his presidential exit. He emerged, faintly smiling, onto the pavement, his telephone call neatly concluded, his suit crease-less and expertly cut to flatter his bulky frame, a slim leather briefcase held lightly in one hand. As the chauffeur drove on to the car park, Lazenby took a deep breath of the damp Washington air, then strode into the building, its door yielding before him, either by magic or the agency of some attentive lackey within.

'Do you know why he always does that, Roger? I mean, get out of the car out front instead of taking the elevator from the car park?'

'Likes to make a grand entrance, I guess.'

'Could be. But I reckon he dislikes those dark corners down in the basement.'

'Afraid somebody might be lying in wait for him, you mean?'

'Something like that.'

'Heaven help anyone who was.' Roger sniggered. 'Getting the jump on Byron has to be the original mission impossible.'

194

THIRTY-EIGHT

Harry left Starbucks in a daze and wandered south-west along New Hampshire Avenue. His only aim was to quit Dupont Circle without heading back to the Hay-Adams. No destination – no purpose, let alone a plan – had formed in his mind. The probability that Lazenby would recognize him rendered the whole Page-Muirson pretence unsustainable. And his objective in setting up their meeting unachievable. His fond notions of simultaneously defeating Lazenby, rescuing Donna and saving David were in ruins.

He reached Washington Circle and shambled round it, uncertain which direction to take. A down-and-out clutching a half-bottle of Jamaican rum and smelling strongly of the contents propositioned him for a hand-out, no doubt deceived by his gleaming shoes and cashmere overcoat. Harry gave him a dollar and seriously contemplated asking him for a swig of rum in return.

He chose 23rd Street more or less at random, trudging down through the university precincts and on past dour well-spaced government buildings towards the distant bulk of the Lincoln Memorial. The working day was in full swing now, the administrative machine up and cranking. Back at Globescope, Byron Lazenby was probably sipping a cup of freshly filtered coffee and casting an eagle eye over his diary for the day. A call on this influential politician; a check on that province of his empire. A meeting here; an appointment there. And at four o'clock: Messrs Page and Cornford of Page-Muirson Ltd. One way or the other,

195

it was unavoidable. The only question was: should Harry call it off or simply not show up? Postponement was obviously the sensible course. But the cut and run option was sorely tempting.

He found himself on Constitution Avenue, separated by surging traffic from the greenery of the Mall. A view of the Washington Monument above the trees gave him a fix on where he was in relation to the Hay-Adams. Then, through the bushes on his left, he saw a familiar face gazing benignly at him. It was a statue of Albert Einstein.

Harry walked round to the giant bronze likeness of the physicist, depicted lounging on a low wall in sandalled feet, holding a parchment in his left hand with the final workings of his most famous theory inscribed on it. Harry sat down beside him and smoked a cigarette. He recalled Einstein's photograph on Dr Tilson's study wall, along with his own vague and partial understanding of relativity. Something to do with tiny amounts of matter containing vast amounts of energy. Hence the atom bomb. Something to do with the elasticity of time. Hence clocks moving faster on an orbiting spaceship than on Earth. Or was it slower? He could do with a slowing down of time just now, he really could. He could do with four o'clock never coming. But he did not suppose Einstein could have arranged that even before he was cast in bronze.

Suddenly, time's status as a higher dimension in its own right burst into Harry's thoughts. In some sense he did not comprehend, that was the key to relativity. And it had placed previously undreamt-of power in human hands. But time itself remained invisible and untouchable, just like all those other preposterously numerous higher dimensions the theoreticians had conjured up. What if each of them could unlock just as much power as time? Or more? At last he felt he grasped something of their meaning. And something of the irresistibility of their appeal to David. $E = mc^2 \times n$. The universe, not just the world, made his oyster. And he became . . . scarcely less than a god.

But the god was sleeping. And his father was no nearer finding a spell to wake him. Harry crossed Constitution Avenue and walked out through the scattered yellow leaves of late autumn onto the Mall. A path led him down past the Vietnam Wall, where the tourists and grieving relatives had not yet gathered in force, then up to the circle enclosing the Lincoln Memorial. He climbed the steps and stood at the top, gazing back along the Reflecting Pool towards the Capitol, its dome no more than a smudge of grey against the pastier grey of the sky. A cold wind was blowing and there were spits of rain in the air. The prospect, both real and metaphorical, was bleak.

Once more, Harry confronted the intractable question of what he should do. With Woodrow beside him, he would have advocated going through with it, since Woodrow could have distracted Lazenby whenever recognition seemed to be dawning on him. But there was nobody beside him. And no reason to think Lazenby would fail to place him long before he had had a chance to retrieve the tape. Risk was one thing, certain failure another. He would be doing nobody a favour by embarking on a task he knew to be hopeless.

But what were the alternatives? There were none he could envisage that were not equally hopeless. Every choice was a counsel of despair. He needed a friend who would stand by him in crisis; an ally in a fragile cause; a *deus ex machina*. But squint as far into the Washingtonian distance as he pleased, he could not see one. And nothing in his experience encouraged him to think he ever would. Except the perverse reflection that providence had so seldom smiled on him that the statistics of its workings must some day turn in his favour.

He heard a muffled fragment of commentary drift up from a tourist shuttle bus as it drew to a halt near the foot of the memorial. Most of the few tourists on board emerged to camcord the sights. Several crossed the road and headed up the graded flights of steps towards him. He started down, unwilling to find himself suddenly part of a noisy crowd.

As he reached the broad platform at the foot of the second flight, a couple appeared directly ahead of him who seized his attention almost before he was aware of the reason. One was a slightly built middle-aged woman in a bright red coat, with curly ash-blond hair and a serene smiling face. The other was a man of about Harry's own age, a thick-set figure in raincoat and hat, puffing at a cigarette. He pulled up as soon as he saw Harry, causing the woman to do the same. Harry stopped in his tracks at the same instant and stared astonished into the man's darkly twinkling forever untrustworthy eyes. Beneath them, a mischievously disbelieving grin was slowly forming.

'Harry, old cock?' said Barry Chipchase. 'Is that really you?'

197

THIRTY-NINE

'Remarkable,' trilled the ash-blond woman, beaming at Harry and Barry in turn. 'You mean to say you know each other?'

'We certainly do,' Harry replied, smiling at his lapsed friend and former partner with a meaningful beetling of the brow.

'But I thought you said you'd never been to the United States before, Barry.'

'I haven't.' Chipchase's laugh had a nervous edge Harry felt sure only he could have detected. 'Harry and I go way back. We were in the RAF together.' Strangely he did not go on to mention their ill-fated spell as co-proprietors of Barnchase Motors, Swindon. 'Longer ago than either of us would like to admit.'

'And this is the first time you've met since? That really is extraordinary.'

'Not exactly the *first* time. But I'm forgetting my manners.' He waved a hand between them. 'Harry Barnett; Gloria Bayliss.'

'Pleased to meet you, Harry. What brings you to Washington?'

'Oh, business. And you?'

'Absolutely the reverse. Barry is escorting me on the holiday of a lifetime.' Gloria's capped and crowned smile burst forth once more. 'We're going on from here all the way through the Carolinas and Georgia to Florida, then across to New Orleans and back home in time for Christmas.'

'And where is home?'

'Easingwold, near York. What about you?'

'Oh, wherever I lay my head.'

198

'Another globetrotter, like Barry? You *do* remind me of each other, as a matter of fact. Itchy feet and a sparkle in the eye. Yes, I can see that.'

'Really?' Harry was not sure he cared for being likened to Barry Chipchase in any way.

'Why don't I take a snap of this rare encounter?' Without waiting for their agreement, Gloria ushered the two of them together, then retreated down the steps and began trying out angles through the viewfinder of her camera.

'What the bloody hell *are* you doing in Washington, Harry?' muttered Chipchase through a cheesy grin.

'I told you. Business.'

'Business my left buttock. You don't know the meaning of the word.'

'Don't I? Well, what about bankruptcy, fraud, embezzlement and repossession? Think I might have any experience of them? Think of anyone, can you, who might have *given* me some experience of them?'

'*Take your hat off, Barry,*' shouted Gloria. '*I can't see your face for the brim.*'

'Talking of business, Barry, what line are you in now?'

'Mind your own – whatever it is.'

'Aegean time-share when we last met, wasn't it? Is that how you met Gloria?'

'*Put a comb through your hair, would you, Barry? It's all over the place.*'

'I think we ought to have a word in private. I really do.'

'Not on. Gloria's got a full day's sightseeing planned.'

'Does she know about Barnchase Motors? Or Jackie? Or me – and the lurch you two left me in?'

'*Smile for goodness' sake! Anyone would think you weren't pleased to see one another after all these years.*'

'I have a suspicion she knows nothing about what we could charitably call your chequered career. Nothing accurate, anyway. Want me to enlighten her?'

'Christ almighty, Harry, it's more than twenty years ago. I never took you for the vindictive type.'

'Needs must. Now what do you say to that chat?'

'There's nothing to chat *about*.'

'Let me be the judge of that.'

'*Splendid! Hold there.*' The camera shutter clicked. '*You can relax now.*'

'Well?'

'Can't you see how bloody awkward this is?'

'Yes. Which is why I'm hoping you'll agree.'

'Oh, bloody hell.'

Gloria Bayliss turned out to be as enthusiastic a talker as she was an energetic a sightseer. Undaunted by a chill wind and incipient rainfall, she led Harry and Barry on a thorough inspection of the memorials and vistas of Constitution Gardens, reaching the Washington Monument three-quarters of an hour later with an unguarded description of her nascent relationship with Barry Chipchase threaded into recited extracts from a Michelin guidebook.

She was, it transpired, a widow, wealthy by Harry's inference, comfortably off by her own admission. Her late husband, Fred Bayliss, had been a third-generation undertaker. The family firm, now managed by their son Eric, owned funeral parlours throughout Yorkshire and Humberside, with subsidiary interests in floristry and monumental masonry. She had gone on a Mediterranean cruise back in the spring to avoid spending the first anniversary of Fred's death in the family home. Among her fellow passengers she had met a widower of about her own age, a man of charm, tact and ebullience who had recently taken early retirement from an Anglo-Turkish property company. It did not sound like Barry Chipchase to one who had known him longer and better than most, but a true account of Barry's past would have prompted Gloria to check her credit cards rather than her make-up, so Harry was not unduly surprised. As for the motive behind Barry's proposal of an autumn holiday in the American South, Harry thought he knew what it was. So did Gloria. Fortunately for Barry, though, they did not think the same. 'Two lonely people who've had the good fortune to meet and discover they're compatible,' she had announced as they crossed 17th Street. 'That's us, isn't it, luv?'

'I reckon it is,' Barry had replied, meeting her affectionate glance so directly that Harry had been unable to catch his eye. 'I can't tell you how glad I am I booked that cruise. It's turning out to be one of the best decisions of my life.'

The weather had shrivelled the queue at the Washington Monument to bus-stop proportions. Gloria proposed an ascent to the observation room at the top. Prompted by a faint nudge from

Harry, Barry urged her to go alone while they discussed old times over a cigarette. Blithely unsuspecting and with a parting smile of unalloyed trustfulness, she went. Leaving the partners in a long since bankrupt Swindon garage to prowl the windy lawn at the foot of the monument and pretend an interest in the view south of the Jefferson Memorial.

'You're looking bloody prosperous, Harry. Better than the last time we met.'

'Appearances can be deceptive. Rather like shipboard acquaintances' accounts of themselves.'

'Now hold on a—'

'Jackie's alive and well, legs just as long and lovely as ever. So what's with the widower bit?'

'A minor inaccuracy.'

'And early retirement? Come off it, Barry. I shouldn't think you've ever done anything you *could* retire from. Early *or* late.'

'No call to look down your bloody nose at me. I just didn't want to . . . disappoint her expectations.'

'This is about your expectations, not Gloria's. Marriage to a moneyed widow. A taste of well-heeled Yorkshire squiredom. A Chipchase finger in the undertaker's till. That's what you see looming on your horizon, isn't it?'

'What if it is? What's it to you, anyway?'

'She seems a nice woman.'

'She *is* a nice woman.'

'Pity to let her be snared by a fortune-hunter, then . . . for the lack of a word to the wise.'

'You wouldn't.'

'I'm afraid I would, Barry.'

'But she's having a good time. I'm giving her a good time. Why spoil it?'

'What does son Eric think of you?'

'The same as I think of him. He's been whispering sour somethings about me into her ear all summer. To no bloody effect, I might add.'

'Ah, but I don't expect he has the sort of hard evidence I can bring to bear.'

'I can't believe you'd punch so low. We're both too old to harbour grudges, Harry. And we need to think about our declining years. This is my personal pension plan. You wouldn't try to queer it for me, would you?'

'I would.'

201

'Why, for Christ's sake? Surely not for revenge. Mellow pliable genial old Harry wouldn't stoop to that, would he? Think of all the scrapes I got you out of in the RAF.'

'Only because you got me *into* them in the first place.'

'The favours I did you.'

'I don't remember any.'

'For the love of Mike! Just give me a break will you? Times have been tough lately, even for old Chipchase.'

'For me too.'

'If there's anything I can do . . . You know, a loan or something. I mean, I'm not completely un-bloody-reasonable.'

'There *is* something, as a matter of fact.'

'What?'

'You *could* call it a loan.'

'How much?'

'Oh, about six hours.' Harry glanced at his watch. 'Yes, about six hours of your invaluable time is what I need, Barry. And a bravura piece of play-acting. Should be no problem for a widower who's just taken early retirement from an Anglo-Turkish property company.'

FORTY

Just after a quarter to four that afternoon, a limousine pulled up outside the Watergate Hotel on Virginia Avenue. Two smartly dressed middle-aged men emerged through the revolving door from the hotel lobby and clambered into the car, which then drew slowly away. It eased out into the traffic, hung a gentle left at the lights into New Hampshire Avenue and cruised steadily northeast in the direction of Washington Circle and, beyond that, Dupont Circle.

'What did you tell Gloria?' Harry enquired, as much to ease the tension as to satisfy his curiosity. 'She seemed suspiciously reasonable about being left to her own devices.'

'I told her you wanted me to cast my expert eye over a luxury homes development out at Forestville you're thinking of investing in.'

'*Where?*'

'Forestville, Maryland. I saw an advert for it in the paper this morning. Old Chipchase likes to keep his eyes peeled.'

'Just as well she didn't want to come along.'

'The Freer Gallery held more appeal. She knows I hate footslogging round a load of grimy works of so-called bloody art. Why not just buy postcards of the bloody things? That's what I say.'

'Quite the old married couple, aren't you?'

'Not yet. Nor likely to be if any more skeletons come rattling out of my cupboard. Not that anyone could mistake *you* for a skeleton. Still keen on the beer, I see.'

203

'You don't exactly look like a famine victim yourself, Barry.'

'Financiers don't tend to. And it's a financier you want me to play, isn't it? So don't bloody complain.'

'I'm not about to. But remember you have to sound the part as well as look it.'

'Piece of cake. Pulling the wool over friend Lazenby's eyes doesn't bother me.'

'What does, then?'

'You do, Harry old cock. Dressed up like a Mayfair divorce lawyer with a haircut that looks as if it's been *styled*, for God's sake. And undertaking some hush-hush find-and-remove mission on behalf of . . . well, who exactly?'

'Best you shouldn't know.'

'It's never best for old Chipchase not to know. I think you're out of your depth and quite bloody possibly out of your mind as well. Which would be fine by me, except I seem to be diving into the deep end with you.'

'And all for the love of a good woman.'

'Sneer as much as you like, Harry. But remember our deal. I do the talking. You do the half-inching. And if you're caught in the act I'll make it plain as a puritans' picnic that I haven't the remotest bloody clue what you're up to. Which won't be difficult, since it happens to be the gospel truth.'

'I know. You said.'

'You're too old for whatever kind of game this is. You should have settled down years ago. Got a proper job. Married. Had some children. Taken up lawn mowing and D-I-bloody-Y.'

'I know. You said.'

'You should have settled for second best. You should have folded in your hand and faced up to reality. Like me. That's what I'm doing. Late in the day, but not too late, I'm coming to terms with life. Why not knock this bloody charade on the head? Call it off. Throw in the towel. We could go somewhere and get drunk together. Better use of the time all round.'

'I know. You said.' The limousine entered Dupont Circle and cruised slowly round towards the Globescope Building. 'And you're probably right.'

'Make that definitely.'

'But we're going through with it.'

'I know.' Chipchase sighed. 'You said.'

* * *

Harry had to announce their names and business through an entry-phone before the imposing doors of the Globescope Building hummed open. The foyer was an equally imposing expanse of reflective marble, presided over by a receptionist and two security officers who needed only a change of costume to pass as Cleopatra and her bodyguards.

They were required to sign a register and clip colour-coded badges to their lapels, then directed to take the middle elevator of three to the top floor, where they would be met. Seemingly at the last moment, one of the security men asked Harry to open his briefcase. The contents – pocket calculator, investment magazine and Page-Muirson paperwork thoughtfully prepared by Make-peace Steiner – excited no interest. They were invited to proceed.

'What happens if they search you on the way out?' muttered Chipchase as the elevator started on its journey.

'Search me.'

'Ha-bloody-ha. We're no match for them. You do realize that, don't you?'

'What became of your famous confidence, Barry?'

'I left it in my other suit.'

'Pity.' The elevator eased silkily to a stop and the floor indicator clicked. 'Too late to go back for it now, I'm afraid.' Then the doors slid open.

A tall curvily built middle-aged woman with grey hair, high cheekbones and eyes Harry felt he could take a warm bath in was waiting to greet them. 'Hi, I'm Ann Mather. Mr Page? Mr Cornford?'

'That's right.'

'Would you care to follow me? Mr Lazenby can see you right away.'

Following Ann Mather would ordinarily have been a pleasant occupation in itself, but Harry felt obliged to concentrate on their surroundings. Wide pale-carpeted spaces communicated in a series of leisurely right-angles past pastel-doored offices, some glass-panelled to reveal gadget-rich seminar rooms, others revealing nothing beyond an informally styled name on the door. Buzz somebody. Kitty somebody else. Names – but nothing else.

They reached an area Ann Mather evidently shared with another secretary and paused before a set of double doors. Ann went ahead to announce them, then ushered them into Byron E. Lazenby's concept of a presidential space.

Space there predictably was in abundance, plus a considerable

205

panorama of north-west Washington courtesy of raked windows set in the mansard roof. These plus a significant acreage of oak desktop and tabling gave the room something of the feel of a Nelsonian captain's cabin. But the grey metropolitan light, the graph-spattered world map covering most of one wall and above all the presence of Byron Lazenby imposed their own contemporary order.

'Come in,' he boomed, striding forward to meet them. 'Glad you could make it.' His low but powerful tone, his suppressed but palpable energy, were exactly as Harry had unconsciously expected. He was a man accustomed to having his way and seeing it clear before him; a man whose surest prediction would always be his own success; a man not to be crossed.

'Norman Page,' Harry announced, steeling himself to meet Lazenby's gaze and shake the proffered hand firmly. He detected no glimmer of recognition. Perhaps, he thought, he could rely on somebody so immensely self-confident to be immensely unobservant as well. 'And my colleague, Bill Cornford.'

'Pleasure,' declared Chipchase, stepping between them as it had been agreed he would.

'You sound more than a little British to me, Mr Cornford. I thought—'

'I was in business over here before Norman proposed we work together. He calls me his American partner, but we're both born and bred Brits.'

'Right. And what business was that?'

'Mobile phones.' Harry's heart lurched at this sudden invention. What in the wide world did Barry know about mobile telephones? More than Harry, it was devoutly to be hoped. 'I got in at the ground floor. And out before the whizz-kids started piling into the elevator.'

Lazenby laughed, too loudly for comfort. 'Maybe you don't need my services if you can spot a hot prospect so unerringly.'

'Oh, it was mostly luck. You need a healthy dose of judgement as well to stay ahead.'

'Which is where I come in, right?'

'Exactly.'

'Great. Well, I'll have my projects manager, Cherie Liebermann, join us later to run over the specifics of what we can offer. To start, I thought I'd familiarize you with Globescope's founding concepts. Set the scene, so to speak.'

'Sounds ideal,' Harry woodenly enthused.

206

'Why don't you gentlemen take a seat? I'll have Ann fix us some tea. Guess that might appeal to you, right?'

'Fine.' Harry turned in the direction of Lazenby's extended hand, moving ahead of Chipchase to claim the armchair nearest the windows, the '*huge and squashy*' armchair Hammelgaard had recounted concealing the tape in. '*Soft cream leather constructions*,' according to Makepeace Steiner. '*Over-sized and none too comfortable*.' Harry had caught a sort of presumptive glimpse of them on entering the room while his mind was still fixed on verbal ploys and distractive techniques. Now all he had to do was—

They were different. Large and obviously expensive, but not the same. Classically styled and upholstered in a delicately hued gold and grey fabric, they were patently not the chairs Harry had expected to see, planned to see, above all *needed* to see. The other ones had gone, God and Byron Lazenby alone knew where. They had been removed – along with anything and everything hidden within them.

Harry stopped in his tracks and gaped at the farcical reality before him. His face might well have lost most of its colour. His jaw could easily have dropped. He was too dismayed to sense his own reaction. It might have ended with a bang or a whimper. But instead fate had held back a sour and scornful laugh for this moment when he least needed to hear it.

'Are you OK?' Lazenby asked. 'You sure don't look it.'

FORTY-ONE

Forty minutes had passed. Harry could only hope he had made some faintly coherent contributions to the discussion, though he could remember virtually nothing of it. He had drunk some tea without tasting it, introduced himself to Cherie Liebermann without absorbing the slightest impression of her character or appearance beyond the extreme brightness of her lipstick and had listened to every word uttered in the room without retaining one of them in his memory.

Gripped by a paralysis of thought as well as action, he had imagined David and Torben sitting there, smiling at Byron Lazenby every bit as falsely as he and Barry. He had seen, as distinctly as the glossy brochures placed in his lap, David's hospital room, its motionless occupant wired and monitored in the bed; and the bridge in Copenhagen where Torben had died, the water seeming to lap at its piers loudly enough to blot out the conversation around him.

Always Lazenby seemed to be either smiling or laughing outright, at some joke of Barry's or some drollery of his own. It was as if he knew the absurdity of Harry's plight and was savouring it. Helpless and squirming like a worm on a hook, Harry sat where he was, waiting for his futile pretence to run its course. Sustained by Cherie Liebermann's eager resumé of Globescope's forecasting techniques and prolonged by Barry's energetic impersonation of a self-satisfied big spender, it was brought finally to a close by Lazenby's grinning conclusion: 'I think I can safely say, gentlemen, that Globescope could put you several steps ahead of the opposition in your field. It's up to you to decide whether you want to take advantage of our services. They're not inexpensive, but I hope we've persuaded you of their unique value to the truly far-sighted players in the game.'

Whether he genuinely thought that was what his two guests were hardly mattered. Nor did it matter whether his Olympian assertions of where the world was going were any better founded than Cherie Liebermann's number-crunching econometrical projections. Page-Muirson Ltd was about to vanish into the computerized void it had been summoned up from. And Harry's half-chance of saving his son was about to go the same way.

'We'll get back to you very shortly,' Barry declared as they rose to leave. 'Norman and I just need to talk this through.'

'Of course,' said Lazenby. 'Decisions like this shouldn't be rushed. Don't hesitate to contact us if you need any supplementary information before making your minds up.'

'Thanks,' mumbled Harry as he shook Lazenby's hand. 'Very interesting.'

'Hope it was. Cherie, would you show our guests to the elevator?'

'Surely. This way, gentlemen.'

They moved out into the secretarial ante-room, the double doors swinging shut behind them. Ann Mather said something to Cherie which Harry did not catch. Cherie stepped across for a word with her, giving Chipchase the opportunity to wink at Harry and whisper: 'Got it?' But all Harry could do was shake his head numbly in reply.

'Sorry about that,' said Cherie, rejoining them. She smiled at Harry, then a tinge of puzzlement at his blank expression crossed her intent bespectacled features. Harry seemed to see her clearly for the first time. A lively and perceptive individual holding her vivacity in check, she had probably already written him off as a dull-witted nonentity who did not matter to her beyond the fee he might bring in. But his insignificance was also his opportunity. And it was the last one he was going to get. The realization was like a douche of cold water. He blinked and stepped back. 'Mr Page?'

'Sorry. Yes?'

'Shall we go?'

'Of course.' They began to move, Harry slowing the pace as much as he dared. 'Kind of you to spare us . . . so much of your time, Miss Liebermann.'

209

'My pleasure.'

'Ours, I assure you. Mr Lazenby . . . has a lovely office, doesn't he?'

'It is kinda grand, isn't it?'

'I particularly liked the chairs we sat in.' He sensed a momentary falter in Chipchase's stride beside him. 'Elegant as well as . . . comfortable.'

'Glad you liked them.'

'They seemed pretty new.'

'I believe they are.'

'And expensive.'

'Quality doesn't come cheap.'

'Were their predecessors . . . the same style?'

'No. Cream leather, as I recall. Kinda lower slung. More contemporary. But why—'

'He replaces costly items of furniture quite frequently, does he?'

'Pardon me?'

'I mean, what use have the old chairs been put to?'

'That seems a strange question, Mr Page.' Cherie's puzzlement was deepening. And the elevator was already in sight.

'Humour me, Miss Liebermann. Please.' He would have fallen at her feet if necessary. But it was vital she should not know just how desperate he was to extract an answer to his question.

'Since you ask, I believe the previous suite was moved to Luke Brownlow's office. Luke's our vice-president in charge of recruitment. But why do you—'

'Good housekeeping's the point. I appreciate thrift as much as hospitality. Economy as well as economics. I'm reassured to learn Globescope doesn't run on throwaway principles. That's important, believe me.'

'I suppose it is.' She smiled hesitantly. 'Glad it was the right answer.'

'Me too.' Cherie called the elevator, which arrived almost instantly. Chipchase stepped inside and Harry followed, turning to avoid his gaze. 'Thanks again, Miss Liebermann. We'll be in touch.' The elevator doors closed and their descent began.

'Did that bloody carry-on mean what I thought it meant, Harry?' Chipchase growled.

''Fraid so.'

'So that's why you acted like a zombie – leaving me to prattle on nineteen to the bloody dozen about the state of the Mexican bond market.'

'You probably enjoyed it.' Harry reached past Chipchase to the controls and stopped the elevator at the fourth floor, keeping his finger on the DOORS CLOSED button. 'And the fun isn't over yet.'

'You're planning to pay Luke Brownlow a call?'

'What do you think?'

'I think you're bloody mad.'

'Then stay in the lift.' Harry pressed the button for the top floor and stepped back. 'But hold it for me, would you? I might need to leave in a hurry.'

'You don't know where his office is.'

'Vice-president, she said.' The elevator stopped. The doors opened. There was no sign of Cherie Liebermann or, for the moment, anyone else. 'Somewhere up here, don't you reckon?'

Chipchase groaned. 'Matter of fact, I saw the name on one of the doors when we arrived. You'd better follow me.'

He led the way at an anxious lope that was just the businesslike side of a bolt. A serious young fellow who looked as if he could be Superman in his spare time passed them, tut-tutting over a computer print-out. Then, after one more turn of the hall, they were at Luke Brownlow's door.

Harry took a deep breath, knocked once and went straight in, praying that Brownlow had been called away, leaving the coast clear for just as long as it would take.

But it was not clear. Brownlow, a lean balding figure in a black suit and jazzy tie, looked up in surprise, as did his guests, a pair of well-groomed young Globescopers seated in the large cream leather armchairs facing his desk.

Brownlow frowned. 'Can I help you?'

'Sorry. Wrong room.' Harry recoiled into the corridor, slamming the door behind him. He hurried away, grimacing forlornly at Chipchase. 'There are people sitting in the damn things,' he whispered.

'Well, they are chairs.'

'Thanks for that helpful observation.'

'What now?'

'I don't know. We'll draw attention to ourselves if we hang around much longer. But if we just give up and leave . . .'

'You won't get a second chance.'

'Not a hope.'

'Then you'd better shift their arses from those chairs, hadn't you?'

'How do you suggest I do that?'

211

'Lateral thinking.' Chipchase pulled up and grinned at Harry. 'The answer's right behind you.'

Harry turned slowly round and found himself looking at a bright-red metal lever fixed to a junction-box mounted on the wall. Stencilled on the lever were the words PULL DOWN IN CASE OF FIRE.

'I should get on with it if I were you,' said Chipchase. 'You don't want the bloody fire to get out of control, do you?'

FORTY-TWO

The managing director of Page-Muirson Ltd and his senior partner stood in the lift car, hands poised close to the controls in case any member of the Globescope staff forgot the injunction against using elevators during a fire. Predictably, however, they had been well trained in evacuation procedure, as the audible march of feet towards the stairs demonstrated. Soon, the sound of their good-humoured exchanges – *'Is this a drill or what?'*; *'One hell of a time for it to happen'* – faded away. The top floor – and no doubt the ones below it – fell silent save for the tireless wail of the alarm. The managing director of Page-Muirson Ltd and his senior partner were left in sole occupation.

Harry opened the doors and stepped gingerly out into the hall. It looked and more importantly *felt* deserted. Signalling for Chipchase to follow, he started at a jog towards Brownlow's office, arriving a few breathless moments later. It was empty, the desk disordered. The low fat leather armchairs still bore the crinkled imprints of recent use. But their use had been abruptly suspended.

Harry dropped his briefcase, flung the cushions off the nearer of the two chairs and forced his hand into the narrow gap between the seat and the base of one of the arms. A void of sorts revealed itself within the arm. But the gap was so narrow that exploring it was both awkward and time-consuming. The sudden and ludicrous fear that he might end up with his hand trapped did little for his thoroughness. And nothing more substantial than dust and what felt like biscuit crumbs met his questing fingers.

213

'Trouble,' said Chipchase from behind him. But Harry could not stop to ask what trouble there was. As he moved to explore the other arm, he heard Chipchase leave the room. Then his voice carried from further down the hall. 'Perhaps you can help me, squire.'

'Can't you hear the alarm, sir?' came another voice. 'The idea is to leave the building.' A security officer, Harry assumed. Deputed to check the evacuation was complete. Or to find the source of the alarm. Either way, Harry's activities were going to look just about as suspicious to him as they possibly could.

'I'm a visitor, actually. A colleague and I had just left a meeting with Mr Lazenby when this happened.'

'Page and Cornford?'

'That's us. I'm Cornford.'

'Yeh, you're on my list. Where's Page?'

'That's just it. He went to find the men's room. Then the alarm went off. I didn't like to leave without him. But I'm not sure where—'

'*I'll* check the men's room, sir. *After* I've seen you safely to the emergency staircase.' There was an exasperated tone to his voice. 'Follow me, would you?'

Harry reckoned he had a few minutes at least. If he kept calm, it was enough. If there was anything to find, he should find it. Abandoning the first chair, he moved on to the second, tossing the cushions aside and shoving his hand into the gap so fiercely that he had to stifle a cry of pain as a rigid framing bar came off better in a contest with his knuckles.

'This is bloody ridiculous,' he complained under his breath. 'I've been involved in some fiascos in my time, but this has to be—'

A small cool solid metal object, about the size and shape of a matchbox, just as Hammelgaard had promised. There it was, exactly where it had been all these weeks, safe, secure and waiting. Harry's fingertips burned at the touch of it. And all the fear and mounting panic left him. Even the alarm seemed to stop ringing in his ears. Cocooned in the silence of his own concentration, he gripped it firmly in his fingers and pulled his hand and forearm free, oblivious now to the scraping of the bar over his knuckles. It was just a tiny black box, but when he held it up and saw the miniature spool of tape visible through a transparent plastic window at its centre, he smiled broadly.

'Bugger me,' was the only thing he seemed capable of saying by way of celebration. Then urgency resumed its grip. He dropped

214

the recorder into his pocket, hoisted the cushions back onto the chairs, grabbed his briefcase, strode out into the hall and started towards the lift.

Rounding the first corner, he cannoned straight into the security officer and rebounded like a rubber ball hitting a tree. 'Mr Page?' the man flintily enquired.

'Er . . . yes. I'm looking for . . .'

'Mr Cornford?'

'That's right. How did—'

'Hold on one moment, would you, sir?' He raised a hand to the walkie-talkie clipped to his lapel and spoke into it. 'I've located the other one, Mr Fredericks . . . Yuh . . . OK. I'll wait for you here.'

'Shouldn't we, er, be leaving?'

'There's no fire, sir. It was a false alarm.' As if on cue, the bell was cut off in mid-wail. 'Triggered from this floor. Kinda co-incidental, wouldn't you say?'

'In what way?'

'Well, this is also the floor I found you and Mr Cornford wandering around . . . after everyone else had gone.'

'I lost my way. Simple as that.'

'Same as Mr Cornford?'

'Exactly.'

'In that case, you won't mind co-operating in a straightforward security precaution.'

'What sort of precaution?'

'We have to be on our guard against theft; industrial espionage; that kinda thing.'

'What's that got to do with me?'

'Nothing, I expect, sir. As searching you will no doubt confirm.'

FORTY-THREE

They were back in Lazenby's office. Harry, simulating affronted dignity in his refusal to submit himself to a search. Barry, wearing the look of choirboy innocence he reserved for such occasions. Cherie Liebermann, as perplexed by their behaviour as she seemed irritated by having to spend time analysing it. And Lazenby himself, a baffled frown lending an ugly cast to his face. Plus the security officer who had waylaid Harry; and Fredericks, his boss, a beady-eyed petty tyrant exhibiting a brewing suspicion that something was in danger of eluding him.

'You have to see this from our point of view, Norman,' said Lazenby. 'Our clients – of whom I hope you'll become one – rely on the absolute confidentiality of our work here. Security precautions are essential to that. And they have to be observed without fear or favour.'

'I came here in good faith,' Harry blustered. 'I don't care to have that called into question.'

'It's not being. But the circumstances under which you were found on the premises *after* their evacuation require explanation.'

'I have explained them.'

'Not to our satisfaction. Cherie tells me you interrogated her about my taste in office furniture.'

'To find out whether your fee levels – high by your own admission – are subsidizing corporate extravagance. And it was much less of an interrogation than this is.'

216

'But why did you return to this floor after she'd escorted you to the elevator?'

'To verify what she'd told me. Bill bet me it was a cover story.'

'A chair-cover story,' put in Chipchase with a frail grin. But nobody laughed.

'As soon as I saw the chairs she'd described in Luke Brownlow's office, I was satisfied.'

'Yet you still didn't leave.'

'I happen to have a slight prostate condition. Use of your men's room counts as suspicious behaviour, does it?'

'If Mr Page won't consent to being searched,' said Fredericks, as unmoved by Harry's explanation as he had clearly been determined to be, 'I recommend we call the police and ask them to take him and Mr Cornford downtown for questioning. I don't see there's any other way to settle the issue. The alarm was manually tripped on a lever-switch halfway between Mr Brownlow's office and the elevator. And that's exactly where they were at the time.'

'Any member of your staff could have done it,' protested Harry.

'Why should they?' countered Lazenby.

'A prank. A dare. Perhaps they were just bored and wanted a break.'

'I do not employ people who indulge in practical jokes, Norman. And those I do employ are never bored.'

'I'll have to take your word for that. Just as you'll have to take mine that I didn't set off the alarm. Why in heaven's name should I?'

'I don't know.' Lazenby glanced at Fredericks. 'What does Luke say?'

'Nothing taken or disturbed. As far as he can tell.'

'Weird.' Lazenby looked back at Harry, his gaze narrowing, his brow furrowing. 'One other thing. Why do I get this feeling we've met before, Norman? Why is that, huh?'

'As far as I know, we never have.'

'Norman has that kind of face,' contributed Chipchase. 'He tends to remind people of their favourite uncle.'

'I don't have an uncle,' snapped Lazenby.

'No? Well, you won't have many clients either if you go on treating them like this. I'm sure I speak for both of us when I say we're prepared to write this off as an unfortunate misunderstanding – provided it goes no further. If it *does* go further . . .'

'Yuh? What then, Bill?'

Barry eyed Lazenby nonchalantly. 'A lawsuit for harassment, detention and assault. Whatever our attorney recommends. He's like you, Byron. Expensive *and* effective. Gives up about as easily as an Israeli Nazi-hunter. Know what I mean?'

'Then there's the publicity,' contributed Harry, warming to Barry's theme. 'An old school chum of mine writes for the *Financial Times*. He'd be happy to describe our experiences. Coming on top of all that no doubt groundless speculation about the death rate among your former employees, it might put a significant dent in your share price.'

Lazenby scowled. 'You didn't mention you knew about that.'

'Because I didn't think it was relevant.'

'It isn't. The situation we have here is—'

'Oh, for God's sake!' With a forcefulness that clearly surprised Chipchase, Harry slammed his briefcase onto Lazenby's desk and flung it open. 'Anything there I didn't come in with?' Then he unloaded his pockets onto the desk as well: wallet; passport; cigarettes; matches; pen; comb; diary; handkerchief; a bunch of keys; some loose change. 'Or there?' Next he pulled out the lining of his pockets one by one. 'Or here?' He glared at Lazenby, then Fredericks, then back at Lazenby. 'Well?'

Lazenby gave him a long glowering look, weighing his baffled exasperation against the possibility that these two fast-talking Englishmen represented a genuine threat. One he ought logically to defuse at this low ebb of his public reputation. In the end, logic won. 'Like you say, gentlemen. An unfortunate misunderstanding. Let's leave it at that, shall we?'

'But sir—' protested Fredericks.

'*Let's leave it.*' Lazenby turned to Cherie Liebermann. 'Show them out, would you, Cherie?' He allowed himself a weary smile. 'Again.'

'I'm glad this has been amicably resolved,' said Harry, gathering up his possessions from the desk. 'Really I am.' He gave Lazenby a conciliatory smile that was secretly self-congratulatory. For he was holding a Marlboro cigarette pack in his hand at the time. And he could feel through the cardboard something heavier and harder and squarer than the few cigarettes that remained.

FORTY-FOUR

'Tell me, Harry old cock, why do I seem to spend my entire bloody life saying goodbye to you for what I *think* is going to be the last time?' There was a trace almost of affection in Chipchase's protest, delivered on the concourse of Union Station half an hour after their hasty departure from Globescope. A homeward flood of commuters was in spate around them, bathing them in reassuring anonymity. They had bolted down the escalator into Dupont Circle Metro station largely on instinct, representing as it did the handiest and swiftest means of quitting the area. Now, five stops along the Red Line, sheltering by a pillar in an eddy of the workaday tide, they paused to recover their nerves as well as their breath. 'And another thing. What was that about Globescope staff dropping like bloody flies? You never mentioned that to me.'

'I didn't want to worry you,' Harry replied with a smile.

'Didn't want me to twig how risky the whole barking bloody mad escapade was, you mean.'

'Well, that too, I suppose.'

'What's on the tape, Harry?'

'I don't know.'

'Liar.'

'Look, Barry, you're better off not knowing, believe me. Go back to your hotel, wine and dine Gloria, then get on with your holiday. That's all you have to do. In fact, I thought it was all you *wanted* to do.'

'Yeh, well . . .' Chipchase sighed. 'It's not exactly life on the

219

edge, is it? Easingwold's hardly a thrill a bloody minute, take my word for it.'

'What's the matter? Not sure you want to settle down after all?'

'Well, it was something, wasn't it? What we did back there. Quite something. Just like old times. Remember those triumphs of private enterprise we pulled off at RAF Stafford? The same bloody technique, Harry. You and me. The old firm. We should never have split up.'

'Your decision, as I recall.'

'No, no. It was a combination of . . . unfavourable circumstances . . . and Jackie's evil little mind. You know how persuasive she can be. When you boil it down, it wasn't really any of my doing.'

Harry could not help himself. He laughed so suddenly and uproariously that he had to bend over, tears starting into his eyes.

'What the bloody hell's the matter?'

'Nothing, Barry . . . Nothing at all.' He straightened up and did his best to look serious. His success was little short of miraculous, given the expression of trampled sincerity on Chipchase's face. 'Let's go and find a cab. Before I start remembering all the grudges I should still be bearing.'

'Where are we going?'

'*You're* going to the Watergate Hotel. Via the best hi-fi store in town. Which is where *I'll* be getting out. And don't worry. This probably is the last time you'll be saying goodbye to me. Unless you invite me to the wedding, of course.' Chipchase's eyes widened in horror. 'Just joking, Barry. Just joking.'

For different reasons, Harry was equally sorry they had come to a parting of the ways. When he clambered out of their taxi at G Street and 13th, it was with a queasy awareness that he was relinquishing the lucky charm of Chipchase's unquenchable self-confidence. Without his Smart Alec sarcasms, the immediate future looked altogether more hostile and uncertain. And Harry would have to face it alone. Solitude was no stranger to him. But nor was it any kind of friend.

Capital Sound & Vision lived up to the cab driver's recommendation as a repository of all things audio-technological. A dedicated young assistant identified the kind of headphones Harry would need and assured him they were a bargain at nineteen dollars and ninety-five cents. 'This is state of the art, sir. Where the competition's still not at.' He was equally enthusiastic in explaining how to operate the recorder and Harry left with a

220

reasonable idea of which buttons to press, if only he could find something small enough to press them with. His fingers clearly would not do. But the tip of his pen just might.

Seated at a café table in the converted shell of the Old Post Office on Pennsylvania Avenue, surrounded by chattering groups of shoppers and office workers, Harry rewound the tape to near the beginning, then donned the earphones, tapped the play button and waited to hear his son's voice for the first time.

It was actually Lazenby's voice he first heard, in all its syrupy familiarity, so distinct and authentic that he could have been sitting at the same table. There was no static on the recording, only an eerie pin-sharp clarity that transcended normal hearing.

'*—serves no purpose. Well? I'm waiting. And I won't wait much longer. I run to a tight schedule, as you two ought to know. Why don't we come to the point? Sybil's dead and buried. And there's no way she's going to be exhumed. Why can't you and your friends just accept that?*'

'*We do,*' said Hammelgaard.

'*But they don't.*' It was David. Disembodied but somehow instantly recognizable as the voice of the silent figure in the hospital bed, he spoke at last. But he did not speak to Harry. '*We've come to warn you, Byron. They mean to dig her up. And make her dance to their tune.*' This was it, then. The tonguetip of treachery. The recorded moment of imminent betrayal.

'*The hell they do.*'

'*There's nothing you can do to stop them. It'll take time to reassemble the material, of course. But it can be done.*'

'*Not if they want to hold on to their jobs. I have a lot of friends in the academic world. I can make it real tough for them.*'

'*Not tough enough, Byron. These are dedicated people. They mean to go through with it.*'

'*Why are you telling me this, David?*' Lazenby's tone grew suddenly emollient. '*What's in it for you?*'

'*We could sabotage their efforts. Dispute their findings. Deny you tried to gag them.*'

'*Why would you do that?*'

'*To help you out of a hole.*'

'*A very deep hole,*' put in Hammelgaard. '*Seeking to tamper with genuine predictive endeavour is a serious charge for somebody in your position to answer. If it stuck, it could . . .*'

'*Ruin me?*'

221

'*Maybe.*'

'*So you need our help, Byron,*' said David. '*Don't you?*'

'*Seems I might.*'

'*And in return . . .*'

'*Oh, you do want something in return, do you?*'

'*Naturally. What we're proposing is a business transaction. And in business everything has to be paid for.*'

'*Yuh. It does.*'

'*The only difficulty is agreeing a price.*'

'*What did you have in mind?*'

'*Start-up money for a pet project of ours. I've told you about it before. HYDRA.*'

'*Why did I know you were going to say that?*'

'*Because I've asked you to help fund it on several occasions. And you've never seen any advantage in becoming involved. Only now—*'

'*You've supplied the advantage.*'

'*That's right.*'

'*Well, I have to admire your gall, David. I surely do. How much are you hoping to squeeze out of me?*'

'*Significantly less than your commercial survival would justify.*'

'*That's what we're discussing,*' said Hammelgaard. '*Not so much the planet's future – as yours.*'

'*Bull. Your friends can't prove a thing. I've had all trace of Project Sybil erased. As far as Globescope's concerned, it never was. Which makes your threat as hollow as a Presidential policy statement.*'

But David was undaunted. '*They're respected specialists in their own fields, Byron. They'll be believed, evidence or no evidence. The rumour mill will start grinding. The word will go out. Your client-list will start to shrink.*'

Hammelgaard joined in. '*Then the clients who commissioned Sybil in the first place will realize they've been taken for a ride. Once that happens . . .*'

'*You've thought this out very cleverly, gentlemen,*' said Lazenby. He paused, then added: '*You realize what you're doing amounts to blackmail?*'

'*Report us to the police, then,*' David replied. '*See how far that gets you.*'

'*It could get you two as far as a prison cell.*'

'*Unlikely.*'

'*And even if it did,*' reasoned Hammelgaard, '*it wouldn't solve your problem. You'd still have the others to deal with.*'

'I suggest you deal with us,' said David. 'We're so much more reasonable.'

Several seconds of silence followed, during which Harry found it easy to imagine the exchange of eloquent glances. Then Lazenby said: 'How much do you want?'

'Three million dollars.'

'Jesus! You have a—'

'And your help in seeking other sponsors.'

'You're crazy.'

'No. Sane, sober and entirely serious. You can afford it.'

'I can afford many things. That doesn't mean I buy them.'

'Look on this as one of life's necessities.'

'How do I know you two aren't just shooting a line?'

'Easy. Wait until the others are ready to publish their allegations in the scientific press. We'll give you prior notice. That's when you pay up – and we deliver.'

'And when's that likely to be?'

'Early next year. Until then, all we need is a little pump-priming money. Let's call it a deposit. What do you say to ten per cent?'

There was another lengthy pause. At the end of it, Lazenby said: 'What I say, gentlemen, is that you don't appear to leave me much choice.'

Harry switched the machine off, removed the earphones and sat back in his chair. He had heard enough. It was there, if you were looking for it. The seed of Lazenby's intentions. The space between his words in which their true meaning was revealed. He had been threatened. And he had chosen to neutralize the threat.

Harry slipped the recorder into his pocket. Then he headed for the nearest telephone, called the Hay-Adams Hotel and asked to be put through to Ms Cornford. He half-expected Donna to have left. It would have been a sensible precaution. But no. She was where he had left her that morning.

'It's me, Donna.'

'Thank God.' Then her relief turned to anger: 'Have you any idea what kind of a day I've had to endure? What the hell did you mean by—'

'There's no time for this. I have the tape. And I've played it. I think it'll do the job.'

'How did—'

'Just listen! The less said now the better. Did you hire a car as planned?'

223

He sensed the effort with which she limited her reply to the needs of the moment. 'Yes.'

'How soon can you pick me up?'

'Ten minutes.'

'All right. Ten minutes. Corner of Constitution and Twelfth, eastbound side. I'll be waiting.' And with that, before she could say another word, he put the telephone down.

FORTY-FIVE

Movement imposed security – and a distance between them neither seemed sure they wanted to cross. Donna drove slowly east as far as the Supreme Court, then turned west along the southern side of the Mall as she listened to the tape. She must have listened to it two or three times, while Harry watched her from the passenger seat and tried to read her reaction from her face. Sorrow at the recorded proof of her onetime lover's treachery. Elation at the escape from her fugitive existence it promised to deliver. Gratitude for Harry's recovery of it. She might have felt them all. But her expression revealed nothing.

Eventually, out on a dark and empty stretch of road near the Jefferson Memorial, she pulled in long enough to stop the tape, remove the earphones and say, still without looking at Harry: 'This will destroy Lazenby. I doubt it's proof in the legal sense. But it's good enough.'

'You don't seem very pleased.'

'I don't feel very pleased. I loved David. And Torben was a good friend. Their reputations won't look much better than Lazenby's when this is over.'

'That can't be helped.'

'We're talking about your son, Harry. Doesn't it matter to you what people think of him?'

'Not as much as what he thinks of me.'

'There you go with that stubborn present tense again. As if I can summon up a miracle for you.'

225

'Last night you seemed to believe you could.'

'I wondered whether you'd mention last night – or simply pretend it never happened. Walking out on me was a kind of denial, wasn't it?'

'Donna, I . . .'

'Don't say you're sorry. Please don't say that.'

'I left without waking you so you wouldn't have the chance to stop me keeping my appointment with Lazenby. No other reason.'

'You felt guilty, Harry. That's the truth. And that makes me feel guilty too. Which I don't like. For somebody old enough to be my father, you don't handle your emotions with much maturity.' She sighed. 'But you do work miracles, it seems. Even if the one you really want's beyond you. How did you pull it off?'

'It was easy.' Though not as easy as he was about to make it sound. He had already decided Donna did not need to know – or worry – about Barry's involvement in the affair. 'I told Lazenby my partner was ill. During our meeting, he left the room for a few minutes. That's when I retrieved the tape. It was where Torben said it would be. No problem.'

'No problem? Come on. Lazenby would never leave a stranger alone in his office. It can't have been that simple.'

'He must be losing his touch. There's the tape to prove it.'

'Yuh.' She tapped the cassette against the rim of the steering-wheel. 'Reel-to-reel salvation. And you just hand it to me. Like shelling a pea.'

'It worked. Sometimes things do.'

'And now you're going to say we need to move fast. That sitting here is just a waste of time.'

'Well, we agreed—'

'Don't tell me what we agreed. I remember. And you're right. On just about every count. I would have tried to talk you out of it this morning. I happen to care about you. That's why I haven't already driven off into the night with the tape in my purse. Because I think you're trying to get rid of me. And the reason has to be you're afraid Lazenby will come after you. So you want me out of the way.'

'Of course I do. But only for safety's sake. Lazenby suspects nothing.'

'I don't know you well enough to tell if you're lying.'

'I'm not lying. Take the tape and go. I'll book us both out of the hotel tomorrow. Then I'll catch a train to New York, call on Woodrow to set his mind at rest, and fly back to England. I'll tell

Iris you're going to contact Hector Sandoval and do your level best to persuade him to consider David's case. Fair enough?'

'Oh, it's fair. And I'll do it. Just as soon as there's so much adverse publicity slewing around Lazenby that coming after us no longer makes sense. But—'

'How long?'

'A few weeks, I guess. Maybe less. The newspapers will bite our hands off for the story. But you can come back with me to Dallas and call Iris from there. Doesn't it make sense to stick together now we've come this far?'

'It's not what we planned to do. And the plan's worked. Let's not abandon it now.'

'This isn't about the plan, Harry. There's something you're holding back.'

'There's nothing.'

'What is it?'

'You ought to be on your way, Donna.' He looked at her, the shadows veiling her mouth and eyes, and steeled himself to go on lying as long as he needed to. He did not fear Lazenby. Not as much, anyway, as he feared the thicket of conflicting emotions he and Donna would enter if they stayed together. To go now was best. For them *and* David. But it hardly felt like it. 'I ought to be on my way too.'

'I haven't even thanked you, have I?'

'Make good use of the tape. And don't take no for an answer from Sandoval. That's the only thanks I need.' He opened his door and started to slide out, meaning to forestall their farewell. If they kissed, his resolution might crumple. If they said goodbye, they might fail to part.

'Harry—' Her hand touched his sleeve. He hesitated and looked back at her. She had leant towards him, into a shaft of yellow light cast by a street-lamp twenty yards away. She was confused and weary, as fearful as she was hopeful. She was not sure what to do. She trusted him. But she did not believe him. She needed time. But there was none to spare. 'Look after yourself now. Not me. Not David. Not anyone. Just you.'

'Don't worry. I've always been a selfish bugger.'

'I'll be in touch as soon as I can.'

'I'm relying on it.'

'Do you really have to—' She stared at him, silently imploring him to make up her mind for her. 'Can't we—'

'It's OK, Donna. Go now.' He climbed out onto the pavement

227

and closed the door, then stood in the inky overhang of the roadside trees and waited for her to drive away. A few moments passed, then the engine started and the car moved slowly off. Only when he was certain she did not mean to stop did he wish she would, instantly and intensely.

FORTY-SIX

Harry slept badly, alternating between shallow descents into fretful dreaming and long wakeful ruminations on the success of his visit to Globescope. The totality of that success – the simplicity it had acquired in his mind – was in some ways its most worrying feature. Could it really be so easy?

He rose well before dawn, bathed, shaved, breakfasted on black coffee and Marlboro cigarettes, then packed his bags and prepared to book himself and his absent neighbour out of the hotel. His departure was needlessly early for the itinerary he had proclaimed to Donna. But that had been a drastically edited version of his true intentions. If she had known what they were, she would have refused to leave without him. And the errands he had in mind were best run alone.

The first would take him to David's house in Georgetown, which he had promised Hammelgaard he would search for records of David's most recent hyper-dimensional research. He was hardly the ideal candidate to carry out such a task. Nor was this the ideal time to attempt it. Donna, who would have known what to look for a lot better than him, would have denounced it as fool-hardy when there was so much still to be lost and gained. But a promise was a promise, especially one given to a dead man. And Harry was about to leave Washington, conceivably never to return. He could scarcely bear to go without seeing his son's home. The place had been unoccupied and unvisited for more than two months. It was not likely Lazenby was keeping it under

229

surveillance. As risk-running went, this was small beer.

Besides, Harry told himself, if there was anything of value there, it ought to be removed for safe-keeping. Dr Tilson would know what to do with it. One day, David might thank him for going to such lengths. That half a hope of earning his son's gratitude was perhaps the clinching factor. And the one he could least have afforded to confess to Donna. She would not have said it was foolish and futile. But she would have thought it.

It would not take long. He could be there and back within the hour. And still make Union Station in time for the ten o'clock Metroliner to New York. That would allow him to spend a couple of hours in Philadelphia tracking down Isaac Rosenbaum before carrying on to see Hackensack. Carl Dobermann remained a loose end in David's recent past. One Harry felt unable to ignore.

Donna would be at some Midwest airport by now, waiting for the first flight of the day to Dallas, with the tape safely stowed in her bag. He wondered if she was thinking of him just as he was thinking of her. But his habit of self-denigration would not allow him to believe it. She was probably already glad to have seen the back of him, grateful he had not tried to prolong the intimacy she should never have encouraged. Old enough to be her father, as she had pointed out with wounding accuracy, but emotionally immature. It was not much of a testimonial. But he supposed it was the one he would have to settle for.

Maple Place was a cul-de-sac on the north-eastern fringe of Georgetown, within walking distance of Dupont Circle, a fact which lent a furtive haste to Harry's approach. The taxi dropped him at the end of the road on Q Street, just short of the Rock Creek bridge which he envisaged David crossing each morning on his way to Globescope, formerly perhaps with Donna beside him, more recently for certain alone.

The properties were well-to-do townhouses, with expensive cars parked outside beneath trimmed and well-spaced trees. A man in an elegant overcoat was walking a King Charles spaniel before setting off for his no doubt prestigious place of work. And the pavements were so clean Harry felt obliged to stub out his cigarette meticulously and nudge the remains into the gutter with his toe. He had been told Globescope paid generous salaries. And now he saw the proof of it.

Number 18 Maple Place was a whitewashed brick replica of its neighbours, with sash windows and an imposing bottle-green front door. Harry stepped up to it, took the keys from his pocket and examined them: a Yale and a mortise – matching the locks on the door – and another smaller type. He wondered idly what it was for as he opened the door and stepped inside. Then an alarm started bleeping ominously. There was a box on the wall with lights flashing on a panel beside a small keyhole. Harry wrenched the key out of the door behind him, dropped the bunch in the process and only managed to switch off the alarm after it had given several ear-splitting wails.

He glanced out into the street and saw, to his relief, no signs of neighbourly concern. He closed the door with exaggerated care and moved down the hall. There were stairs ahead of him, an open door leading into a kitchen at the far end and another closed door to his left. He opened it and went through into a large lounge-dining room looking out onto the street.

A sofa and an armchair were arranged in front of the fireplace. A dining table stood against the right-hand wall, beneath a serving hatch, with four chairs tucked in around it. Another smaller gate-leg table stood by the window, one flap raised. A television, video and hi-fi occupied the space behind the door. Enough books and magazines to fill several bookcases were stacked in orderly piles either side of the fireplace. The room had a moved-in-but-not-yet-finished-unpacking feel to it.

There were no pictures or ornaments, unless the blade-end of an oar propped in a corner counted as one. To judge by the inscription on it, David had rowed with some success at Cambridge, a fact Iris had never mentioned. For one self-indulgent split-second, Harry imagined standing with Iris on some windy stretch of Cambridge riverbank, cheering their son on in a race. Then he fended the thought off, shaking his head like a horse troubled by a fly that will not give up. He reached out absently and touched the radiator next to the doorway.

It was warm. Scarcely hot, but certainly warm. It reminded him that the house did not have the musty chill he might have expected after so long a desertion. Then he noticed the post on the table by the window. Two months' worth of letters and circulars that should have been littering the hall had been neatly stored there, awaiting David's return. But stored there by whom? A friend? A neighbour? Where were they? How often did they call in?

Harry hurried on. He glanced into the kitchen, which revealed only a bachelor sparseness of kettle, cupboards and cooker, then climbed the stairs. There were two bedrooms and a bathroom, the rear bedroom serving as a study. More books and magazines were piled there, with a less orderly appearance than in the lounge. Colour copies of computer-generated imagery – vivid seahorse swirls spiralling in dazzling patterns – were Blu-Tacked around the walls. A computer, telephone, fax machine and sundry other electronic gadgetry filled a large table at one end of the room. A more modestly proportioned desk stood by the window, which looked out over the small backyard and a patch of straggling woodland beyond the rear wall that dropped away towards the creek.

Harry sat down at the desk. The top was bare save for an anglepoise lamp and a Charles-and-Di wedding mug filled with pens and pencils. It looked as if it had been cleared in preparation for a lengthy absence. He slid his fingers across the wood. There was no trace of dust. Then he opened the deep drawer beneath the desk. It was fitted with a filing cradle, occupied by bulging manilla folders, subject headings recorded in felt pen on their facing edges. The first few were innocuous enough. *Tax. House. Mortgage. Car. Insurance.* The thickest of the lot was *Divorce.* With a respectful squeamishness, Harry resisted the temptation to delve into it. *Globescope* he pulled out and examined. It turned out to contain an unremarkable clutch of formal letters about David's conditions of employment, most of them signed by Luke Brownlow. But the last item in the file – a curt three-liner dispensing with David's services as of 12 April – was signed in Lazenby's sprawling hand. The next file, *HYDRA*, Harry leafed through eagerly. But it comprised only letters written to multifarious individuals and organizations over a period of five years or more seeking funding for HYDRA's establishment. The replies were uniformly discouraging.

The last few cradles were empty. Unused, presumably, although a split in the cardboard at the base of one was faintly inconsistent with that conclusion. Harry sat where he was for several minutes, wondering why there was so little in the way of working material. Where were the disks for the computer? Where were the voluminous jottings he imagined a mathematical theorist would naturally surround himself with? There had been the notebooks, of course. But were they really all there was?

He rose, walked across to the piles of books and magazines and bent over to examine their titles. Most of them were as impenetrably technical as he assumed the contents to be. Particle physics and quantum theory; superstrings and twistor space;

232

topology and cohomology: the whole mind-bending tangle of higher mathematics Harry instinctively shrank from. Plus a couple of medical texts about diabetes, some science fiction paperbacks, several of them by Isaac Asimov, and a few fat runs of *Scientific American* and suchlike journals. It was what he might have expected. But it was not what he was looking for. Maybe there was simply nothing to find. Maybe the notebooks were the beginning and end of it.

He walked into the bedroom. A sheet had been laid right across the bed. The outline of pillows and folded blankets could be seen beneath it: further proof that David had not intended to return for quite a while. There was a wardrobe and bedside cabinet, but no other furniture. A large watercolour of what Harry thought could be the Californian coast dominated the wall facing the window. He glanced out into the street, satisfying himself that the alarm really had roused nobody. The man he had seen earlier walking his dog was hanging his jacket in the back of his BMW, prior to departure. The mailman was doing his rounds. Nothing else was stirring.

Harry opened the cabinet drawer. It contained a box of tissues, a pocket-watch that had stopped at 11.42 one day, a slim paperback of a script for a Tom Stoppard play Harry thought he might have heard of . . . and a spiral-bound notebook with a stub of pencil beside it. He took it out to leaf through. But every page was blank. If David had kept it there to record nocturnal flashes of mathematical inspiration, he was evidently more of a lark than an owl.

Then Harry noticed a tell-tale scrap of paper caught in the wire spiral – all that was left of an earlier page. One that had been torn out, perhaps one of several. According to the specification printed on the cover of the notebook, it contained seventy sheets. Quickly, he counted them. Sixty-four. Six sheets were missing. It meant nothing, of course. David might have removed them himself. And yet . . .

Harry walked over to the wardrobe and opened it. That was all it was: a wardrobe filled with clothes. Suits; jackets; trousers; jeans; shirts; sweaters; ties. But they somehow conveyed more to Harry of the strangeness of his relationship with David than anything else he had seen. The owner of the clothes was only what he had always been to Harry: an absence; a costume without a wearer; an amputated life.

Glancing down at the boots and shoes stowed in the base of the wardrobe, Harry noticed a hatbox propped on its side at the back.

Almost certainly, then, a hat was not what it contained. He lifted it out onto the floor, unfastened the string and removed the lid.

A chaos of paper met his gaze. Old bank statements and pay-slips were interleaved with maps, travel brochures, newspaper cuttings and photograph wallets. The wallets turned out to contain only negatives. The snapshots themselves were long gone. Harry held one strip up to the light and made out the unmistakable figure of Hope Brancaster reclining curvaceously on a beach in a dramatically minimal swimsuit. A print, better still an enlargement, would have been well worth seeing. He discarded it and began sifting through the rest.

Then he saw something he recognized: a tour guide to Lindos. A picture of the medieval castle on its hill above the white-walled dwellings of the town framed by the familiar deep-blue Aegean sea and sky adorned its cover. Study the scene long enough and he would be able to spot the Villa ton Navarkhon, where he had lived for nine lost years. He picked the guide up and looked at it. David had bought it for 750 drachmas from Papaioannou's gift shop. There was the old rogue's name on the label. He should not have asked more than 500 by rights. Harry fanned idly through the pages. As he did so, a photograph fell out of the centre-spread: a snapshot that had served as some kind of page-marker. It landed face upwards on the floor and Harry stared down at it.

It was a picture of David, sitting at a table beneath one of the fig trees outside the Taverna Silenou. He was wearing a yellow open-necked shirt and a casual grin. A glass of beer was visible on the table in front of him, beside what was almost certainly the same Lindos guidebook, held open by a plate containing a half-eaten slice of one of Kostas's dubious pizzas. But Harry's attention did not linger on the foreground. It drifted towards the shadowy interior of the bar and focused on the figure of a man propped against a door-pillar: none other than Harry himself, a few drink-fuddled minutes short of his disastrous encounter with Torben's girlfriend. Harry as he had been six years ago, near the bottom of his mid-life trough. Harry as he had seemed ever since in his son's recollection.

'May I ask what exactly you're doing?'

Harry started with surprise and looked up to find a woman of seventy or more regarding him levelly from the doorway. She was small, spry and sharp-featured, with dove-grey hair, keen blue eyes and a faint Parkinsonian tremor. She was wearing a rag-bag outfit of frayed yachting gear, but her voice and bearing implied she would be equally at ease in a ballgown and pearls.

'How did you get in here?' She spoke with the eardrum-tingling loudness of the hard of hearing. 'Well? Explain yourself, young man.'

'Sorry.' Harry could not help smiling at her description of him as young. He scrambled to his feet, hastily composing a lie, or at any rate recycling one. 'I'm . . . er . . . Harry Venning. David's uncle.'

'His *uncle*?'

'Yes. That's right. And you are?'

'Nona Stapleton. David's next-door neighbour. Hasn't he mentioned me to you?'

'No. I don't think so.'

'Really? I should have thought he must have done.'

'Well, I haven't seen that much of him these last few years, to be honest. I've tried to, er, rally round since his illness, of course. Give Iris as much support as I—'

'I wrote to David's mother expressing my sympathy and explaining that I'd be happy to continue keeping an eye on the house until he recovered or it was decided what to do with it. You would be her brother-in-law?'

'Sort of. I had to come over on business, so I offered to check that everything was all right. She gave me the keys.'

'Without mentioning my letter?'

'She's been under a lot of strain lately, as I'm sure you can imagine.'

'Indeed I can. How is David?'

'Oh, the same. Neither better nor worse.'

'My heart goes out to her. Such a fine boy. Nevertheless, I do think you might have made a few enquiries before . . . Well, I feared the worst, I must say, when I found the door unlocked and the alarm switched off. Then I heard a noise up here. I had half a mind to go back to my house and call the police. I'm not exactly sure why I didn't. I guess . . .' She shook her head and looked away, revealing a hint of sentiment. 'I guess I hoped it might be David.'

Harry attempted a consoling smile. 'He's been a good neighbour to you?'

'More of a friend, I'd like to think. Since my husband died and Donna left . . . You've heard of *her*, I take it?'

'Yes. Look, I'm sorry about just barging in,' he continued, eager to change the subject. 'It was thoughtless of me.'

235

'That's OK. You weren't to know you'd nearly give me cardiac arrest.' She nodded down at the hatbox. 'Looking for something?'

'This snapshot, actually. It's one Iris particularly likes.' He slipped the photograph into his pocket. 'And some of his, er, working papers. For a colleague of his.'

'Really? Are you sure David would approve?' Then she waved her hand. 'Well, it's none of my business. You must do as you think best.'

'Maybe you can help me. I don't seem to be able to find the stuff.'

'Lord, I wouldn't know about that sort of thing. Isn't it all in the study?'

'Not what I'm looking for.'

'He must have taken it to England with him, then.'

'Apparently not.'

'It has to be one place or the other.'

'Yes. That's what I thought. Nobody else has . . . been through his papers . . . have they?'

'You mean here? Absolutely not. No-one but me's crossed the threshold since David left.' She frowned. 'Unless they had a key, of course. I wouldn't have known you'd been here if I hadn't come in.' Her frown deepened as her gaze moved to the hatbox. 'Depending how well you plan to clear up after you, that is.'

'So it *is* possible someone's been in?'

'I guess so. But we keep a pretty close watch on comings and goings here in Maple Place. Have to, the number of crazies there are wandering the streets. Especially lately.'

'Why lately?'

'Oh, a gruesome-looking old hobo showed up last month and just wouldn't go away. I know a lot of people were worried about their children. The police must have moved him on a dozen times, but he kept coming back. Like he was waiting around for something. Though we'll never find out what. Not now.'

'Why not?'

'The police seem certain he was the man they pulled out of Rock Creek last weekend. He must have fallen in and drowned. Maybe off one of the bridges. Drunk, I daresay, or high on drugs. You'd have to be to drown in that depth of water. Mad would help as well, of course. According to this morning's *Post*, he's been identified as an escaped inmate from some lunatic asylum up north. So I suppose—'

'Did they give his name?'

236

'Probably. I don't recall.'

'Was it Dobermann?'

She looked at him sharply. 'Why yes. Now you mention it, I believe it was.'

'Carl Dobermann. From the Hudson Valley Psychiatric Center, near Poughkeepsie.'

'Yes. That's exactly right. You must have read the report.'

'No.' He shook his head. 'I didn't read the report.'

'Then how do you know? Were you acquainted with him?'

'Never met him in my life.'

'I don't understand.'

'Neither do I. But I think you're right. He *was* waiting for something. Or someone. And it looks like he waited too long.'

FORTY-SEVEN

The body recovered from Rock Creek on Sunday just south of the Q Street bridge has now been identified as that of Carl Victor Dobermann, 59, a long-stay patient missing from Hudson Valley Psychiatric Center, Poughkeepsie, NY, since September 5. He had no known connexions with the Washington area. Police are treating his death as an accidental drowning. They believe Mr Dobermann may have been the prowler complained of in recent weeks by residents of Maple Place, Georgetown, who confirm that they have not seen—

Woodrow Hackensack tossed the newspaper aside and made a quizzical face at Harry. 'So Mad Dog Carl's gone to meet his maker. You won't be getting any answers from him now, will you?'

Harry shrugged. 'Perhaps I don't need any. He was looking for David. That's obvious. And he was disturbed enough for the reason to be well-nigh unfathomable. That's equally obvious. What more do we need to know?'

'You've sure swapped hymn sheets. A few days ago you were all for turning over every stone Dobermann ever trod on.'

'Not much point now, is there?'

'What about Rosenbaum? He might still be able to tell you something.'

'I decided to give him a miss. I think Donna was right. Dobermann's just a red herring.'

'Fish can't drown, Harry. Didn't they teach you that in school?'

238

'Certainly not. Mine was a classical education.' Harry lowered his voice. 'The point is, Woodrow, Donna has the tape and a good chance of dishing Lazenby. She's promised to do her very best to persuade this hot-shot neurosurgeon, Sandoval, to take on David's case as soon as she's free to approach him. So, the sooner I get back to England and convince Iris there really is some hope of progress, the better.'

'And maybe you'll eventually be able to ask David to explain his interest in Dobermann for himself.'

'Exactly.'

'You handled Lazenby better than I'd have given you credit for, y'know.' Hackensack nodded at him in puzzled appreciation. 'Smooth as silk. Which I'd never have said you were in a million years. Must have taken real nerve to go through with it on your own.'

'More a case of desperation. Plus a lot of luck.'

'So you say. But—'

'Tell me the medical news. When do you get out of here?'

'Oh, after the weekend, they reckon. The stairs back home are gonna be a problem, o'course. But good ol' Martha's offered to fetch and carry for me. That'll be non-stop entertainment, let me tell you. But don't worry. I'll have plenty of time to scour the papers for the first signs of Lazenby's well-earned downfall.'

'They won't be long in coming. I'm sure of it. All you have to do is sit tight and watch it happen.'

'Sounds easy.'

'It is, believe me. I have a feeling everything's going to come right from now on.'

'Yeh? Well, I have a feeling you're holding out on me. But since it's a sure bet you're not gonna tell me why . . . I'll just have to shake your hand and wish you *bon voyage*. Happy landings, Harry. Reckon you deserve 'em.'

Harry agreed with Hackensack. Happiness – or at least peace of mind – seemed a fair reward considering everything he had gone through in recent weeks. Unfortunately, peace of mind eluded him. During the long subway ride out to JFK Airport, he tried as hard as he could to reason his way to such a condition. But something stronger than reason held him back, something founded in what Hackensack had correctly deduced was being kept from him.

Harry had not lost interest in Dobermann now he was dead. Quite the reverse. The circumstances of his death were too eerily

239

reminiscent of the caprices of fate that had overtaken four out of the seven participants in Project Sybil to be ignored. Harry had left Maple Place that morning with every intention of breaking his journey to New York in Philadelphia and trying to track down Isaac Rosenbaum.

Only to discover, standing on the Q Street bridge and gazing down at the stretch of Rock Creek where Dobermann had drowned, that he had somehow mislaid the piece of paper on which he had recorded Rosenbaum's address. It had been in his pocket two days ago, tucked inside the cover of his diary. Now it was no longer there. He had turned out his pockets since, of course. In Lazenby's office, the previous afternoon. It was possible the piece of paper had slipped out then. It was hard to imagine where else it *could* have slipped out.

Harry could still have gleaned Rosenbaum's address from some other source. The telephone directory; Columbia University. Its loss had not been an insurmountable obstacle. But where he had lost it had been. There was no logical cause for concern. A scrap of paper with a Philadelphia address scrawled on it would mean nothing to Lazenby. He had probably not even noticed it. Yet *probably* was not quite good enough. He *might* have seen it fall from Harry's diary. He *might* have kept it. If he had, then he would remember it when scandal broke around his head and Norman Page's consuming interest in his choice of soft furnishings at last made sense. It would be the only trail he could follow. A trail that was bound to peter out – so long as Rosenbaum had no visit from an inquisitive stranger to report. Whatever he might or might not recollect about Dobermann's long-ago crack-up would have to remain an open question. '*A good poker-player knows when to fold,*' Chipchase had told Harry more than once. Now, Harry reckoned, it was time to break a forty-year habit – by following his friend's advice.

FORTY-EIGHT

Higher than a transatlantic flightpath on duty-free booze, Harry's misgivings floated away into the pressurized ether as the homeward journey passed in a blur of rapid-reverse time zones. As seasoned travellers around him donned the bizarre paraphernalia of in-flight slumber, Harry drifted into a hazy dreamland where he, David and Iris shared a harmonious domestic existence, went for long country drives in the Riley 4/44 he had once owned and picnicked languidly in flower-carpeted Wiltshire meadows.

Dreams end as inevitably as journeys. But even the dismal tumult of Heathrow Airport at dawn could not crush Harry's spirits. He felt strangely alert and clear-headed, as if jet-lag and a hangover had slugged each other into mutual submission. Rattling into London on the Piccadilly line and out again on the Bakerloo, he had ample time to plot his strategy for the day. He did so with something close to relish. He had good news for Iris and even better news for his opinion of himself. He had returned. And he was not empty-handed.

For Mrs Tandy he had two surprises. One was a litre of Bailey's Irish Cream, her favourite tipple. The other was his well-groomed and smartly dressed appearance. It was not clear which pleased her more. Either way, his reward was a breakfast fit for a trencherman. 'I went out specially to buy these sausages after you called last night,' she announced. 'Though why I should want to pander to your unhealthy tastes I cannot imagine, considering the previous lack of so much as a postcard by way of proof that you were still in the land of the living.'

'Sorry, Mrs T. Force of circumstance.'

'Profitable circumstance, judging by that overcoat. Cashmere, isn't it?'

'Shouldn't think so. Taiwanese lookalike, I expect. You'd be surprised how cheap it was.'

'Taiwanese? I find that hard to believe.'

'The bangers are great,' lisped Harry evasively through a mouthful of one.

'Good. When you've finished, I hope you'll telephone Mrs Hewitt, by the way. The poor lady is anxious to hear from you.'

'Mrs Hewitt?' For a moment, Harry did not recognize the name. 'Oh, Iris.'

'Yes. She's called several times.'

'Don't worry. I plan to see her later.'

'Do I take it from that you *won't* be phoning her?'

'Put it like this. She'll want to hear what I have to tell her face to face. And when she's heard it, I reckon she'll agree it was worth the wait.' He stirred the yolk of his fried egg with a forkful of sausage and grinned at Mrs Tandy across the table. 'Believe me.'

Harry grabbed a couple of hours' sleep, then had a bath and a second breakfast before setting off for the hospital. He planned to arrive about half an hour earlier than Iris's customary two o'clock visiting time and to share his high hopes of Sandoval's expertise with the patient before sharing them with the patient's mother. It was less than three weeks since he had said good-bye to David en route to Copenhagen, but it felt far longer. *'I'll do what I can,'* had been his parting promise. And he had been as good as his word. Pride was stirring unfamiliarly within him. There were grave difficulties ahead, but it was no longer inconceivable that they would be surmounted. Thanks to the father he had never known, David's future might yet be retrievable.

Harry took the tube to Piccadilly Circus and cut through Soho to Theophilus's shop near the top of Charing Cross Road. Theophilus claimed not to recognize him at first, then asked if he had come into an inheritance. If so, would he be switching to Cuban cigars in future? Because it just so happened . . .

Harry bought two hundred *Karelia Sertika* and smoked the first ambling through Bloomsbury towards Queen Square. The afternoon was cold and grey. London was at its late autumn bleakest, traffic fumes souring the dank and bitter air. But Harry was undaunted. He stopped off at the Museum Tavern in Great Russell Street for a couple of pints, then headed on, reaching the hospital on schedule just after half past one.

He took the lift to the third floor and followed the well-remembered route to room E318. He did not stop at the nursing station, merely smiled and said 'Hello' to the nurse who was sitting there, immersed in form-filling, as he passed. 'Mr Barnett?' he heard her say in a surprised tone from behind him.

'Yes. Long time no see, eh?'

'But—' He reached the door to the room and opened it. 'Mr Barnett!'

The room was empty. David was not there. Nor was anyone else. The bed was bare. The shelves were clear. Harry glanced stupidly at the number on the door to reassure himself he had not somehow taken a wrong turning. But there was no mistake. And no reassurance. This was room E318. But the name-panel was blank. David had gone.

'Mr Barnett?' The nurse had caught up with him. She spoke softly, her hand tugging gently at his elbow.

'Where is he?' he mumbled.

'You mean David?' But his look of baffled alarm must have made that obvious. 'Haven't you . . . I mean . . .'

'Where is he?'

'Don't you know?'

'What's going on?'

'Surely Mrs Hewitt . . . I mean, we assumed she would have . . . Do you really not know?'

'Know what?'

She stared at him in disbelief for a moment, then said, her face colouring as she spoke: 'Mrs Hewitt decided . . . acting on Mr Baxendale's advice, of course . . . that there really was no point . . . in artificially prolonging his life.'

'They switched him off?'

'He was taken off the ventilator . . . earlier this week.'

'He's dead?'

'I'm afraid so.'

'When? When did they do it?'

243

'Tuesday.'

'But that's only three days ago.' He fell back against the doorpost behind him and closed his eyes, feeling the tears start into them. 'Only three bloody days.'

FORTY-NINE

They found him a chair in a rest room and gave him a cup of tea. Staff Nurse Kelly was sent for to have a quiet word with him. Embarrassed consolation was tentatively plied. But none of it made much impact on Harry. The shock drained into a grief sharper than anything he would have expected to feel for somebody he had strictly speaking never even met. Then a darker thought filled his mind. He had kept his word. But Iris had broken hers. *'I'll do nothing until I've heard from you,'* she had assured him. Yet she had brought herself to end their son's life. And she had not heard from him. Only now she would. By the time Staff Nurse Kelly arrived to offer her starched brand of sympathy, Harry was on his way out.

'Mr Barnett?'

'Sorry. Can't stop.'

'Wait a moment. Let's sit down and—'

'Waiting's over, Rachel. Didn't they tell you? Three days ago.'

He hailed the first taxi he saw outside and demanded to be taken to Chorleywood. The driver declined, quoting some regulation or other, and suggested Marylebone station. 'You can get a train out to Chorleywood from there, guv.' Harry did not bother to argue.

He had twenty minutes to wait at Marylebone. These he spent in the Victoria and Albert bar, drinking scotch at a rate the barman clearly found alarming. He remembered meeting Zohra there years ago, in a different life, in a world he had not known he

245

shared with David and had forgotten he shared with Iris. '*I'll do nothing without consulting you first*.' She could not shrug off this breach of faith and nor could he. This was worse than all the disappointments of his life gathered and surveyed. This was the extinction of what might have made every one of them worthwhile.

The 14.57 to Aylesbury crawled out late through the suburbs into the patchy beginnings of Home Counties countryside. The sallow light thinned. The day faltered. The chill of a premature dusk crept into Harry's soul. Just after half past three, the train reached Chorleywood, a well-bred commuter town consumed by the eerie stillness of a workday afternoon. There were no taxis to be had. He gleaned directions from a fishmonger's shop opposite the station and started walking, fast and hard, uphill along select residential streets.

Chalfont Lane represented another degree of selectness again, large tree-screened family homes spaciously lining a broad-verged road. About halfway along, he found the one he was looking for: Squirrels, a gabled pile with lamplight already gleaming warmly in the windows, a scent of woodsmoke drifting out to him across the immaculate lawns. He marched straight up to the deep-porched door and yanked at the bell-pull.

The woman who answered was plumper and redder-haired than Iris, but unmistakably her sister. She had the same dress sense, the same cautious bearing. In her gaze, enlarged by the violet-framed lenses of her glasses, there was an appalled hint that she knew who he was as well, without need of introduction.

'Mrs Tremaine?'

'Yes.'

'I'm looking for Iris.'

'Oh. I'm sorry, but—'

'I'm Harry. I expect she's told you about me.' It was obvious she had. Not least because of the glance Blanche Tremaine cast over her shoulder and the blush of confusion that came to her face. 'Is she here?'

'No. No, she isn't.'

'I won't leave without seeing her.'

'But you can't. I'm sorry, but it's quite impossible.' She stepped back and was about to close the door when Harry moved into its path. 'Please, for goodness' sake! If you don't go at once, I'll call the police.'

246

'Fine. Do that. I know how reluctant they are to become involved in family disputes.'

'This isn't a family dispute.'

'No? Will they agree, do you think, when I tell them my son was allowed to die this week at his mother's bidding – and Iris is the mother who did that to him?'

'This is outrageous!'

'Too right. And I'm the one who's outraged.'

Blanche's resolve faltered. It seemed for an instant as if some part of her shared his indignation at what had been done. Maybe his opinion was not the only one Iris had failed to seek.

'He was your nephew, Blanche. Your nephew and my son. Are you seriously saying there's nothing for us to discuss?'

'It's too late for discussion.'

'Where is she?'

Blanche closed her eyes for a moment, then stepped back into the hallway. 'You'd better come in.'

He followed her the short distance to a flock-papered drawing room where a fire was burning and the light from numerous side-lamps was falling flatteringly on richly patterned rugs and deep-cushioned sofas, on the fittings and furnishings of stockbroker-belt respectability: his son's world – one he had only ever entered as a passing stranger.

Blanche went across to the fireplace and stood there, staring down at the burning logs to avoid his gaze. But her fretful fiddling with the ornaments on the mantelpiece defeated her evasiveness. She was not as sure her sister had acted for the best as she was likely to claim. Doubt – and vicarious guilt – squirmed within her. 'David's condition was quite hopeless. You do realize that, don't you?'

'No. I don't.'

'The doctors were unanimous. There was nothing to be done.'

'Nothing can be done for him now. I realize *that*.'

'It was Iris's decision, of course. It had to be. The rest of us . . . could only advise.'

'Except for those of us who weren't *allowed* to advise.'

'I understood you'd . . . disappeared.'

'You all wished I had, you mean.'

'Your . . . relations . . . with my sister are none of my business, Mr Barnett. I—'

'She promised to do nothing until she'd heard from me again. Did she tell you that?'

247

Blanche looked up at him in surprise that almost amounted to shock. 'No, no. That can't be right. Ken said you'd . . . washed your hands of the matter.'

'Oh, *Ken* said, did he? Good old Ken. Well, it would suit him to, wouldn't it? Since washing his hands of David is what was at the top of his agenda all along. I don't suppose a stepson on money-no-object life support struck him as good business, do you?'

'Money was never an issue.'

'Sure of that, are you, Blanche? Absolutely sure?'

She flushed and pursed her lips. 'This is pointless. David's—'

'Dead? Yes. I know. But what I don't know is why.'

'I told you. There was nothing they could do for him.'

'Where's Iris?'

Blanche sighed. 'She's gone back to Wilmslow to make arrangements for the funeral.'

'Give me her address.'

'I couldn't possibly.'

'I'll get it anyway. You may as well tell me.'

'This won't help anyone, Mr Barnett. Surely you see . . . ' But the message was sinking in. Harry did not see. 'I think I'd better telephone Iris and ask her to speak to you.'

'Yes. I think you had.'

She crossed to a bureau in the corner, picked up the telephone and dialled the number. Harry watched as she waited for an answer – and he waited with her. 'Iris? . . . Yes . . . Look, I'm sorry, but . . . Harry Barnett's here . . . Yes, he's with me now . . . He wants to speak to you . . . Well, of course, but . . . Yes, I think you probably should . . . Hold on.' Expressionlessly, she passed the handset to him.

'Iris?'

'Harry, I—'

'Why did you do it?'

'I . . . I had no choice.'

'You promised to wait. You could have chosen to keep your promise.'

'There was no point.'

'Promises are never pointless.'

'You don't understand.'

'No. But I intend to. I'm not going to let you – or that bastard you're married to – walk away from this. Do you hear me?'

'I hear you.' She sounded subdued and weary, as if she had

foreseen these exchanges. 'Don't come here, Harry. Please. You and Ken . . . I couldn't bear any . . . unpleasantness.'

'You're going to have to.'

'Please, Harry. What's to be gained by it?'

'As little as there is to be lost.'

'For God's sake—'

'He was our son, Iris. *Our* son. Not yours alone.'

'You never knew him.'

'And you've made sure I never will. You and Ken between you.'

There was a lengthy silence. Then Iris said: 'We could meet, perhaps. Next week. I could come down to—'

'Now. We'll meet now. Whether you like it or not.'

'I can't leave here. Not as things are.'

'Then I'll come to you.'

'No. Ken would— Listen. OK, we'll meet. If we must. Tomorrow morning. In Manchester.' He could almost hear her mind plotting the lies she would tell Ken, the stratagems by which she would keep them apart. 'Albert Square at ten o'clock. The benches in front of the Town Hall. Can you make that?'

'The time and place don't matter. I'll be there. You'd better be too.'

'I will be.'

'Be sure you are. If not, I'll come looking for you, Iris. That's a promise. And I keep *my* promises.'

FIFTY

Saturday morning in Manchester. The shoppers were out in force, defying a cold wind and the threats of a louring sky. Christmas was still more than a month off, but electronic carols were drifting out from tinselly shopfronts as Harry made his way from the cheap hotel he had spent the night in towards Albert Square and his rendezvous with Iris.

It was not yet a quarter to ten by the Town Hall clock when he arrived. There were plenty of people in the square, but they were passing through, intent on gift-hunting and queue-beating. The Gothic splendour of the Town Hall and the Albert Memorial facing it were of no interest to them. And it was too cold for idle occupation of the benches spaced around the perimeter of the square, even had they been able to spare the time. Harry, however, had time in greater abundance than any other commodity. And he found the chill of the air strangely comforting. He sat down near a statue of Gladstone, lit a cigarette and prepared to wait.

But he did not have to wait long. Iris too was early for their appointment. She approached from his blind side and sat down hesitantly at the opposite end of the bench. She was wearing a grey coat and a black fur-trimmed hat. Her shoes and tights were black as well. Why Harry should find these hints of mourning so jarring he could not have explained, beyond the sense in which it seemed perverse of her to mourn what she had herself brought about.

'Hello, Harry.' She looked pale and drawn, thinner than when

250

they had last met. Her grief was genuine enough, he knew, but still he resented it. And his resentment forbade him to make any attempt to understand what she had done.

'I don't know what to say to you, Iris. Do you know that? After what you've done, I just don't know what to say.'

'It wasn't easy, Harry. In fact, it was the hardest thing I've ever done.' She plonked a well-filled John Lewis carrier-bag on the bench between them as a kind of barrier. 'But it was for the best. It really was. You have to understand that.'

'Why? Why do I have to?'

'Because . . . he's at peace now. And he never could have been, hooked up to that machine. They weren't keeping *him* alive. They were keeping *my hopes* alive. Well, I had to let them die. It's as simple as that.'

'Oh no. Simple is one thing it isn't.' He turned and looked at her directly for the first time. 'Why didn't you wait?'

'Because I had no idea how long I'd have to wait *for*. The papers reported Hammelgaard was dead and the Danish police were looking for an Englishman called Barnett. Can you imagine what Ken made of that? I couldn't give him your side of the story because I didn't know it. You ask why I didn't wait. Frankly, Harry, I thought your silence meant I'd have to wait for ever before I'd hear from you again. Ken reckoned—'

'Yes? What did Ken *reckon*?'

'That you'd got into serious trouble in Copenhagen and decided to go to ground.'

'Not far wrong. But that doesn't let you off the hook. I'm back. As I said I would be. As you should have known I would be. And the Danish police had written off Hammelgaard's death as natural causes long before you had David . . . what's the word? . . . terminated. So that won't wash, will it? Try something else, Iris. Try the truth.'

'All right.' She stretched her neck back as if it ached and gave a long sigh. 'This is the truth. David was never going to recover. I had to let him go. Reaching that decision and sticking to it took more out of me than I thought I possessed. But once I'd got there . . . waiting was impossible. I couldn't have gone through the whole process again. I wouldn't have had the strength to. I'm sorry I had to break my word. I'm not trying to deny I broke it. I'm just trying to explain why I felt I had to.'

'For David's sake?'

'Yes. His suffering's over now.' She stared straight at him.

251

'You'd have preferred me to prolong it indefinitely, wouldn't you? To chase the dream of a miracle cure for ever because for you it was the dream of something you'd never had: a son. I don't blame you for that. But I couldn't indulge you or myself any longer. I had to put an end to it. And yes, if I'm really honest, I suppose I was afraid you might come back and talk me out of it if I postponed the decision.'

'What if I told you I'd gone some way towards turning your dream into reality these past few weeks?'

'I wouldn't believe you. I took the finest advice available. A second opinion. A third and a fourth. They all said the same.'

'I found Donna.'

'And what did she say?'

This was the moment he had secretly craved; the moment he crushed her excuses beneath the revelation of just how much he had gained – only for her to throw the prize away before he could win it. Yet now, looking at her in the cold grey light, studying the signs of her age and weakness, he hesitated. What would the knowledge do to her? What would the realization leave her to treasure in her son's memory? What was the point in taking his revenge on her?

'Well? What did she say?'

He bowed his head and opened his hand in a helpless gesture of concession. There was revenge coming for her, all right, whatever he said or did. Once the truth about Globescope was out, David's reputation was going to be a poor sullied tattered thing for any mother to wrap herself in. And that also would be Harry's doing. Suddenly he felt so much sorrier than angry. Sorry for Iris and David and himself. Sorry for everything.

'Thank you for trying, Harry. It's not your fault you've come back empty-handed.'

'If only you knew,' he murmured, unsure from her lack of reaction whether she had caught the words – but certain she could not have grasped their meaning.

'If you want to . . . see David . . . before the funeral . . . I could . . .'

'Wouldn't Ken object?'

'He needn't know. I could take you straight to the chapel of rest from here.'

'But then you'd be late home from your shopping expedition. Wouldn't that look suspicious?'

'If you must know, Ken isn't at home this morning. He's putting

252

in some time at the factory. Clearing things up so he can take Monday off.'

'For the funeral?'

'Yes.'

'Where's it to be?'

'St Bartholomew's, in Wilmslow. Then . . . Manchester Crematorium. But Harry—'

'I'm *persona non grata* for the event. Is that it? A hole-in-the-corner visit to the chapel of rest while Ken does his bit for the export drive's just about acceptable. But shaking hands with the vicar while you explain who and what I am isn't. Have I got the message, Iris? Or have I got the message?'

'Don't be angry. Please. You know you never really . . .'

'Knew him? Or even met him, right?'

'Well, you didn't, did you?'

'Take a look at this.' He handed her the photograph he had found at Maple Place of David at the Taverna Silenou – with Harry visible in the background. 'It was at his house in Washington.'

'You've been to Washington?'

'I've been to many places. But you don't want to know where or why. Believe me.'

'This photograph . . . When was it taken?'

'August eighty-eight. On Rhodes. He looked me up after all, you see.'

'But . . . you never mentioned it.'

'I never knew. He looked. But he didn't like what he saw.' The photograph was shaking in Iris's fingers. Gently, Harry retrieved it. 'You don't mind . . . if I keep it, do you?'

'No.' She frowned at him in her confusion. 'Of course not.'

'It's all I have of him. You have a lifetime of memories. I have . . . as much as you let me have.'

'That's not fair.'

'No. But life isn't fair, is it? Nor's death. You should have waited. You really should.'

There were tears in her eyes. A single photographic glimpse of her son as he had once been – bizarrely juxtaposed with the father he had always disclaimed the slightest scrap of interest in – had proved too much for her self-control. The realization that she had known David less well than she had supposed served only to sharpen her grief. She took out a handkerchief and dabbed away the tears. 'I'm sorry,' she said. 'So stupid. It happens . . . quite

253

often at the moment.' She took a deep breath. Order was restored to her voice. 'Do you want to . . . see him, then?'

'No.' It would have been more accurate to say he could not bear to see him. He would look as he had in the hospital, serene and untroubled. And that would only remind Harry of how close he had come to saving him. Besides, to accompany Iris now to wherever David's coffin was standing really would imply he somehow accepted the justice of his exclusion from the funeral. Sparing her the bitterest portion of the truth was one thing; conspiring in the salving of her conscience quite another. 'You kept me out of his life. Better keep me out of his death as well.'

'I *am* sorry, Harry.'

'I know. So am I. And we'll both be sorrier yet.' He rose and fastened his coat. 'If you'd waited, I'd have done everything I could for you. You *and* David.'

'There's nothing you *could* have done.'

'There's nothing I can do now. That much is certain.'

She looked up at him. 'Goodbye, Harry.'

He returned her gaze levelly, squeezing condemnation and forgiveness into a grudging blankness. There was nothing to say. Parting was merely a turning away, a closing of a door. Time, the hidden dimension, was reeling them in. What they had shared was over. What he was about to do was simply a silent statement of the obvious.

He raised his hand as if to wave, then let the gesture fall to his side. He took his leave of her in a single glance – unconsoling, unaccepting, unreconciled. Then he turned and walked away. He did not look back. And she did not call after him.

FIFTY-ONE

The London train had barely cleared the end of the platform at Manchester Piccadilly station and was rattling and swaying across the points when Harry presented himself at the buffet and ordered a scotch. He stood by the narrow carriage window, watching the grey Mancunian vista of streets and house-backs slide past him as the train gathered speed. Was the city moving or was he? He pondered this relativistic nicety as he swallowed the first of the whisky. It made nothing clearer. Which was, after all, the point of drinking it. He had no need of clarity. Much more of that and he would regret letting Iris off so lightly.

'*Good morning, ladies and gentlemen,*' crackled a voice through a microphone somewhere above him. '*This is your conductor speaking. Welcome aboard the eleven-thirty West Coast Intercity service to London Euston. This train will call at Stockport, Macclesfield, Stoke-on-Trent, Watford Junction and London Euston.*'

Why, Harry wondered, as he raised the plastic tumbler to his lips again, had he not made Iris suffer for what she had done? Because he had always been too soft – too gentlemanly in his own way. Lazy and unambitious maybe, but never cruel or vengeful. Faintly chivalrous, perhaps, though his chivalry had often been ignored or misunderstood. Come to that, it had never been tested to the limit. Would he have stood by her all those years ago, if she had told Claude she was pregnant by another man and he had thrown her out? Would he have done his best by her and David?

255

It was easy to say yes and to blame her for not giving him the chance. But at least she had enabled him to give himself the benefit of the doubt. And doubt was always a two-edged sword.

Yet the anger remained. Indeed, it seemed to grow as the whisky sapped his sorrow. He had tried so hard. He had achieved so much. Yet still he had failed. Perhaps it would have been better not to try at all. Better by far, he reckoned, draining the tumbler and turning to order a refill, if this sterile churning anger was all he had to show for his efforts. As it seemed it was.

The buffet attendant raised his eyebrows at Harry, but served him obligingly enough. Harry went back to the window and gazed out again at the unyielding view. There was nothing in its colourless portion of the world to comfort him. No sticking-plaster for his wounds; no target for his anger. Just a drab suburban haul through playing fields and shopping centres, trading estates and recreation grounds, cul-de-sacs and flyovers. It was all—

HEWITT ENGINEERING. His eyes focused suddenly on the name, starkly lettered on a factory wall. There it stood, amidst a jumble of industrial premises beside the track. Hewitt Engineering – where good old Ken was even then checking his profits and losses, making up for the time he would spend at his stepson's funeral on Monday, a funeral he had worked so assiduously to bring forward. Yes, of course. Ken Hewitt ran an engineering business. Iris had told him so. In Stockport.

The train began to slow at that moment. They were on a viaduct, crossing a motorway and a stretch of the Mersey. The factory fell away behind. '*This train will shortly be arriving at Stockport,*' came the conductor's announcement. '*Stockport will be the next station stop.*'

Harry emptied the tumbler, turned around and slapped it down onto the counter.

'Don't you think you've had enough, sir?' the attendant gently enquired.

'Yes,' Harry replied. 'Definitely.'

FIFTY-TWO

Hewitt Engineering occupied a triangular site between the M63 and the railway line, a redundant spur of which could be seen rusting away on a patch of weed-choked wasteland to the rear. The car park was nearly full, suggesting a healthy order-book; Ken Hewitt was not the man to pay time and a half without good cause. A fork-lift truck was active over by the loading bay. A sound of welding could be heard from the region of the workshop. The place seemed busy enough. It certainly looked more prosperous than most of its neighbours. Good old Ken doubtless had a shrewd head as well as a hard heart. And he was there all right. Harry recognized the racing-green Jag in its reserved berth by the office entrance.

Harry pushed the main door open and walked into a pot-planted reception area decorated with framed certificates of technical excellence. Hewitt Engineering had apparently won a Queen's Award for Technological Achievement. Ken would be in line for an OBE if he played his cards right, maybe something more prestigious still. No wonder he had not wanted his wife dragging him into Globescope's murky affairs. Not when the New Year Honours List might be beckoning.

The receptionist was evidently one member of staff who did not work on Saturdays. No reps to fob off, Harry supposed. It left the coast clear for him, though. He started up the stairs, which looked as if they might lead to the boss's lair.

There was a long straight corridor at the top, running past a

257

series of doors to the right and windows to the left looking out over the dip-and-scarp roof of the workshop. A door stood open at the far end of the corridor, giving onto an office large enough to be that of the man himself. Who, talk of the Devil, chose that moment to emerge from one of the intervening doorways, tossing some remark to a junior over his shoulder. 'Be sure they do. Maybe's not good enough.' He looked even more arrogant and domineering in pinstripe trousers, straining blue shirt and taut red braces, bestriding his home turf, than he had in tweed and twill at the Mitre Bridge Service Station. Harry struggled for a moment to call to mind all the excellent reasons for hating him. Then their eyes met.

'Barnett!'

'Morning, Ken.'

'What are you doing here?'

Harry stopped at the top of the stairs. They stared at each other along half the length of the corridor. 'Came to pay my respects. Felt I couldn't leave Manchester without looking in.'

'You've seen Iris?'

'You bet. We had an appointment. Didn't she mention it? Must have slipped her mind. Well, I suppose she's had a lot to think about lately. Arranging the funeral and everything. Arranging a death, come to that. Or was that down to you?'

'I warned you before to leave my wife alone.' Hewitt started advancing slowly towards him. 'Listening to your worthless ramblings is the last thing she needs to do at a time like this.'

'Ah, but she did listen. Do you know why? *Because* it's a time like this. Because our son is dead. Like you wanted him to be. Dead – but not yet buried.'

'Get out of here.'

'Gladly. Once you've answered a couple of questions.'

'Your questions don't warrant answers.'

'You haven't heard them yet.'

'I don't need to.' Hewitt came to a halt three feet away and stared at Harry in a manner his employees doubtless found intimidating. He lowered his voice, perhaps to ensure none of them caught what he was about to say. 'You're a spineless shit, Barnett. You *had* a connection with my wife. A foolish and regrettable connection, now sundered. That's all I need to know. I don't allow myself to be questioned by the likes of you.'

'Why were you so eager to have David killed?'

'It's only out of consideration for Iris I don't call the police and have you arrested. You're drunk, you're offensive and this is private property. I'm telling you to leave. Now.'

'Because of the cost of his treatment? Because he was *our* son rather than yours? Because he was the son *you* were never capable of having?' This last was an impulsive jibe he had not even thought of uttering until the words were out of his mouth. He was not even certain Hewitt had no children. But the look on the other man's face suggested he had hit home. 'Which one of us is really the spineless shit, Ken, eh? Me or—'

Hewitt telegraphed the punch by the sudden gritting of his teeth and the widening of his eyes. Harry saw it coming and felt pleased in that instant to have provoked it. Pathetically late, his reflexes got in on the act and jerked him out of the line of the blow, which struck nothing but thin air. Hewitt was evidently in even worse shape than Harry, because the effort left him red-faced and off-balance, clutching at the top of the banisters for support. As he turned Harry hit him hard with his fist on the bridge of the nose. He heard something crack and found himself wondering if it was a bone or a banister. Hewitt grunted and fell backwards, subsiding onto the top step of the stairs like a punctured zeppelin. Blood began to stream from his nose. He coughed, groaned and raised a hand to his face. His eyes rolled for a moment before focusing on Harry. The arrogance in them had gone now. It had not taken much to dislodge it.

'What the hell's going on?' A figure had emerged from a doorway down the corridor and was moving hesitantly towards them. He was a tall shambling man of forty or so, wearing just the expression somebody would wear when called upon to rescue an employer he probably feared more than he respected.

'Call the police, John,' roared Hewitt through a blood-flecked handkerchief and what sounded like a heavy cold. 'I think the bastard's broken my nose.'

'As a matter of fact,' said Harry, grinning inanely, 'I think *this* bastard's broken my thumb.' Certainly it was throbbing painfully. He flexed it experimentally and winced. 'But I reckon it was worth it.'

'Don't just stand there goggling,' Hewitt shouted, when John still made no decisive move. 'Get to a bloody phone.'

'Which is undoubtedly preferable to a bloody nose, eh?' Harry was tempted to administer a boot to Hewitt's groin, but the futility of even talking to the man, let alone kicking him, washed over him in that instant. He shook his head dismissively at him and started down the stairs.

'Don't think you can get away with this,' Hewitt bellowed after him.

Harry paused long enough on the half-landing to grin back at Hewitt and raise two contemptuous fingers at him. Then he headed for the door.

Outside, the world was cold and grey and unaltered. At a chapel of rest in Wilmslow, his son's body still lay in its coffin. Nothing could change that. Nothing at all. Hitting Hewitt had made Harry feel better. But he knew the sensation would not last. Crossing the car park, he noticed a half-brick lying at the foot of the low boundary wall from which it had been dislodged. He picked it up in his left hand, his right now protesting at any movement, and looked back at the office building. He could see John in an upper window, speaking on a telephone and glancing down anxiously at him. Harry caught his eye and smiled, then took aim and lobbed the brick towards the windscreen of Hewitt's Jaguar. It hit dead centre. The sound of smashing glass blotted out the breaking of so much else in Harry's heart and mind. But only for a second. Only for a fraction of a second.

FIFTY-THREE

Ten days later, at noon, near the chill grey heart of Kensal Green Cemetery, Harry was sitting on the steps leading up to the east front of the Anglican Chapel, smoking a cigarette with his left hand while his right, encased in plaster save for the top two joints of his fingers and the tip of his thumb, rested on his knee, the thumb fixed ludicrously in a hitch-hiking position. But there were no rides to hitch here. And he had no destination to name even if he had been offered one. The fading of the year and the slow silent crumbling of the catacombs and sarcophagi around him perfectly matched his mood.

Death, he understood in the aftermath of his own son's, was not merely extinction, but erasure. The broken pillars still stood, the hollow helmets still echoed. But the thousands of names – and the thousands of people they had once been – vanished, sooner or later, beneath the lichen of utter forgetfulness. The memorials outlasted the memories. They alone remained, in this petrified forest of ceremonied mortality.

He ground out the cigarette beneath his heel on a lower step and tackled the complicated task lighting another had become on account of a broken thumb. As he did so, he thought fondly of the day he could throw away the lighter he had recently bought and revert to honest-to-goodness matches.

A figure, he noticed, had appeared far off along the central avenue that led from the chapel towards the east gate. A sightseer, he surmised, for there were always more sightseers than mourners,

261

though few of either on days as cold as this. Strangely, however, this one did not seem to be interested in the memorials lining the path. He or she kept up a steady pace in Harry's direction, looking neither to right nor left and becoming, somewhere near John St John Long's Grecian monument, identifiably female. She was a slim slightly built woman dressed in jeans and a dark coat with a hood, carrying a bag of some kind over her shoulder. By the time she had passed George Birkbeck's mausoleum, Harry knew who she was.

'Hi, Harry,' said Donna as she reached the foot of the steps. 'Good to see you.' She gave him a faltering smile that was somehow the more moving because of its uncertainty. 'Mind if I join you?'

'Be my guest.'

'Your landlady told me where to find you.' She climbed to where he was and sat down beside him. 'She said you'd been spending quite a lot of time here lately.'

'Well, none of the residents object to Greek tobacco, you see. Can't say that of many places these days.'

'Don't joke about it.' She squeezed his arm through the sleeve of his coat. 'I know what you must be feeling.'

'But that's the point, Donna. A joke is what I feel. Or the butt of one. I plod around here trying to see the funny side of it. But laughter seems in short supply. Plenty of weeping angels. But not a grinning one to be found.'

'I came as soon as I could.'

'But not sooner than was safe, I hope.'

'Haven't you read about it in the papers?'

'Mrs T said there was something. But I . . . couldn't seem to face the chapter and verse. What have they done? Turned the story into a major theatrical production – with Lazenby as the villain of the piece and a discreditable bit-part for David?'

'Something like that. The *Washington Post* went for it in a big way. Now all the media have joined in. Globescope's closed its doors and Lazenby's gone into hiding. Pretty ironic, given that we've just come *out* of hiding.'

'You're sure he won't try anything?'

'He'd be crazy to. I mean, *Newsweek* are assassinating him in print, film crews are besieging his house, Globescope's clients are taking out law suits against him and his senior staff are probably trying to set up book deals to compensate for the redundancy money they won't be getting, but it's all so much less excruciating than he deserves. Criminally, he's fireproof. None of the deaths fall under US jurisdiction and I doubt the British, French, Canadian and Danish authorities have the basis of a case between them, let alone adequate grounds for extradition. If Lazenby sits tight and keeps his hands clean, he can't be touched. And by the same token . . .'

'You can't be touched either.'

'Exactly.'

'I'm glad my efforts achieved that much, Donna. Really.'

'We wouldn't have got out of this without you, Harry. You know that, don't you?'

'Well, you wouldn't have got into it either, would you? Ultimately.'

'You can't take responsibility for David's actions. He was his own man.'

'But what sort of man would he have become if I'd raised him as my son, eh? That's the real question. And the answer? I can't help wondering. Dead and disgraced at thirty-three? I don't think so. I'd *like* not to think so, anyway.'

'I reckon you're probably right. He would have been better for having you as his father.'

'Kind of you to say so.'

'I happen to believe it. David had so many gifts so early he was blind to his own fallibility.'

'Well, I could certainly have taught him about *that*.' He held up his plastered hand. 'I've never made much of a fist of anything, have I?'

'That's garbage. You saved me, Harry. Makepeace and Rawnsley too. We owe you our lives. As for David . . . God, I'm sorry they let him die, even though I don't suppose Sandoval could have done much for him. Talking of whom, Iris didn't seem to know anything about him. How come you didn't mention him to her?'

'There didn't seem much point.'

'So you went easy on her, despite her broken promise. See what I mean? Not such a bad example to set. I tried to explain how grateful we all are to you, but I'm not sure she took much of it in. The publicity's hit her hard. It's one hell of an obituary. What with that and Ken Hewitt for a husband, her future must look pretty bleak. But I gather she's put a stop to your prosecution for assault, so she evidently realizes you're not to blame for what's happened.'

'Really? I assumed Ken had withdrawn his complaint for fear

263

of what I might say in court. But you're probably right. Iris isn't a malicious woman. In some ways, I wish she were. Then I might feel less sorry for her.'

'Not to mention yourself?'

'Ah, self-pity. That's your diagnosis, is it?'

'You tell me. David's dead. That's a fact. He's dead, but not for the want of trying on your part. That's a fact too. There's plenty to regret, but nothing to be ashamed of. You don't seem to realize what an altogether remarkable man you are. I didn't go to bed with you just because you happened to be there at the time, you know.'

Harry half-smiled and ran the fingertips of his right hand down her cheek, remembering as he did so the unbearable softness of her flesh. If only it were all as simple as what had happened that night. If only the ghost of his dead son and her abandoned lover did not stand between them, along with the small matter of more years than he cared to count. Then almost anything would seem possible. But to pretend such things could be set aside was the first step along a path leading to greater desolation than he already felt. He had pursued one fantasy in vain. He knew better than to chase another.

'What are you going to do, Harry?'

'Oh, this and that. The daily round. You know. Get on with life.'

'Is sitting here in this mouldering necropolis what you call getting on with life?'

'I suppose so. Well, these people are as real as anyone else in this city, aren't they? Or they were. And since time is just a dimension like any other, that means they still are, doesn't it? Time is the only thing separating us. Maybe if I sit here long enough . . . it won't.'

'I don't like the sound of that.'

'I know quite a lot about some of them,' Harry went on, undaunted. 'See that marble sarcophagus down there on the right?'

'Yes. What about it?'

'It's the tomb of Princess Sophia, daughter of George the Third. She had the sort of repressed royal upbringing you'd expect, then fell in love with a court equerry, General Garth. Got pregnant the only time they slept together. Gave birth in secret. Never told her father. Never lived with Garth. The son turned out a worthless scrounger. She went blind in old age and lived as a solitary recluse. Died nearly a hundred and fifty years ago. But nothing changes in human nature, does it? There are plenty of Garths in this world.

264

In a way, you're sitting next to one. Perhaps he got his come-uppance too. The guidebook doesn't say.'

'For God's sake, Harry—'

'Don't worry. They say things get easier to bear. With time.'

'I'd like to help.'

'You can.' He swivelled round on the step to look at her. 'Go home, Donna. Get on with *your* life. Start enjoying it again. Sign yourself up for a million-dollar book deal. Globescope, the full story. Should be a bestseller. Might even change the future. There's more chance of changing that than the past.'

'But what *about* the past?'

'Forget it. It's over.'

'This isn't the Harry I met in Chicago talking.'

'No. Because I'm not the Harry you met in Chicago. Or the Harry who was happily frittering away his life just six weeks ago, unaware he had a son lying comatose in hospital.'

'So what's Harry now?'

'A man with his eyes open. Looking into a mirror. And not much liking the view.'

'Well I'm looking over your shoulder. And I don't reckon the view's so bad.'

Harry managed a rueful grin. 'Thanks.'

'When all this is over . . . why don't you fly out to California . . . and stay a while?'

'That's an invitation you might come to regret.'

'I don't think so. What's the answer?'

'The answer's maybe. You mightn't think it was such a good idea if it came to the point.' He leant over and kissed her gently on the cheek. 'Let's wait and see.'

Harry walked Donna to Kensal Green station and waited with her on the southbound platform. She was heading for Heathrow and a flight to Copenhagen. Margrethe Hammelgaard was owed an explanation. Perhaps by Harry most of all. But he was happy to leave such matters to Donna. He had not even contacted Athene Tilson, as he had promised to do. What she had made of the affair he could not summon the energy to contemplate. The same applied to every other ramification of the Globescope scandal. His part in its exposure had left him drained and directionless, aware of little save the mockery David's death had made of his grand pre-tensions. He knew he had succumbed to self-pity. But he also knew that was preferable to accepting the pity of others. When he kissed

265

Donna goodbye, saw the doors slide shut behind her and watched the train accelerate out of the station, he was certain he would never take up her invitation. If he looked in the mirror now, there would be no-one smiling over his shoulder. It was not as he would have wanted. But it was as he had chosen.

He walked slowly out of the station and stopped by the entrance. Foxglove Road lay to the right, the cemetery straight ahead, the Stonemasons' Arms to the left. After a lengthy delay for the lighting of another cigarette, he turned left, quickening his pace as he went.

FIFTY-FOUR

December had always been Harry's *mois noir*. Dark, dreary and dominated by the familic frenzy of Christmas, it contained all the elements of Englishness he most hated. He had often suspected that the disruption of normality it entailed was a conspiracy to turn contented loners such as himself into suicidal depressives. His usual policy was to ignore it as far as humanly possible.

This December was different, however. It needed no conspiracy to lower his spirits. With no job to distract him, no responsibilities to discharge and no future worth looking forward to, he sank with little resistance into general despondency and occasional despair. The media hounding of Byron Lazenby largely passed him by. He glimpsed a harassed-looking photograph of him on a cover of *Time*, with the caption A PREDICTION TO DIE FOR: *Globescope's Self-Destruct Message for the Millennium*. And he was aware, because Mrs Tandy told him, that the Fleet Street Sundays were delving gleefully into the affair, even to the extent of door-stepping Iris in Wilmslow. But she was saying little. And absolutely nothing about her late son's natural father. So Harry was safe from the news-hounds, if not from the black dog of hopelessness.

The creature was still on his trail when Christmas arrived with all its goodwill-laden inevitability. Mrs Tandy departed, as was her wont, for a ten-day sojourn with her niece in Leamington. Harry customarily spent the holiday with his mother in Swindon and could think of no acceptable reason to make this year an exception. He would have preferred to pass the festivities in glum solitude at Kensal Green, but to explain such a preference to his mother was quite simply unthinkable, so to 37 Falmouth Street, Swindon, the house he had been born in and sometimes feared he might die in, he obediently travelled on Christmas Eve.

It was unclear whether his mother noticed any deterioration in his appearance or state of mind. The plaster having recently been removed from his right hand, Harry was spared the need to explain away a broken thumb. He maintained a jovial front to the best of his ability, retreating to the Glue Pot Inn even more eagerly than usual, but no more frequently than she was used to. Globescope – and the name David John Venning – meant nothing to her. And Harry was determined they never would. A scapegrace son was only what she had long known she had. But a dead grandson was a trick she did not deserve to have life play on her.

Three days after Christmas, Harry was soaking gently at the bar of the Glue Pot, trying to achieve the level of mild intoxication he deemed necessary for an afternoon of his mother's undiluted company, when just about the last person he ever expected to see on the premises walked through the door.

'Zohra! This is . . .'

'A surprise?'

'Yes. But a pleasant one, believe me.' It was true. Zohra, who he thought of as a friend rather than the wife a legal fiction declared her to be, was looking not merely well but radiant. She had changed her hairstyle, swapped her glasses for contact lenses and acquired a more adventurous wardrobe since moving to Newcastle. The plum-coloured coat and matching Tudor hat she was wearing were outrageously elegant for their present surroundings. But the confidence to wear them was what stood out. She was no longer the insecure young woman Harry had rescued from deportation. She had gained a belief in herself along with a British passport. And it showed. 'What, er, brings you to Swindon?'

'You do, Harry. Would you like to come out to tea with me? There's something we need to discuss.'

Tea was taken beside a roaring fire in the cosy surroundings of the Castle and Ball Hotel, Marlborough. The smart little car Zohra drove there in was a further surprise to Harry. Clearly, life was treating her rather better than him. But he had never been prone to envy. He felt pleased for her. Doubly so because of the help

268

he had once given her. It was much-needed proof that at least some things he did worked out for the best.

'Your mother's never liked me, has she?' said Zohra as she filled Harry's cup. 'She looked daggers at me when you told her we were going out for the afternoon.'

'She's never understood why I married you, that's all. I've tried to explain, of course, but marriage other than for lifelong union and the procreation of children is an alien concept to her.'

'In a sense, I agree with her.'

'Well, so do I, but . . .'

'As a matter of fact, it's what I want to discuss. I've met somebody. A new junior in the practice. He . . . well . . . he wants to marry me. And I . . . want to marry him.' She smiled at Harry nervously, as if he were a guardian whose approval she was seeking, though his co-operation was actually what she required. 'You and I have lived apart for more than three years now. It should be relatively straightforward to . . . take the necessary steps.'

'Divorce, you mean?'

'Well, yes. I'd make all the arrangements, of course. I'd make sure you weren't put to any trouble or expense. It's only a formality.'

Zohra was right, of course. It *was* only a formality. He had been her saviour. But salvation was no longer required. It was understandable. It was natural. But still he could not help wishing it had happened sooner or later, any time but now, when further proof of his expendability was the last thing he needed.

'I'll never forget what you did for me, Harry. I've told Neil all about it. You'll like him, you really will. And we'll stay in touch, won't we? This won't change anything.'

'No. I don't suppose it will.'

'So . . . you'll help speed things along?'

'Oh yes. Don't worry, Zohra. I won't cause you any trouble at all.'

In the wake of Zohra's visit, Harry found it difficult not to think more than just another year was ending in his life. Events had prodded him into looking forward as well as back. And the road seemed empty in both directions. On New Year's Eve, he walked out to the house in Holyrood Close that Claude Venning had hired him to paint back in the long-ago summer of 1960. It looked remarkably unchanged, except that the garden was more overgrown and the wooden doors and windows had been replaced with double-glazed UPVC units. They had no need of a painter now. His day was done.

Harry saw in the New Year with desperate gusto at the Glue Pot and spent the first day of it too hung over to speak much, let alone concentrate on the challenges awaiting him back in London. First among them would be finding a job. There was certainly nothing like economic necessity to take a fellow out of himself, as Harry knew from experience. He assured his mother it would be a top priority. She looked sceptical, but still gave him a farewell breakfast next morning that would have been sufficient to sustain a railway navvy for a week.

'You've been looking pasty to me ever since you arrived, Harold. Is something ailing you?'

'Age, Mother. That's all.'

'You should take better care of yourself.'

'*What for?*' Harry was tempted to ask. But instead he summoned a reassuring smile. 'I will. From now on.'

The man sitting opposite Harry on the train to London spent the journey immersed in a newspaper. Harry found himself studying the articles on whichever page was folded towards him. To his horror, he spotted the word *Globescope* in a headline presented for his inspection just after Didcot and could not refrain from reading on. It turned out to be a speculative piece on whether Project Sybil's dire predictions for the year 2050 should be taken seriously. Expert opinion was evidently divided on the point. Byron Lazenby, it seemed, was not the only forecaster who believed in telling people what they wanted to hear. Which merely served to underline the pointlessness of David's death. The only comfort it gave Harry was to remind him he would not be around in 2050 to find out how right or wrong David, Donna and the rest of them had been. Time would tell. But it would not tell him.

It was a bank holiday, the last in the long Christmas and New Year sequence. The Stonemasons' was open all day on the strength of it. Stopping off there on his way home, Harry found himself staying longer than he had planned. It did not matter unduly. Mrs Tandy was not due back from Leamington until Wednesday. He could arrive as late as he chose – and in whatever condition suited his mood.

It was, in fact, gone four o'clock on a cold and already frosty afternoon when he slid his key into the lock at 78 Foxglove Road. He stepped into the passage and dumped his bag, then turned back to close the door, resolving in his mind to spend no more lunchtimes that stretch till dusk in the Stonemasons'. They were no way to initiate the overdue process of pulling himself together. He would not continue January the way he had begun it. That much was—

The door flew open as he moved towards it and a figure burst into the passage, flinging him back against the wall and pinning him there, a hand grasping him by the collar of his shirt, a knee wedged between his legs. Which he saw first – the gun pointing at him from such close range that the barrel was blurred, or beyond it the sweating contorted face of Byron Lazenby – was hard to tell. But suddenly he felt stone-cold sober – and very very frightened.

'Hi, Norm,' said Lazenby in a breathless rasp. 'Or is it Harry?'

'I . . . Look, for God's—'

'Never mind that now. I have a more important question for you. A real brain-teaser.' Lazenby grinned and cocked the revolver. 'Can you think of a single reason – I mean a single goddam one – why I shouldn't blow your fucking head off?'

FIFTY-FIVE

They had moved awkwardly, like two tangled crabs, into Mrs Tandy's sitting room, knocking one of her Indian brass trays off the wall in the process. It had hit the floor with the noise of a clashing cymbal, convincing Harry for a strangely serene split-second that Lazenby had fired the gun. Death, it seemed, was like travelling on the tube: noisy but painless.

In reality, however, death was still only a threat, evident in the cold hard prod of a gun-barrel beneath his jaw. But the threat was real and horribly immediate. Lazenby had backed him up against the sofa, tightened his grip on his collar and repeated the question to which he could not seem to articulate any kind of answer.

'What do you say, Harry? I'm tempted – oh so tempted – to pull this trigger. Aren't you going to try to convince me I shouldn't?'

'Look, can't we talk? I mean—'

'We *are* talking. Not very persuasively in your case.'

'All right, all right.' Harry gulped, feeling the gun like a lump in his throat. 'Let's be reasonable. I hear . . . the law can't touch you. Why change that? Why become . . . a wanted murderer?'

'Why?' Lazenby grinned. 'For the satisfaction, you sonofabitch. Don't you know what you did to me? I almost wish I *was* being prosecuted rather than eaten alive by the piranhas of every newspaper, magazine and TV current affairs show in the western world. My business has been bankrupted. My reputation's been shredded. My entire life's been taken apart. I'm public enemy

272

numbers one, two, three and keep on counting. I don't even get a chance to clear my name in court. All that's down to you, Harry. So don't ask me why. Tell me why *not*.'

'Because . . . you did it to yourself. You killed four people and got away with it. You wouldn't . . . get away with this.'

'Don't give me that crap. Everybody else thinks I'm guilty. Naturally. But you *know* I'm not.'

'You're surely not trying to—'

'To hell with this! *I'll* give you the reason your brains aren't already splattered over that wall over there. Because I want the truth, Harry. I want the goddam truth. Why did you do it to me? Just tell me. Just give me the full story and maybe – if I'm sufficiently moved by your candour – I'll let you live.'

'I don't know what you're talking about.' Lazenby had asked for the truth and Harry had spoken it. But it was not what Lazenby wanted to hear. His cold blue eyes bored into Harry's, their unblinking message clear to see. He was in earnest. And there was no way out – for either of them. 'Honestly. I don't. I stole the tape to stop you killing anybody else. To expose what you were doing. David Venning was my son.'

'I heard all that from Ablett. I don't want to hear it again. We both know you're playing a deeper game. But I'm blowing the whistle. The game's over.'

'Ablett? I don't understand.'

'If you expected a slimeball like him to keep his mouth shut, you're an idiot, which I don't happen to think you are. He told me the lie you peddled them in Dallas about Hammelgaard's dying message. About being Venning's father. He told me everything. And I didn't even have to hold a gun to his head to make him.'

'It wasn't a lie.'

'Listen to me, Harry. Listen good. The world believes I commissioned four murders. And I can't convince the world it's wrong. But I know it is. Because I know I didn't do it. I'm an innocent man. You and I are both well aware of that.'

'No. I'm not. This is—'

'Your last chance. That's what this is. I'll make it easy for you. I'll tell you what I've already figured out. It's something to do with Slade, right? Something to do with higher dimensions. Hammelgaard and Venning researched them. Slade bragged about using them in his act. That's the connection. It has to be. Nothing else fits. And I've done *my* research. You were in Copenhagen when Hammelgaard died and Slade was the last person to speak to

273

Venning before he fell into a fatal coma. That's on the record. Plus Slade was in Paris the day Mermillod got his. And you . . . well, where were you when Kersey breathed his last? Montreal, by any short stretch of the imagination? I know Slade was on stage here in London at the time. So it has to be you, doesn't it?'

'I've never been to Montreal in my life. I don't know anything about this.'

'Drop the act, Harry. I'm your audience. And I can do much worse than throw rotten fruit.'

'It's no act. It's the—' There was a sound elsewhere in the house. A clunk, followed by a slither. Harry knew what it was at once. Neptune, fed in his and Mrs Tandy's absence by Mrs Edwards from number 75, was making his entrance via the cat-flap, in search of whatever gourmet dish Mrs Edwards had prepared for him. But Lazenby was ignorant of such pet-minding trivia. His eyes narrowed suspiciously.

'What the hell was that?' he whispered.

'I don't know. I'm not sure.'

The kitchen door creaked. It sounded as if Neptune had detected their presence and was coming to investigate.

'There's someone out there,' murmured Lazenby. He half-turned towards the door. The barrel of the gun slipped away from Harry's throat. It was the glimmer of a chance he knew he had to take. He lunged to one side, swung his right arm back and struck Lazenby across the jaw with his elbow. Lazenby grunted and fell against the sofa, then down onto the floor as if stunned. Hoping he was – for the few seconds needed to escape – Harry flung himself towards the door.

He was halfway there when he tripped. He knew from the squeal behind and beneath him that Neptune – the stupid overweight interfering mouser – was the cause. He heard the cat scampering away as he toppled onto all fours. Then his ears were booming and his brain whirling in the gale of an explosive roar. There was a crater in the wall where the light-switch had been. Plaster was raining down around him, brick-dust and cordite stinging his eyes and nostrils.

'Stand up very very slowly,' said Lazenby.

Harry stood up just as slowly as his trembling muscles could manage, fixing his eyes on the mangle of exposed wires in the wall where the bullet had hit and imagining the bloody mess it would have made of his bones and arteries.

'Turn round.'

Harry obeyed and found himself staring straight into Lazenby's face. Hollow-eyed, unshaven and wearing a suit so crumpled and creased he might well have slept in it, he was a far and desperate cry from the slick-toned businessman Harry had met in Washington. A horrible realization was seeping through the fear. Lazenby was telling the truth. He had been set up. And he had every reason to believe Harry was one of those who had set him up.

'Guess you borrowed one of the cat's nine lives there, Harry. You won't get lucky a second time, believe me. It just doesn't work like that. Let me explain something to you. Whether I kill you or not is a marginal decision. It could go either way. Depending how much my jaw aches when the numbness wears off, for instance. Or whether I like your choice of phrase. Know what I mean? You're on a fraying tightrope, friend. Over the deepest drop there is. I don't advise you to try anything that might tip the balance.'

'This is the truth, Byron. As God's my witness. I *am* David's father. Hammelgaard *did* ask me to carry a message to his friends about the tape. I had nothing to do with his death or any of the others. I stole the tape in good faith, to prevent more of the murders I believed *you* were responsible for. I thought you had to be stopped. I thought you were behind it all.'

'What do you think now?'

'I don't know what to think. If it wasn't you . . . then who? And why?'

'It was you and Slade. Like I told you. As to the why, *you* tell *me*.' Lazenby stepped closer, raised the gun and pressed the point of the barrel against Harry's forehead. For a second, Harry felt sure he meant to pull the trigger without another word. He wondered if his heart would stop from sheer fright before the bullet entered his brain. Then Lazenby said: 'Come on, Harry. What's it all about?'

'It's about Project Sybil and David's attempt to blackmail you. It's about the steps you took to stop their report seeing the light of day. What else can it be about?'

'That's not good enough.'

'It's all I know.'

'It can't be.'

'It is.'

'This is no time to hold out on me. You're bluffing with a losing hand.'

'I'm not bluffing.'

'Goodbye, Harry.'

'Wait. For Christ's sake . . .'

'I'll squeeze the truth out of Slade. D'you realize that? I'll find out anyway. You'll die for nothing.'

'I've told you as much as I know.'

'This is your last chance. Your very last chance.'

The gun seemed to bore into Harry's skull as Lazenby's stare bored into his eyes. His last chance was no chance. There was nothing he could say or do. Instinctively, he closed his eyes and took a deep final breath. There was a click, the prelude, he assumed, to oblivion. Then—

'OK. You win.'

Harry breathed out and opened his eyes. Lazenby was frowning at him curiously, as if events had surprised and puzzled him. He slowly withdrew the gun to his side and cocked his head.

'You thought I was going to kill you, right?'

'Yes.'

'Well, I was. But you worry me. I thought you'd tell me everything I wanted to know.'

'I can't.'

'That's what worries me. The possibility you might be on the level. The chance you might just be somebody else's dupe.'

'I think I must be.'

'Slade's?'

'I don't know.'

'Neither do I. But I reckon we ought to find out. Time we paid the magician a call.'

'*We?*'

'That's right, Harry. You and me. Right now. I have an automobile outside. I need a driver. And you just volunteered for the job.' He took a car key from his pocket and tossed it to Harry, who fumbled the catch but somehow managed to hold on to the key. 'Let's go.'

FIFTY-SIX

Harry was out of practice behind the wheel of a car. Even had he not been, nightfall on the streets of London, with a passenger aiming a loaded gun at his midriff, would have sufficed to spoil his technique. The only meagre blessing was that they were heading into the centre while everybody else seemed to be heading out. Told to aim for Mayfair, he set off south along Ladbroke Grove, riding the clutch at every stop for fear of stalling the engine and steering semi-blind on account of a fogged windscreen – until Lazenby took pity on him and started the demister.

'Do I really need to tell you Slade's address?' mused Lazenby as they tracked east along Bayswater Road. 'Maybe you know it anyway. Maybe you're a frequent visitor.'

'I've met Slade just once. At a restaurant in Soho. I've no idea where he lives.'

'So you say.'

'You're going to have to tell me.'

'OK. Waverley Mews. Near Berkeley Square. Go down Park Lane and hang a left by the Dorchester. You know that, I suppose.'

'Yes. I know it.' Harry's mind cast back to his meeting with Hope Brancaster at the Dorchester less than three months that seemed like years ago. Hindsight was a bitter business. But maybe foresight was even worse. 'Can I ask a question?'

'You can *ask*.'

'If you really are innocent—'

'Of this crime, I'm innocent as a new-born babe.'

277

'All right, then. So what did you plan to do about David and Torben? Pay them enough to set up HYDRA? Allow yourself to be blackmailed by them?'

'Not a chance. Giving in to blackmail's not my style. Nor's murder. Too messy. I prefer . . . circumvention.'

'What does that mean?'

'It means I already had someone to do what Venning and Hammelgaard were offering to do – at a cheaper price. It means I'd already catered for the contingency they thought they were springing on me. Gerard Mermillod was acting as my spy inside their camp from April on.'

'*What?*'

'You really didn't know, did you? Keep the surprise going, Harry. It's doing a lot for your chances of getting out of this alive. Yuh, Mermillod was my mole. I figured there was a chance the others would get together and try to publish their findings after I'd dispensed with their services. Mermillod was my insurance against that happening. He was to supply early warning plus a dissentient voice if and when the time came. He'd already told me what they were planning before Venning and Hammelgaard came to see me. I acted dumb for their benefit. Turns out I acted too well for my own good, though, thanks to the goddam tape.'

'Mermillod was the real traitor all along?'

'Yup. I kept him on the payroll with a covert and – it has to be said – generous salary. He had expensive tastes. I like people like that. It makes them easily corruptible.'

'But in that case—'

'I had absolutely no interest in seeing him dead. You've got it in one. I never had any intention of paying Venning and Hammel-gaard three million dollars. Instead, I meant to use their attempt at a side-deal to discredit them in the eyes of the others. And I planned to make them look like screwballs to the outside world by subjecting their hyper-dimensional research to some cogently reasoned rubbishing by the scientific establishment. I put Mermillod onto arranging that. He had contacts all over academia. Plus a blank cheque from me for cases where a little encourage-ment was needed. With two out of the seven lined up to lose all credibility and another happy to say whatever I told him to say, I had every option covered. Without the least need of putting out a contract on anyone's life.'

'What did you think when you heard about David's illness?'

'Same as I thought when I heard Mermillod was dead. That

278

events weren't going according to plan. But what could I do? After Kersey died, the others made themselves scarce. I came over here in an attempt to pick up their trail, but it ended at Venning's bedside – where you and I first had the pleasure of bumping into each other. I had no way of tracing Hammelgaard and Co. – or second-guessing them. I just had to sweat it out. I knew the media couldn't make their conspiracy theory stick because I knew there wasn't a conspiracy. Leastways, not the kind they wanted to believe in. As to what the hell *was* going on – if it wasn't just an incredible series of accidents, that is – I was as much in the dark as anyone else. Till the tape appeared and a landslide of unanswerable allegations hit me. It didn't take long for me to realize Globescope was finished. But whose doing was it? I've had more than a month of living out of a suitcase to ponder that one.'

'Whatever Rawnsley Ablett may have said, I can assure you I had no hand in it.'

'But what are your assurances worth, Harry? I know for a fact you've been holding out on Ablett, Steiner and Trangam. The guy scheduled to play Cornford to your Page broke his leg, right? And you told them you went through with it alone. But you didn't, did you? So, who *was* Cornford?'

They were at Marble Arch now, Harry drifting uncertainly between lanes as he steered into the southerly flow. Struggling in his mind with the problem of how to answer Lazenby's question when the truth might sound less plausible than any number of lies, he suddenly had to brake violently to avoid rear-ending a coach. The engine cut out on him as they shuddered to a halt.

'Jesus, will you watch what you're doing?' Lazenby glared at him, his face bathed in the blood-red glow of one of the coach's giant brake-lights. 'You won't get out of this by staging a crash, if that's what you're thinking.'

The coach moved on. A taxi behind them blared its horn. Harry started the car and drew jerkily away. Smooth acceleration and noiseless gear changes were beyond him because of the tension that had gripped every muscle in his body, but in Park Lane things were simpler. He headed south, training his eyes on the traffic in front.

'Who was Cornford, Harry?'

'A fellow-countryman I met in a bar in Washington and paid to act the part. I never told him why I wanted the tape – or what was on it.'

'You should have carved out a career for yourself as

279

straight-man to a comedian, you know that? I just can't tell if you're as dumb as you seem. It's worthy of a pro. But then maybe you *are* a pro. What kind, though, I wonder.'

'No kind.'

'What is it you and Slade have going?'

'Nothing. Nothing at all.'

'It doesn't matter. I'll find out soon enough. We're nearly there.'

'What if he isn't in? There's no saying he—'

'Pray he *is* in, Harry. Pray he hasn't gone away on vacation. I want answers. And I want them now. If I don't get them, somebody will suffer for it. Care to take a guess who that somebody might be?'

FIFTY-SEVEN

Waverley Mews seemed quieter and emptier than anywhere so close to Park Lane had a right to. The air was cold and still, the atmosphere discreet and affluent. There was no way to tell from the porch-lit exteriors who was in and who was out. The curtains were drawn, the garage doors closed, the shutters up. And Harry's number quite possibly with them.

But outside number seventeen, where Adam Slade lived, there was a hopeful sign, in the form of a casually parked jet-black Porsche, registration number AS 100. The front wheels, their tyres looking as fat as they were squat, had been left angled towards the street, ready for the swiftest of getaways. At least one resident of Waverley Mews did not believe in denying his neighbours the opportunity to admire his purchasing power.

Lazenby walked Harry from the car, the gun prodding ominously in his back, past the Porsche and up to the front door. There he pressed the bell and nodded at the entry-phone. 'You talk our way in,' he whispered, apparently still labouring under the illusion that Harry was qualified to do so.

A few seconds passed. Lazenby was reaching out to press the bell again when the entry-phone crackled into life. 'Yeh?' It was Slade, sounding like a man in a hurry. Perhaps, if they had been a few minutes later, he would already have vanished into the night on a gust of high-performance exhaust fumes. If so, his luck was out. But Harry's was in.

'Could I have a word with you, Mr Slade?'

'Who's that?'

'Harry Barnett. Remember? David Venning's father. We met . . . some while ago.'

'Barnett? Christ, yes, I remember. Get lost, will you?'

'It's important I speak to you.'

'Not to me.' The entry-phone went dead.

'Get us in there,' snapped Lazenby.

'How?'

'I don't care. Just do it.'

Harry pressed the bell, waited for a second, then pressed it again.

'You still there, Barnett?' Slade sounded angry now as well as impatient. 'Get off my doorstep, will you? This is becoming ever so slightly boring.'

'It could become ever so slightly expensive if you don't open up. I'm about to take a bradawl to the paintwork of your Porsche.'

'You what?'

'Just a brief chat, Mr Slade. That's all I want. It comes a lot cheaper than a respray.' But the last remark was addressed to a dead line. Slade was already on his way.

A few seconds later, the door was flung open by a barefoot figure wearing a dragon-patterned bathrobe. The left side of his face was pink-flushed and newly shaved, the right still covered with soap. His eyes darted from Harry to Lazenby and back again, then slowly tracked down to the gun in Lazenby's hand.

'What the—'

'That's right,' said Lazenby. 'It really is a gun. It's loaded. And I won't hesitate to use it. Why don't we all step inside?'

Slade's mouth sagged open. He stepped back into the hall. Lazenby signalled for Harry to follow. He brought up the rear, closing the door behind them.

They found themselves in a narrow passage, leading towards a kitchen. An open door on their left led into a lounge. Lazenby nodded towards it and Slade backed his way in. Harry went after him. The room was rectangular, with the shutters closed on its windows. It was furnished in clean-cut contemporary style, with glass-topped tables, chrome-limbed sofas, matt black hi-fi towers and a glossy green cactus in one corner reaching nearly to the ceiling. A matching pair of wall-mirrors faced each other across the width of the room, reflecting an endless regression of themselves. An infinite number of ever smaller Slades stumbled into view as Harry glanced into the one opposite him.

'You,' said Slade, frowning at Lazenby and running a hand

round his chin, apparently unaware of the soap still covering it. 'Don't I . . . Haven't I . . . Shit, you're Byron Lazenby, aren't you?'

'That's right, Adam. What's the matter? Thought I wouldn't figure it out so quickly?'

'He thinks you arranged the murders and let him carry the can,' put in Harry. 'Matter of fact, he thinks *we* arranged them.'

'*We?*'

'Harry denies it,' said Lazenby. 'And I'm almost tempted to believe him. Why don't you settle the matter? Are you in it together? Or is it just you?'

'I don't know what you're talking about.'

'The murders, Adam. Venning, Mermillod, Kersey and Hammelgaard. Your handiwork? Murder by magic, was it?'

'Are you crazy? I never—'

'Shove the denials! I'm serious.' Lazenby stepped close to Slade and prodded the gun into his groin. Slade crouched forward in a reflex reaction, then slowly straightened up, the breath hissing frantically through his clenched teeth. 'Why did you do it?' For a second, Harry was tempted to make a run for it. He was closer to the door than the others. But something stronger than the memory of what had happened at Foxglove Road held him back, something closer to sheer curiosity. 'Come on. I want the truth. Just fractionally more than I want to blow your balls off.'

'I haven't murdered anyone. I know nothing about any of those deaths.'

'You were the last person to speak to Venning before he was found in a coma.'

'He invited me to dinner, for Christ's sake. What's the big deal? Somebody *had* to be the last person to speak to him.'

'But that somebody was also in Paris nine days later when Mermillod was killed on the Metro.'

'I was filming a routine for French television.'

'But were you in the studio when Mermillod fell under a train? Or was he pushed – by you?'

'Of course not. I'd never met him. Why should I want to kill a man I'd never met?'

'Why should Venning want to have dinner with you?'

'We shared an interest in hyper-dimensional science. He enjoyed discussing it with me.'

'Are higher dimensions behind this, then? Something linking Venning's research and your act? Are they what made it worth your while to pin four murders on me?'

'No. No, no. They're just—' Slade glanced desperately at Harry, pleading for help, in words if not in actions. He was a professional performer, an illusionist *par excellence*. But surely his gaping terror was beyond simulation. If there was a secret to be spilt, he would have spilt it now. Yet he could find nothing to say. Harry knew the feeling – all too well.

'Just what, Adam?'

'Just a stunt. A trick. A come-on for the audience. You have to have something different to single you out from the card-sharps and spoon-benders. Higher dimensions are my . . . novelty, you could say. I don't have any hyper-dimensional powers. Nobody does. It's just . . . hocus-pocus.'

'Hocus-pocus? Then why should a brilliant mathematician be interested in them?'

'Because he thought my powers were real. Shit, that's what I *wanted* him to think. Scientific backing would have got me a hell of a lot of publicity. I was trying to con him.'

'Like you're trying to con me.'

'No. It's the truth.'

'But you're a trickster by trade. Truth is the last thing you're capable of telling.'

'Say something, Barnett.' Slade's eyes flashed imploringly at Harry. 'Christ almighty, help me convince this guy, will you? I didn't murder your son. I didn't murder anyone.' In that instant, Harry was certain. Slade was just a publicity-hungry illusionist using a spurious scientific claim to promote his magic act. A con artist with an oversized ego – but not a murderer.

'I believe him, Byron. I think you should too.'

'Why?'

'Because he's just admitted his stage-show's a fraud. Don't you see? His higher powers are just . . . hot air. If they weren't, he wouldn't be at your mercy.'

'It has to be one or the other of you – if it isn't both.'

'It's neither of us. We haven't even tried to blame each other, have we? We haven't lied to you.'

'Somebody has.'

'Not us.'

'Who, then?' Lazenby whipped the gun away from Slade and stepped back to face them. 'Who?'

'Maybe no-one. Maybe they really were just . . . accidental deaths.'

'That's bullshit.'

'But this isn't,' put in Slade, his voice sounding marginally calmer. 'You're ruined, but you're not finished. Kill us and you will be. If there really is someone out there who engineered your downfall, they'll have the last laugh then, won't they? You'll have let them have it.'

'You're a free man,' said Harry. 'You still have a chance of nailing your enemy. You still have a chance to rebuild your life.'

'Why blow it?' echoed Slade.

'Why not?' Lazenby glared at each of them in turn. He still held the gun firmly in his right hand, but his left was flexing and stretching, as if seeking some object to grip. The fingers slowly closed around an imaginary shape and crushed themselves into a fist. He raised it to his mouth and rubbed the back of his thumb across his lips. He was thinking hard and fast, weighing their lives against his desire to hit back at whoever had brought him down. 'The tape did for me. And you stole the tape, Harry. I haven't forgotten that.'

'Whatever Barnett did,' said Slade, 'I had no hand in it.'

'Shut up.'

'What I'm trying to say is—'

'Shut your mouth!' Lazenby's arm jerked up. He pointed the gun straight at Slade and seemed to be struggling for a moment against a compelling instinct to shoot him. Then his expression lost some fraction of its intensity. His grip on the gun slackened. He lowered it to his side. 'You're not worth it. That's the real joke. I've ended up chasing a spineless creep . . .' He glanced at Harry. 'And somebody who's been made almost as big a fool of as I have. Jesus Christ! I was so sure it had to be you. There was nobody else it could be. But there is, isn't there? And I haven't a clue who they are.'

'Byron,' Harry began. 'Why don't we—'

'Shut up, Harry. Just don't say a word. You too, Slade. Save your breath. It's all right. I'm not going to harm you. Unless you provoke me. I advise you to do and say absolutely nothing. Now or later. I'm leaving. And I don't expect to see or hear from either of you again. Contact the police and you'll regret it, I promise. Then I really will have nothing to lose. For the moment, I have just enough at stake to save your necks. Be grateful. I'm sure as hell not.' He stepped past Harry to the doorway and through it into the hall. There he stopped and looked back at them. 'If I ever find the trail and it leads to either of you, I'll make you wish I'd finished it tonight. If you're lying, I'll find out and come after you.

285

I'll dedicate my life to it. You have my word.' With that, he turned and strode away.

They heard the front door slam behind him and, a few seconds later, the sound of his car accelerating away down the mews. Slowly, Harry's muscles relaxed. The tension drained out of him. It was over. He was going to stay alive. But there was a price to pay even for that. Like Lazenby, he was not going to learn the truth tonight. Or any other, it seemed.

FIFTY-EIGHT

Ten minutes had passed since Lazenby's departure; nine and a half since Slade had blundered from the room; four or five since the sound of vomiting and coughing had ceased to carry to the lounge. Harry felt none of the magician's nausea, merely a numb sense of defeat. There was to be no answer, no allocation of guilt, no pinning of blame. Some part of the truth remained always out of reach.

He was helping himself to a scotch from the glass-shelved drinks bay when Slade walked back in, tucking a turquoise dress-shirt into black evening dress trousers. The soap was gone from his chin, but the skin beneath was still unshaven, giving his face a sinister lop-sided shadow. The grimace of fear was also gone, but there was still a discernible tremor in his hands. His panic was ebbing, but his swaggering arrogance was not yet back in place.

'Haven't you gone, Barnett? I thought you'd have crawled out of here by now.'

'I needed a drink. You don't mind, do you?' Harry was careful to make it clear by his tone that he was not really asking for permission.

'Looks like it wouldn't matter if I did. Pour me one too. A large one. With some ice.'

'Besides, I didn't know if you'd want me to wait while you called the police.' He handed Slade a glass and drank from his own.

'Are you crazy? You heard what he said.'

'You believed him?'

287

'Yeh. I believed him. Apart from which . . . there *is* such a thing as bad publicity. Getting mixed up in the Globescope scandal is the kind of exposure I don't need.'

'Because you might be forced to repeat your confession that your hyper-dimensional powers are pure eyewash?'

'No way. And if you're thinking of broadcasting what I may or may not have said under extreme duress, let me warn you not to. I'll deny it – and sue you for every penny you've got.'

'That won't bring you in much.'

'Anyway, I had to tell him something of the sort. I was trying to talk him out of shooting me, for Christ's sake.'

'Which is precisely why you told him the truth.'

'Back off, Barnett.' The whisky was beginning to restore Slade's self-confidence. 'As far as I'm concerned nothing happened here tonight. Except an uninvited visit from you. A visit that's just ended. Finish your drink and go. OK?'

'What did you and David talk about at the Skyway Hotel?'

'Don't you ever give up? It's over. Let it lie.'

'You're right. It is over. So you may as well tell me. After all, I did do my best to stop Lazenby killing you.'

'Huh!' Slade eyed himself in the mirror and rubbed the unshaven half of his chin. 'Shit, I look rough. At this rate, I'm going to be late for the opera. I can't go till I've finished shaving. And I can't finish shaving till my hands have stopped shaking.' He looked round at Harry. 'Why don't you leave me alone?'

'Why don't you tell me what you discussed with my son?'

'What do you think?' Slade slammed his glass down on the mantelpiece beneath the mirror and glared at Harry. 'Higher fucking dimensions. He believed in them. In the possibility of accessing them. He *almost* believed I already had the secret. But I could never quite get him to give me a public vote of confidence. It was the same that night. Except . . . he seemed to think he was much closer to the answer than before. He seemed to think he was very nearly there.'

'Not depressed? Not suicidal?'

'No way. He was right at the other end of the scale. Elated. Excited. *Eager*. Like he knew something I didn't know.' Slade paused to drain his glass. 'I've never seen anyone like that before. It was as if . . . he could see right inside your head. As if he could reach through you if he wanted to. There was this . . . sensation of power. And . . . something really weird.'

'What?'

'I kept getting these . . . shocks. You know? Like static electricity. Off the furniture, the cutlery. Off David when I shook his hand. Like I was . . . charged up. Or he was.'

'Did he ever explain his theory to you?'

'Not in terms I could understand. He talked a lot of higher maths that night. And he talked so fast. So *fluently*. It was like watching another magician performing an act you don't know. You don't believe what you see, but you can't see what the trick is either. I felt I understood while he was with me. I've had to familiarize myself with hyper-dimensional theory as part of my stage spiel, so it wasn't all new to me. I even wrote down a summary of what he'd said, sitting in the car park, before I drove away. I thought I might be able to use it to put extra scientific gloss on my act.' He grunted. 'Some hopes.'

'What was the problem?'

'When I read it in the morning, it was all . . . gobbledegook.'

'Still got it?'

'The note? Yeh, probably. Somewhere.'

'Could I see it?'

'You? What the hell for?'

'Curiosity.'

Slade snorted derisively. 'Be like giving an orang-utan *The Origin of Species* for bedside reading.'

'Nevertheless . . .'

Slade stalked across to the drinks bay to refill his glass, then said: 'Will handing over a page full of gibberish get you off my back, Barnett?'

Harry shrugged. 'Yes.'

'Then you can take it with you.' He sniggered bitterly. 'I won't want it back.'

In a quiet corner of the first pub he came to after leaving Waverley Mews, Harry took several calming gulps of beer, lit a *Karelia Sertika* and unfolded the page Slade had plucked from his Filofax and handed over a touch too willingly for Harry's peace of mind. As he scanned the page, covered in Slade's small neat handwriting, one reason for that willingness was revealed. But it was about all that was revealed. The contents were impenetrable. Doggedly, Harry read the words. Without grasping more than the merest hint of their meaning.

Human mind most complex/sophisticated organism so far discovered. Human consciousness straddles quantum mechanical/classical physics. Unitary evolution of particles at quantum level posits simultaneous existence of identical objects in form of complex-number-weighted co-existence of alternatives. Real-number squared moduli of complex-number weightings act as relative probabilities. State-vector reduction functions as dimensional compression. Alternatives apply in humanly unobservable dimensions. Leap to classical level illusory, because all alternatives are equally real, orthogonally superposed and reduced to one by macroscopic observation of quantum entanglement.

Fractal geometry of apparently chaotic natural phenomena reveals systems responsive to multi-dimensional attractors. Such systems ∴ exist fully only in multi-dimensional phase space, experienced by humans as 4-dimensional cross-sections of mental phase space. 4 conscious dimensions ∴ mirrored by minimum of 6 subconscious, through which topologically enfolded physical presence of 4-dimensionally unobservable reality can theoretically be accessed. Consciousness and com-pactification ∴ intimately related. Further refinement of hyper-dimensional complex maths will enable humanity to unlock enfolded matter as energy.

Slade had stopped there and driven away, while behind a closed hotel-room door, as the Heathrow jets climbed into the sky, infinity drew David Venning down into its velvety grip. Where he was, all secrets were known, but none could be told. All were equally real – and equally unobservable.

Harry sat for a long time, sipping beer and smoking cigarettes while he stared at the unyielding pageful of words. What did they mean? What – in the name of God or whatever universal organizing principle the physicists had put in his place – did they amount to? He looked at the smoke and the darkness and the dim lights around him. He looked at his face in the window and the figures moving at the bar behind him. He looked and looked – but he did not see.

He left the pub well before closing time and walked slowly back to Kensal Green through the amber-black London night. Several times he had the feeling there was something or someone just ahead or behind, lying in wait or closely following, no more than a curtain's thickness from his side, barely a whisper away; as if, in the invisible wall of his world, there was a two-way mirror through which he could be seen, but could never see – even so much as a reflection of himself.

It was an illusion, of course. Then, as on those other occasions when it had troubled him. An illusion, conjured up by his own anxieties. In the final analysis, there was nothing else he could allow himself to believe it might be. Reality, however bleak, was a cross-section of the world he could trust. And he was not about to desert it.

FIFTY-NINE

Harry woke early next morning, more exhausted by a succession of turbulent dreams than he was revived by sleep. Grateful to have a practical task to address himself to, he skipped breakfast and went straight down to clean up Mrs Tandy's sitting room. He swept up the brick, Bakelite and plaster fragments, vacuumed the carpet and peered into the crater in the wall in vain search of the bullet. Then he pondered the urgent problem of how to repair the damage before Mrs Tandy returned from Leamington the following afternoon. He was neither an electrician nor a plasterer, but he reckoned the services of both would be required that very day if he wanted to avoid explaining why he had let an armed madman into the house.

A cigarette and a cup of strong black coffee goaded his mind into some kind of constructive thought. Surely Mike, a regular at the Stonemasons', was an electrician, or at any rate an odd-job man who might be willing to cobble something together for him. He would phone Terry for his number when the hour was a little more godly. Better still, he would slide down there at opening time and ply him for the information face to face. Meanwhile, he supposed he ought to prise some tuna from a tin for Neptune. He plodded off towards the kitchen to summon the brute.

As he entered the hall, the post plopped through the letter-box. Assuming it would as usual be for Mrs Tandy, he retrieved the single item from the mat. Only to find that it was for him: a hand-addressed airmail letter, postmarked New York, 23 December. He

292

tore it open, made out Woodrow Hackensack's jagged signature at the bottom – looking like the electro-encepholograph of a disturbed brain – and began to read.

Hi Harry,

Thought you'd like to know I'm well on the road to recovery and getting barrel-loads of sympathy by telling strangers my stiff leg's a legacy of distinguished service in Vietnam. Should be a great Christmas.

Donna told me about David, so I guess yours isn't going to be so great. What can I say? It's tough. David was a good friend to me. I'm real sorry he's gone. Anything I can do— Well, I don't need to say it. You know where I am.

The other reason for writing is I felt sufficiently mobile this week to take a train-ride to Philadelphia. Tracked down Isaac Rosenbaum and tapped him for recollections of our late and loony friend Carl Dobermann. Rosenbaum's a tiny old guy with a face like a monkey and a memory that doesn't set much store by chronology. We had to sift through one hell of a lot of chaff before we turned up any grain.

The long and short of it is that Rosenbaum *does* remember Dobermann, as a head-in-the-clouds Ph.D. student who suddenly went crazy in the fall of '58. Well, maybe not so sudden, because the kind of rumours David said were running around Hudson Valley – the vanishing acts and second sight stuff – had already stuck to Dobermann back then. Which proves David didn't make them up. Static electricity was another thing. Dobermann was charged up worse than a nylon turtleneck. Rosenbaum claimed other students actually got shocks off this guy. A bright spark in more ways than one, seemingly.

Anyhow, the bottom line is Dobermann turned weirder and weirder, then went totally berserk one day. Wrecked a couple of laboratories. Had to be straitjacketed off to the asylum. A real men-in-white-suits job. Rosenbaum was put onto clearing up the mess afterwards. Reckoned the labs looked like a German panzer division had been through them. A one-man demolition team was our Carl. After he'd gone, the word was put out that the less said about him the better. Nothing official, but unofficially Dobermann became an off-limits subject.

That's more or less it, bar one tantalizing detail.

Rosenbaum said the mathematics lecturer supervising
Dobermann's thesis left right after Carl, low-key and
sudden. When he named the party, I realized it could be
the connexion with David you'd been looking for. I
remember David mentioning the same name when he
talked about how he got hooked on higher math in the
first place. Could mean nothing, but I thought you'd like to
know. Athene Tilson. Ever heard of her?

   Feel free to ignore all this if you've lost interest in the
subject. It'd be understandable if you had. But I reckoned
I owed you one, so I thought I'd make the effort. As for
Lazenby, well, we sure cooked his goose, didn't we?
   All the best,
   Woodrow

Harry did not get round to reading the last paragraph of Hackensack's letter properly until he was standing amidst the milling
commuters on the southbound platform of Kensal Green station,
waiting for the next Bakerloo line train. 'Lost interest in the
subject?' he murmured to himself, smiling grimly. 'No chance,
Woodrow.' The state of Mrs Tandy's sitting room was a matter of
small consequence now. He did not know what this latest revelation meant. But he knew he would have to find out. That very
day.

SIXTY

A winter's morning of frozen stillness slowly revealed itself as the train sped north through snow-patched Essex. Harry breakfasted on black coffee, a microwaved bacon bap and the tangle of his own thoughts. He re-read Hackensack's letter and Slade's note. He recalled as much as he could of the last time he had come this way. He remembered Athene Tilson's words – *'If you really want to understand higher dimensions, you could do worse than my own foray into the subject'* – and the inscription in the book she had given him. *For Harry*, she had written. *May you find as well as seek*. It had always seemed a strange choice of words. And now the strangeness was becoming sinister.

The Norfolkman reached Ipswich at nine o'clock. It was the same train Harry had travelled up on back in October, so he knew he was in ample time for the Southwold bus. But still he hurried across the footbridge and along the platform towards the exit. Haste was more a state of mind now than any kind of necessity.

Then, as he passed the windows of the buffet on his left, a glimpse of something oddly familiar stopped him in his tracks. A plump figure in a bell-tent raincoat was sitting at one of the window tables, staring out at him as he stared in. Her face was pale as a new moon, her hair bright as flame where a cold lance of sunlight fell upon it. And in her eyes was a startled look that amounted almost to fear.

He pushed open the door and stepped inside. The air was a

warm fug of coffee steam and cigarette smoke. At one end of the room, a track worker was caught in the eager embrace of a fruit machine. At the other, beyond a wasteland of empty tables, sat Athene Tilson's housekeeper, dwarfed by a mountainous grubby pink holdall that looked like a Brobdingnagian's cast-off and a cello case sporting more multi-coloured labels than a globetrotter's trunk.

'It's Mace, isn't it?' Harry asked, moving across to her. 'Remember me?'

'I remember,' she murmured.

'Been away for Christmas?'

'What makes you think so?'

'Well, the bag. And . . . being here.'

'I've not been away. I'm going.'

'Oh, right. Holiday?'

'I'm going for good.'

'Really. Why's that?'

'Ask Athene. It was her decision.'

'Sorry?'

'She threw me out.'

'You're joking.'

'Does it look like I am?' The forlornness in her was almost palpable, from the tiny mittened hands cradling her mug of tea to the bitter skittering anguish in her eyes. Assuredly, she was not joking. 'Athene gets rid of a lot of things she's had the best out of. I suppose I shouldn't have been surprised to be next on the list.'

'She . . . sacked you?'

'If you like. But since I was never exactly her employee . . . evicted is nearer the mark.'

'I don't understand.'

'Who ever understood Athene? Not me, that's for sure. Not even after thirteen years.'

'You worked for her – sorry, lived with her – for *thirteen years*?'

'Yeh. Unlucky for some, eh?'

'It's a long time, certainly. I'm on my way to see Dr Tilson now. Do you—'

'Don't go.' Her face suddenly flushed. She reached up and clasped his forearm. 'Please don't.'

'Why not?'

'Just promise me you won't.'

'I can't do that.'

296

'You have to.'

'Not without an explanation.'

'*The next train to arrive at platform two will be the nine-twelve service to London Liverpool Street,*' interrupted the station announcer. Mace looked up sharply, then glanced down at her alarm-clock-sized wristwatch. '*This train will call at Manningtree, Colchester and London Liverpool Street.*'

'Your train?'

'I suppose so.'

'Where are you going?'

'Not sure.'

'Not *sure*?'

'I mean . . . it doesn't matter.'

'It must do.'

'Not compared with—' She released his arm and let her hand fall back onto the table. 'Take my advice. Don't go to Southwold.'

'Why not?'

She looked up at him, her eyes huge and imploring. 'Is it true David was your son?'

'Yes.'

She nodded. 'There's a resemblance. I can see it.'

'You knew him . . . quite well?'

'I loved him.'

'What?'

'I loved David. Worshipped him from afar. At Cambridge . . . and since. Unrequited passion isn't actually very poetic. More . . . corrosive, as a matter of fact.'

'You were at Cambridge with David?'

'Yes.' Her eyes unfocused dreamily. 'Athene was my tutor. And David's supervisor. You could say she brought us together. And kept us apart.'

'I had no idea.'

'Why should you?' The London train rattled into the station, but Mace made no move to get up. 'Why should anyone?'

'Tell me about it.' Harry sat down beside her. 'I'd like to understand.'

'I'll miss my train.'

'There's always another.'

'That's what my friends said about David. Plenty more fish in the sea. Lots more pebbles on the beach. Pull yourself together; come to a party and pick up a boy. You know? The usual platitudes. And no help at all.'

297

'Why didn't it work out?'

'Not because of my weight, if that's what you're thinking.'

'I never—'

'I was slim then. Beautiful, some people thought. Positively Pre-Raphaelite.' She frowned and raised a hand to her forehead. 'Sorry. I've always been over-sensitive. Especially since— Well, the fact is David just wasn't interested in me. For a start, I was a musician, not a mathematician. He thought anyone who preferred counterpoint to calculus had to be either perverse or stupid – or both. I suppose, looking back, it should have been obvious it was hopeless. We simply didn't have enough in common.' She summoned a faint smile. 'But I wasn't very level-headed at nineteen.'

'Who is?'

'David, for one. Level-headed. Single-minded. And chillingly mature. As well as irresistibly attractive.'

'Was there . . . somebody else?'

'Oh yes. There was somebody else. I just didn't know it at the time. I thought he was . . . unattached. Which made rejection pretty hard to take. So much so that . . .' She sighed and shook her head. 'I proved him right about being stupid.'

'How?'

'Gave up serious study. Followed him around. Bombarded him with love poems. Oh, and took up shoplifting. Books and clothes mostly. The psychiatrist said it was attention-seeking. It certainly attracted the attention of the police. And the university authorities. After they'd finished with me, there wasn't much left.' She stroked the neck of the cello case affectionately. 'Not even a half-decent cellist.'

'You must have had a rough time.'

She nodded. 'All the rougher for being self-inflicted.'

'How did you end up living with Dr Tilson?'

'She'd just bought Avocet House in preparation for her retirement. Needed somebody to look after the place during the week, while she was in Cambridge. I was on probation and didn't have much option. It was either take up Athene's offer or go back to live with my parents. No competition, let me tell you. I'd probably be in an institution by now if I'd gone down that road.'

'Are you going back to them now?'

'For a few days. Then . . . I don't know.'

'But why stay in Southwold all this time? You can't have been on probation for thirteen years.'

298

'I like it there. And I like Athene. She has a . . . quality of peace . . . that can be quite contagious. I wanted to hide from the world and she wanted to retire from it. It was a sensible arrangement for both of us. I was grateful to her as well, of course. For getting me off the hook. I suppose I didn't realize I was effectively swapping one hook for another.'

'What do you mean?'

'Well, living with Athene meant I could still see David from time to time. He wasn't a frequent visitor. But he kept in touch. With Athene, I mean. So, I always had the chance – the hope – of impressing him. I had this fantasy that when she died, he'd take pity on me and carry me off somewhere. Pathetic, isn't it?'

'I don't think so.' Harry smiled at her almost paternally. 'We all have fantasies.'

'Yeh? Well, mine's over now. David's dead. And I'm not going to be nursing Athene into her dotage. The door of my cosy seaside retreat from reality's just been slammed in my face.'

'Why? What was the problem?'

'I must have asked too many questions, I suppose.'

'What about?'

'Her recent travels, mostly.'

'Travels? I thought she was a virtual invalid. Housebound, I assumed.'

'Far from it.' Mace chuckled humourlessly. 'The arthritis and emphysema seem to come and go at will. They're part of Athene's disguise. She says there's nobody people are less suspicious of than a doddery old woman. Nobody more *ignorable*. Which is what she likes to be. Ignored. Forgotten. Neglected. Overlooked. Underestimated.' She paused. 'Perhaps fatally so.'

'What do you mean by that?'

'I mean she was away from home the night David fell ill. Attending a college dinner in Cambridge, she said. But I checked. She wasn't there. She was away quite a lot in September. And she lied about her destination every time. She went away again about a week after your visit in October.'

'How long for?'

'A fortnight or so.'

'Where did she go?'

'She didn't even bother to lie to me that time. She just . . . declined to say.' Mace let out a long slow sigh. 'I didn't much care by then. It was the day I'd telephoned the hospital – prompted by

299

some kind of instinct, I think – and learnt David was dead. Just a few hours later, Athene walked through the door. Quiet, regal, ghostly as ever. A little like death herself. Cold. Remote. Above it all. Like . . . a visitor from another planet. She's always had this . . . unearthly quality. I think it's what drew David to her. Not mathematics so much as . . . magnetism.' Mace's eyes flicked up to meet Harry's. 'She was the somebody else in your son's life. Always and for ever. Oh, don't worry. I'm not alleging some bizarre sexual relationship. It was her mind he couldn't resist. I once asked him why he kept coming to see her. I had some frail hope he might say it was an excuse to see me. But instead he replied, with utter sincerity: *"Because Athene's the real thing. A mathematician several generations ahead of her time. The most brilliant, original and innovative numerical thinker since Cardano."* '

'Who?'

'Gerolamo Cardano. An Italian mathematician of the sixteenth century. I looked him up. He was the discoverer of probability theory and complex numbers – whatever they are.'

'I've never heard of him.'

'Just as most people have never heard of Athene Tilson. *"She knows more than she'll let me understand,"* David said. *"But one day, when I've learnt enough, I'll persuade her to unlock her secrets."* '

'But I thought . . . she said . . . David's work had left her behind.'

'The way he told it, he was still trying to catch up.'

'Or maybe he *had* caught up.' As Harry's thoughts were doing, with the implications that were beginning to thread themselves between the facts he had so far failed to connect. 'At long last.'

'How do you mean?'

'Did their relationship seem . . . different in any way . . . the last time he visited her . . . in early September?'

'I wouldn't know. I wasn't there. Athene sent me to Cambridge that day to collect some books she'd ordered. I didn't find out about David's visit until I got back. She said he'd turned up unexpectedly. But that wasn't true either. They'd spoken on the phone only the night before. She wanted me out of the way for some reason. Like now, I suppose. Except that was just for the day. This is for good. Or bad.'

'Did David ever mention anyone called . . . Dobermann?'

'What name?' Mace frowned, as if struggling to pin down an errant familiarity.

300

'Carl Dobermann.'

'No. Never. But . . . it's funny. You knowing the name. While Athene was away, some time early in November, a man telephoned, asking for her. Long distance. He gave his name as . . . Carl Dobermann.'

'Highly strung, was he? Unbalanced, maybe?'

'Maybe. Odd, certainly. But we only exchanged a few words. He wanted Athene, not me.'

'Did he leave a message?'

'Yes. After a fashion. He asked me to tell her he'd . . . remembered.'

'Remembered what?'

'He didn't say. That was all there was to the message. He'd remembered.'

'You passed it on?'

'No. As a matter of fact, I didn't. I meant to, of course. But . . . other things put it out of my mind. I think I may have assumed it was some kind of wrong number.'

'But he asked specifically for Athene?'

'Yes. He did.'

'Then it can't have been, can it?'

'No. I suppose not.'

'What's your Christian name, Mace?'

'Phyllida. Why?'

'It's a pretty name.'

She blushed. 'No-one ever uses it.'

'That's a pity.'

'A pity. But not a tragedy. Sounds like it could be my epitaph.'

'Why don't you want me to go to Southwold, Phyllida?'

'For the same reason part of me was glad to leave. Lately, Athene . . .' Mace's eyes fell. Her voice sank close to a whisper. 'She frightens me. She used to be . . . comforting. Now . . . I don't know. Something's changed.'

'I have to go.'

'Why?'

'For David, I suppose.'

'But you never knew him.'

'That's why I have to go.'

'Don't. Please.'

'I must.'

'I'm pleading with you.' She laid her mittened hand on his. 'Don't go.'

'What harm can it possibly do to visit a little old lady who lives by the sea?'

'More than either of us can imagine.' Her grip tightened. 'That instinct I had. To phone the hospital the day David died. It's the same feeling I have now. About you. And Athene.'

'What feeling?'

'That if you go to see her . . .' Slowly and sadly, Mace shook her head. 'You won't come back.'

SIXTY-ONE

By the time he had seen Mace off on the next train to London, Harry had missed the 99 bus. But such minor obstacles no longer troubled him. Courtesy of a thirty-six-pound taxi ride, he reached Southwold while the bus must still have been chugging through Saxmundham.

The morning seemed colder and dazzlingly brighter than it had in Ipswich. The low winter sun danced and glinted on the sea, invading and confusing Harry's senses as he made his way from the busy market place down towards the green at the southern end of the town, where Avocet House stood on a minor crest, hedged off and withdrawn from its neighbours.

He marched straight up to the door and tugged at the bell, heard its echo in the hall merge with the chime of a clock striking the half hour and waited for the sound of footsteps or an answering voice. But there was no response. Nor when he rang again. And again. He stood baffled in the porch, rubbing his hands for warmth, aware – to his own bemusement – that he had been confident Athene would be there because of a subconscious suspicion that she had known he was coming and had sent Mace away to ensure there would be no witness to their encounter.

Unwilling either to leave or merely to wait on the doorstep, he walked round to the rear of the house, past a wind-carved broom hedge and so into the garden, overlooked by the conservatory where she had received him last time. Her wicker chair was empty and there were no walking-sticks propped against the table beside it. He peered in through the window. There was no sign of movement. He tried the door. It was locked. The key was visible on the other side and the way the door yielded at top and bottom implied that the bolts, if there were any, had been left unshot. Crouching down to squint beneath the weatherboard, he made out a shrinkage gap above the threshold of nearly half an inch. That, plus the bundle of old newspapers resting on the lid of the dustbin over by the garage, constituted a virtual invitation. He went over and prised one free of the string, glancing in through the garage window as he did so. The bulky shape of a vast old Humber revealed itself through the gloom. Wherever Athene had gone, it was evidently not far. But Harry did not propose to wait for her any longer.

He went back to the conservatory, folded the front few pages of the newspaper flat and slid them beneath the door, then prodded at the keyhole with the nib of his pen until the key plopped out obligingly onto the paper. He smiled at the simplicity of the ploy, recalling how sceptical he had been when seeing it used too many times for plausibility in Hollywood B movies. Then his smile stiffened. Carelessness, after all, could just as easily be deliberation. And Athene Tilson had not struck him as the careless type. As he inched the newspaper back out and saw the key emerge with it, he saw also the close-packed typesetting of the *Wall Street Journal*. It was the edition for Tuesday 8 November, the edition he had himself bought in Chicago on account of a front-page article reporting a fall in Globescope's share price following Hammelgaard's sudden and unexplained death in Copenhagen. Harry grabbed the key and whipped the newspaper over to the front page.

And there – where the article should have been – was instead a neatly clipped rectangular hole.

Athene's possession of the newspaper was suspicious enough, but her meticulous removal of the Globescope article raised suspicion to a pitch of confounded disbelief. Harry wrenched the door open and rushed through the conservatory into the drawing room, pausing only to listen to the stillness of the empty house. She was not there. But she had so often been there that the walls and furnishings – the very air itself – seemed ingrained with her presence. She was not there. But Harry did not feel entirely alone.

He followed his instincts along the hall to the study. It was as he remembered, the desk loaded with papers, the shelves with

304

books. The photograph of Princeton Institute luminaries *circa* 1953 still hung above the mantelpiece. And the blackboard . . . was blank. Harry goggled at it in a kind of wonder. Where were the equations, the formulae, the jumbled Greek letters? Where was the work in progress? Erased, apparently. But why? What had made erasure necessary?

He rounded the desk and cast aimlessly through the stacks of paper. Here too blankness was the norm. The clutter had more than a hint of contrivance about it. Even the blotter contained fresh unmarked paper. And the desk diary, lying where it could not be missed, was for the old year. Somehow, Harry would have expected such a rigorous thinker as Athene Tilson to have replaced it with a new one promptly on 1 January. Her failure to have done so struck him as a portent, both indefinable and undeniable.

He opened the diary and leafed through it to the date she had given him for Hammelgaard's visit: 20 September. *David's friend*, she had scribbled. *3.30*. He leafed on to his own visit, unsure for the moment of the date. Then it was there, in front of him. But it was not what he was prepared for. Beneath the heading for 25 October was written: *David's father 11.45*.

He had not told her he was David's father until he had arrived. He had not told her and she could scarcely have guessed. The diary entry was either made after the event – which seemed singularly pointless – or she had known all along. She had known what Iris had fondly believed no-one *could* know. She had known even before Harry had known himself.

He wrenched at the drawer beneath the desk, anger adding to his impatience. It was locked and stoutly constructed. But locks were not going to stop him. He strode out into the hall and along to the kitchen, where he hunted down a carving fork and an old butcher's steel that looked as if they would do the job between them.

A strange sensation ran through him as he retraced his steps along the hall. It was as if he had walked into a cobweb; as if a brush had been passed over his head or a razor been slid across his unshaven chin. He pulled up and examined himself in a full-length mirror that hung beside a barometer next to the telephone table. As he reached up to rub his forehead, his hair frizzed out to meet his hand. The telephone tinkled faintly, just once, then fell silent.

He went on, then stopped again. The door ·to the study stood ajar, whereas he had surely left it wide open. There were no open windows to create a draught. And there was no-one else in the house. Was there?

Hesitantly, he pushed the door away from him and entered the room, turning slowly to look towards the desk. Where Athene Tilson sat smiling expectantly. 'Hello, Harry,' she said mildly. 'Looking for something?' She slid the desk drawer open as she spoke, lifted out half a dozen identical blue cloth-bound notebooks held together with a rubber band and dropped the bundle in front of her on the blotter.

'You know what these are, don't you, Harry? You were asking about them last time you came here. They're David's notebooks. All of them. Just waiting for you.'

SIXTY-TWO

At first glance, Athene Tilson was just as she had been ten weeks before. Grey-haired and thin to the point of gauntness, dressed in guernsey, tennis shirt and corduroy trousers, she could easily have been taken for a frail old woman surrendering shabbily to advancing years.

But a second glance told a different story. Gone were the round-shouldered stoop and arthritic stiffness, gone too a clutch of implied weaknesses and suggested failings. She was a woman transformed. Or one revealed, perhaps, for what in truth she had always been. There was nothing cosmetic about it. Artifice had been abandoned. That certainty communicated itself to Harry in the erectness of her bearing, the intensity of her gaze, the intimidating placidity of her presence. He felt like some bucolic intruder confronting a high priestess. What she knew he could scarcely hope to understand. And what he understood she already knew.

'Sit down, Harry,' she said calmly, pointing to a chair. 'Let's talk.'

Numbly, Harry obeyed, dropping the carving fork and steel onto the carpet beside him. 'I didn't . . . hear you come in,' he murmured.

'You've done well,' she said. 'Really. Exceptionally well. I think David's tenacity must have been an inherited trait, don't you?'

'How would I know?' Harry managed to toss back. 'I never met him.'

'I'm sorrier for that than I can ever say. He asked my advice, after tracking you down in Rhodes. He asked what I thought he should do about you. I recommended him to forget you, to exclude you from his life. I was wrong. I did to you what so many others have done to me. I underestimated you. I mistook the superficial for the substantial. I am so very sorry. It was unforgivable. More so, perhaps, than other more drastic actions I've taken since.'

'What actions?'

'There's no need for me to tell you, Harry. You already know.'

'Tell me about Dobermann.'

'So that's what brings you here. You made the connection, did you? After all my efforts to prevent you.'

'I want the truth.'

'Really? Are you sure about that?'

'What was it with you and Dobermann and David?'

'What was it? It was a dream. Their dream and my nightmare.'

'You're talking in riddles.'

'It is a riddle. But it's no game.'

'Dobermann phoned here while you were away in November. Mace took a message.'

'She never told me that.'

'She told *me*.'

'What was the message?'

'He said he'd remembered. After more than thirty years, he'd remembered.'

'My fault,' Athene said in an undertone. 'Entirely mine.'

'What had he remembered?'

'Something he would have done better to forget for ever.'

'*What?*'

'The answer to the riddle.'

'*Just tell me.*'

'Very well.' She reached out and ran her hand across the cover of the topmost notebook. 'But it's so difficult to explain. There are no words to describe the structure of the world as it has become apparent to my mind. The range and acuity of my perception have grown with age. Once, all was dazzle and confusion. Now, the clarity is . . . incredible. The ability is latent in your mind as well, Harry. And in the mind of every shopper walking the streets of Southwold. If it became actual, you'd be like a blind man given telephoto sight. There's a scale difference – a phase shift – you literally can't envisage.'

'You're talking about higher dimensions.'

'I am.'

'Hocus-pocus, according to Adam Slade.'

'Everything is – in the mind of a charlatan. Believe that's what *I* am, if you wish. It's probably safer. Believe what I'm about to tell you is an old woman's fantasy. But it isn't. I *know* it isn't.'

'Convince me.'

'I can't. You're not a mathematician. You don't understand. You never will. Good. I'm glad for you.' She smiled. 'What did you make of my book?'

'Nothing. It was way over my head.'

'Exactly. But the book is where it begins. Numbers are the key. Their nature and behaviour – their possession of a level of reality mathematicians learn to use and respect without ever quite comprehending – are shadows cast in the four-dimensional world by the forms above and around and within it. We see their shadows, not their shapes. But there cannot be a shadow without a shape. In that book, in the work that went into it, I began to feel my way towards them, as you might feel your way towards the door in a darkened room, slowly and painstakingly. My knowledge has grown exponentially since. It reads to me now like a child's scribbling-pad, even though it contains secrets no twentieth-century mathematician could hope to understand.' She paused. When she began again, a tiny inflexion of guilt had entered her voice. 'None living, I should say.'

'You mean David?'

'And perhaps one other: Srinivasa Ramanujan, the genius from Madras. His surviving work on modular functions suggests that, if he'd lived to read *The Implicate Topology of Complex Numbers*, its significance would not have been lost on him. But Ramanujan died two years before I was born, aged just thirty-three.'

'The same age as David.'

'Yes.' She caressed the notebooks once more. 'Thirty-three. A magic number, mathematicians call it. One that recurs in calculations when least expected, for reasons that cannot be fathomed.'

'Except by you?'

Her hand slipped away. She leant back in her chair. 'My work attracted distinguished attention, despite its esotericism, or perhaps because of it. I was invited to Princeton largely on account of Gödel's interest in the book, which in turn aroused Einstein's curiosity. It was there that I made two important discoveries. Firstly, that it might be possible to train the mind to the point where its grasp of the numerological underpinnings of higher dimensions became so sure, so natural, so *instinctive*, that one might take the mental leap to direct experience of them.'

'That's crazy.'

'Think that if it will help you sleep at night. But I'm only describing to you a path I've already trodden. The existence of higher dimensions has been mathematically verified many times. The compactification theory is a *post hoc* rationalization. It evades the issue. Ask Miss Trangam how much of the brain we fully understand. If she answers honestly, she will say: hardly any of it. What we call consciousness is partial awareness. The rest is locked up here.' She tapped her forehead. 'Waiting for us to turn the key.'

'As you've done?'

'In a sense. But a key can lock as well as unlock. That was my second discovery.'

'What do you mean?'

'I mean that what's possible is not necessarily desirable. Imagine you are aware of only two spatial dimensions: length and breadth. Then imagine I take a hula hoop, pass it over your head and lower it to the floor around your feet. You have thus become my prisoner. You cannot escape.'

'Why not? I only have to step over it.'

'But you can't. Height – and therefore the idea of raising your foot, the very act of stepping itself – is beyond your conception. You don't believe height exists. The hula hoop is to you an impassable barrier. You're trapped by the limitations of your own senses.'

'You're just playing with words.'

'I'm not *playing* at all. If this room had neither doors nor windows, you would agree we could never leave it?'

'I suppose so, but—'

'I could simply step out of it, as you would step out of the hula hoop.' For a moment, Harry could think of no riposte. Athene smiled at him, a smile not so much of superiority as of protectiveness. 'Don't you see, Harry? The power conferred on those who attain an awareness of higher dimensions is a power *over* those who don't. To entrap. To manipulate. To spy. To hurt. And ultimately to kill – without the slightest fear of detection. Who would know – who could ever find out – if I squeezed your heart until it stopped beating?'

'That's not . . . possible.'

'Why not? If skin and bone are no more a barrier than a hula hoop encircling your feet.'

'But they are more. What you're saying is . . . madness.'

'The attempt may end in madness, certainly. It did in poor Carl's case. The intellect is a fragile thing. It cannot take too much pressure.'

'You're saying an attempt to become aware of higher dimensions . . . drove Dobermann mad?'

'I'm saying there are clues to be found in *The Implicate Topology of Complex Numbers*. Clues that form a trail two of my students have, over the years, tried to follow. I can't erase the clues. Only time can do that. When I am dead as well as forgotten, and the last copy of my book has mouldered on some dusty shelf of some obscure library, *then* mankind will be safe from the secret.'

'*Mankind?*'

'Is worth protecting from its own folly. Wouldn't you say?'

'I'd say it depends who's doing the protecting. And why.'

'I am, Harry. As to why, I found reason enough at Princeton in the fifties. First there was Oppenheimer, willing – nay, eager – to confess what it felt like to have placed immense destructive power in the hands of his fellow humans. Remember what he said at the time. "I am become Death, the destroyer of worlds." Well, he meant it. He had known sin, he told me. He had brought evil to life. From a single atom of uranium. If we'd sat here a century ago and I'd told you a glob of matter no larger than a grapefruit could lay waste half of Suffolk, you'd have said it was – what was your word? – madness. But that madness became the linchpin of this country's defence strategy. And MAD was the acronym used to describe it.

'Then there was Einstein, who'd paved the way for the atom-smashers fifty years before with the chilling simplicity of the equation he's universally remembered for. Energy equals mass times the speed of light squared. With that, he laid the fuse for Oppenheimer to ignite. And he too recoiled from the consequences.

'I became a regular afternoon caller at Einstein's office, ostensibly because he valued my contribution to his work on unified field theory. Actually, he wanted an audience for his doubts about the desirability of scientific progress. And he was shrewd enough to sense that I needed to be warned. Hiroshima and Nagasaki had proved to his satisfaction that the human consequences of scientific inquiry are always incalculable and are never as positive as the scientist predicts. His biographers generally interpret the inconclusive nature of his work on unified field theory

311

as evidence of his mental decline in old age, but I suspect he may have deliberately dragged his feet. And may have picked holes in quantum theory for much the same reason. He feared a widening gap between knowledge and the moral maturity of mankind. And he foresaw disaster if the gap was not narrowed.

'I've no doubt Einstein was right. Some discoveries are best avoided. Or delayed. Or hidden. Carl's disintegration proved that and I wish for no more compelling illustration. I've published nothing on the subject of higher dimensions since *The Implicate Topology of Complex Numbers*. I've taught only what others can teach. It has not been easy. I've often craved recognition and reward for what I've achieved, though with age such cravings – like most others – have diminished. If I were a man, I might have given way. But women take a broader view. I've held my tongue and my brain in check. And my reward is freedom from the guilt that troubled Einstein and Oppenheimer and their fellow physicists who lived in the shadow of the mushroom cloud.

'You'll think it odd that I should claim to feel no guilt in view of what I'm about to tell you. But it's true. I've examined my conscience and am clear on the point. What I did had to be done. The sin would have been to do nothing. To while away my days here and let the next generation grapple with the consequences. It was tempting, believe me. I wanted none of this. But it had to be.'

'None of *what*?'

'Murder, in the strict legal definition. I've murdered three men. And your son was one of them.'

'You admit that?'

'Would there be any point denying it?'

'But . . . *why*?'

'I've told you why. Like Carl, David saw the true significance of my work. But much more clearly. His intellect was equal to the task. And piercing enough to see through my concealments. I can follow his progress in these notebooks, edging ever closer over a decade and more. The wrong turnings and the false hopes. But also the slow advances, the brilliant intuitions and the flashes of pure genius. Till in the latest of them he was only a few short steps behind me.

'When he came here last September, it was to proclaim his discoveries and to unveil his plans for HYDRA. I tried to preach caution to him, but he wouldn't listen. He already saw himself as the founder of a new scientific generation of the hyper-dimensionally aware. He was terribly convincing. I could see he would make it happen. The promise of funding he'd extorted from Lazenby and the originality of his most recent work would have opened the door. Within his lifespan, mankind would have had to cope with the creation of a powerful élite of hyper-dimensionally trained mathematicians.'

'I thought you said the ability was latent in all of us.'

'So it is. But accessible only to the mathematically gifted. At least to begin with. A beginning that would certainly last several generations. During which those denied such training – or intellectually incapable of benefiting from it – would inevitably be reduced to a position little short of servitude. David saw none of that, of course. He anticipated only universal prosperity and the general advancement of the species. My fears were dismissed with the confidence – and the myopia – of youth. I was left with no alternative. To safeguard the future, I had to act. In short, I had to stop him. And there was only one way to do it.'

'You *killed* him? Because of the effect his work *might* have had on the future?'

'*Would* have, for certain. He didn't suffer, Harry. I made sure of that. He was sleeping. Dreaming, perhaps, of the better world he fondly supposed his discoveries would usher in. A dream he never woke from. It's as generous a fate as any of us can hope for.'

'You call two months on life support . . . *generous*?'

'I call it a tragic misfortune. It was never my intention that his life should have such a pointless epilogue. I left a DO NOT DISTURB sign on his door that was evidently removed. Who knows why or by whom? If it had gone on hanging there . . . But we are all, including me, the playthings of chance. And of our own mis-judgements.'

'Oh, so you're not infallible, then?'

'Far from it. If I'd ever thought I was, Hammelgaard's visit a week later disabused me. He was looking for the notebooks, mystified by their absence from David's hotel room. It became apparent as we talked that he knew too much about David's work to let it lie. He'd have pressed on with it. More slowly, it's true, and probably less coherently. But he'd already gleaned enough to get there in the end. And to persuade others to join him in the endeavour. By the time he'd left, I'd reluctantly concluded that he too had to be stopped.' She paused, reading the dismay in Harry's face. 'I had to finish what I'd started. Don't you see? I was trading two lives against a catastrophic future.'

313

'Two? A moment ago, you admitted to *three* murders.'

'Yes. Because one sudden death in mysterious circumstances, as David's was supposed to have been, made nobody very curious, whereas two – when both victims were researching higher dimensions – carried the risk of arousing unhealthy suspicion. I needed to lay a false trail. Mermillod had come to see me a few weeks before, trying to buy information with which to blacken David's name. He'd even had the effrontery to offer me some kind of sinecure at IHES in exchange for lending my name to a campaign ridiculing David's hyper-dimensional theories. He was an unpleasant man and had obviously been put up to it by Lazenby. I wasn't susceptible to his bribes, of course. But they gave me an idea. Three deaths *would* look suspicious. But if all three victims were former employees of Globescope, *that's* where the suspicion would be directed. Mermillod had angered me. So, indirectly, had Lazenby. I decided to use them to solve my problem. I persuaded myself that Mermillod was asking for it. As I rather think he was.'

'And Kersey? Was he "asking for it"?'

'Not at all. But then I didn't kill Kersey. His death really was an accident. A singularly untimely one, since it convinced the other participants in Project Sybil that there was a plot against them. They went into hiding. And suddenly Hammelgaard was out of my reach. Lying low in Copenhagen, I had no doubt. But if I went in search of him, there was a danger of undermining the Globescope conspiracy theory just when it was gathering momentum. How could I go looking for him in a strange city without my name becoming known there, my face recognized, my interest in him remembered and remarked upon? No, no. I could only travel in secret and strike covertly. I needed somebody else to hunt him down. And I chose . . . you.'

Harry opened his mouth to speak, but could find no words to express the conflict he felt between doubt and understanding. She had asked him at the outset whether he was sure he wanted the truth. Now, his answer might have been different.

'I was the one who phoned the Mitre Bridge Service Station on the seventeenth of October and left the message for you. I calculated – correctly – that once you knew David was your son, you wouldn't stop until you'd led me to Hammelgaard. You're the sort who never gives up, you see. The sort with so little to lose you'll move mountains when somebody offers you something to care about. I'd read about you in the papers when you were implicated in the disappearance of that girl in Rhodes. I'd noted

314

how the story ended. I'd remembered you as the kind of man who won't take no for an answer. And last October I realized I needed such a man.

'I sent you the newspaper cutting a few days later to make sure you'd follow the trail here. You'd have done so eventually, anyway, but time was beginning to press. I knew you'd follow my advice and go looking for Hammelgaard in Copenhagen. It was inevitable. When you did, I went with you. No doubt you thought you travelled alone. But not so. I was with you, every step of the way. Except when *I* was waiting for Hammelgaard on Knippelsbro – and *you* still hadn't arrived.'

'That can't be true.'

'But it is. He didn't see me. He didn't know it was about to happen – even a split-second before it did. There was no pain and no anticipation. I think you glimpsed me on the bridge, didn't you – sensed how close I was?'

'No,' Harry insisted in the teeth of his own memory's evidence. 'I sensed nothing.'

'Have it your way. At all events, it culminated there. With Hammelgaard's death, the secret was sealed. Everything you went on to achieve in America was merely window-dressing, I'm afraid. Or should have been. Unfortunately, it wasn't as simple as that. David's contact with Carl – and Carl's subsequent abscondence from Hudson Valley – were shocking discoveries to me. David had clearly been more suspicious of me than I'd given him credit for. As for Carl, the connection with me he represented was a real danger. I knew that if you learnt of it, you'd start to piece the truth together. I did all I could to stop you. Hackensack's accident; your loss of Rosenbaum's address: every distraction I could think of. But I suppose I knew all along they could only really be delays. You were bound to work your way back to me in the end.'

'Did these "delays" include murdering Dobermann?'

'No. I'm not sure how he met his death. I didn't know he was keeping watch on the house in Maple Place. He must have seen me when I went there to retrieve the remaining notebooks and papers. What effect that had on him I can only imagine. And, to be honest, I'd rather not.'

'Oh, you'd rather not, would you?' Harry knew his anger was partly synthetic: a mask for his inability either to accept or deny what Athene had said. But he knew also he had to indulge it. Anger was his last defence. 'I thought you claimed to be serving the future, not your own sensibilities.'

315

'And I thought you claimed to want the truth. Have you changed your mind?'

'I haven't heard the truth. If you believe everything you've told me, then you must be mad.'

'You know I'm not, though, don't you?'

'I know nothing of the kind.'

'Why do you think I let you into the secret?'

'You tell me.'

'Because David was your son. You of all people should know the truth about him. His life *and* his death. That truth lies between us now, literally as well as metaphorically. In his notebooks. And in the knowledge I've shared with you – but with no other living person.'

'Your possession of the notebooks proves nothing. You didn't need access to higher dimensions to become a thief. And if their contents were as earth-shattering as you say, you'd have destroyed them by now.'

'I should have done, certainly. But I too have my weaknesses. The notebooks are a unique record of David's work. His ticket to immortality. If they go into the fire, his memory goes with them. And some part of me goes too.'

'What are you saying, then? That you expect me to walk meekly away and keep my mouth shut? While you sit here with my son's discovery rotting in a locked drawer?'

'Hardly. Even if you agreed to do that, the time-bomb would still be here, ticking away, waiting to explode when I died and the drawer was opened.'

'What's it to be, then?'

'I have to end this. You do understand, don't you? Much as you'd prefer not to.' She gave him a consoling smile. 'You should leave now, Harry. You really should.'

'Without the notebooks?' Slowly, Harry stood up. He glanced past Athene and out through the window, where the gate leading onto the road and the stone wall beside it and the rooftops opposite and the distant outline of a water tower against the pale-blue Suffolk sky assured him that the familiar physical world still existed, obeying its four-dimensional rules, rebuffing as madness the powers and perceptions this old woman laid claim to. One way or another, madness was the answer. His, if he believed her. Hers, if he did not. 'I'm not prepared to do that.'

He reached out and touched the notebooks. His fingertips tingled. His scalp contracted. Nervous tension, he told himself.

316

Nothing more. He hooked his forefinger round the rubber band and slid the bundle towards him.

'Aren't you going to stop me?'

'You want me to?'

'I want you to prove you can.'

'I can't let you leave here with the notebooks.'

'Then you'd better do something about it. Right now.'

'Don't you believe I could – if I wanted to?'

'I don't believe anything any more.' He picked the bundle up and stepped back from the desk. 'Beyond the evidence of my own senses.'

'They're as treacherous as any other kind of evidence.'

'They're all I've got.' He turned, strode to the door and stopped there, looking back at her over his shoulder. 'Well?'

'Well what?'

'I mean to walk out of here with these, you know.'

'Oh, I know. Believe me, I know.'

Her eyes held his for a compulsive moment, communicating not the slightest doubt that she would have her way. But she made no move. She did not even stir in her chair. Relief flooded over Harry. Hers was the confidence of the utterly mad. It had to be. For it seemed there was nothing she meant to do to stop him. And nothing she thought she needed to do.

'Goodbye, Harry.'

'I'll take these to the police,' he said, holding up the bundle in triumph as his apprehensions faded. 'I'll get them to check their forensic records for some trace of your presence in David's room at the Skyway. A fingerprint. A hair. A fibre. There'll be something.'

'You're probably right.'

'Then they'll come for you.'

'No doubt.'

'And you'll answer for what you did to him.'

'I'm sure I will.'

'Do you understand?'

'Completely.'

She was staring at him with a strange and compassionate soulfulness that touched him more deeply than he would have been prepared to admit. She seemed to be urging him on even as she was calling him back. Still she did not move.

'Goodbye, Harry.'

'Go to hell.' He tore himself free of her gaze and plunged

317

through the doorway, aware as he moved of a crackling in the fabric of his clothing and a crawling as of insects across his skin. But even as the sensations reached his mind, the rational part of it flung up its defences. Pay them no heed, it insisted. Just go, while you still can.

A spark of static jolted his fingers as he grasped the handle of the front door and pulled it open. Then he was out, striding through the clear cold air towards the gate, trusting his own judgement yet not daring to look back. As he reached the pavement beyond the gate, he realized he really had thought she was capable of stopping him. But she had not been. Athene Tilson had been bluffing all along. And he had called her bluff.

SIXTY-THREE

Life had often perplexed Harry, but never more so than now. Seated at an alcove table towards the rear of the Lord Nelson as the early lunchtime trade picked up slowly at the bar, he stared at his half-drunk pint of Adnams' Broadside and the six notebooks held together by a rubber band that stood on the table in front of him. He lit a cigarette, watched the first lungful of smoke drift up into the landlord's collection of antique soda syphons and forced himself to consider a question he dearly wished he knew the answer to. Was Athene Tilson a liar or a madwoman – or exactly what she claimed to be?

Insanity was his preferred choice. Age, isolation and neglect could have made her so eager for fame and recognition that she had assembled a bizarre confession to fit the undeniably bizarre facts. There was no saying she had stolen the notebooks at all. Harry only had her word for it that David had not left them with her for safe-keeping, as he might well have done if suicide had been in his mind. If so, they were unlikely to contain any startling hyper-dimensional discoveries. Not that Harry would be able to tell if they did. But others would. As Athene well knew. Yet she had let him walk away with them. Presumably for the plainest of reasons: she had not the means to stop him.

This display of her impotence, contradicting the sweeping vigour of her words, had vitiated Harry's threat to go to the police. What would he go to them with? Ten years' worth of his son's inconclusive mathematical jottings were unlikely to have them

319

rushing round to Avocet House with handcuffs at the ready.

But what if those jottings were not inconclusive? What if David really was up there with Euclid and Newton and Einstein? What if the notebooks fixed in Harry's line of sight proved his son was a pioneer of mathematical thought? It all came back to the same point in the end. What did they contain? Gold or dream-dust? Something . . . or nothing? Tracing their cloth-bound spines with his fingers, Harry knew he would have to find out – soon. The rest hinged on this.

He would take them to Donna. Yes, that was the answer. She would be able to judge whether they were dealing with shadow or substance. She would know if this was the real thing. He peeled the rubber band off and picked up the topmost notebook, assuming it would be the latest of them: the one in which David had reached either an apotheosis or the deadest of dead ends. He toasted the boy's ambivalent memory in beer and flipped open the cover.

A blank page. Then another. And another. And another. They were all blank, Harry saw as he turned them over with mounting anxiety. Every last one. There was not a word, a number, an equation, a clue. There was not a single thing. He grabbed up the next book in the pile, fanned through the pages and saw that it was the same. And even as he cast it aside and snatched at the next, the realization burst into his mind. There was nothing here. There never had been. They were *not* the notebooks. Athene had tricked him.

Harry rushed out empty-handed into the street and turned towards the sea. The esplanade, and the lane linking it with South Green, represented the quickest route back to Avocet House. As he ran, he wondered why Athene had deceived him. What was the point, when it must have been obvious he would discover what she had done before he left Southwold? What did she hope to gain – except too little time to be of the slightest use?

He reached the green, lungs straining, heart racing. As he paused to catch his breath, an acrid scent drifted on the air to meet him. Something was burning. Then he heard a distant crackle as of igniting timber. He ran on, glimpsing a reflection of flame in a window on the other side of the road as he neared Athene's gate. Turning, he saw a churning tangle of fire and smoke in the study. The room was ablaze. And was far enough gone for the rest of the house to follow if it was left unchecked. What had happened? What had she done?

A car pulled up behind him at the roadside. Harry looked back at the anxious face within. 'Call the Fire Brigade,' he bellowed. Then he flung the gate open and raced across the garden to the study window. Inside, fire was encroaching from the corners, as if it had started simultaneously in several different locations. But Athene was sitting exactly where he had left her, staring impassively at the empty blackboard as fire climbed its frame like some vine whose life is compressed into a minute.

Harry hammered on the window and shouted Athene's name. Slowly, with the reluctance of a waking dreamer, she turned and looked at him over her shoulder. On her face was a calm smile of irony and recognition, lit like stained glass by the leaping flames. She shook her head, but went on smiling. It was a warning not to interfere, entwined with a gentle farewell.

There was a trowel propped in a broken flowerpot at Harry's feet. He grabbed it and struck at the window, then again with greater force. The glass splintered and he knocked out the shards. 'Quick,' he shouted, even as the curtains caught with a whoomph and heat punched into his throat. 'Over here.' But she made no move.

The window was mullioned. Realizing he would have to open it for anyone to climb in or out, Harry smashed another pane next to the handle and reached in to turn it. But it would not shift. A lock had been fitted, he saw, and the catch closed. There was no sign of the key. She had done this deliberately. She had planned the whole thing. He glanced in at her desperately. As he did so, she looked away and he noticed, stacked on the blotter in front of her, six blue cloth-bound notebooks.

Harry whirled round and made for the side of the house. She had the notebooks, the *real* notebooks. And he would be damned if he stood by and watched her destroy them along with herself. The conservatory door might still be open. Even if it was not, the conservatory windows were plain glass and too large for locks to keep him out.

He reached the rear and barged at the door. But it did not yield. She had locked it. He retreated to the garage, heaved the dustbin up by its handles and stumbled across to the largest of the conservatory windows, thrusting the base of the bin through it like a battering-ram. The bin crashed down inside amidst a shower of broken glass. Harry clambered in after it, ignoring a cut to his hand as he clasped the frame, then crunched his way past the wicker chairs and table where he and Athene had taken coffee –

and such unequal stock of each other – ten short weeks before.

The smoke was a throat-catching mist in the drawing room, but a choking fog in the hall, pierced by a wavering line of flame that led from a sparking light-switch by the study door up the wall and across the ceiling. Harry ran forward, stooping as he went, his forearm braced in front of him.

Entering the study was like stepping into a furnace. The bookcase had caught as readily as a stand of drought-stricken timber. Fire had consumed the panelling beneath the mantelpiece and was roaring in the chimney. Flames were licking at the legs of the desk. While Athene still sat behind it, motionless as a shop-window mannequin, with the notebooks before her on the blotter. Harry started towards her, but the heat and smoke beat him back. He recoiled into the hall, coughing and blinking. The front door was to his left, offering the swiftest of escapes. But he ran back down the hall to the kitchen, determined not to give up. He would save the notebooks at least. Athene could do as she pleased – but not with his son's property.

He grabbed a towel from a rail by the sink, soaked it under the tap, then draped it over his head and returned to the hall. The smoke was thicker now. And there was more than one jagged line of flame flickering through it. Holding a damp end of the towel to his nose and mouth, he closed his eyes, plunged recklessly forward and opened them again to find himself at the study door.

As he entered, the top half of the bookcase, unbalanced by the fire eating at its lower shelves, gave way, spilling books onto the floor, where sparks ignited the rug between him and the desk. Smoke billowed up from the debris of the bookcase, stinging his eyes and singeing his ears. With every breath he swallowed more. Through his tears and heaving coughs, he saw Athene's clothes catch and heard a whoof as fire suddenly engulfed her. She stretched forward, her whole right arm ablaze, and laid her hand on the pile of notebooks. Some instinct of preservation – some pointless flare of hope – drove Harry towards her. But there was another whoof of ignition and instantly she and the desk and the notebooks were part of a single flame that jetted to the ceiling.

Harry recoiled, the failure of his attempt releasing fear and confusion in his mind. As he swung towards the door, his foot caught in a curled corner of the rug. He stumbled and fell, the side of his head striking the edge of one of the fallen bookcase shelves as he rolled. There was a moment of dazed disorientation. Then he realized where he was again.

322

But the realization was not enough. There seemed no air left to breathe, only heat and smoke and choking weakness. The doorway blurred and seemed to turn, as if on an axis. But he was the one turning, rolling slowly onto his side, a hood of darkness and helplessness closing around his head, the will to move draining away as his lungs and muscles failed him. The doorway vanished. Then the skirting-board by which he lay. Then the tufts of the carpet beneath his face. Recognition of the moment for what it was – the end of consciousness, the brink of death – was a frail and fleeting thought. And it was also his last.

SIXTY-FOUR

'Goodbye, Harry.'

'I'll take these to the police,' he said, holding up the bundle in triumph as his apprehensions faded. 'I'll get them to check their forensic records for some trace of your presence at the Skyway. A fingerprint. A hair. A fibre. There'll be something.'

'You're probably right.'

'Then they'll come for you.'

'No doubt.'

'And you'll answer for what you did to him.'

'I'm sure I will.'

'Do you understand?'

'Completely.'

She was staring at him with a strange and compassionate soulfulness that touched him more deeply than he would have been prepared to admit. She seemed to be urging him on even as she was calling him back. Still she did not move.

'Goodbye, Harry.'

'Go to hell.' He tore himself free of her gaze and plunged through the doorway.

Back into the study. The room he had just left. With the same contents and dimensions. And the same occupant, smiling benignly at him from behind the desk. 'Give me the notebooks, Harry,' she said, her voice echoing behind and around him. In that instant, he saw a difference in her face and in the room. The arrangement of her features and the positioning of the furniture were reversed, as

324

in a mirror. 'Give them up.' He whirled round and saw her again, waiting for him back in the original study. 'You have to.' Her voice reverberated in his head and suddenly the room telescoped into an infinitely receding succession of its own image, like the reflections he had seen of Slade's lounge in the magician's self-regarding mirrors. 'You have no choice.' He looked down at his hand where the notebooks should have been and saw that it was empty. 'None whatsoever.' Fear filled him and he tried to scream, but no sound came. His throat was dry and voiceless. 'You cannot keep them.' He opened his mouth wide, struggling to force out a cry, struggling and writhing and straining. And then—

'Hello, Harry.' Donna smiled at him soothingly. 'I came in a while back, but you were sleeping and I didn't like to wake you. You looked as if you were dreaming.' A concerned frown displaced the smile. 'Was it about the fire?'

'The fire?' His brain wrestled with the shards and scraps of his memory. 'Yes. I expect it was.' The fire at Avocet House; his vain attempt to rescue the notebooks; the despair he had felt at the failing of his strength: the components of what had happened reassembled themselves in his mind's eye like the reversed film of a demolition. As they did so, he remembered regaining consciousness in the ambulance, an oxygen mask held to his face by a paramedic. And being put into the bed he now lay in and told how lucky he was. And that he was going to be all right. And that he should sleep if he could. 'What . . .' His throat was excruciatingly sore. His voice, he realized, was not much more than a hoarse croak. 'What time is it?'

'Just gone eight.'

'In the evening?'

'Yuh.'

'So . . . it's still Tuesday.'

'That's right.' She grinned, as if his inane questions were a source of immense pleasure to her. 'Still Tuesday.'

'Where am I?'

'In hospital.'

'But . . . where?'

'Oh, the James Paget, it's called. At Gorleston. About twenty miles from Southwold. Just over the county border in Norfolk.'

'Boundary,' he said, pointlessly. 'English counties aren't grand enough to have borders.'

'Right.' Her grin broadened. 'That's a good sign. Picking me up on little bitty turns of phrase.'

'What are you doing here?'

'It's a long story. But since you're supposed to rest your throat, you may as well hear some of it. I flew in this morning and went out to Kensal Green to see you. There was nobody home. So I went to the cemetery, but you weren't there either. I tried that pub you use, but they hadn't seen you since before the holiday. Reckoned you must still be in Swindon. I was going to catch a train down there, but I decided to give Mrs Tandy's place one last try. While I was there, ringing at the bell, a patrol car pulled up and a policeman got out. He asked if I knew you. They were trying to trace your next of kin. Well, that sounded pretty alarming, I can tell you. And it didn't get a whole lot better. All he knew was that you'd been pulled out of a house fire in Southwold and rushed to hospital. They'd got the Foxglove Road address from a letter in your pocket.' A letter? She must mean Woodrow's. Did she know what was in it? he wondered. Was that why she had flown over? 'I high-tailed it up here and what do I find? That you're in miraculously good shape. You're a lucky guy, Harry. If Southwold didn't have its own fire station . . . If they hadn't got to the scene so quickly . . . If a fireman with breathing apparatus hadn't gone straight in . . . Well, as it is, you've only got a few cuts and bruises and the odd minor burn – plus a mild case of smoke inhalation – to show for playing the hero.'

'Sounds trivial.'

'It isn't exactly that.'

'Smoke inhalation's no problem. I've done it all my life.'

'Maybe. But this would be a good time to give up.'

'Can't see why. As a matter of fact, a cigarette's just what I need.'

'Absolutely not.' She shook her head disapprovingly. 'You've got to take care of yourself. And if *you* won't, *I* will.'

'Is that a promise?'

'Kind of. But tell me. What were you doing in Southwold in the first place?' So she did not know what Woodrow had discovered in Philadelphia. She really did not know. 'I mean, why go back there? What unfinished business did you have with Athene Tilson?'

'She is . . . dead is she?' he asked, partly to evade the issue, partly to confirm what he could not quite bring himself to believe.

Donna nodded. ' 'Fraid so.'

'Do they know what caused the fire?'

'It's too early to be certain. They haven't even ruled out arson.'

'Arson?'

'Well, I gather there was a live-in housekeeper. You must have met her last fall. Girl by the name of Mace. She's gone missing. A neighbour drove her down to Ipswich early this morning and she evidently told him the old lady had sacked her. So, anything's possible.'

'That isn't. I saw her onto the London train myself before taking . . .' He hesitated, deliberately amending the record of his movements to remove the element of urgency. He did not know how much he would eventually tell Donna, but he knew it was a decision best delayed. For the moment, he was simply unable to muster all the factors in his mind. 'Before taking the bus to Southwold.'

'You saw her in Ipswich?'

'Purely by chance.' At least, he supposed it was by chance. But Athene's calculations had run so far and so deep that almost every chance seemed now like one more cunning contrivance. 'She's got nothing to do with it.'

'I'll mention that to the police. They'll want to take a statement from you soon.'

'It'd be good if you could hold them off until tomorrow. I'm tired and . . . I need to collect my thoughts.' He congratulated himself on the euphemism. What he really needed to do was settle on a story and stick to it.

'No problem. They'll understand. But I'm not sure I do. You still haven't said why you were in Southwold.'

'Haven't I? Sorry. Well, I . . . er . . . told the old girl I'd let her know what came of my . . . enquiries . . . and . . . I finally got around to it . . . today.'

'Oh, so she was expecting you?'

'Yes. We had . . . an appointment. But of course I never . . . actually spoke to her.'

'Guess not. The fire had got quite a hold before you went in, right?'

'Yes.' He thought back. 'It had.'

'It was a brave thing to do. Trying to rescue her.'

'Or stupid. Depends how you look at it.'

'Do you want me to contact your mother?'

'No. Better not worry her. I'll be out of here before she knows I'm in.'

'What about Mrs Tandy?'

'She's still at her niece's in Warwickshire. Gets home tomorrow. I'll phone her then. Unless you're . . . going back that way.'

'Going back?' She smiled and shook her head, as if amused by the slightness of his trust in her. 'I'm staying until you're fit enough to be discharged, Harry. I've already booked into a hotel just up the road in Great Yarmouth. Unless you'd rather . . .' Her face fell. '. . . I booked out again.'

'Of course not.' He patted her arm with his bandaged hand. 'I just didn't know how long . . . I mean . . . Hell's teeth, *you* haven't explained either. Why the flying visit?'

'Ah, that's tricky.' She traced the bindings of the bandage with her fingers. 'I have some news. Kind of unexpected. But let's get you better first, shall we?'

'Suspense isn't going to speed my recovery.'

'It won't hold it up, either.' She glanced along the ward. 'This isn't the time or place, Harry. When you get out of here, we'll find both. OK?' Then she bent forward and kissed him on the cheek. 'That's a promise.'

SIXTY-FIVE

Within twenty-four hours, Harry's experiences at Avocet House had assumed a dreamlike quality in his mind. He suspected some form of subconscious defence mechanism was at work, enabling his memory to assimilate and cope with what had happened. It reinforced his reluctance to think too deeply about the things Athene Tilson had said. What he could not quite bring himself either to believe or disbelieve was safer unscrutinized. Later, he might come to regret turning his back on the central mystery of his son's life. But that time was not now. And he had never believed in looking too far ahead.

To Detective Constable Waller of the Suffolk Police he proffered a pragmatic lie, hoping nobody had seen him arriving at Avocet House a full hour before he claimed to have done. Waller's reaction suggested he had nothing to worry about. The Fire Brigade were evidently content with faulty wiring as an explanation. And Athene Tilson's frailty was assumed to account for her failure to escape before the blaze took hold. It was an assumption Harry was happy to conspire in. He remained unsure what the truth really was. But he felt certain it was a truth best allowed to die with the woman who had stood guard over it for so long.

When he telephoned Mrs Tandy with a self-effacing report of his futile heroics, she was so concerned for his well-being that she forgot to complain about the state she had found her sitting room in. Harry refrained from mentioning it, trusting his powers of invention to carry him through when the time came.

Two days after being rushed into the James Paget Hospital, Harry was discharged with as clean a bill of health as his lifestyle allowed and a solemn warning to eschew cigarettes for at least a month. He assured the doctor he would and decided not to push his luck by asking what had become of the pack he had been carrying when he was admitted.

Donna was waiting to collect him, looking sophomorically youthful in scarf, sheepskin jacket, jeans and pixie boots. Harry felt happier to see her than he knew to be wise. She would soon be on her way back to California and the best way of reconciling himself to the fact was to crush any preposterous hopes that might enter his head before they had a chance to establish themselves. So intent was he on doing this that he discounted the news she had promised before he had even heard it and overlooked the clues that her manner might have revealed. She was nervous, as if she knew the day held something more momentous than he could have imagined, as if she were confronting a challenge before she was ready to meet it – a challenge in which Harry was somehow involved.

His wish to thank personally the fireman who had rescued him from Avocet House necessitated a diversion both seemed to welcome. Donna had hired a car to drive them down to London, but was by her own admission in no hurry. 'We've got all day,' she said. 'There's no need to rush.' *Her* need, her tone implied, lay all the other way.

A change in the weather had brought grey clouds and spitting rain to Southwold, borne on a keen east wind. A call at the fire station established that Dave Moorhouse was off duty, a call at his home that he could be found on the beach repairing the family's storm-damaged beach-hut.

He was a phlegmatically amiable forty-year-old unwilling to admit he had done anything out of the ordinary, but reluctant to reject Harry's gratitude. 'You were lucky,' he said deflectively. 'If we'd got there a few minutes later . . . There was no hope for the old lady, of course. It's a funny thing, that. When I went into that room, do you know what I thought? What my first impression was, like? That she was the source of the fire, the centre of it, y'know?' He shook his head. 'She wasn't just alight. She was . . . blazing.'

330

'I thought an electrical fault was suspected,' put in Donna.

'Yeh.' Moorhouse shrugged. 'Well, that's the kind of thing they *would* go for – when they haven't the foggiest idea what really happened.'

The house was a blackened ruin, the external walls and chimney-stack still standing, but the roof, ceilings, staircase and most of the internal walls gone. A gang was already at work on the place, moving cautiously through the ash-heaped wreckage to make it ready for demolition. Two large skips stood in the road, filled with charred wood, broken glass, rolls of scorched carpet, tangles of twisted pipework, hollow frames of lost paintings, sodden remains of burnt books. And, somewhere midst the chaos, a walking-stick spared from the flames as if by an oversight.

'Dave was right,' said Donna. 'You *were* lucky.'

'Yes,' said Harry, staring around him. 'I certainly was.'

'What do you think he was getting at? That business about Dr Tilson being the source of the fire. Do you reckon he was implying . . . spontaneous combustion?'

'Do professional fire-fighters believe in such things?'

'Wouldn't have thought so. Not a level-headed guy like Dave, anyway.'

'Even level-headed guys have to believe the unbelievable if they come smack up against it.'

'What's that supposed to mean?'

'I'm not sure.' He smiled, eager to defuse the moment. 'Fancy a drink? They told me I should keep the throat lubricated.'

'They did?'

'Actually, no.' His smile turned into a sheepish grin. 'I think it must have slipped their minds.'

The Lord Nelson was busier than it had been on Tuesday. It was market day, the barmaid explained. Harry and Donna retreated to a small table sandwiched between a fruit machine and a settle-back, where Harry eased his sore throat with several enthusiastic swallows of beer while Donna took one tentative sip at her Perrier water.

'How's Makepeace?' he enquired, just as the ebb in their conversation began to stretch towards an awkward silence.

'Disappointed. She thought – like me – that with all the publicity the Globescope story's been getting there'd be a genuine world-wide debate about the predictions we made. Which is about the

331

only way the issues are going to be looked at with the seriousness they deserve. Instead, it's become just another big business crime story. And the media are rapidly losing interest even in that now it's become obvious there isn't going to be a trial. I mean, why worry about whether the planet's still going to be habitable a hundred years from now when you can spend all day plugged into one cable station or another pondering the vital mystery of whether a retired footballer murdered his ex-wife? That seems to be the rationale.'

'You sound even more cynical than me.'

'Not cynical. Just depressed by people's lack of concern for the needs of the next generation – and the one after that.' She frowned at him. 'When I came over a month ago, you were the one who was depressed. But you seem to have bounced back since. Quicker than I'd have expected.'

'I think I'm just pleased to be alive.' He grinned at her over the rim of his glass, conscious as he was that his mood amounted to more than relief at cheating death. His unwonted contentment stemmed rather from a posthumous pact with Athene Tilson. One he was only now fully aware he had entered into. He and a dead mathematician *had* helped the next generation – and the one after that. They would never know they had been helped. But nevertheless they had been. And Harry had played his unwitting part in the process. 'What about that news you promised me, Donna?' he continued. 'Aren't you going to put me out of my misery?'

'Get yourself another pint first. You might need it.'

'OK.' Needing no second invitation, he rose and ambled through the ruck to the bar, glass in hand. The barmaid was busy, but the landlord emerged from the rear to serve him as if on cue. 'Pint of Broadside, please.'

'Certainly, sir. Weren't you in here a couple of days ago?'

'Er . . . Maybe.'

'Yeh, you're the fellow who left those notebooks behind. Have you had them back yet? We put them by somewhere.'

'Notebooks?' Harry tried to look as uncomprehending as he could. 'Sorry. I don't know what you're talking about.'

'You must do. It was definitely you.'

''Fraid not. You've got the wrong man. Not the first time it's happened.' Harry paid for his beer and took a sip from it. 'I think I must have one of those faces. You know? Strangely familiar.'

'Strange is right.'

'Yeh, well, there you go.' He took another sip. 'The beer's very good, by the way. Thanks a lot.' He turned and strolled non-chalantly back to the table.

'What was all that about?' Donna asked as he sat down.

'A case of mistaken identity. Don't worry about it.'

'If you're sure.'

'I am. Honestly. And you won't get round to telling me your news by going on about it, so why don't—'

'I'm pregnant.'

Harry slowly lowered his glass, which had been halfway to his lips, back onto the table and stared at her. 'What?'

'I'm seven weeks pregnant.'

'Seven weeks? You mean . . .'

'That's right, Harry. I'm carrying your child.'

'But . . . you can't be. I mean . . . I thought . . . you must have . . .'

'I don't think either of us was expecting what happened in Washington to happen, do you? And sex wasn't exactly top of my agenda while I was on the run. I was taking precautions against getting killed, not pregnant. Besides . . . ' She laughed, a bitter-sweet laugh mixing irony and regret in a stubborn blend of hope. 'Besides, a man of your age and habits has no business being so damned fertile.'

Harry grimaced. 'Sorry about that.'

'Are you?'

'Well, that depends . . . I suppose . . . on how you . . . feel about it.'

'Shocked. Taken aback. Thrown off balance. Hit by a train when I didn't even know I was standing on the track. I reckon that about covers it.'

'Not what you'd call an entirely welcome development, then?'

'Not at first. I even considered . . . terminating it.'

'Still considering it?'

'No. I wouldn't have told you if I had been. I thought it all through over Christmas with my folks in Seattle. Weighed up my needs, the child's needs – and yours – as best I could. I guess the Globescope affair played its part. I guess it prompted me to show some faith in the future. Mine, anyway. Or should I say ours?' She leant towards him. 'I mean to have this child, Harry. I'm not exactly sure of all the reasons. The future. The past. You. Me. David. Plus a bundle of hang-ups and hormones. But I'm going to go through with it. Alone, if I have to.'

'If you *have* to?'

333

'Nobody's going to cut you out of fatherhood this time. Unless you cut yourself out.'

He reached across the table and took her hand tentatively in his. 'What are you saying, Donna?' Part of him already knew. But he needed to hear the words in order to believe them.

'I'm saying you might like to think about swapping the catacombs of Kensal Green Cemetery for the streets of San Francisco. I'm saying we can have a future together.'

'The three of us?'

'Exactly. But I can only speak for two of us. It's up to you now.'